STAR TREK®
NEW FRONTIER

SP

STAR TREK®
NEW FRONTIER

HOUSE OF CARDS
INTO THE VOID
THE TWO-FRONT WAR
END GAME

Peter David

GUILDAMERICA
B O O K S

HOUSE OF CARDS Copyright © 1997 by Paramount Pictures. All Rights Reserved. Printing History: Pocket Books paperback July 1997

INTO THE VOID Copyright © 1997 by Paramount Pictures. All Rights Reserved. Printing History: Pocket Books paperback July 1997

THE TWO-FRONT WAR Copyright © 1997 by Paramount Pictures. All Rights Reserved. Printing History: Pocket Books paperback August 1997

END GAME Copyright © 1997 by Paramount Pictures. All Rights Reserved. Printing History: Pocket Books paperback August 1997

Published by arrangement with:
Pocket Books
A division of
Simon & Schuster Inc.
1230 Avenue of the Americas
New York, New York 10020

ISBN # 1-56865-502-9
Printed in the United States of America

CONTENTS

HOUSE OF CARDS   1

INTO THE VOID   113

THE TWO-FRONT WAR   225

END GAME   327

To The Fans . . .
You Know Who You Are

EDITOR'S ACKNOWLEDGMENT

I would like to thank Paula Block for her help in turning *New Frontier* into a reality, Peter David for the fantastic new characters he peopled the *New Frontier* with, and Gene Roddenberry, whose sandbox we're playing in.

—John J. Ordover,
Senior Editor

HOUSE
OF
CARDS

TWENTY
YEARS
EARLIER . . .

M'K'N'ZY

I

Falkar regarded the remains of his troops and, as the blazing Xenex sun beat down upon them, decided to wax philosophical about the situation. "It is not uncommon to desire killing a teenager," he said. "However, it is not often that one feels the need to send soldiers to do the job."

His men regarded him with a surprising amount of good cheer. It was surprising they had any left, for the battle between themselves and the Xenexians had not only been brutal, but also extremely unsatisfying. Although not particularly unsatisfying for the Xenexians.

They were a somewhat bedraggled lot, these survivors. Their armor, their clothing, hung in tatters. Their weapons were largely energy-depleted, and when they had fled the scene of their final rout, they had done so depending heavily on short swords and knives to hack their way to safety (or what passed for safety). Weapons that hung at their sides largely for ornamentation, for decoration, for a symbol of achievement. Most of them had never touched the bladed weapons except to polish them for display purposes. Not one man in fifty could remotely consider himself expert with their use. As Falkar studied the barely two dozen men remaining to him, it was as if he could read what was going through their minds.

Falkar drew himself to his full height, and as he was six and a half feet tall, there was something to be said for that. His skin was a dark bronze, as was that of all the people of his race. His build was an interesting combination of both muscle and economy. There was no denying the power in his frame, but it stretched across his body in such an even manner that—despite his impressive height—it was easy to underestimate just how strong he was. His hair was long and black, and usually was tied neatly, but now it hung loosely around his shoulders in disarray. When one is beating a hasty retreat, it's hard to pay attention to keeping one's hair properly coiffed.

His eyes were solid black, his nose was wide and flared, and his incisors were particularly sharp.

"Perhaps we deserved our fate," he said tightly.

His men looked up at him in surprise. If these were words meant to comfort an already dispirited band, they were not doing the job.

"We have ruled the Xenexians for over three hundred years," he said tightly. "Never, in all that time, has there been any uprising that we were unable to quash. Never has our authority been questioned. And because of that, we have allowed ourselves to become sloppy. Become overdependent on hand weapons." He was striding back and forth in front of his troops. "We came to believe," he continued, "that we would be able to win battle upon battle, not because we were the better prepared or the better armed . . . but simply because we were *entitled* to do so, as if by divine right. Well, the Xenexians showed us differently, didn't they?"

"It was that damned boy," one of the soldiers muttered.

Falkar spun and faced him, his dark eyes glittering. "Yes," he said, voice hissing tightly from between his teeth. "That damned boy. That *damned* boy. The one who rallied his people. The one who outthought us at every turn. The one who anticipated our moves, who was not intimidated by us, who gave his people hope. *Hope,* gentlemen. The worst thing people such as these could have. Because hope leads to action, and actions lead to consequences. And the consequence of these actions is that we are now faced with a people who stand on the brink of liberation. We fight them and fight them, and they keep coming back and defeating us. Our government, gentlemen, has made it clear to me that they are beginning to consider Xenex more trouble than it is worth. And that damned boy is the cause.''

Falkar had been standing on the uppermost reaches of a plateau. Now he pointed out at the formidable terrain before them. It stretched on for hundreds of miles, seemingly in every direction. The ground was hard and cracked. Small mountains dotted the landscape, and there were small bits of vegetation here and there clinging desperately for life.

''He's out there, gentlemen. Out there in the Pit. Providence has potentially put him within our reach. His vehicle was seen spiraling out of control in that direction during the battle's waning moments. He's separated from his troops, from his followers. He is alone. He is no doubt scared. But he is also very likely dangerous, as would be any trapped and injured animal.'' Falkar turned and looked back at his men. ''I want him. Alive, if possible. Dead, if not. But if you capture him alive and he 'accidentally' meets his demise in transit, make certain that all injuries he sustains are to his body. I want his face pristine and uninjured, easy to identify.''

One of his soldiers frowned. ''I don't understand, sir. Certainly he could be identified from DNA records in any event.''

''True,'' said Falkar. ''But I'm referring to being able to identify his face . . . when his head is stuck upon a pole in the great square of Xenex.'' He surveyed the terrain one more time and then said, ''Find him. Find M'k'n'zy . . . and let's put an end to this rebellion once and for all.''

M'k'n'zy felt his left arm stiffening up again. The blood that covered his biceps had long since dried; the large piece of metal that had embedded itself in his arm had cut him rather severely, and it had been a hellish few minutes to pry it out of where it had lodged itself. That wasn't the major problem though. The big difficulty was that he had dislocated the damned limb. The pain had been excruciating as M'k'n'zy had braced himself and, agonizingly, shoved it back into place. It had been so overwhelming, in fact, that M'k'n'zy had fainted dead away. When he came to a few minutes later, he cursed himself for his weakness.

He treasured the small bit of shade that he'd managed to find for himself as he extended his fingers and flexed them, curved them into a fist and straightened them once more. ''Come on,'' he muttered to himself through cracked lips, expressing annoyance with the uncooperative portions of his body. "Come on." He worked the fingers, the wrist, and the elbow until he was satisfied with the movement in them. Then he surveyed the territory, trying to assess his situation.

While Falkar was wild of mien by the moment and by happenstance, M'k'n'zy had that look to him all the time. His skin also had a burnished look to it, but had more of a leathery texture to it than Falkar's, most likely due to the fact that he spent so much time out in the sun. His hair was wild and unkempt. The Xenexians had a reputation for being a savage people, but one look into M'k'n'zy's purple eyes bespoke volumes of intelligence, cunning, and canniness. No one who thought him a simple scrapper could hold to that opinion if they looked into his face for more than a moment.

One would never have thought that M'k'n'zy was merely nineteen. The years of hardship he had endured gave him a weathered look, with several deep creases already lining his forehead. And more . . . there was something in his eyes. Whatever innocence he had once possessed was long gone.

Those savage eyes scanned that section of Xenex called the Pit. It was an area approximately thirty miles across that was well known to the people of M'k'n'zy's home city of Calhoun as someplace from which people should—under ordinary circumstances—steer clear. For starters, it was extremely inhospitable, filled with small life-forms that had developed various nasty abilities required for surviving in the desert environment. Moreover, the weather was severely unpredictable, thanks to a combination of assorted fronts which would slip in and become trapped within the mountains that ringed portions of the terrain. Fierce dust storms would whip up at any time, or torrents of rain would fall—sometimes for days—to be followed by such calm and dryness that one would think that there had been no precipitation there for ages. In some areas the terrain was cracked and dry, while in others the ground was exceedingly malleable.

Beyond the physical challenges the place presented, there was something else about the area as well. Something that bordered on the supernatural. Those who were advocates of pseudoscience would claim that the Pit was a source for a rift in reality. That it was a sort of nexus, an intersection for multiple realities that would drift in and out as easily as dust motes caught up in vagrant breezes. Those who were not of a pseudoscientific bent just figured the place was haunted.

Either way, it was the most unpredictable piece of real estate on Xenex.

But although modern Xenexians gave the Pit a wide berth, centuries previously it had been part of a fundamental rite of passage among Xenexian youth. When a Xenexian reached a certain age, he or she would trudge into the midst of the Pit to embark on what was called the "Search for Allways." It was believed that, if one wandered the Pit for a sufficiently long enough time, visions of one's future would reveal themselves and one would come to understand one's true purpose in life.

However, the Search for Allways began to take a significant death toll as young Xenexians would fall prey to the dangers that the Pit presented. As a consequence, the Search disappeared from the practiced traditions of the Xenexians. This did not mean, however, that it vanished from practice altogether. Instead, it went underground. A sort of dare, a test of one's bravery and character . . . and, if truth be told, ego. Those who felt that they had a destiny—whatever that might be—would take it upon themselves to embark on a Search of their very own. Parents would try to emphasize to their children the folly of such actions, just as their parents had before them. And in most cases they were no more successful in dissuading their own children than their own parents had been in discouraging them.

By the time M'k'n'zy was thirteen, he had no parents who could try and talk sense into him (although, to be fair, even if his parents had been alive, the odds are that they would have not been successful). Loudly proclaiming to his peers that he was a young man of destiny, M'k'n'zy set out for the Pit to discover just what that glorious future might be. As the (unofficial) tradition dictated, he went out into the Pit with no supplies save for a supply of water that would last him—under ordinary circumstances—one day.

Even with rationing, by the fifth day he had used up the entire supply.

It was day eight when his big brother D'ndai found him, unconscious, dehydrated, and muttering to himself. D'ndai brought him home and, when M'k'n'zy was fully recovered, he told his friends of the remarkable visions he had seen. Visions of his people free from Danterian rule. Visions of a proud and noble people rising up against their oppressors. And he recounted these visions with such force, such conviction, and such belief that they were attainable goals, that it became the basis for the eventual uprising of the Xenexian people.

The truth was, he hadn't seen a damned thing.

It was his great frustration, his great shame. It was the last thing he wanted to admit. And so, when his friends had pressed him for details of what—if anything—he had seen, he began to string together a series of fabrications which grew with every retelling. In fact, somewhere along the way even M'k'n'zy allowed himself to believe that his claims were reality.

Deep within him he knew this wasn't the case. But, like most men of destiny, he wasn't going to allow trivialities such as truth to stand in his way.

The Danteri made their way slowly through the Pit's northwest corridor. They moved with caution, surveying literally every foot of land before them. All of them knew that the Pit could be merciless on anyone who didn't keep his guard up at all times.

Falkar kept a wary eye on the skies overhead, trying to be alert to any sudden change in the weather. He'd never actually explored the Pit, but its reputation was formidable.

Falkar's aide, Delina, suddenly stiffened as he studied the readings from a sensor device. "What is it?" Falkar demanded.

Delina turned and looked at his superior with a grim smile. "We've got him," he said. He tapped the sensor readings. "He's stationary, approximately one hundred yards west."

"He's not moving?"

"Not at all."

Falkar frowned at hearing that. "I don't like the sound of it. He could be sitting there, knowing we're looking for him, trying to lure us into a trap."

"But isn't it just as likely, sir," suggested Delina, "that he's injured? Helpless? That he's resting in hopes of remaining in hiding? How does he even know he's being pursued, sir?"

Thoughtfully, Falkar stroked his chin and stared in the direction that the sensor indicated. Stared with such intensity that one would have thought he could actually see M'k'n'zy with unaided gaze. "He knows, Delina."

"With all respect, sir, you don't know that for sure. . . ."

Falkar fixed his gaze on Delina. "When our troops moved in for the surprise raid on Calhoun . . . he knew, and the city's defenses repelled us. When we were positive that we had them cornered in the Plains of Seanwin . . . he knew, outflanked us, and obliterated five squadrons. When my top advisors assured me that the Battle of Condacin could not possibly be anticipated, that it was—in fact—the preeminent military strike of the century . . ."

Delina's face darkened. "My brother died at Condacin."

"I know," said Falkar. "And the reason was that M'k'n'zy knew. I don't know how. Maybe he trucks with the spirit world. Maybe he's psychic. All that matters is that he knew then, and he knows now."

"Let him," said Delina fiercely. "Let him for all the good it will do him. If you'll allow me, sir, I'll rip his heart out with my own hands."

Falkar studied him appraisingly. "Very well."

"Thank you, sir." Delina snapped off a smart-looking salute.

With confidence, the Danteri headed after their prey.

The confidence lasted until they moved through a narrow passageway that led to the hiding place of M'k'n'zy. Then there was a faint rumble from overhead, which quickly became far more than faint. They looked up just in time to see a massive landslide of rocks cascading toward them. There was a mad scramble forward as they tried to avoid the trap. Screeches were truncated as soldiers disappeared beneath the heavy stones. There was a brief moment of hesitation as the Danteri tried to decide—with death raining down around them—whether they should advance or fall back. Falkar was shouting orders, but was having trouble making himself heard above the din.

Falkar, in turn, did not hear Delina's shout of warning. All he knew was that suddenly Delina slammed into him, knocking him back against a wall. For a split second his breeding objected strenuously to such handling, but it was only a split second that he felt that way. Because a moment later the boulder that would have struck Falkar instead landed squarely on Delina, who hadn't been able to get himself out of the way in time. Delina vanished under the boulder, wearing an expression of both outrage . . . and satisfaction.

All of it happened within seconds. Ultimately the Danteri overcame their hesitation and did indeed drive forward, or at least the handful of survivors did.

They plunged headlong to safety, or so they thought.

In fact, what they plunged headlong into was ground that gave way beneath their feet. Falkar, bringing up the rear, stopped himself barely in time as he heard the alarmed howls from his men. The rumbling of the rockslide behind him was fading. On hands and knees, Falkar slowly edged forward and peered into the hole. Far below he saw the glint of some sort of underground cavern, and the broken bodies of his men down there. He glanced back over his shoulder and saw assorted hands and feet sticking out from between the rocks from the avalanche.

"Bastard," he hissed between clenched teeth.

M'k'n'zy mentally patted himself on the back. He could not have picked a better spot for an ambush. In the week he'd spent in his futile (and yet, curiously, productive) Search for Allways, he'd familiarized himself with much of the Pit. When he'd taken refuge there now, he had done so knowing that he was capable of outthinking and outmaneuvering anyone who might be so foolish as to try and chase him down. A simple, small explosive charge which he'd detonated from hiding was more than enough to do the job of bringing the rocks down.

As for the hidden cavern, M'k'n'zy himself had almost fallen victim to it several years previously. Fortunately he had, of course, been alone, so his far lesser weight resulted in only one leg going through the insubstantial covering above the caves. It had scared the hell out of him when it happened, but a scare was all it had been.

For the warriors who had been pursuing him, however, it had been a good deal more lethal.

Still, caution was called for. He had no intention of making the same sort of foolish mistake that his opponents had made.

M'k'n'zy left the hiding place that he'd staked out in the upper reaches of the passageway and slowly made his way to where he could see the devastation. He peered down; thirty feet below, there didn't seem to be anyone moving. There were limbs protruding from beneath rocks, and farther beyond, there was the massive hole through which the remaining soldiers had fallen.

He nodded approvingly, but decided that it would probably be wiser to maintain altitude where he could. The high ground was always preferable, after all.

So M'k'n'zy began to make his way back to his home, back to Calhoun. He wondered what sort of reception would be there for him. He further wondered—hoped, prayed—that the Danteri had finally had enough. That this latest and greatest defeat had finally convinced them that the Xenexians would never give up, never surrender, never stop believing in the rightness of their cause. Sooner or later, the Danteri would have to get the message. If it took repeated pounding in of that message, then so be it.

He sniffed a change in the air around him, and he definitely didn't like it. He had the hideous feeling that a storm was beginning to brew, and he knew from firsthand experience just how quickly such things could come up. There were outcroppings of rocks around him, plenty of places where he could anchor himself and not risk being carried away by the fierce winds that a typical Pit storm generated. As a matter of fact, he had passed what seemed to be a particularly likely sheltered area only minutes before. Smarter to retrace his steps and secure himself there until the storm had passed.

He turned around and, sensing danger, came within a millimeter of losing his life.

The blade was right at his face. It had been sweeping around, aiming toward his neck. If he hadn't unexpectedly turned at that very moment, the blade would have severed the jugular vein. As it was, he reacted just barely quickly enough to survive as the gleaming blade sliced across his face, from right temple down across his cheek, down to the bone. Blood fountained out across the right half of his face as M'k'n'zy backpedaled frantically. But with him blinded by his blood, with pain exploding in his mind, the ground went out from under the normally surefooted M'k'n'zy. He fell, landing badly and aggravating further the already existing injuries to his arms.

And during all that, not a sound escaped from his lips.

"No cry of pain," Falkar said, pausing to survey his handiwork. As an afterthought, he wiped the blade of his short sword on his garment. "I am impressed, young man. As impressed, I should hope, as you are by my ability to have crept up on you without you hearing. What with your being a savage and all, I'd think you'd pride yourself on your instincts and ability not to be surprised. So . . . were you surprised by being surprised?'' he added, unable to keep the smugness from his voice.

M'k'n'zy didn't say anything. He was too busy denying his deep urge to scream. He fought for control, breathing steadily, pushing away the agony that was eating away at him, dulling his senses, making it impossible for him to concentrate on the simple business of staying alive. His right hand was slick with blood; he was literally holding his face together.

"Did I take the eye out?'' asked Falkar, in no hurry to finish the job. He had suffered far too many losses at the hands of this young twerp. In a way, he was glad that he had missed the initial killing stroke. That had been generated as a result of rage and—he hated to admit it—a tinge of fear in facing this crafty killer man-to-man. This way was better, though. Worthier. It was the best of both worlds, really: he could face his victim, and at the same time, not worry about him. "Perhaps I'll take the other as well. I could give you that intriguing choice. Kill you . . . or leave you, but alive and blind.''

Truthfully, there was so much blood, so much pain, that M'k'n'zy couldn't even tell if he'd lost the eye altogether. His red-coated hand was clasped over the right side of his face. He felt himself dangerously close to succumbing to the ungodly torment that threatened to paralyze him. And he also knew that there was no way, despite what Falkar had just said, that Falkar was going to leave him alive. Oh, he might blind him first. Watch his progress with sadistic amusement and then kill him. Desperate for time, M'k'n'zy said, "I have . . . no love for my eyes.''

"Indeed?'' said Falkar. The steadiness of M'k'n'zy's voice was slightly disconcerting to him. "And why is that?''

And M'k'n'zy started to talk. Every word out of his mouth felt thick and forced, but he spoke and kept speaking to focus himself, to stave off the pain, to buy time . . . maybe even to remind himself that he was still alive.

"These eyes,'' he said, "in their youth . . . saw rebel leaders punished by having their unborn children . . . ripped from the wombs of their mothers. They've seen villages burned to the ground. They've . . . they've seen 'criminals' convicted of minor crimes . . . punished by having limbs lasered off . . . one at a time, screaming for mercy . . . receiving none. . . . They've seen my . . . my father tortured in the public square, punished for crimes against the state . . . a punishment ordered by you, you bastard . . . my father, beaten and whipped until a once proud man . . . was reduced to screaming even in anticipation of the blows. . . . They . . . they saw the look of pure shock on his face . . . just before his mighty heart gave out in the midst of the beating. . . . The last thing my father ever heard . . . was my begging him not to leave me . . . begging for a promise he couldn't keep. . . .'' His voice choked as he said, "These eyes . . . have seen the hand of tyranny . . . and before I grew to manhood, I wanted to lop that hand off at the wrist. . . .''

M'k'n'zy's words made Falkar exceedingly nervous. Despite M'k'n'zy's continued ability to outthink and outscheme Falkar's own war chieftains, he had always harbored the image of M'k'n'zy as a grunting savage, operating mostly out of luck and a native wit beyond anything his fellow tribesmen might possess.

But what he had just heard was hardly the speech of a barely artic- ulate savage. What the hell kind of person was capable of sounding erudite while losing blood out of his face by the pint? Suddenly all thoughts of toying with his victim, all intentions of dragging things out, evaporated. He just wanted this . . . this freak of nature dead, that was all. Dead and gone, and his head as a trophy.

What Falkar had not realized, however, was that M'k'n'zy's little speech served one additional purpose: a stall for time that allowed the coming storm to arrive. The storm that M'k'n'zy had sensed, which Falkar was oblivious of. But he was not oblivious any longer when the full blast of the storm abruptly swept down upon them.

It roared across the near plain, up through the canyons, and ham- mered down around M'k'n'zy and Falkar just as Falkar was advancing on M'k'n'zy to carve him to pieces. The wind was howling around Falkar, and he had no idea which way to look. Without having any time to prepare for it at all, Falkar was suddenly at the heart of a whirlwind. He staggered, buffeted by the powerful forces around him, and insanely he actually tried hacking at it with his sword. The wind, in turn, knocked the sword away from him. He heard it clatter away, turned in the di- rection that he thought it had fallen, but wasn't able to track it. Instead he found himself helplessly staggering around, unable to seek it out. He snarled *''I hate this planet!''* under his breath, and at that moment came to the conclusion that the Xenexians were welcome to the damned place. If he never saw it again after this day, he would count himself fortunate.

He couldn't see anything. He went to one knee, squinted fiercely, and bowed his head against the blasting of the wind. He felt around, hoping against hope that he would be able to locate his weapon. He'd probably have to track down M'k'n'zy all over again, because certainly the little barbarian would use this convenient cover to escape. That was the problem with Xenex: Nothing on the planet was ever simple.

And then wonderfully, miraculously, his questing hands discovered his fallen weapon. As the wind shrieked around him, his fingers brushed against the unmistakable metal of the blade as it lay on the ground. He let out an exclamation of joy and tried to reach over for the hilt so he could pick it up.

Suddenly the blade was lifted off the ground and for a moment he thought that the wind had tauntingly snatched it away once again. He lunged after it . . .

. . . and suddenly found that it was buried in his chest, up to the hilt.

And there was a mouth speaking softly in his ear, a nearness that almost seemed to imply a degree of intimacy. A voice that whispered, "Looking for this?"

Falkar tried to reply, but all he managed to get out was a sort of truncated gurgle. The sound of the storm diminished, replaced by a pounding in his head that blotted out all other noise. And then he rolled over onto his back, and the last thought on his mind was—unsurprisingly—the same thought he'd had only moments earlier. . . .

I hate this planet. . . .

II

Trying not to think about what he was doing . . . trying not to let the pain overwhelm him completely . . . M'k'n'zy held his face together until he was reasonably sure that blood was no longer fountaining from the gaping wound. He had no idea just how temporary the stoppage was. He was certain that the only thing preventing more bleeding was the pressure that he was applying, and considering the fact that he was fighting off unconsciousness, he had no clue how long he could continue to apply that pressure. He had visions of slumping over and bleeding to death through his sliced-open face.

He wondered if he would dream in that state. He wondered what he would dream of. Would his father and mother come walking out of swirling mists, extend a welcoming hand to him and bring him to wherever it was their souls resided (as the priests of Calhoun preached)? Or would there be blackness and oblivion (as M'k'n'zy suspected)? Then he realized his thoughts were drifting and he forced himself to focus once more.

The storm had begun to subside, and M'k'n'zy began rummaging around Falkar's body, using one hand while continuing to apply pressure to his face with the other. He was reasonably sure by this point that his right eye was intact, if for no other reason than that he didn't think anything was oozing out of the socket. But he could still barely see worth a damn, and he was operating more on feel than on sight.

He had already stuck Falkar's sword into his own belt. He felt the ornate hilt, and decided it was so elaborate that it was probably connected somehow to the royal house from which Falkar hailed. He checked around Falkar's belt and discovered some sort of pouch attached to it. He pulled on it, and it refused to yield. He yanked again, this time channeling some of the pain he was fighting off into the motion, and the pouch obediently came free. He rummaged through the pouch, hoping to find something along the lines of a first-aid kit. But there was nothing like that. Instead it appeared to be a tool pouch of some sort. Not unusual even though someone of Falkar's rank could hardly be considered a common repairman. Danteri prided themselves on being prepared for all manner of situations, and being able to make quick fixes would certainly fall under that consideration.

Then his fingers curled around something that he immediately realized could very well be of use. It was a small laser welder, handy for repairing any cracked metal surface (such as, for instance, a broken sword, or perhaps a vehicle with a hole torn in the side).

It was not, of course, intended for flesh. Unfortunately, that was the use that M'k'n'zy intended to put it to.

M'k'n'zy sat down, bracing his back against an outcropping of rock. He brought the hilt of the sword up to his teeth and bit down on it. And then he raised the welder to his face and flicked the switch. From the two prongs which extended from the top, a small, intense beam of light flickered for a moment and then held steady. He adjusted the controls, trying to bring it down to its lowest intensity, but even that looked daunting. He could not allow himself hesitation, however, for he felt blood starting to flow anew from the wound. He had no idea how much blood he had already lost, but if he didn't do something soon, there was no question in his mind that he was going to bleed to death.

The one comfort he took was that his face was already feeling so numb, he doubted he had much sensitivity left in it.

He brought the welder up to his face and took several deep breaths, once again doing everything he could to push away whatever pain he might feel. Then he touched the laser welder to his skin at his temple, at the top of the gash.

He immediately discovered that he was still more than capable of feeling pain. A sharp hiss of air exploded from between his teeth even as he fought to keep his hands steady, struggled to make sure that his head didn't move. He bit down even more tightly on the hilt. He smelled meat burning and realized that it was him. He kept telling himself, *Detach. Detach. Ignore it. The pain is happening to someone else very far away. It's not happening to you. Watch it from a great distance and do not let it bother you.* And as he kept repeating this, slowly he drew the laser welder down the side of his face. It was delicate work, because—working entirely by touch—he had to hold the pieces of his traumatized face together and heat-seal them, while at the same time keeping his fingers out of the way of the laser itself. Once he got too close and nearly bisected his thumb.

He had no idea how long it took him to complete the grisly task. When he finished, the laser welder dropped from his numbed fingers. He slumped over, the world spinning around him, and it was only at that point that he realized he was still chomping down on the hilt. He opened his mouth slightly and the short sword clattered to the ground. He noted, with grim amusement, that he had bitten into the hilt so hard that he'd left tooth marks.

He was still chuckling over that when he passed out.

When he awoke, his first thought was that he had been lying there for about a week. He couldn't even feel his mouth; his lips had completely swollen up and gone totally numb. Blissfully, night had fallen. The cool air wafted across him, gentle as a lover's embrace.

His mind informed him that this was the time to move. This was the time to haul himself to his feet and get the hell out of the Pit. It was always easier to travel at night. And he decided that that was exactly what he was going to do . . . as soon as he had rested up just a little more. He closed his eyes and—when he opened them once more—the sun was just starting to come up above the horizon.

And a creature was coming toward him.

It was small, scuttling, and seemed particularly interested in the pool of blood that had coagulated beneath his head. And, as a secondary curiosity, it also appeared to have taken a fancy to the newly soldered gash in his face. It had a hard shell, black pupils eyes, and small pincerlike claws that were clacking toward M'k'n'zy's eyes. Given another few seconds, it would easily have scooped out M'k'n'zy's right eye as if it were ice cream.

M'k'n'zy didn't even realize that he was still clutching the sword. All he knew was that, instinctively, his hand was in motion and he brought the gleaming blade swinging down and around, slicing the creature efficiently in two with such force that the two halves of the beast literally flew in opposite directions.

He smiled grimly to himself, or at least he thought he did, because he couldn't feel anything in his face.

Slowly he forced himself up to standing, his legs beginning to buckle under him before he managed to straighten them out. He tentatively rubbed the caked blood out of his eye and was pleased to discover—upon judicious blinking—that the eye was most definitely in one piece. He surveyed his surroundings, confident in his ability to find his way around in the Pit.

That self-possession lasted for as long as it took him to get a look at his whereabouts. That was when he came to the sudden, horrendous realization that he had no clear idea where he was. "It can't be," he muttered through his inflamed lips. "It can't be." He had been certain that he knew every mile, every yard of the area.

But he had collapsed right in place . . . hadn't he? No. No, apparently not. Because now, as M'k'n'zy ran the recent events through his head, there were brief moments of lucidity interspersed with the unconsciousness. He realized that, even barely conscious, he had started trying to head for home. It was as if he'd been on autopilot. But because he'd been operating in an ill, semidelusional state, he hadn't gone in any useful direction. He supposed he should count himself lucky; after all, he might have walked off a cliff. Still, he had lost enough blood to float an armada, he had a gaping wound on his face, he felt a throbbing in his forehead, and his pulse was racing. He had a suspicion that he was running a fever. Well, that was perfect, just perfect. In addition to everything else he probably had a major infection of some kind.

He looked at the position that the sun held in the sky. Knowing beyond any question that he wanted to head east, he set off determinedly in that direction. He didn't know, however, that he was concussed, confused, still in shock. Consequently, weary and bone-tired, he'd hauled himself east for nearly a day before he suddenly realized that he wanted, in fact, to head west.

By this time he couldn't move his arm at all, and he felt as if his face were on fire. But the sun had set, and he knew that there was no way he was going to survive another day of trekking through the heat. He could not, however, simply stay where he was, which meant that night travel was his only option. That suited him better, actually, because—despite his exhaustion—he was afraid to go to sleep for fear that he would not awaken. It was a concern that had some merit to it. And so, memorizing the point over the distant ridges where the sun had set, and using the stars as his guide, M'k'n'zy set off west.

He heard the howling of the storm mere moments before it hit, giving him no time at all to seek shelter, and the winds hammered him mercilessly. M'k'n'zy was sent hurtling across the ground like a rock skipping across the surface of a lake. And finally M'k'n'zy, who had endured so much in silence, actually let out a howl of fury. How much was he supposed to take? After everything that had been inflicted upon him by the Danteri, now the gods were out to get him, too? Couldn't he be the recipient of the smallest crumb of luck?

And the gods answered him. The answer, unfortunately, was to try and make clear to him that he was something of an ingrate. He was, after all, still alive. The gods, if gods there were, had permitted him to survive, and if that was not sufficient for him, well then here was a reminder of how grateful he should be. Whereupon the winds actually lifted M'k'n'zy off his feet. His hands clawed at air, which naturally didn't provide him with much support.

"Stoppppp!" he shouted, and then he did indeed stop . . . when the wind slammed him against a stone outcropping. And darkness drew M'k'n'zy in once more.

And the darkness tried to hold on to him as well, keeping him there as a permanent dweller. After what seemed an eternity, he fought his way back to wakefulness. By the time he awoke it was day again. His fever was blazing, his wound red and inflamed. He felt as if the only two things inside his skull were the constant pounding and a tongue that had swollen to three times its normal size. He now had a ghastly purpling bruise on the left side of his head to match the mangling of the right side of his face.

By this point he had no clear idea where he was supposed to go, in which direction lay safety, or even what safety was. His own identity was beginning to blur. He fought to remember his name, his home, his purpose. He was . . . he was M'k'n'zy of Calhoun . . . and he . . .

And then, like an insect wafted by a breeze, it would flitter away from him before he could quite wrap himself around it. He tried to chase it, as if he were capable of actually laying hands on a passing thought, and then he collapsed while at the top of a small hill. He tumbled forward, rolling down gravel which shredded his abused body even further. By the time he lay at the bottom of the hill, he was beyond caring.

He might have lain there for hours or days. He wasn't sure. He wasn't interested. All he wanted was for the pounding to go away, for the heat to leave him, for the pain to cease. How much was he supposed to endure, anyway? How much was he supposed to take?

He was tired. Tired of people depending upon him. Tired of people looking to him for decisions. All his life, as far back as he could remember, he had been fired with determination and singularity of vision. Obsession, some would likely have called it. Still others would have dubbed it insanity.

But behind the obsession or insanity or whatever label some would attach to it was his own, deep-rooted fear that he would be "found out." That deep down he was nothing more than a frightened young man, rising to the demands or expectations held by himself and others. As he lay there, feverish and dying, all the midnight fears visited themselves upon him, boldly displaying themselves in the heat of the midday sun. Fears of inadequacy, fears of not measuring up to the task he had set himself and the standard others now held for him.

It had been so easy at first. There had been no expectations. He had fired up his followers based solely on conviction and charisma. He had predicted success in battle, and then provided it. He had told his people that the Danteri would soon find themselves on the defensive, and he'd met that promise as well.

But as he'd taken the Xenexians step by difficult step closer to their goal, paradoxically that goal became more and more frightening even as it drew constantly closer. For two fears continued to burn within him. One was that, after all the effort and striving, the goal would be snatched from them at the last moment. And the second was that, if the goal was achieved . . . if the Xenexians won their freedom from the Danteri . . .

. . . then what?

He'd never thought beyond it. Indeed, the fact that he never had thought beyond it was enough to make him wonder whether he himself, secretly, deep down, didn't consider it a true possibility.

Get up.

His eyes flickered open, wondering at the voice within his head. It was the first thing he'd detected inside his skull in ages aside from the pounding.

His father was standing nearby, standing in profile. His back was raw with whip marks. The sun shone through his head, and a small creature scuttled uncaring through his foot. He didn't seem to notice. *Get up, damn you,* he said, his mouth not moving.

"Go away," said M'k'n'zy. "Go away. Just want to sleep."

Get up. I order you to . . .

"Save your orders!" snapped M'k'n'zy. At least, that's what it sounded like to him. Truth to tell, he was so dehydrated, his lips so swollen and cracked, his tongue such a useless slab of overcooked meat, that anyone else listening would have been able to discern nothing much beyond inarticulate grunts. "I begged you to stay! Begged you! Where were your orders, your pride, when I needed you, huh? Where? *Where?*"

Get up.

"Go to hell," he said, and rolled over, turning his back to his father.

There was a woman next to him. A naked woman, with thick blond hair and a mischievous grin on her face. She was running intangible fingers across his chest.

Get up, sleepyhead, she said. There was a playfulness in her voice, and something told him that it wasn't her usual tone. That it was something she reserved for him, and only for him. That in real life, she was tough, unyielding, uncompromising. Only with him would she let down her guard.

He blinked in confusion. He had never seen her before, and yet it was as if he knew her intimately. It was as if she filled a void that he didn't even know he had. "Who—?"

Get up, Mac, she admonished him. *We have things to do.* . . .

He stared at her. She had a beautiful body. A flat stomach, firm breasts. M'k'n'zy had never, in point of fact, seen a naked woman before. Oh, there had been women, yes. But it had always been rushed, even secretive, under cover of darkness or with most clothes still in place. He had never simply relaxed with a woman, though. Never lain naked next to one, never idly run his fingers over her form, tracing her curves. Never been at ease . . . with anyone. . . .

. . . *What are you thinking, Mac?* she asked him.

He reached a tentative hand over to cup her breast, and his hand passed through and came up with sand. There was no sign of her.

With a howl of frustration (or, more realistically, a strangled grunt) he lunged for the place where she'd been, as if he hoped to find that she had sunk straight into the sand and was hiding just below the surface. Some sand got in his eye, and it felt like someone had jabbed pieces of glass into his face. He blinked the eye furiously until the obstruction was gone, but now his vision was clouded.

The world was spinning around him and this time he did nothing to fight it off. All he had to do was get some rest and he'd be okay. That was the one thing of which he was absolutely positive.

Yes . . . yes, just a little rest . . .

The ground seemed softer than he'd thought it would. Everything was relaxing around him, beckoning to him to relax, just . . . relax. That was all he had to do.

That's not an option.

It was a different voice this time, and it certainly wasn't female. He looked up in confusion.

There was a man standing there, shimmering as if from a far-off time and place. He wore some sort of uniform, black and red, with a gleaming metal badge on his chest. He was more or less bald, and his face was sharp and severe. Yet there was compassion there as well.

"Go away," whispered M'k'n'zy.

You're a Starfleet officer. No matter what you are now . . . that is what you will always be. You cannot turn away from that.

M'k'n'zy had absolutely no idea what was happening, and he certainly was clueless as to what this . . . this transparent being was talking about. "What's . . . what's Starfleet? What . . . who are you? What . . . ''

You have a destiny. *Don't you dare let it slide away. Now get up. Get up, if you're a man.*

There was a gurgle of anger deep within M'k'n'zy's throat. He didn't know who this shade was, didn't comprehend the things he said. But no one questioned M'k'n'zy's bravery. No one . . . not even hallucinations.

M'k'n'zy hauled himself to his feet, adrenaline firing him. He staggered forward, and the bald taunter didn't disappear as the woman had. Instead he seemed to float in front of M'k'n'zy, M'k'n'zy steadily pursuing him. He continued to speak to M'k'n'zy, but M'k'n'zy wasn't really paying attention to the details of his words. Indeed, they all seemed to blend together.

And he heard ghosts of other voices as well, although he didn't see the originators. Voices with odd accents, saying strange names . . .

. . . and there was one word repeated. It seemed to be addressed to him, which was why it caught his attention. And the word was . . .

. . . *Captain.*

He tried rolling the unfamiliar word around in his mouth, to say it. As before, nothing intelligible emerged.

Time and distance seemed to melt away around him as he followed the floating, spectral figure. Every step brought newer, greater strength to his legs, and soon his pain was forgotten, his dizziness forgotten, everything forgotten except catching up with his vision.

It all came rushing back to him. The stories of the Allways, the visions of one's future that one could come upon in the Pit if one was open enough to them. The visions which had refused to come to him when he had sought them out. And now, when nothing concerned him— not even his own survival—that was when sights of the future presented themselves.

But was it the future? Or was it just . . . just fanciful notions from deep within his subconscious? That certainly seemed the more reasonable explanation. In his youth (odd that a man barely past nineteen summers would think in such terms) he had believed in fanciful mysticism. But he'd seen too much, stood over too many bloodied bodies. The fancies of his younger days were far behind.

But still . . . it had seemed real . . . so real . . .

And it was still there.

Still there.

That floating, bald-headed son of a bitch was *still* there, floating away, leading him on, ever on. M'k'n'zy let out a roar of frustration that, this time, actually sounded like something other than a grunt, and he ran. If he'd actually been paying attention to what he was doing, he would have realized the pure impossibility of it. He was suffering from exhaustion, blood loss, dehydration, and fever. There was no way that someone who was in that bad shape should be able to move at a dead run across the blazing surface of the Pit, yet that was precisely what M'k'n'zy was doing. And it was all happening because he refused to let that ghostly whatever-it-was taunt him this way.

"Who are you?!" he shouted. "Where are you from? Where's the girl? What's happening?! What's going to happen! Damn you, I am M'k'n'zy of Calhoun, and *you will not run from me!"*

There was a gap in the ground directly in his path. If he'd fallen into it, he could easily have broken his leg. It was five feet wide and eight feet deep. He leaped over it without slowing down in the slightest, and he wasn't even really aware that it was there.

And then he saw that the phantom, which was still some yards ahead, was beginning to shimmer. He got the sense that it was fading out on him altogether, and the knowledge infuriated him all the more. "Get back here!" he shouted. *"Get back here!"*

The specter faded altogether . . . but there was something standing in its place. Something of far greater substance, accompanied by a few other somethings.

M'k'n'zy's brother, D'ndai, stood there and waved his arms frantically. Around him were several other members of the search party, which had been wandering the Pit for some days in what had seemed increasingly futile search for M'k'n'zy.

D'ndai was a head taller than M'k'n'zy, and half again as wide. He was also several years older. Yet from the way in which D'ndai treated his brother, one would have thought that D'ndai was the younger, for he seemed to regard M'k'n'zy with a sort of wonder. In many ways, truthfully, he was in awe of D'ndai. M'k'n'zy had always taken great pride in the fact that D'ndai was such a confident, trusting soul that he didn't feel the least bit threatened by the fact that his younger brother's star shone far more brightly than his own.

The relief which flooded over and through D'ndai was visible for all to see. He choked back a sob of joy and threw wide his arms, shouting his brother's name.

M'k'n'zy ran up to him . . .

. . . and pushed past him.

"Get back here!" he shouted at thin air.

The rescue party members looked at each other in confusion. On the one hand M'k'n'zy looked to be in absolutely hideous shape; on the other hand, he certainly seemed peppy enough for a man who was at death's door.

"M'k'n'zy?'' called D'ndai in confusion.

M'k'n'zy didn't appear to hear him, or if he did, he simply ignored him. Instead he kept on running, gesticulating furiously, howling, "You don't get away that easily!'' By the time the rescuers had recovered their wits, he was already fifty paces beyond them and moving fast.

They set out after him at a full run, and it was everything they could do to catch up with him. D'ndai reached him first, and grabbed him by the arm. "M'k'n'zy!'' he shouted, keeping him in place. He gasped as he saw the huge gash in his brother's face close up for the first time. He tried not to let his shock sound in his voice. "M'k'n'zy, it's me!''

"Let me go!'' he shouted, yanking furiously at D'ndai's arm. "Let me go! I have to catch him!''

"There's nothing there! You're hallucinating!''

"He's getting away! *He's getting away!*''

D'ndai swung him around and fairly shouted in his face, "M'k'n'zy, get hold of yourself! There's *nothing there!*''

M'k'n'zy again tried to pull clear, but when he turned to attempt further pursuit of whatever it was that existed in his delusional state, he seemed to sag in dismay. "He's gone! He got away!'' He turned back, hauled off and slugged D'ndai with a blow that—had he been at full strength—would damn near have taken D'ndai's head off. As it was, it only rocked him slightly back on his feet. "He got away and it's all your fault!''

"Fine, it's my fault,'' D'ndai said.

M'k'n'zy looked at him with great disdain and said, "And what are you going to do about it?''

"I'm going to take you home . . . help you . . . cure you . . .'' He put his hand against M'k'n'zy's forehead. "Gods, you're burning up.''

M'k'n'zy tried to make a response, but just then the exhaustion, the fever, everything caught up with him at the exact moment that the adrenaline wore off. He tried to say something, but wasn't able to get a coherent sentence out. Instead he took a step forward and then sagged into his older brother's arms. D'ndai lifted him as if he were weightless and said, "Let's get him out of here.''

"Do you think he'll make it?" one of the others asked him.

"Of course he'll make it," said D'ndai flatly as he started walking at a brisk clip in the direction of their transport vehicles. "He's got too much to do to die."

III

M'k'n'zy heard them talking in quiet, hushed tones outside his room, and slowly he sat up in bed. He was pleased to see that, for the first time in days, all of the dizziness was gone. He didn't feel the slightest bit disoriented. The pounding had long faded. In short, he finally didn't feel as if his head were about to fall off at any given moment, a state of affairs that could only be considered an improvement.

D'ndai had been cautioning him to stay put, to take it easy, to rest up. He was being extremely solicitous of his younger brother's health, and it was starting to get on M'k'n'zy's nerves. His impulse was to get out of bed and back on his feet, but D'ndai was always cautioning him not to rush things. It was advice that M'k'n'zy was having a hard time taking. It didn't help that it was, in fact, very solid advice indeed. Particularly considering the fact that the first time M'k'n'zy had defiantly sprung from his bed, proclaiming that he was fit and ready to go, the room promptly tilted at forty-five degrees and sent him tumbling to the ground. That had been over a week ago.

Now, though, the room graciously stayed put. M'k'n'zy padded over to a closet, pulled out fresh clothes, and dressed quickly. He didn't feel the slightest twinge of pain or dizziness as he did so, and considered himself on that basis fully recovered.

He stepped out into the hallway and startled D'ndai and the three other Xenexians who were holding a whispered conference. "Oh! You're up!" said D'ndai.

"How could I be anything but, considering the yammering going on out here," M'k'n'zy replied good-naturedly. "What's going on? What are you whispering about?"

D'ndai and the others looked at each other momentarily, and then D'ndai turned to M'k'n'zy and said, "Danteri representatives are here."

"Excellent," said M'k'n'zy. "You hold them down, I'll hack their heads off."

"They're here under flag of truce, M'k'n'zy."

M'k'n'zy gave him an incredulous look. "And you *accepted* it? Gods, D'ndai, why? They'll think we're soft!"

"M'k'n'zy . . ."

"If we showed up at their back door under a flag of truce, they'd invite us in, pull up a chair, and then execute us before we could say a word. I say we do them the same courtesy."

"M'k'n'zy, they have Federation people with them."

M'k'n'zy leaned against the door, weighing that piece of news. "The Federation?" he said. *"The* Federation?"

D'ndai nodded, knowing what was going through M'k'n'zy's mind.

Their father had told them tales of the Federation in their youth. Stories passed on to him from his father, and his father before him. An agglomeration of worlds, with great men and women spanning the galaxy in vast ships that traversed the starways as casually as mere Xenexians would cross a street. Explorers, adventurers, the like of which had never been seen on Xenex except fleetingly. Every so often there would be reports that one or two or three Federation people had shown up somewhere on Xenex . . . had looked around, spoken to someone about matters that seemed to be of no consequence, and then vanished again. It was almost as if the Federation was . . . studying them for some reason. Sometimes it was difficult to decide whether certain such reported encounters were genuine, or the product of fanciful minds.

But this . . . this was indisputable. And then a chilling thought struck M'k'n'zy. "They're here on the Dentari side? Here to aid them in suppressing us?" A frightening notion indeed, because the stories of the

Federation's military prowess were many. They might very well have been based on conjecture and exaggeration, but if even a tenth of what they'd heard was accurate, they could be in extremely serious trouble.

D'ndai shook his head. "I don't think so, no. They claim they're here to try and smooth matters over."

"Well . . . let them try," said M'k'n'zy. "Shall we go speak to them?"

"Are you sure you're . . . ?"

M'k'n'zy didn't even let him get the question out, but instead said quickly, "Yes, I am fine, I assure you. Perfectly fine. Let's go."

They headed down the short hallway to the conference room. The structure in which they were was, of necessity, rather small. Building materials were at a premium, nor was there any desire to make such an important building too big and, hence, an easy target. M'k'n'zy confidently strode into the conference room . . .

. . . and he stopped dead.

He recognized two of the three individuals he found waiting for him in the conference room. One was a member of the royal house of Danteri; his name was Bragonier. And the other . . .

. . . the other was the bald man from the Pit.

M'k'n'zy couldn't believe it. He resisted the impulse to walk over and tap the man on the chest to see if he was, in fact, real. He looked straight at M'k'n'zy with that level, piercing gaze which M'k'n'zy had found so infuriating. Standing next to him was the only one in the group he didn't recognize. He had thin brown hair, a square-jawed face, and wore a similar uniform to the bald man.

Bragonier took them in with a baleful glare. When he spoke he did not address the Xenexians, but rather the men at his side. "Are the people of Xenex not exactly as I promised, Captain?"

That word . . . *captain.* It so caught M'k'n'zy's fancy that, for a moment, he blithely overlooked Bragonier's snide tone of voice. But only for a moment. "We may not have your polish and breeding, Danteri," said D'ndai with a mock bow, "but we also do not share your string of defeats. We accept the one as the price for the other." At that moment M'k'n'zy wished that he had the sword with him. The one he had taken off Falkar. The sight of that would have likely sent Bragonier into total apoplexy.

But he needn't have worried, for his brother's words were more than enough to rile Bragonier, who began to rise from his seat. But the bald man standing next to him had a hand resting on Bragonier's shoulder. It was a deceptively relaxed hold. For when Bragonier tried to stand, the bald man was able to keep him stationary with what appeared to be no effort at all. And Bragonier was powerfully built, which meant that the bald man was stronger than he looked. And he radiated confidence.

"I am Captain Jean-Luc Picard of the Federation starship *Stargazer*," he said, and nodded in the direction of the man next to him. "This is Lieutenant Jack Crusher. We represent the United Federation of Planets . . . an alliance of starfaring worlds."

Crusher said, "We have been . . . surveying your world for some time, and have made tentative first contact in the past. We feel you are culturally prepared to understand and interact with the UFP and its representatives."

"In other words, we've risen up to your level," D'ndai said without a trace of irony.

Nonetheless the irony was there, and Picard stepped in. "No offense meant. The fact is . . . the Danteri have asked us to aid them in this . . . difficult situation."

"Aid how?" D'ndai asked.

"To be perfectly candid," the man identified as Crusher said, "the Danteri Empire represents a rather strategically situated group of worlds. The Federation has been in discussion with the Danteri about their possibly joining us."

"But the Danteri seemed skeptical that the Federation had anything to offer," Picard now said. "However, they felt themselves stymied by the recent upheavals on this world. And their innate pride hampered their ability to discuss peace settlements with you in any sort of workable fashion."

"We could have," Bragonier said with a flash of anger. "It's not simply pride. It is them! They're savages, Picard! Look at them!"

Picard regarded them a moment. His interest seemed most fixed on M'k'n'zy, and M'k'n'zy met his level gaze unwaveringly. "I've seen worse," Picard said after a moment. "And you would be . . . M'k'n'zy, I assume?" His pronunciation was hardly the best; he tripped over the gutturals in M'k'n'zy's name.

M'k'n'zy made no attempt to correct how his name was spoken. He merely nodded, his lips pressed tightly together. It was a surreal situation for him, to be standing and conversing with a being who, barely a week ago, had been little more than a figment of his imagination.

"Your reputation precedes you," Picard said. "The Danteri have little good to say about you. About any of you. But that is of no interest to me whatsoever." His voice was sharp and no-nonsense. "I do not care who began what. I am not interested in a list of grievances. One thing and one thing only concerns me, and that is bringing you all together so that you can reach an accord. An understanding. A compromise, if you will, so the bloodshed will end."

There was silence for a long moment, and then M'k'n'zy finally spoke his first words to the in-the-flesh incarnation of Jean-Luc Picard.

"Go to hell," he said.

Bragonier's face purpled when he heard that. Crusher blinked in surprise, for he was somewhat unaccustomed to anyone, from lowliest yeoman to highest-ranking admiral, addressing Captain Jean-Luc Picard in that manner.

Picard, for his part, did not seem disconcerted in the slightest. Instead he said nothing; merely raised an eyebrow and waited, knowing that M'k'n'zy wouldn't let it rest there. Knowing that M'k'n'zy would have more to say.

And he did. "I know their idea of compromise," he said flatly. "Promise us a limited presence on our world. Promise us a slow pull-out. Promise us that we'll have self-government within six months. Promise us riches and personal fortune. And then yank it back at your convenience. Well, damn your promises and damn your lies. We want one thing and one thing only: the Danteri off our world for good. No contact. No overseeing. Forget we exist."

"I would gladly do so," said Bragonier tersely.

"Ohhh no you wouldn't," said M'k'n'zy. He leaned forward on the table, resting his knuckles on it. He was very aware of Picard's watching him, appraising him. "I know your kind. You will never forget. And you will never rest until my brethren and I are eliminated, and my people are subjugated. Well, I am here to tell you that it will not happen. These are my people, and to concede to you, to compromise with you, will be a betrayal of their faith in us. We will give them Xenex for Xenexians. If that is what you have come to offer, then offer it. Anything less, and you can leave."

"I am Bragonier of the royal house," Bragonier informed him archly. "You cannot simply dismiss us as if—"

"Get out," M'k'n'zy replied, and he turned and walked out. From behind him, Bragonier blustered and shouted. But he did so to an empty room as the rest of the Xenexians followed M'k'n'zy out.

They walked out into the hallway and started down it. And then, from behind them, Picard's firm voice called out to them. They stopped and turned to face Picard. Although Picard addressed all of them, his focus was upon M'k'n'zy.

"That was foolish," said Picard. "And you do not strike me as someone who does foolish things."

"Look . . . Captain," M'k'n'zy replied, "you've just gotten here. I know these people. They are arrogant and deceitful, and think us fools. If we immediately listen to what they have to say, we will have to tolerate more of their condescension. There can be no peace, no talks, no rational discourse, until they are willing to understand that we are not their subjects, their slaves, or their toys."

Picard's hawklike gaze narrowed. "We will return tomorrow," he said. "And I shall make certain that Bragonier is in a more . . . positive mood."

"Whatever," M'k'n'zy said, sounding indifferent.

Picard hesitated a moment, and then said, "M'k'n'zy . . . may we speak privately for a moment?"

M'k'n'zy glanced at the others. D'ndai shrugged. M'k'n'zy headed to his room, with Picard following him. They entered and M'k'n'zy turned quickly. He never let his guard down for a moment, a trait that Picard noticed and appreciated. Picard took a step closer and told him, "These people listen to you, M'k'n'zy. They obey you. The capacity for leadership is one of the greatest gifts in the universe. But it brings with it a heavy burden. Never forget that."

"I have not . . ."

"You are in danger of doing so," Picard told him. "I can tell. You're filled with rage over past grievances. It's understandable. But that rage can blind you to what's best for your people."

"My rage fuels me and helps me survive."

"Perhaps. But there's more to life than survival. You must believe that yourself; otherwise you'd never have come this far or accomplished all you have."

Slowly, M'k'n'zy nodded. "Nothing is more important than the good of my people. All that I do . . . I do for them."

Picard smiled. "Save that for them. That's the sentiment they want to hear. But you and I both know . . . you do it for you. No one else. You take charge, you lead, not because you want to . . . but because you have to. Because to do any less would be intolerable."

Remarkably, M'k'n'zy felt a bit sheepish. He looked down, his thick hair obscuring his face.

"You're an impressive young man, M'k'n'zy," Picard said. "Rarely have I seen so many people of power speak a name with such a combination of anger and envy. You've accomplished a great deal . . . and you are only . . . what? Twenty-two?"

"Nineteen summers."

Picard's composure was rock-steady, but he was unable to hide the astonishment in his eyes. "Nineteen?"

M'k'n'zy nodded.

"And your goals are entirely centered around overcoming the Danteri hold and freeing your people."

"Nothing else matters," M'k'n'zy said flatly.

"And after you've accomplished that?"

" 'After?' " He pondered that, then shrugged. " 'After' isn't important."

And in a slightly sad tone, Picard said, " 'And he subdued countries of nations, and princes; and they became tributary to him. And after these things he fell down upon his bed, and knew that he should die.' " When M'k'n'zy looked at him in puzzlement, Picard said, "A problem faced by another talented young man, named Alexander. For people such as he . . . and you . . . and me . . . the prospect of no new worlds to conquer can end up being a devastating one. In other words . . . you should give serious thought to goals beyond the short term."

"Perhaps I shall continue to lead my people here."

"Perhaps," agreed Picard. "Will that satisfy you?"

"I . . ." It was the first time that M'k'n'zy actually sounded at all confused. "I don't know."

"Well . . . at the point which you do know . . . let me know."

He turned to go, but stopped a moment when M'k'n'zy demanded, "Why are you so interested in me?"

Now it was Picard who shrugged. "A hunch," he said. "Nothing more than that. But captains learn to play their hunches. It's how they become captains."

"I see. So . . . if I had a hunch . . . that you were important to my future . . . that in itself might be indicative of something significant."

"Possibly," said Picard.

M'k'n'zy seemed lost in thought, and Picard once again headed toward the door.

And then M'k'n'zy said, "Captain?"

"Yes?"

"You, uhm," and M'k'n'zy cleared his throat slightly. "You wouldn't happen to have brought a naked blond woman with you . . . ?"

Picard stared at him uncomprehendingly. "I beg your pardon?"

Waving him off, M'k'n'zy said, "Never mind."

"If you don't mind my saying so, that was a rather curious question."

"Yes, well . . ." M'k'n'zy smiled slightly. "Call it a hunch, for what that's worth."

Picard considered that, and then said, "Well . . . I didn't say all hunches were good ones. A captain has to pick and choose."

"I'll remember that," said M'k'n'zy.

He watched Picard walk out and thought for a time about what had transpired . . . certain that something important had happened here this day, but not entirely sure what. Then he looked over at his bed, thought about what Picard had said about dying in it . . . and exited the room as quickly as possible.

TEN
    YEARS
        EARLIER . . .

        SOLETA

I

She ran the tricorder for what seemed the fiftieth time over the sample she had taken of the Thallonian soil. She was confused by the readings, and yet that confusion did not generate frustration, but rather excitement. She had not known what to expect when she had first arrived on Thallon to conduct her research . . . only that the rumors which had reached her ears had been most curious. Most curious indeed.

Anyone watching would have found themselves spellbound by her exotic looks. Her face was somewhat triangular in its general structure, and her eyes were deep set and a piercing blue. She had thick black hair which was pinned up with a pin that bore the symbol known as the IDIC. Her ears were long, tapered, and pointed.

She had chosen what seemed to her a fairly deserted area, far away from the capital city of Thal. Nonetheless, despite her distance, she could still see the imperial palace at the edge of the horizon line. It was dusk, and the purple haze of the Thallonian sky provided a colorful contrast to the gleaming amber of the palace's spires. One thing could definitely be said for the Thallonian ruling class, and that was that they had a thorough command of the word "ostentatious."

There was a fairly steady breeze blowing over the surface of her "dig." A small, all-purpose tent, which collapsed neatly into her pack when not in use, was set up nearby, its sides fluttering in the breeze. She did not intend to stay overly long on Thallon, for she knew that an extended stay would be exceedingly unwise. For that matter, even an abbreviated stay wasn't the single most bright thing she had ever done.

She couldn't resist, though. The things she'd heard about Thallon were so intriguing that she simply had to sneak onto the home world of the Thallonian Empire and see for herself. She had been most crafty in arriving there. Her one-person craft, equipped with state-of-the-art sensory deflectors, had enabled her to slip onto Thallon undetected. Now all she had to do was finish her work and get off before she was . . .

The ground was rumbling beneath her feet. Only for a moment did she think it was a quake. Then she realized the true source of the disruption: mounted riders, obviously astride beasts sufficiently heavy to set the ground trembling when they moved. And from the rapidly increasing intensity of the vibrations, it was painfully obvious to her that they were heading her way.

She had been so preoccupied with her studies that she hadn't noticed it earlier. This was disastrously sloppy on her part; with her accelerated hearing, she should have heard intruders long before she felt them. However, mentally chastising herself wasn't going to accomplish anything.

Her pack was usually quite organized, with pouches and containers carefully chosen for every single item she might be carrying with her. And if she'd had the time—any time at all—she would have maintained that organization. But she had no time at all, so she quickly gathered her materials together, stuffing everything into her pack with no heed or care. She could have left it all behind, but she had no desire to abandon the scientific data she had gathered. One had to prioritize, after all.

She slung the pack over her shoulders and bolted for her craft . . .

. . . and stopped.

The craft was gone.

Her eyes narrowed and then she saw the nose of the craft protruding just above the ground. The entire thing had descended into what appeared to be a sinkhole of some kind . . . a sinkhole large enough to swallow her entire vessel.

She stared at the sinkhole and said flatly, "That was *not* there before. If it had been there, I would have not landed my ship on it."

Suddenly she looked up as, just over the crest of a nearby rise, several riders appeared. They were five of them, astride great six-legged beasts with gleaming ebony skin. One of the riders, curiously, was a young girl, several years shy of adolescence. She kept near one of the adults, a man who . . .

Well, now, he was definitely an interesting-looking individual. He held the reins of his mount with one hand, as if imperiously certain that the creature would not dare to throw him. It was hard to get a reading for his height since he was riding; if she'd had to guess, she'd have pegged him at just over six feet. His skin was the typical dark red of the Thallonian upper caste, and his brow was slightly distended. His head was shaven, and he had small, spiral tattoos on his forehead. His jaw was outthrust, his eyes rather small. Indeed, she would have not been able to see his eyes at all, had he not been looking directly at her. He sported a thin beard which ran the length of his jawline, and came to a point that made him look slightly satanic.

The girl to his right had skin a slightly lighter shade of red. Her head was not shaved, and her hair grew thick and yellow. But she had a single tattoo on her forehead.

Neither of them spoke, however. Instead the lead rider, a massively built Thallonian astride a mount who looked as if his back would break, said imperiously, "I am Thallonian Chancellor Yoz, and you are under arrest." He had guards on either side of him who glowered at the woman as if annoyed that she was disrupting their day.

As if he hadn't spoken, the woman pointed at the area where her ship had vanished and said again, "That was *not* there before. That sinkhole. The topography simply cannot change that way, not so abruptly."

Yoz stared at her as if she'd lost her mind. "I said you are under arrest. Submit to my authority."

"I'm busy," she said brusquely, her immediate difficulty forgotten.

The imperious-looking man at the girl's side half-smiled at Chancellor Yoz. "You have her nicely intimidated, Lord Chancellor. She should be begging for mercy at any moment now."

"Worry not, Lord Cwan. She will not retain her insolence."

"I was not worried," said the one called Cwan. "Worst comes to worst, she can always replace you as Lord Chancellor."

Yoz did not appear amused by the observation. Angrily he demanded of the defiant female, ''What is your name?''

''Soleta. Now please leave me to my work. This is a scientifically curious situation, and it takes precedence over the famed Thallonian inhospitableness.'' She began to unsling her pack so she could pull out her tricorder.

With annoyance, Chancellor Yoz urged his steed forward and it moved with confidence toward the woman who'd called herself Soleta. She glanced with impatience at him and said, ''Go away.''

''Now you listen here . . .'' he began.

With an impatient blowing of air between her teeth, Soleta reached over and clamped her left hand at the base of the mount's neck. The creature let out a brief shriek of surprise and then collapsed. It rolled over to the right, pinning Chancellor Yoz beneath it.

Surprisingly, Soleta heard a peal of laughter from the girl. It drew her attention just long enough for one of the guards to pull out a weapon and fire it, point blank, at Soleta. It knocked her off her feet with such force that she felt as if she'd been slammed with a sledgehammer in the chest. She hit the ground and was busy making mental assessments as to just what precisely the nature of the weapon was when she fell into unconsciousness. And the last thing she heard was the voice of Cwan saying, ''You certainly showed her who was in charge, Chancellor. Perhaps she *should* replace you at that . . .''

II

Soleta stared at the four walls of the dungeon around her and wondered just how much one was reasonably supposed to suffer in the pursuit of scientific knowledge. Unfortunately, the skeleton lying next to her didn't seem inclined to provide an answer.

She suspected the Thallonians left skeletons lying around their dungeons for dramatic effect. Perhaps even to intimidate prisoners. Certainly it didn't seem to serve any logical purpose.

The dungeon itself was hideously primitive-looking. The floor was strewn with straw, the walls made of rock. It was a contrast to the other parts of the palace, which had a far more contemporary look. Far in the distance, her sharp ears were able to take in the sounds of celebration. The Thallonian royal family was having one of their famous "do's."

"Pity I wasn't invited," she said dryly to no one in particular.

She pulled experimentally on the bonds that attached her wrists to the wall. They weren't anything as arcane as chain, which would have been consistent with the decor. Instead they seemed to be some sort of coated cable. They were, however, rather effective. They seemed solidly attached to the wall, without the slightest interest in being broken by her efforts. They were firmly attached to her wrists by means of thick wristlets. The key was securely in the possession of the guards outside. She was having trouble brushing her hair out of her face since her movement was impeded. Her IDIC pin was gone; she had no idea whether someone had stolen it or if it was just lost in the desert. She was saddened by the loss. The pin had no intrinsic value, but she had had it for quite some time and had become rather attached to it.

Her chest had stopped hurting a while back. She was reasonably sure that the weapon had been some sort of sonic disruptor device. Very primitive. Also very effective.

She heard footsteps approaching the door as she had many times in the two days since she'd been tossed in here. She wondered if, as had been the case those other times, they would just walk on past. But then they seemed to slow down and stop just outside the door. There was a noise, a sound of an electronic key at a lock, and then the door swung open.

Standing framed in the doorway was the guard who had tossed Soleta into the dungeon upon the instructions of no less prestigious an individual than the Chancellor of Thallon. Standing next to him was another individual whom Soleta could not quite make out. He was cloaked and robed, a hood pulled up over his head.

"You have company," said the guard. "You can rot together."

Soleta said nothing. Somehow it didn't seem the sort of comment that really required a reply.

The guard seemed to display a flicker of disappointment, as if hoping that she'd beg or plead or in some way try to convince him that she should be released. It was a bit of a pity; in times past, he'd been able to milk the desperation of some female prisoners for his own . . . advantage. Ah well. If she was made of sterner stuff than that, it was of no consequence to him. For that matter, it meant that if she eventually came around it would make her capitulation that much sweeter.

He guided the hooded and robed figure over to the opposite corner of the dungeon. "Sit," he snapped, his hand tapping the sonic disruptor which dangled prominently from his right hip. The newcomer obediently sat and the guard snapped cuffs identical to Soleta's into place around the newcomer's wrists. The guard stepped back, nodded approvingly, then turned to Soleta. "In case you're wondering, you had a trial today."

"Did I," Soleta said levelly. "I do not recall it."

"You didn't attend. Thallonian law feels that matters proceed more smoothly if the accused is not present. Otherwise things are slowed down."

"Far be it from me to stand in the way of efficient Thallonian justice. I was found guilty, I assume."

"The charge was trespassing," the guard said reasonably, arms folded. "You're here. That makes it fairly indisputable. The penalty is death, of course."

"Of course. Is an appeal possible?"

"Naturally. Thallonian law may be strict, but we are not unreasonable barbarians. As a matter of fact, your appeals hearing is scheduled for tomorrow."

"Ah." Soleta nodded and, with a sanguine tone, said, "You will be certain to come by and tell me how I did."

He inclined his head slightly in a deferential manner and then walked out, the door slamming shut solidly behind him.

Soleta turned and stared at the figure in the shadows. "Who are you?"

The figure was silent for a moment. When he spoke, it was in a tone that was flat and level, and just a touch ironic. "A fellow guest. And you are the famed 'Soleta,' I assume."

She made no effort to hide her surprise. "How did you know?"

"Word of you has spread. Apparently you dispatched the high chancellor in a manner not keeping with his dignity. Si Cwan informed anyone who would listen. He was more than happy to—what is the expression—take Chancellor Yoz 'down a few pegs.' " He paused a moment. "May I ask why you are here?"

She sighed. "Scientific curiosity. In my wanderings, I'd heard some rather odd reports about the surface structure of Thallon. Some very unique geophysical, high-energy readings."

"Your 'wanderings,' did you say?"

"Yes."

From within the folds of his hood, he seemed to incline his head slightly. "You are a Vulcan. Vulcans do not generally 'wander' aimlessly. There is usually more direction and purpose in their lives."

She was silent for a moment. "I am not . . . entirely Vulcan. My mother was Vulcan . . . but my father, Romulan." She shrugged, a casually human gesture which was in contrast to her demeanor. "I'm not sure why I'm telling you. Perhaps because you are the last individual with whom I shall hold a relatively normal conversation. I have very little to hide.''

"Indeed." He paused. "You are far from home, Soleta."

She raised an eyebrow and said—with as close to sadness as she ever got—"I have no home. Once, perhaps, Starfleet. But now . . ." She shrugged.

"Ah," said the newcomer.

" 'Ah' what?''

" 'Ah,' the guard is returning as I had surmised he would."

There was something about the voice of the man in the cell with her that she found almost spellbinding in its certainty. For Soleta had undergone a tremendous crisis of confidence, and a man who was so clear, so in control . . . she could not help but be fascinated by such a man. Sure enough, a moment later—just as he had said—the door opened and the guard entered quickly. He glanced at Soleta and the newcomer. Neither had budged, of course. Soleta was on her feet but still nowhere within range of the guard. And the newcomer was seated on the floor with such serenity that it appeared he was ready to stay there until the end of time. Quickly the guard looked around on the floor. As he did so, he was patting down the pockets in his uniform.

"Problem?" asked Soleta. Not that she cared.

"It's none of your concern," the guard said brusquely.

And the newcomer, from his position on the floor, inquired, "Would you be seeking this, by chance?"

The guard glanced over and his jaw dropped. For the prisoner was holding up the electronic key. The multipurpose device that opened the door of the cell . . .

. . . and also the prisoners' shackles.

Barely did the guard have the time to register this fact when the stranger was on his feet. It did not seem possible that anyone could move so quickly. A second, two at the most, had passed in between the time when the guard realized his peril and when the newcomer was actually making his move. Soleta hadn't even blinked. It seemed to her that the newcomer had not even really moved with any apparent haste. It was simply that one moment he was upon the floor, and the next moment he was upon the guard. His hand snaked out, lightning fast, and for a moment Soleta thought that the newcomer was in the process of strangling the guard. Had he done so, Soleta would not have mourned the guard's loss in the slightest. Oh, she couldn't have done the deed herself, but she wasn't going to shed a tear if someone else dispatched him on her behalf.

But the guard did not die. Instead his head snapped around in response to a hand clamping securely on his right shoulder. Reflexively his hands came up, grabbing the hand at the wrist, but by the time his hands clamped onto the arm of his assailant, it was already too late. His eyes rolled up and, without a sound, he slumped to the floor.

"That was a nerve pinch," said Soleta.

The newcomer made no immediate reply, but instead took the electronic key, which he clasped securely in his palm, crossed quickly to Soleta, and opened the shackles that held her. She rubbed her wrist. "Who *are* you?" she demanded.

He pulled his hood back and Soleta found herself staring into the eyes of an individual who looked as if he could have passed for a Thallonian. His skin had the dark, almost reddish tint and arched eyebrows that were distinctive to Thallonians. His hair was long on the sides, and she looked inquisitively at it. In silent response, he pulled back the hair just a shade to reveal distinctive pointed ears. Vulcan. An older Vulcan, to be sure. He had the face of one who had seen every reason in the galaxy to give up on logic and surrender oneself to disorder . . . and yet had refused to do so.

"The skin tone . . ." she said.

"Simple camouflage, to blend in with Thallonians," he said. "However . . . your predicament put me in something of an ethical bind. I could have remained an impostor . . . blending in with the Thallonian people . . . but that would have required my allowing your demise. The security into the dungeon is too effective. Revealing that I myself was likewise a trespasser onto Thallon was the only means I could discern to get sufficiently near you to be of assistance."

"What is your name?"

"I am Spock," he said.

She looked at him, her inability to disguise her amazement a sure tip-off to her mixed lineage. A purebred Vulcan would have made do with a quizzically raised eyebrow. "Not . . . *the* Spock. Captain Kirk's Spock?"

And now he did, in fact, lift an eyebrow, in a manner evoking both curiosity and amusement. "I was unaware I was considered his property."

"Sorry. I'm . . . sorry."

"Your apology, though no doubt sincere, is both unnecessary and of no interest." He glanced briskly around. "There is no logical reason for us to remain. I suggest we do not."

She nodded in brisk agreement. "You lead the way."

"Of course."

They headed quickly out of the cell, pausing only to securely close the door behind them. The guard lay on the floor, insensate.

They made their way carefully down a hallway. In the far distance they could still hear the sounds of merriment. The party was apparently in full swing. With no one around, Soleta could indulge herself in a low whisper. "I studied so many of your exploits, back in the Academy. It . . . it's difficult to believe that everything they told us really happened."

He paused, his back against the wall of the corridor. "Do not believe it," he said.

"So you're saying it didn't happen."

"No. It happened. But if it simplifies your life to disbelieve it, then do so. It is of no consequence to me. Of far greater concern is our departure." He started moving again, and gestured for her to follow.

"You said security was tight."

"Coming in, yes. Departing, on the other hand, may prove a simpler matter."

Indeed, Spock's theory was correct. There were guard stations placed at intervals along the way, but the guards were lax. Never within recent memory had there been any sort of breakout from the dungeon area, so no one anticipated any now. To exacerbate matters, the sounds of the not-too-far-off party were a sort of aural intoxication. The guards could hear the sounds of laughter and merriment and—most distracting of all—peals of feminine laughter. It was, to say the least, distracting.

Cataclysmically distracting, as it turned out, for Spock and Soleta had no trouble sneaking up on the guards and dispatching them from behind. Indeed, Spock found himself in silent admiration of Soleta's technique. She moved so quietly that it almost seemed as if her feet did not touch the floor. Her technique with the nerve pinch was not as sure and smooth as his, however. Spock had so fine-tuned his ability that the merest brushing of his fingers in the appropriate area was enough to dispatch his victims. Soleta, on the other hand, would grab her target with an almost feral ferocity. If there was a more deft means of taking down an individual by means of nerve pinch, Soleta didn't seem interested in learning it. She noticed Spock watching her at one point.

"Problem?" she asked.

"Increase the spread of your middle fingers by point zero five centimeters," he said. "You will find that you will render a subject unconscious precisely eight-tenths of a second more rapidly."

They came around a corner and suddenly found themselves face-to-face with a guard. He opened his mouth to let out a shout of alarm. Soleta's right arm swung around so fast that it seemed nothing more than a blur. It cracked solidly across the guard's jaw, breaking it with a loud snap that ricocheted up and down the hallway. He dropped insensate to the floor, unconscious before he reached it.

"Of course," Spock continued as if there had been no interruption, "there is something to be said for brute force."

"Thanks," she said. She had already unloaded a disruptor from the belt of one of the guards. She pulled this guard's disruptor from his belt as well and extended it to Spock. He took it, glancing at it in a sort of abstract distaste . . . as if he saw little use for it, but nonetheless had no desire to simply toss it aside. He tucked it safely within the folds of his cloak. "Why are you here?" she asked, taking the brief lull to inquire. "You're an ambassador now, but the Federation doesn't have diplomatic ties with Thallon. No one does. So why are you here?"

"As of late, I have been making inroads into such situations as these precisely because there are no diplomatic ties," he said. "Absence of presence does not require absence of interest. The Federation considers the Thallonian Empire of . . . interest. There has been much rumor and innuendo. It was felt that someone capable of passing as a Thallonian would be of use in investigating the territory."

"So you're a spy," Soleta said.

"Not at all. I am merely an operative for an outside government, who adopted an undercover persona and entered restricted territory through subterfuge for the purpose of discreetly gathering information that might be of use to my superiors."

"So you're a spy," Soleta repeated.

He gazed at her levelly. "Were I a spy," he advised her in an even tone, "you would still be in your cell, as I would be most unlikely to jeopardize my mission simply for the purpose of rescuing a single un-related female whose own sloppiness placed her in harm's way.''

"All right," she sighed. "Point taken. So . . . how do we get off of Thallon?"

"I have arranged transportation."

"What kind?"

"Swift."

She quickly realized he had no intention of going into detail. In the unfortunate happenstance that she should be recaptured, he had no desire to risk her being forced to tell her captors information that could prevent them from getting offworld . . . provided, of course, that she were still capable of getting offworld. She nodded, acknowledging the brevity of the answer but not pursuing it.

As they got farther and farther away from the dungeon, Soleta was struck once more by the opulence of their surroundings. The royal fam-ily of Thallon was collectively every inch the image of the ruling upper class. There were tapestries hanging on walls, ancient pottery inset into the wall, assorted chairs lining the walls apparently for the convenience of any exhausted passerby who needed to take some pressure off his feet after an extended trek through the castle.

The sounds of the party were deafening, and Soleta momentarily wondered if Spock had lost his mind. Did he intend to audaciously walk into the middle of the celebrations? There was a boldness to such a plan that was almost attractive. It would mean that he intended to hide in plain sight. A cunning strategy that, indeed, might work.

But most likely wouldn't.

And it quickly became apparent that it was not his intention at all. There was a cross-corridor, and Spock gestured for her to follow him down. She kept pace with him, following quickly behind.

And then from around the corner stepped Si Cwan.

Spock and Soleta stopped dead in their tracks. Si Cwan did likewise. Cwan was dressed differently than he had been before. In the desert he'd been clad in riding leathers, but here he was sumptuously done up in thick, gorgeously patterned clothes. A long flowing cape hung down from his shoulders. There was also a disruptor dangling from his hip.

Soleta did not wait for him to draw it. Instead she had one of the stolen disruptors in her hand, and she was aiming it squarely at Si Cwan. "Do not move or I will shoot," she said briskly.

"Are you serious?" he asked with unfeigned amusement.

His tone of voice annoyed her, and it was all the excuse Soleta needed. She squeezed the trigger.

Nothing happened.

She glanced at the level indicator in confusion. It read that the weapon was fully charged.

As if reading her mind, he said calmly, "Genetically encoded to its user. Just in case a situation such as this should present itself."

Of course, Si Cwan's weapon would work just fine. And there was no question whatsoever that he could draw the weapon and fire it, and Spock and Soleta were too far away from him to do anything to stop him short of groveling. And neither of them were the groveling type.

He had them cold. They knew it, he knew it, and he knew they knew it.

Yet Spock sounded so calm that one would have thought it was he who had the upper hand. "There is nothing to be gained by our continued incarceration," he informed Si Cwan. "You would be well advised to release us immediately, so that we may take our leave."

"Indeed," asked Si Cwan. "I doubt the Chancellor would feel the same way."

Before Spock could reply, Soleta drew herself up to her full height (which was still a head shorter than Si Cwan). "I want you to know," Soleta said stridently, "that I believe your so-called civilized society to be anything but. Your xenophobia and controlling impulses are ultimately self-destructive."

"Soleta," Spock said warningly.

Unheedingly, she continued, "I believe that your society will crumble within the next twenty years. From my reading of the outlying worlds of your empire, it cannot possibly sustain itself. Do with us as you will. Sound the alarm or, if you will, shoot us down where we stand. But be aware that our downfall will be followed, sooner or later, by your own."

Si Cwan eyed her with unrestrained curiosity. She wasn't quite sure, but it appeared as if, for a moment, the edges of his mouth were starting to go upward. Then his hand went toward the disruptor, and Soleta and Spock steeled themselves. Spock caught her glance and, with an almost imperceptible movement of his head, indicated to her that she should break to the left upon Cwan's firing, while Spock angled to the right.

Perhaps, in that way, they wouldn't both be hit and a rescue could still be salvaged.

And then Si Cwan's hand went past the weapon and thrust into his pocket. He pulled something out in his closed fist, and then he opened his hand. Soleta looked in surprise to see her IDIC pin in Cwan's hand.

"My sister removed this from you without my knowing," said Si Cwan. "I informed her that theft was inappropriate behavior for a princess, and was on my way to return it. Thank you for saving me the extra distance." And with a flick of his wrist he tossed the IDIC to her.

She caught it expertly and looked at it with clear surprise. "I had not anticipated getting this back."

"Life is not anticipation. Death is anticipation. Life is constant surprise."

Soleta considered the situation and then struck a defensive posture. Her arms were cocked, her legs poised and ready to lash out. Spock, standing to her side, looked at her with as close to confusion as he ever allowed himself to come. "What are you doing?"

"In the event he intends to attack us by hand . . ."

This actually prompted Si Cwan to laugh. "As sporting as that might be, it seems a bit unnecessary." Then he pointed off to his left. "Go."

Soleta tilted her head slightly. "What?"

"Go. Leave. The way is clear, I believe. Depart." He paused and said in barely restrained amusement, "Unless you would prefer that I attempt to stop you."

Spock immediately said, "That will not be necessary." He put a firm hand on Soleta's shoulder and guided her past Si Cwan, who stepped to the side, arms folded.

As they headed off down the hallway, he suddenly called to them, "Wait." They turned and Si Cwan removed his cloak and tossed it to Soleta. She caught it reflexively and looked at it in confusion, and then at him. He gestured for her to drape it up and over her head, sporting it as if it had a hood. "It will make your departure simpler," he said.

Soleta couldn't help herself. "Why?" she demanded. "Why are you helping us?"

He smiled. "A typical scientist. You can take nothing for granted; you have to have explanations for everything, even good fortune." He stroked his chin thoughtfully. "It will annoy the Chancellor. There. Hopefully that will suffice. Now go . . . before I change my mind."

They did not wait around to see if that possibility occurred. Within minutes they were outside the palace. A couple of passing guards made no effort to stop them. It was entirely possible that they simply did not realize that these were escaping prisoners. On the other hand, it was also remotely possible that Si Cwan had somehow cleared the way for them. Either way, it was not a turn of events that either Spock or Soleta was in the slightest inclined to challenge.

They moved at a miles-eating clip until the palace was safely distant, and then Spock slowed his gait a notch. Soleta followed suit. "That was unexpected," she said.

"When I was in Captain Kirk's 'possession,' the unexpected became somewhat routine."

She winced inwardly. "Sorry about that."

"Apologies are . . ."

"Unnecessary and of no interest, right, I know," Soleta sighed. "How do we get off the planet?"

"I have made arrangements. A private vessel, primarily a freighter servicing the Thallonian Empire. Sufficiently resourceful to slip in and out past border patrols. The freighter captain will meet us shortly and escort us from the planet surface."

She turned to face him. "Ambassador Spock . . . thank you. I have no idea whether thanks fall into the same category as apologies, but . . ."

"You are . . ." He paused, dredged up the word. ". . . welcome."

III

Si Cwan stood at the window of a high tower and watched them go. His eyesight was exceptionally sharp; even from this distance, he could see them leaving.

Soon, quite soon, the fallen guards would likely be discovered. Si Cwan had no sympathy for them; if they had gotten so sloppy that two departing prisoners were capable of dispatching them, then they certainly did not deserve to remain conscious. They probably didn't even deserve to retain their jobs. He would give serious thought to firing every single guard and replacing them.

On the other hand, although he hated to admit it, he felt some degree of indebtedness to his guards' inability to keep the prisoners locked away. After all, if they'd been successful, Si Cwan wouldn't have had the amusement of letting them go.

Why *had* he let them go? He wasn't entirely sure. Perhaps it was the reason he had stated, for he truly was not a great supporter of the Chancellor.

Or perhaps it was simply a matter of repayment for the laughter that Soleta had brought to Kally. When Soleta had knocked the Chancellor's mount unconscious, Kally had erupted in peals of laughter that were extremely rare for such a serious-minded young girl. Si Cwan didn't hear her laugh nearly often enough. Yes, perhaps that was the reason after all.

Still, there was one dark aspect to it all: the woman's prediction that their society would crumble in . . . what? Twenty years? He was not particularly sanguine about *that* little prediction. No, not at all.

But it was just speculation, surely. And not even tremendously likely speculation at that.

There was a stirring at his side and he looked down. "Little sister," he said. "What are you doing here?"

Kally pulled at his robe. "Everyone at the party is wondering where you are, Si Cwan."

He bowed deeply, almost bending in half. "Merely awaiting the honor of being escorted by you."

She took his arm and, as they headed down a corridor in the direction of the merrymaking, she asked, "Where is your cape?"

He smiled, pictured Soleta's face, and said, "I gave it . . . to a friend."

TWO
YEARS
EARLIER . . .

SELAR

Selar barely remembered any of her trip from the *Enterprise* to Vulcan. Instead, all of her attention was focused inward: inward to the urges that were rampaging through her body, to the drives that were sending her home as fast as the transport was able to carry her.

She felt as if her brain were being divided, with one part of her observing the other part in a sort of distant fascination. The cool, calm, emotionless assessment that had enabled her to diagnose so many people with clinical efficiency, was now contemplating her own state of mind. *So this is what* Pon farr *is like,* the Vulcan doctor mused. *A most . . . interesting phenomenon. Accelerated heart rate, unsteady breathing, a curious pounding that seems to mask out all other sensory input. I find it impossible to dwell on any topic other than mating.*

She had known of the Vulcan mating drive, had even seen it in action. But Selar had always imagined that she herself would somehow be less impacted by the primal urge. Actually, that was a common belief (some would say failing) among many Vulcans. So proud, so confident were they in their discipline and logic that, despite their thorough knowledge of their own biology, they had a great deal of difficulty intellectually accepting the concept of *Pon farr*. The problem was that *Pon farr,* of course, was the antithesis of logical acceptance.

Even when the first stages of *Pon farr* were setting in, Selar had not recognized them for what they were. "Physician, heal thyself " was a perfectly fine axiom, but the truth was that a physician was oftentimes not in the best position to judge what was going on in his or her own body. Such was most definitely the case for Selar.

The timing was particularly bad. She had enjoyed her duties on the *Enterprise,* and had looked forward to the many challenges that her position on the medical staff had offered her. But her physiology would not be denied. What had been difficult was having to be less than truthful with Beverly Crusher. She had not lied outright; she had merely told Crusher that certain duties on Vulcan could not be ignored, and that she would have to take an extended leave of absence. Despite the fact that it was one doctor to another, Selar could not bring herself to discuss such personal matters with an offworlder. It simply was not done.

Of course, Crusher wasn't stupid. It was entirely possible that Beverly knew exactly what was up. But if that was the case, then she respected Selar's privacy sufficiently not to press her on the matter.

So the leave was not a problem, and obtaining transport to Vulcan likewise was not a problem.

The problem, unfortunately, was Voltak. Voltak, her husband, Voltak her mate. Voltak, of whom she had only the vaguest of memories.

Despite her drive, despite her desire, there was something that lay at the core of *Pon farr* which was very daunting to her, and that was basically fear. Never in her life had Dr. Selar felt so vulnerable. Actually, never in her life had she felt vulnerable at all. She had always been supremely gifted and capable. But now, with her inner core laid bare for what she felt was all the world to see, she was driven to mate with someone whom she barely knew. Oh, they had kept up a correspondence, as much as her schedule and his had permitted, for Voltak had his own life and ventures to pursue. Voltak was an archaeologist, forever off on one dig or another, frequently in places where any sort of communication was problematic at best.

It was an infantile, childish attitude for her to possess, but Selar nonetheless felt as if this was all profoundly unfair, somehow. She was a private person, as were most Vulcans. And now she was destined to have no privacy, no barrier, nothing to hide behind, to be fully and totally exposed to a male who was, to all intents and purposes, an acquaintance at best.

And so it frightened her. Fear was something that she could deal with fairly easily when she was in her normal state of mind. As she was, though, she was hardly equipped to handle even the most casual of emotions, much less gut-wrenching terror.

The next hours were a blur to her, a red haze. She was met at the port by Giniv, an old friend of hers who was serving as the equivalent of what would be considered the "maid of honor." She was escorted by Giniv to a great hall. As was the custom, her parents were not there. It was not felt appropriate for parents to see their children during the time when such raw, naked sexuality ran rampant through them.

She sensed him before she actually saw him. She turned and saw Voltak enter from the back of the room.

Voltak was tall and strong, and although he was similarly in the grip of *Pon farr,* he was managing to maintain some degree of composure. Intensity radiated from him, drawing her like a beacon. Not only could she not resist, but she had no desire to do so. Instead her desire was for him, and only for him.

"Voltak," she said, her voice low and intense. "I am summoned. I am here."

She looked into his eyes and realized, to her amazement, that he had likewise been seized with similar doubts just before he'd set eyes on her. Oddly it had never occurred to her that the male would have anything approximating her concerns. But it was certainly not unreasonable. Voltak was no less proud, no less confident than Selar, and no less subject to the same apprehensions.

Those worries washed away from both of them when they looked into each other's eyes. They had been joined when they were mere children in a ceremony that neither of them could even really recall. But it all came rushing back to them, as the link which had been forged years ago finally took its full hold on them.

Selar loved him. Loved him, wanted him, needed him. Her life would not be complete without him. She had no idea whether the feelings were genuine, or whether they were a product of the heat of *Pon farr.* Ultimately, she did not care either way. All she wanted was Voltak's body against hers, to have the two of them join and mate, and fulfill the obligations that their race and biology put upon them.

The fear was forgotten. Only the need and hunger remained. Why? Because they were the only logical courses of action.

*   *   *

The Joining Place had been in Voltak's family for generations. Whenever one of Voltak's line took a mate, it was there that the Joining was consummated.

The room was ornate and sumptuously furnished, in stark contrast to the typically more spartan feel of most Vulcan domiciles. The lighting was low, the room temperature moderate. There was not the slightest discomforting element to distract them from each other . . . although, considering their mental and physical state of mind, nothing short of a full-scale phaser barrage could have pulled their attention from one another.

Voltak pulled Selar into the room and closed the heavy door. They stood apart from one another for a long moment, trying to focus on something other than the drive that had taken hold of them . . . although they could not, for the life of them, figure out why they should be interested in anything but that.

"We are not animals," Selar managed to say. "We are . . . intelligent, rational beings."

"Yes," Voltak agreed readily. He hesitated. "Your point being . . . ?"

"My point," and she tried to remember what it was. It took her a moment. "Yes. My point is that, rather than just giving in to rutting impulses, we should . . . should . . . talk first."

"Absolutely, yes . . . I have no problem with that." In point of fact, Voltak looked as if he were ready to paw the ground. But instead he drew himself up, pulled together his Vulcan calm and utterly self-possessed demeanor. "What shall we talk about?"

"We shall discuss matters that are of intellectual interest. And as we do that, we can . . . introduce ourselves to the physical aspect of our relationship . . . in a calm, mature manner."

"That sounds most reasonable, Selar."

They sat near each other on the bed, and Voltak extended two fingers. Selar returned the gesture, her fingers against his.

It was such a simple thing, this touch. And yet it felt like a jolt of electricity had leaped between the two of them. Selar had trouble steadying her breath. This was insanity. She was a rational person, a serious and sober-minded person. It was utter lunacy that some primordial mating urge could strip from her everything that made her unique. It was . . . not logical.

"So . . . tell me, Selar," said Voltak, sounding no more steady than Selar. "Do you feel that your . . . medical skills have been sufficiently challenged in your position on the *Enterprise?* Or do you feel that you might have been of . . . greater service to the common good . . . if you had remained with pure research, as I understand you originally intended to do."

Selar nodded, trying to remember what the question had been. "I am . . . quite fulfilled, yes. I feel I made the . . . the right decision." Her fingers slowly moved away from his and reached up, tracing the strong curve of his chin. "And . . . you . . . you spoke once of teaching, but instead have remained with . . . with fieldwork."

He was caressing the arch of her ear, his voice rock steady . . . but not without effort. "To instruct others in the discipline of doing that which gives me the most satisfaction . . . did not appear the logical course." He paused, then said, "Selar?"

Her voice low and throaty, she said, "Yes?"

"I do not wish . . . to talk . . . anymore."

"That would be . . . acceptable to me."

Within moments—with the utmost efficiency and concern for order—they were naked with one another. He drew her to him, and his fingers touched her temples. She put her fingers to his temples as well, and their minds moved closer.

There was so much coldness in the day-to-day life of a Vulcan, so much remoteness. Yet the Vulcan mind-meld was the antithesis of the isolation provided by that prized Vulcan logic. It was as if nature and evolution had enhanced the Vulcan telepathic ability to compensate for the shields they erected around themselves. As distant as they held themselves from each other, the mind-meld enabled them to cut through defenses and drop shields more thoroughly than most other races. Thus were Vulcans a paradoxical combination of standoffish and yet intimate.

And never was that intimacy more thorough than in a couple about to mate.

They probed one another, drawn to each other's strengths and weaknesses. Voltak felt Selar's deep compassion, her care for all living beings masked behind a façade of Vulcan detachment, and brought it into his heart. Selar savored Voltak's thoroughness and dedication, his insight and fascination with the past and how it might bear on the future, and she took pride in him.

And then their minds went beyond the depth already provided by the meld, deeper and deeper, and even as their bodies came together their minds, their intellects were merged. In her mind's eye, Selar saw the two of them intertwined, impossible to discern where one left off and the other began. Her breath came in short gasps, her consciousness and control spinning away as she allowed the joy of union to overwhelm her completely . . . the joy and ecstasy and heat, the heat building in her loins, her chest . . .

. . . her chest . . .

. . . and the heat beginning to grip her, and suddenly there was something wrong, God, there was something terribly wrong . . .

. . . her chest was on fire. The euphoria, the glorious blood-frenzy of joining, were slipping away. Instead there was pain in her torso, a vise-grip on her bosom, and she couldn't breathe.

Selar's back arched in agony, and she gasped desperately for air, unable to pull any into her lungs, and her mind screamed at her, *You're having a heart attack!* And then she heard a howl of anguish that reverberated in her body and in her soul, and she realized what was happening. It wasn't her. It was Voltak. Voltak was having a massive coronary.

And Selar's mind was linked into his.

She had no command over her body, over her faculties. She tried to move, to struggle, to focus. She tried desperately to push Voltak out of her mind so she could do something other than writhe in pain. But Voltak, his emotions already laid bare and raw because of the Joining, was responding to this hideous turn of events in a most un-Vulcanlike manner. He was afraid. Terrified. And because of that, rather than breaking his telepathic bond with Selar, he held on to her all the more desperately. It is impossible to convince the drowning man that the only chance he has is to toss aside the life preserver.

Calm! her mind screamed at him, *calm!* But Voltak was unable to find the peaceful center within him, that intellectual height from which his logic and icy demeanor could project.

And in her mind's eye, she could see him. She could see him as if he were being surrounded by blackness, tendrils reaching out and pulling him down, far and away. Paralyzed, pain stabbing her through the chest, she didn't know whether to reach out to him as raw emotion dictated, or try to break off as logic commanded so that she might still have a chance of saving him. She elected the latter because it was the only sane thing to do, she might still have a prayer . . .

And as she started to pull away, Selar suddenly realized her error, because Voltak called to her in her mind, *My **katra** . . .*

His soul. His Vulcan soul, all that made him what he was, his spirit, his essence. Under ordinary circumstances a mind-meld would preserve his *katra* and bring it to a place of honor with his ancestors. But these circumstances were far from ordinary.

To accept the *katra* was to accept the death of the other, and Dr. Selar was not ready or willing to accept that Voltak was beyond hope, beyond saving. She was a doctor, there were things she could do, if she could only battle past the accursed mental and physical paralysis that the mind-meld had trapped her in.

And in a fading voice she heard again, *katra,* and she knew that he was lost. That it was too late. Desperately Selar, who only instants earlier had been trying to pull free, reversed herself and plunged toward him. She could "see" his hand outstretched to her, and in the palm of his hand something small and glowing and precious, and she reached toward him, desperately, mental fingers outstretched, almost pulling it from his grasp, a mere second or two more to bring them sufficiently close together . . .

. . . and the blackness claimed him. Claimed him and claimed her as death closed around the two of them. Coldness cut through Selar, and for a moment the void opened to her, and she saw the other side and it was terrifying and barren to her. So much emptiness, so much desolation, so much nothingness. As life was the celebration of everything that was, there was death, the consecration of everything that wasn't. And from the darkness, something seemed to look back at her, and reject her, pushing her away, pushing Voltak and his soul forever out of her reach, for it was too late.

His *katra,* his essence, his life force, extinguished as easily as a candle snuffed out by a vagrant breeze, and Selar called out over and over again in lonely agony, called out into the blackness, raged at the void, felt his death, felt the passing of his life force, clutched frantically at it as if trying to ensnare passing wisps of smoke, and having about as much success.

*No, please no, come back, **come back to me**. . .*

But there was no one and nothing there to hear her.

And Selar felt a sudden jolt to her head even as the pain in her chest abruptly evaporated. Pulling her scattered senses together, she realized that she had fallen off the bed. She scrambled to her feet and there was Voltak, lying on the bed, eyes open, the nothingness of the void reflected in the soullessness of his eyes.

She quickly tried to minister to him, calling his name, trying to massage his heart, trying to *will* him back to life as if she could infuse some of her own life force into him.

And slowly . . .

. . . slowly . . .

. . . she stopped. She stopped as she realized that he was gone, and not all her efforts were going to bring him back.

She realized that her face was covered with tears. She wiped them away, composing her demeanor, pulling herself together, stitching herself back together using her training as a Vulcan and as a doctor as the thread. Her breathing returned to its normal rhythm, her pulse was restored to its natural beat, and she checked a chronometer to establish the time of death.

And Dr. Selar, as she calmly dressed, told herself that something valuable had been accomplished this day. Something far more valuable than just another mating for the purpose of propagating the race.

She had learned the true folly of allowing emotions to sweep one up, to carry one away. Oh, she had known it intellectually from studying the history of her race. But she had experienced it firsthand now, and she was the better for it. She had left herself vulnerable, allowed someone else into her psyche, into her soul. Certainly she had been dragged there by the demands of *Pon farr,* but she was over that now. The demands of her "rutting instinct" had cost a man—a man whom she had perhaps "loved"—not only his life, but his soul.

She would never, under any circumstance, allow herself to be ruled either by arbitrary physical demands, or by anything approaching any aspect of emotionality. She would be the perfect Vulcan, the perfect doctor. That, and only that, would be her new life's goal. For, to Selar, states of mind such as love, tenderness, or vulnerability were more than just an embarrassment or an inconvenience. They were tantamount to death sentences. And the premier credo of medicine was that, first and foremost, the physician shall do no harm.

That was something that Selar was all too prepared to live by.

Forever.

NOW . . .

I

The *U.S.S. Enterprise* 1701-E made her way through space at considerably less than her normal, brisk clip. The reason was quickly apparent to any observer, for the *Enterprise* was surrounded by half a dozen far smaller, less speedy ships. Ships that had only the most minimal of warp capabilities, and at least one whose warp coils had overheated and was being towed along.

Looking at the monitor screen, in regards to their entourage, Commander William Riker commented, "I feel like a mother duck."

Data turned at his station and regarded Riker with such clear befuddlement that it was all Picard could do to keep a straight face. "Don't say it, Data," he pleaded, heading it off.

" 'It,' Captain?"

"Yes. Don't begin inquiring as to whether Mr. Riker will begin quacking, or waddling, or laying eggs or acquiring webbing between his toes. The answer is no."

"Very well, sir," Data replied reasonably. "In any event, it will not be necessary, since you have already voiced all the possibilities that occurred to me."

Picard opened his mouth again, and then closed it. Riker and Counselor Deanna Troi exchanged broad grins.

"Although," Data added thoughtfully, "there is a *slight* tendency toward waddling. . . ."

Riker's face immediately darkened. The fact that Deanna was now grinning so widely that it looked as if her face was going to split in two didn't help matters. *"Mister* Data, I will have you know I do not, have never, and will never, 'waddle.' "

"You do tend to sway when you walk, sir," Data replied, undeterred and apparently oblivious of the imagery he was evoking. "A sort of rhythmic, side-to-side motion that could, under some conditions, be construed as—"

"No, it *couldn't,"* Riker said sharply.

"If you would like, I can demonstrate," Data began, half up out of his chair.

Both Riker and Picard quickly said, *"No!"* Surprised by the vehemence of the reaction, Data sat back down.

"That won't be necessary," Picard added, clearing his throat and trying to sound authoritative. "Data, I have observed Mr. Riker's . . . gait . . . on many an occasion, and I feel utterly confident in stating that the commander does not, in fact, waddle."

"Very well, sir," Data said.

"Good. I'm glad that's sett—"

"Actually, it is more of a swagger than a waddle."

Riker began to feel a distant thudding in his temples. "I do not waddle . . . and I do not swagger . . . I just . . . walk."

He looked to Deanna for solace and received absolutely none as she told him, "Well, actually, you do have a bit of a swagger."

"Et tu, Deanna?"

"There's nothing wrong with it. Actually, I've always considered it part of your charm. An outward display of confidence in yourself, your capabilities, and your position."

Riker drew himself up and said serenely, "Very well. I can live with that."

And then in a voice so low that only Riker could hear, Troi added, "Of course, that may in turn be covering up something . . . a basic lack of confidence, or perhaps insecurity with . . ."

He fired a glance at her, but before he could reply, Lieutenant Kristian Ayre at the conn glanced over his shoulder and said, "Sir, we are within range of Deep Space Five. Estimated time of arrival, twenty-two minutes."

Thank God, thought Picard. Out loud, he simply said, "Inform them that we are within range."

"There's a ton of ion activity in the area," Ayre commented after a moment more. "Thirty, maybe forty ships have passed through here within the last twenty-four hours. They must be having a *lot* of visitors."

Riker glanced at Picard. "More refugees?"

"Without question," Picard affirmed. "Matters should be fairly . . . interesting . . . upon our arrival."

Picard had never seen a space station quite so packed. The place was bristling with ships, docked at every port. Many others were in a holding pattern. Some were in the process of switching places, taking turns so that different ships would be able to take advantage of the station facilities. The *Enterprise* dwarfed all the other vessels. Partly because of that, she wasn't even able to draw near, and settled for falling into orbit around the station, well within transporter range but far enough away that there was no possible danger of collision with a smaller ship.

At tactical, Lieutenant Paige said, "Sir, I have been endeavoring to hail DS5. There's a lot of subspace chatter, though. I'm having trouble punching through."

"With all the ships jamming the area, I can't say I'm surprised. The reports of the Thallonian refugee situation did not begin to approach just how comprehensive the current state of affairs is."

"Incoming signal, sir."

"On screen."

The screen rippled and the image of DS5 disappeared to be replaced by a face that Picard had not been expecting. Picard found himself staring into the stony, perpetually disapproving gaze of Admiral Edward Jellico. Picard could sense Riker stiffening nearby.

Jellico's history with the *Enterprise* was not exactly a happy one. He had never been a particular fan of Picard. Riker had voiced the opinion to Picard that it stemmed not from an assessment of Picard's performance as an officer, but from Jellico's likely jealousy of how well Picard was regarded by personnel both above and below him. Jellico had temporarily taken command of the *Enterprise* at one time, and he'd butted heads directly with Riker the entire time.

Jellico had a reputation for efficiency and for getting the job done, but he and Picard differed on a very core, fundamental issue. Men followed Jellico because, by the chain of command, they had to. They followed Picard because they wanted to, and no amount of blustering or authoritative officiousness on the part of Jellico was going to change that.

What it boiled down to was that Jellico's was a limited personality. He knew that he would go only so far and no further, would accomplish only so much and no more. Picard's vistas, on the other hand, seemed potentially limitless. Jellico would never be able to forgive him for that.

Perversely, Riker took a small measure of happiness in noticing that Jellico's already thinning blond hair was almost gone. Considering Picard's long-standing lack of follicles, Riker wondered why that nonetheless pleased him. He chalked it off to pettiness, but was willing to live with that. He glanced at Picard and saw no flicker of change in Picard's deadpan expression. Whatever was going through Picard's mind in relation to Jellico, clearly he had no intention of tipping it off to any observers. As always, Picard remained the consummate poker player. He got to his feet and faced Jellico, his hands draped behind his back.

"Admiral Jellico," Picard said evenly. "I was unaware that you were now in charge of Deep Space Five. Congratulations on your promotion and new assignment."

Jellico did not look the least bit amused, which was fairly standard for him. He never looked the least bit amused. "This is not a new post for me, *Captain*," he said, emphasizing Picard's rank in a manner that did not indicate respect, but rather was clearly a not-so-subtle reminder of who was the captain and who was the admiral. "Although I've been cooling my heels here for so long that it's beginning to seem that way. Where the hell have you been? We've been here for three days waiting for you."

"We could have been here far more quickly, Admiral," Picard said, unflappable. "However, that would have required abandoning the vessels which we were requested to escort. Since we are supposed to be providing humanitarian aid, we could hardly do so by leaving behind those to whom the aid is to be provided."

Jellico gestured impatiently. "Fine. Whatever. Ready the main meeting room, and prepare to beam us over."

"Here on the *Enterprise,* sir?" Picard asked.

"I thought my orders fairly clear."

"We had been told that the meeting would occur on Deep Space Five. . . ."

"I'm telling you differently. This place is a madhouse. Thallonian refugees everywhere, station facilities stretched to the limit. There are people camping out in the conference rooms, for God's sake."

Riker said in a low voice, "Ah, those irritating needy people."

He thought he'd said it quietly enough that Jellico didn't hear, but Jellico's gaze quickly shifted and homed in on Riker with daggerlike efficiency. Realizing that possible vituperation would hardly smooth matters over, Picard said, "There will not be a problem, Admiral. We can be ready for you by thirteen hundred hours, if that will be sufficient."

Jellico grimaced slightly, which was about as close to a nod of approval as he ever came. "Fine," he said, and blinked out.

"Perfect," said Riker. "Just who we needed to make a difficult situation just that much more difficult."

Picard considered the matter for a moment, and then said, "I shall brief our guest on the change of plans." As he headed for the elevator, he called over his shoulder.

"Be of stout heart, Number One. We've handled the Borg. We can certainly handle Admiral Jellico." He walked out the door.

Riker turned to Troi and noted, "We aren't allowed to blow up Admiral Jellico."

"Regulations can be a nuisance," Troi said sympathetically. Then she seemed to brighten. "Don't worry. Perhaps he'll be sufficiently intimidated by your confident swagger."

Riker caught himself before he let his reply come out of his mouth, but he couldn't stop the thought. *Some of us have reason to be confident, Counselor. Others of us, who—for example—were unable to helm the* Enterprise *for more than two minutes without crashing her, have far less reason to be confident.*

As she sensed his feelings if not his words, Troi's mouth fell into a disapproving frown.

"I sense great sarcasm," she said.

*   *   *

Picard sounded the door chime, and a voice from within said, "Come." The door slid open and he entered the guest quarters. The room was mostly dark, with illumination being provided by a few choice sources of light including a lit mirror and a candle. To one side of the room, a man was seated in a most contemplative manner.

"Ambassador Spock," said Picard. "We have arrived."

Spock looked up at him, seeming to pull himself from his devotions with effort. He stared at Picard but said nothing.

"Admiral Jellico desired that the meeting be held on the *Enterprise*," Picard continued. "Apparently there is an overabundance of activity on Deep Space Five."

"Indeed," Spock said after a moment. "The place is irrelevant."

Picard felt, ever so slightly, a chill in the base of his spine. Morbidly, he wondered . . . if the Borg ever assimilated the Vulcans, would anyone be able to tell?

"Will you require anything before the meeting?" Picard asked.

"No."

"Very well. I will have one of my officers bring you when the time has come."

Spock inclined his head slightly in acknowledgement.

No one had been more surprised than Picard when he had rendezvoused with the transport that had brought Spock to the *Enterprise*. Spock had been on assignment on Romulus. It was a measure of how seriously the Federation took the fall of the Thallonian Empire that they had requested Spock attend the Thallonian Summit. It had taken Spock no small effort to quietly extricate himself from Romulus. Still, Spock was one of the only people Picard knew of who had any familiarity at all with the Thallonians. It was only natural that his presence was desired at the summit.

He continued to gaze levelly at Picard. This was ridiculous. After everything that Picard had been through in his life, one would think that it would take a hell of a lot more than the stare of a Vulcan to leave him discomforted. Nonetheless, Picard felt as if he should say . . . *something* . . . but he had no idea what. "We certainly have our work cut out for us," he ventured.

Spock was silent a moment more, and then he said, "Captain . . ."

"Yes, Ambassador."

"Vulcans do not engage in small talk."

"Ah" was all Picard could think of to say. Then he nodded, turned, and started to walk out. And then, before he could exit the room, Spock stopped him with a word.

"Captain . . ."

Picard turned, waited with a raised eyebrow.

"I find," Spock said with introspection and not a little bemusement, "that I am experiencing a degree of . . . anticipation . . . in working with you again. The human phrase would be that I am 'looking forward to it.' " He paused, contemplating it. "Fascinating."

"The galaxy is infinitely fascinating, Ambassador," observed Picard.

"So it would appear."

"You know, Ambassador," Picard said after a moment, "Mr. Data—who was once even more removed from emotions than you— has recently acquired them. You might wish to take the opportunity to talk with him about his newly refined perceptions. You may find them . . . equally fascinating."

"I shall consider it, should the opportunity present itself."

"I'll see that it does. Oh, and Ambassador . . ." He paused in the door.

"Yes?"

"This," and he waggled a finger between the two of them, "was small talk."

Then he grinned and walked out the door, leaving the ambassador alone in his darkness.

II

Riker remembered a time when he had gone mountain climbing at the age of fourteen, explicitly against his father's orders . . . or perhaps, if truth be known, precisely *because* his father had forbidden it. He'd been halfway up a particularly hazardous peak when his pitons had ripped loose from where they'd been wedged into the rock surface. Riker had swung outward, dangling, one thin rope preventing him from plunging to his death. The moments until his climbing partner had been able to reel Riker in and help him get re-anchored had been fraught with tension.

It was that exact sort of tension that Riker now felt when he walked into the main conference lounge. The sensation that a vast drop loomed beneath all of them, and they were all hanging by one single rope.

Picard was already there, talking with Ambassador Spock and a woman whom Riker immediately recognized as Admiral Alynna Nechayev. Nechayev was some piece of work. She and Picard had first butted heads back when the member of the Borg collective known as "Hugh" was aboard the *Enterprise*. Picard had refused to infest Hugh with a virus which would have effectively obliterated the Borg, and Nechayev had raked him over the coals about it. And they had had any number of fiery clashes since then. Yet now there she was, in the flesh, and she seemed to be perfectly happy to chat things up with the officer she had so mercilessly dressed down before.

Riker watched the dynamics of the Picard/Spock/Nechayev discussion, and it took him no time at all to discern what was really going on. He noticed that Spock was delivering most of his remarks or comments to Picard, treating him with respect and deference. It was only natural—or, if you will, logical—that Spock should do so. After all, Picard had put his own mind on the line to try and help Sarek, Spock's late father. Nechayev, by her rapt attention on the Vulcan, was clearly a major admirer of Spock's. That was understandable. The term "living legend" was overblown and pompous, but in the case of Ambassador Spock, it was also bang-on accurate. The fact that the living legend clearly regarded Picard so highly was obviously raising Picard in Nechayev's own estimation. She actually laughed in delight at some remark Picard made, and although it was obviously supposed to be something amusing, Picard nevertheless looked surprised at Nechayev's reaction.

Well, good. Picard had accomplished so much, and yet sometimes it seemed as if Starfleet regarded him with suspicion. Indeed, that they were suspicious *because* of everything Picard had accomplished. As if it were impossible to imagine that one mere mortal could have done so much. That it was . . . unnatural somehow.

In short, Picard could use all the support that he could get. If that support stemmed from Nechayev being a fan of Ambassador Spock, then fine.

That was when Riker noticed something out of the corner of his eye.

Riker couldn't believe he'd missed him before. There was a Thallonian standing over to one side in the conference room. He was tall, remarkably so. What was even more remarkable was that, even though the room was brightly lit, it seemed as if the Thallonian had managed to find darkness hiding in corners, behind chairs, under the table. Find that darkness and gather it around him, like a shroud, cloaking himself in the shadows as if he were part of them, and they part of him. For that matter, Riker wasn't sure even now whether he had spotted the Thallonian because he was sharp-eyed . . . or because the Thallonian had allowed Riker to see him.

He was tall and mustached, with spiral tattoos on his head. And he was completely immobile, not twitching so much as a muscle. If it weren't for the level, steady gaze he had fixed upon Riker, Riker might have wondered whether he was truly alive or a brilliantly carved statue.

Riker cleared his throat and approached the Thallonian. The Thallonian's gaze never shifted from him, and his face remained inscrutable. Riker came to within a couple of feet and stopped, as if the Thallonian had somehow drawn an invisible barrier around him and hung a large DO NOT CROSS sign on it. "Commander William T. Riker," he introduced himself. "First officer of the *Enterprise.*"

For the first time the Thallonian made a minimal movement: he inclined his head slightly. "Si Cwan," he said in a deep voice that was tinged with bitterness. "Former prince of the Thallonian Empire."

"My condolences on your tragic loss," Riker said.

Si Cwan gave him an appraising look. "How do you know," he asked, "whether the loss is tragic or not? If you believe the rhetoric of those who brought down my family . . . those who . . ." His voice showed the slightest hint of wavering before he brought it firmly back under control. ". . . who slaughtered those close to me . . . why, my loss of station is one of the greatest achievements in Thallonian history." He began to speak more loudly, deliberately capturing the attention of Spock, Picard, and Nechayev. "Our conquests, our good works, our achievements in art and literature . . . the fact that we sculpted order from chaos . . ."

"Gods spare us from more Thallonian rhetoric."

It was a gruff and harsh voice, and it came from the direction of the entrance to the conference room. Riker saw Si Cwan stiffen as he turned to face the person who had spoken.

Standing at the door was Admiral Jellico. Next to him was Data, who had met Jellico at the transporter and escorted him to the conference room. Ordinarily protocol would have required that it be Picard or Riker, the ranking officers, who fulfilled that function. But considering the urgency of the situation, Picard felt it wiser to place himself where he would do the most good.

Next to Data was a squat and bulky young Danterian. His bronze skin glistened in the light. His broad smile displayed a row of perfect and slightly sharp teeth, and Riker found he had a barely controllable urge to knock one of those teeth right out of his head. The Danterian appeared insufferably smug as he studied Si Cwan, not even bothering to glance at Riker. The fact that he was being ignored didn't bother Riker one bit. He felt that if this Danterian looked at him for any length of time, he'd need a long shower just to make himself feel clean again.

Riker was not surprised by the presence of a representative from Danter. The Danteri were the Thallonians' "neighbors" over in Sector

221-H . . . a nearby, rival empire who were as ironfisted in their way as the Thallonians had been in theirs. But, the Danteri claimed, their ambitions were less overreaching than the Thallonians' and their own little empire more compassionate—a contention that did not hold up for anyone with a significant memory capable of recalling some of the fiascoes that occurred during the Danteri reign. (One of the best known was the uprising on Xenex, a rebellion that had lasted several years and wound up costing the Danteri a fortune in men, money, and esteem before they had finally washed their hands of Xenex and given the accursed planet and its inhabitants their freedom.)

"Thank you, Mr. Data, that will be all," Jellico said. His giving an order to one of Picard's officers in Picard's presence—particularly in a noncombat situation—was also a breach of protocol, and he fired a glance at Picard as if daring him to comment on it. Data, for his part, merely looked blandly at Picard. Clearly he wasn't going to budge until Picard had given his say-so. Picard caught Data's look and gave an almost imperceptible nod. Picking up on it, Data turned and walked out of the conference room.

"Admiral Nechayev, Captain Picard, Commander Riker, Ambassador Spock, Lord Si Cwan," Jellico said by way of brisk greeting. "I suggest we get down to business." He nodded toward the Danterian standing next to him. "This is—"

The Thallonian who had identified himself as Si Cwan stabbed a finger at the Danterian. "I know you," he said slowly, his already partly hidden eyes completely obscured by his dark scowl. "You are . . . Ryjaan?"

Ryjaan bowed stiffly from the waist. "I am honored that you know of me, Lord Cwan. One such as I knows of you, of course, but I am flattered that—"

"Save your flattery," Si Cwan said brusquely.

Ryjaan raised an eyebrow. "I was merely endeavoring to pay respects. . . ."

"Oh, Danter will pay," Si Cwan told him. "You and all your people will pay most dearly."

Picard stepped forward. "Gentlemen, little will be served by vague accusations of—"

"You are quite right, Captain." Si Cwan drew himself to his full height. Riker quickly realized that "looming" was Si Cwan's single greatest weapon. "So I will be blunt rather than vague. Our empire has fallen apart. Planets which once honored the ruling class have broken away. Our economy has crumbled, our social organization lies in ruins, and I have every reason to believe that the Danteri have a hand in it.'' He stabbed a finger at Ryjaan. ''Do you deny it?''

''Absolutely,'' shot back Ryjaan heatedly. His cloak of deference was rapidly becoming tattered. ''I completely, totally, and absolutely deny it.''

''Of course you do,'' said Si Cwan. ''I would have expected nothing less . . . from a liar such as yourself.''

That was all Ryjaan needed. With a snarl of anger, he launched himself at Si Cwan, who met the charge with a sneer of confidence. Ryjaan slammed into him, and even as Riker moved to separate them he couldn't help but be impressed to notice that Si Cwan barely budged an inch. Considering Ryjaan's build and the speed with which he was moving, Riker would have thought that Ryjaan would have run right over Cwan. Instead Cwan met the charge and looked ready to lift Ryjaan clear off his feet.

''That's enough!'' thundered Picard, coming from the other side.

Since Ryjaan was the aggressor, Riker and Picard focused their efforts on him. They pulled Ryjaan off Si Cwan as Admiral Nechayev stepped up to Si Cwan and said sharply, ''That was completely uncalled for, Lord Cwan!''

''You do not have to be present at this meeting, Lord Cwan,'' Jellico put in. ''We are extending a courtesy to you. Need I remind you that, officially, you have no standing. Deposed leaders do not rank particularly high in the grand scheme of things.''

Ryjaan pulled himself together, steadying himself and nodding to Picard and Riker that he had regained his self-control. Picard glanced cautiously at Riker and they released Ryjaan, turning their attention to Si Cwan. Cwan studied them all as if they were insects.

And then, just for a moment, a cloud of pain passed over his face as he said softly, '' 'Uncalled for,' you say. Uncalled for.'' He seemed to roll the words around on his tongue. ''Admiral . . . I saw good and loyal people slaughtered by insurgents. I saw family members carried away while I watched helplessly from hiding. *From hiding,''* he snarled with such self-revulsion that Riker repressed an inward shudder. ''From *hiding,* as I foolishly let supporters convince me that it was important I survive. ''For years my family knew what was best to guide the peoples of the Thallonian Empire. And someone goaded them, turned them against us.''

''And you wish to blame it on us,'' said Ryjaan. ''Go ahead, if it will please you, no matter how baseless the accusation.''

For the first time, the ambassador spoke up. "The accusation," said Spock, "while inflammatory, is nonetheless logical."

"*Logical?*" Ryjaan practically spat out.

Spock was unperturbed by the vehemence of Ryjaan's reaction. "The Danteri share borders with the Thallonian Empire . . . or, to be more precise, the former Thallonian Empire. The Danterian desire for . . ." He briefly considered the word "conquest" and discarded it as too inflammatory. ". . . acquisitiveness . . . is well known. Overt action would possibly lead to undesired confrontation, and therefore it would be logical for the Danteri to pursue a course of gradually undercutting the structure of the Thallonian ruling class. Such actions would obtain the same goals as outright conquest without the proportionate risk."

Admiral Nechayev stood with her hands draped behind her back, and said with clear curiosity, "Ambassador . . . are you saying it is your belief that that was what occurred here?"

"I am speculating, Admiral," Spock replied evenly. "One could just as easily speculate that the Thallonian Empire collapsed entirely on its own, through a combination of mismanagement and oppression. The former would have assured the eventuality of disintegration, while the latter guaranteed that—when the fall of the empire did occur—the attitude of the oppressed people would be violent and merciless. I am merely playing devil's advocate."

Considering the slightly satanic look to the Vulcan demeanor, Picard couldn't help but feel that some mild irony was attached to the comment. Seizing the momentary silence, Picard said, "At the very least, let us be seated and discuss the situation like civilized individuals."

"I heartily concur, Captain," Nechayev said. They moved quickly to seats around the large, polished conference table. The only one who seemed to be moving with slow deliberation was Si Cwan, who took a chair as far from Ryjaan as was possible. Nechayev turned to Jellico and said, "Admiral . . . it's your show. Walk us through."

"Thank you, Admiral." Jellico surveyed those gathered around the table. "Staying with what we know and what is beyond dispute: The Thallonian Empire has effectively collapsed. The royal family has been for the most part executed . . ." He paused to see if the harsh word had any effect on Si Cwan, but the Thallonian's expression was utterly deadpan. Jellico continued. ". . . as have local governors. Reports are muddled, however, as to any new government which may have taken the place of the royals."

"There is none." Si Cwan spoke up with authority. "I assure you of that."

"How do you know?" demanded Nechayev.

"There were factions," Si Cwan told her. "Many of them, united only in their hatred for the status quo. Hatred which had its origins . . ." He turned and fixed his gaze on Ryjaan, but then said simply, "God knows where. In any event . . . I know their type. The alliance will hold only as long as it took them to complete their bloody business. But when it comes time to work together, that will be beyond their abilities. They will tear each other to bits. The chaos and confusion which currently grips the Thallonian Empire is as nothing compared to what will ensue in the time to come."

"Lord Cwan's assessment would appear shared by the refugees," Picard now said. "For several weeks now, as you all know, refugees have been streaming out of the Thallonian Empire. At least half of them were sick, injured, barely alive, and many were dead or dying. The *Enterprise* was one of several ships assigned to escort them and lend humanitarian aid wherever we could. My ship's counselor, Deanna Troi, has been speaking extensively with some of the more . . . traumatized . . . individuals. They share stories of disarray, of internecine squabbling. It is not limited to the Thallonian homeworld, unfortunately. Various races, indeed entire worlds, whose antipathies had been held in check by Thallonian rule, are beginning to lapse into old and bitter disputes. Unfortunately our understanding of all that is occurring in the breakdown of the empire is limited by the fact that we know so little of the empire overall. Even the refugees themselves know or understand little beyond what was directly involved in their own day-to-day affairs."

"They had never needed to," Si Cwan said, and Riker actually detected a touch of genuine sadness in his voice. "We took care of them. We told them exactly what they needed to know, and no more. They were happy."

"They lived in ignorance," Ryjaan snapped back. "You did them no favor keeping them in that state."

"There . . . was . . . *order,*" Si Cwan told him, every word a bullet of ice. "That was what was needed. That was what we provided."

"Lord Cwan," Spock now said, "as you well know . . . I have been in Thallonian territory. I have been to your homeworld."

"Yes. I remember," Si Cwan said. Surprisingly, the edges of his mouth seemed to turn upward ever so slightly.

"My time there was far too brief to garner a full understanding of your empire's parameters, and the Thallonian desire for secrecy bordered on the xenophobic. It would be most helpful to these proceedings if you provided us with a more clear picture of what the Thallonian Empire consisted of. The number of systems, the more prominent races."

"The ambassador is correct," said Jellico.

"Of course I am," Spock informed Jellico, saying so with what sounded ever so slightly like amazement that Jellico would feel the need to point that out. As if Spock would ever be incorrect. Picard fought down a smile at Jellico's slightly flustered reaction, and in order to cover his amusement, the *Enterprise* captain said, "Such information would serve to guide us in our decisions. A course of action must be chosen . . ."

"Even if that course is to do nothing," Nechayev said.

"Nothing?" Both Si Cwan and Ryjaan had said the same word at the same time.

"That is certainly an option," Nechayev told them. "I must remind you gentlemen that we have the Prime Directive to consider. As disconcerting, as distressing as the current upheavals must be . . . it is not within our mandate to interfere."

"So you'll just stand around and watch all the star systems within the empire slide into oblivion," asked Si Cwan.

Ryjaan seemed no happier at the notion. "And you will let a member of the Federation—namely ourselves—deal alone with the security threat that the fallen Thallonian Empire represents?"

"You should have thought of that earlier," Si Cwan snapped at him.

Ryjaan was about to fire back a retort, but Jellico quickly cut him off. "We have not made any decision yet, gentlemen. As noted, that is the purpose of this meeting. Lord Cwan . . . will you tell us everything you know about the Thallonian Empire?"

Si Cwan looked slowly around the room. It seemed as if he were judging every single person in the room individually, trying to determine what he could expect from each and every one of them. Finally he said, "There were, at last count, thirty-seven systems within the empire. Each system has at least one inhabited planet; some as many as four."

"Would you be willing to work with Starfleet cartographers to give us a more detailed picture?" Jellico asked.

"Under certain conditions," Cwan said after another moment's thought.

"What sort of 'conditions'?" asked Nechayev.

"Let us save that discussion for another time. We must stay on topic."

"I'm curious, Lord Cwan," Picard said, stroking his chin thoughtfully. "What, precisely, do you feel is the 'topic' under discussion?"

Si Cwan spread his hands wide. "Is that not obvious?"

"Not necessarily," replied Picard.

"Gentlemen and lady," Si Cwan said, looking around the table and pointedly ignoring Ryjaan. "My escape from Thallonian space was aided by dedicated supporters, many of whom died in aiding me in my flight." Clearly the thought that he had, indeed, fled, was anathema to him, but he pressed on. "They felt that I was the last, best hope to restore the Thallonian Empire to its former greatness. And that I would do so by seeking your aid."

"If by 'your,' you are referring to the United Federation of Planets," Jellico noted, "need I point out that the Thallonian Empire is not a member of the Federation."

Si Cwan raised a scolding finger. "Do not confuse isolationism with ignorance. I point out to you that the Klingon Empire, some seventy years ago, also had not joined the Federation at the point that they found themselves in disarray. They were, in point of fact, mortal enemies. Yet the Federation welcomed them with open arms." His face darkened. "Perhaps we Thallonians should have sought conflict with you. Intruded into your territories, fought you for domination of worlds. Made ourselves a threat, rather than simply desire to be left alone. Had we done so, you might be as quick to cooperate with us as you were with the Klingons."

"Your description of the chain of events regarding the fall of the Klingon Empire," Ambassador Spock said with quiet authority, "is somewhat simplistic."

"How do you know?"

"I was there." He paused a moment. "Were you?"

Si Cwan met his gaze and then, to Picard's mild surprise, looked down at the tabletop. "No," he said softly. "I was not."

"For the sake of argument," Riker asked, "how would you have the Federation aid you?"

He looked at Riker as if the answer were self-evident. "Why, provide us with enough force of arms that the royal family can be restored to power. I know the power your fleet possesses. You have it within your power to right this great injustice."

The Starfleet officers looked at each other. Then Nechayev leaned forward and said, "Perhaps you didn't hear what I said earlier. Our Prime Directive forbids our interfering in other societies. . . ."

Si Cwan smacked an open hand on the table with such force that the table shook. "There is no society! There is disorder! Anarchy! I'm not asking you to change anything; merely restore the insanity which currently reigns into the order that previously existed. In exchange for your aid," he continued, "I guarantee you that the Thallonian Empire will be willing to join your Federation."

"It's . . . a bit more complicated than that," Nechayev told him. "There is an extensive approvals process through which any candidate must go. You don't simply snap your fingers and announce that you're in. Furthermore, you are not in a position to make any promises on behalf of the Thallonian Empire . . ."

"We were *the Thallonian Empire, damn you!"* Si Cwan shouted with such force that it shocked everyone into silence. For a long moment no one spoke, and then Si Cwan rubbed the bridge of his nose, looking a decade or so older than he had moments ago. "Pardon the outburst," he said softly. "I have not slept in some time. Being royalty does not make one immune from certain . . . pressures." He lowered his hand and then, with new urgency, he continued, "Let me put it to you this way: It is in the best interest of all concerned to restore the royal family to power. None of you knows what Sector 221-G used to be like. My kinsmen have ruled for two and a half centuries; an unbroken line of ancestors, keeping the peace, keeping order. There are some who might argue with the methods, but none can dispute the fact that for hundreds of your years, the Thallonian Empire thrived. I have many supporters still in place, but they are scattered and afraid. With the armed might of Starfleet behind us, however, it will rally support behind the true line of succession. Believe me, you would not want to see it return to the state that existed before my ancestors forged it into one of the mightiest empires in the history of our galaxy. If it *did* backslide in the anarchy that once existed, the number of dead and dying to which you referred earlier, Captain, would be as nothing compared to what's to come."

And now Ryjaan's voice turned deadly. "That would not be advisable."

This tone did not sit well with the Starfleet officers. As much as he was trying to maintain his impartiality, Picard's tone was icy as he said, "Why not?"

"Because we Danteri have our own security to consider. In point of fact, we were intending to send our own vessels into Thallonian space . . ."

"I *knew* it," Si Cwan said angrily.

Ignoring Si Cwan's outburst, Ryjaan said, "To be completely blunt, several systems within Thallonian space have already contacted us. There is discussion of new alliances being formed. They want protection, and we are prepared to provide it for them. If a fleet of UFP ships enters Thallonian space with hostile intentions, it is entirely possible that they may find themselves in conflict with Danterian ships."

"You think to pick over our bones," Si Cwan said, and he started to rise from his chair. "You are premature, Danterian. We are not as dead as you would desire us to be. And if you come into conflict with us . . ."

"If by 'us' you mean your beloved royal family, need I remind you there is no 'us.' Your time is past, Cwan, and the sooner you come to terms with that, the sooner you can stop wasting our time."

"Sit down, Lord Cwan," Jellico said sharply, and Si Cwan reined in his anger before it could overwhelm him. Slowly he sat once more.

Ambassador Spock, speaking in his slow, deliberate manner, said, "I believe we can all agree that avoiding violence and an exacerbation of an already difficult situation is of paramount importance?" There were nods from all around. "Very well. With that in mind . . . Ryjaan, you are authorized to speak on behalf of your government, I take it?"

"Of course. And you are for yours?"

Spock glanced at Jellico and Nechayev and said, "We have not come into this situation unprepared. I have made a thorough study and report of the likely reactions of both the Danteri and the Thallonians. Thus far they have remained in line with the projected probability curve."

Ryjaan made no effort to disguise his confusion upon hearing this pronouncement. Remarkably, he looked to Si Cwan for clarification. "He's saying we're predictable," Si Cwan explained.

"Quite so," affirmed Spock. "With that in mind . . . I have already made recommendations to the Federation which, if I am not mistaken, Admiral Nechayev is prepared to discuss."

"Thank you, Ambassador," she said. She drummed her fingers on the desk for a moment, gathering her thoughts. "Ryjaan . . . since the Danteri are members of the UFP, I am informing you that the Federation would consider it contrary to its best interests to have Danterian ships entering Thallonian space in any great numbers, inflaming an already inflammatory situation and stirring up hostilities. I am telling you this informally. If you desire, a formal resolution can be delivered by the Council.''

''I see,'' said Ryjaan dryly. ''And you anticipate that the Danteri will simply sit back and take no action, allowing the Federation to enter Thallonian space in force and shift the balance of power in a direction they find more appealing. Is that it?''

''No. That is not it at all. Provided that the Danteri do not, by force of arms, attempt to affect the situation, the Federation has no intention of attempting similar tactics, simply for,'' and she afforded Si Cwan a quick glance, ''the personal benefit of a handful of people.''

Si Cwan stiffened. ''You do not understand,'' he said. ''This has nothing to do with personal aggrandizement. I didn't ask for my station in life. To be relieved of responsibility . . . to be normal . . .'' He took a deep sigh, and there was the slightest tremble to his words. ''It would almost be a blessing.'' Then he seemed to shake it off and, more firmly, he continued, ''It is not for myself that I seek your help. It is for the good of the entire Thallonian Empire.''

''You,'' Ryjaan said coolly, ''are not in a position to decide the welfare of the Thallonian Empire.''

Before Si Cwan could shoot back a response, Jellico quickly stepped in. ''It's irrelevant to discuss the option. Starfleet is not going to send in armed forces to restore you or any surviving members of the royal family to power, Lord Cwan. It simply isn't our way.''

''I see. Instead your way is to allow billions of people to be swallowed by a spiral of chaos.''

Spock replied, ''That, sir, is overstated. It is also inaccurate.''

''We are discussing,'' Jellico continued, ''sending in observers. A neutral vessel with a small crew to observe and report back to the Federation, so that appropriate action can be taken at the appropriate time.''

With utter contempt, Si Cwan said, ''What a disappointment the present human race would be to its ancestors. As opposed to the pioneers and warriors of a bygone day, you are now all tentative and hesitant. When a time calls for the strides of a giant, you take small, mincing steps.''

''Considering you came to us for help, Lord Cwan,'' Jellico said in exasperation, ''I can't say I appreciate your attitude.''

And then Commander Riker said something completely unexpected.

''Cwan is right.''

If Riker had sprouted a third eye he could not have gotten any more of an astounded reaction from Jellico, Nechayev, and Ryjaan. Spock, as was his custom, remained impassive, and Picard was poker-faced.

"Are you saying we should go in there with guns blazing, Commander?" Nechayev said with ill-disguised incredulity.

"No," Riker replied flatly. "Difficult times do not call for extreme measures. But by the same token," and he leaned forward, arms on the table, fingers interlaced tightly, "we are talking about the collapse of an empire. We are, as Lord Cwan said, considering the fate of billions of people. For the Federation response to simply be that of passive observation . . ."

"The Prime Directive . . ." began Jellico.

"The Prime Directive, Admiral, last time I checked, did not first appear on the wall of Starfleet Headquarters in flaming letters accompanied by a sepulchral voice intoning, 'Thou Shalt Not Butt In,' " Riker said flatly. "It's a guide for day-to-day interaction with developing races so that we don't have umpty-ump Starfleet officers running around playing god by their own rules. But this is not day-to-day, Admiral. And we're not talking about playing god. We're talking about showing compassion for fellow living beings. Tell me, Admiral, while you were sitting on Deep Space Five waiting for us to show up, did you actually walk around and interact with the refugees? Did you see the misery in their faces, the fear in their eyes? Did you help patch up the wounded, stand by the bedside of the dying, say a prayer for the dead? Or did you sit isolated in your quarters grumbling over the inconvenience?"

"That is quite enough, Commander!" Admiral Nechayev said sharply.

Jellico smiled grimly. "You'll have to forgive the commander. He and I have some . . . history . . . together. The kind of history that prompts him to throw caution to the wind, even in the face of potentially gross insubordination."

If Riker seemed at all intimidated, he didn't show it. "The Prime Directive was created by men and women, no better or worse than any of us, and I respectfully submit that if our hands are so completely tied by it that we sit around impotently, then we have to seriously reconsider what the hell it is we're all about."

Jellico's anger seemed to be growing exponentially, but the supernaturally calm voice of Ambassador Spock cut in before Jellico could say anything. "I once knew a man," he said quietly, "who would have agreed with you." There was a pause as Spock's words sank in, and then he continued, "What would you suggest, Commander?"

"We assign a starship to enter Thallonian space. A single starship . . . hardly a fleet," he said, the latter comment directed at Ryjaan who already seemed to be bristling. "That ship will serve to report to the Federation about what they find within Thallonian space . . . but will also have the latitude to lend humanitarian aid where needed. Furthermore, if the races in question turn to the captain of this starship for aid in rebuilding their empire through whatever *peaceful* means are available," and when he emphasized the word he looked straight at Si Cwan, "the starship would basically do whatever is necessary—within reason—to try and make Sector 221-G a going concern again."

"And who decides what is 'within reason'?" demanded Jellico.

"The captain, of course."

"You want to send a starship into a potentially incendiary position, with possible enemies all around them, any of whom might want their help one moment and then turn on them the next." Jellico shook his head. "Putting aside the battering the fleet took in the last Borg engagement . . . forgetting for a moment that it would simply be sloppy planning to put a ship on such a detail for the benefit of a non-Federation member, and for an indefinite period of time . . . the bottom line is that Sector 221-G is a powder keg and Commander Riker is suggesting that we ask someone to stick their head into the lion's mouth."

"I would have phrased it without mixed metaphors, but yes, that's correct," said Riker.

Jellico looked unamused; it was an easy look for him. "It's sloppy thinking, Commander. It is a completely unnecessary risk."

And Ambassador Spock fixed Jellico with a dead-eyed stare and said, "Risk . . . Admiral . . . is our business."

Jellico opened his mouth, but there was something in Spock's gaze that caused him to snap it shut again. There was silence in the room for a long moment, and then Admiral Nechayev turned in her chair and said, "Captain Picard . . . what do you think?"

He tapped his fingertips on the table thoughtfully and then said, "I agree with Commander Riker."

"Oh, *there's* a surprise," snapped Jellico.

"With all due respect, Admiral, you know me well enough to know

I would not speak from some sort of knee-jerk loyalty,'' Picard informed him archly. "I have respect for the chain of command, and for personal loyalty, but first and foremost I do what I feel to be right. Might I point out that if that were not the case, the *Enterprise* would never have joined the fleet in the recent Borg invasion and you would have far greater problems to deal with than what to do about Sector 221-G.''

Jellico's face reddened slightly. Nechayev seemed unperturbed as she said, "Point well taken, Captain Picard. Admiral . . . I believe the idea has merit. It may take a bit of doing, but I'm reasonably certain I can sell the notion to the Federation.''

"Admiral,'' began Jellico.

But Nechayev was making it quite clear that she was not looking for further discussion. "Do you have a recommendation for an available starship, Admiral?''

"I . . .'' He started to protest again, but then he saw the look of steel in her eyes. He came to the realization that further dispute on his part was simply going to provide amusement for Picard and Riker, and he'd be damned if he gave them the satisfaction. So instead he switched mental tracks and began running through available ships in his mind. Finally he said, "One comes to mind. The *Excalibur.*''

"Wasn't she damaged in the recent Borg invasion?'' asked Picard.

"Yes, and her captain killed. Korsmo. A good man.''

"We came up through the Academy together,'' Picard said. "And I had the . . . honor of battling at his side in an earlier Borg incident. He was . . . a brave man.''

"Yes, and his last act was to get his ship clear. Otherwise the damage could have been a lot worse. She's currently being refit and repaired. The crew has been reassigned . . . all except the first officer. She's awaiting a new assignment; she's angling for command.''

"Aren't they all?'' smiled Riker.

Jellico fixed him with a stare. "Not all,'' he said snidely. And Jellico took some small measure of satisfaction in watching Riker's face fall. "The *Excalibur* should be ready to go in approximately three weeks. Push comes to shove, we can probably have her ready in two.''

"Very well,'' said Nechayev. "Admiral, Captain . . . under the circumstances, I would look to you for recommendations as to the appropriate captain for this assignment. We shall reconvene in your office, Picard, in two hours. Gentlemen,'' and she looked at Ryjaan and Si

Cwan, "it is our hope that this decision will meet with your approval. It is, to my mind, the best we can offer at the present time."

"My government will be satisfied," Ryjaan said evenly.

All eyes turned to Si Cwan as he sat there for a moment, apparently contemplating empty air. When he spoke, it surprised all of them as he said, "I will, of course, be on this vessel as well."

The Starfleet personnel looked at each other in mild confusion. "Why do you make that assumption, Lord Cwan?" asked Nechayev.

"It is my right," he said. "It is my people, my territory. As you say, you thrust yourselves into a dangerous situation. I still have many supporters, and my presence will give validity to your own. I must be there."

"We protest!" shouted Ryjaan, thumping his fist on the table.

"Save the protest," Jellico said. "Lord Cwan, it's not possible. You're not Starfleet personnel."

"The idea has merit," Picard said slowly. "We are talking about an unexplored, unknown area of space. His presence could offer advantages . . ."

"I said no, Picard. What part of 'no' don't you get?"

"I'm simply saying you should not dismiss the idea out of hand. . . ."

"Look, Captain . . . perhaps some of us are so lax about the presence of non-Starfleet personnel that they'll let teenage boys on their bridge to steer the ship," Jellico snapped. "Others of us, however, know what is and what is not appropriate. Si Cwan has no business serving in any sort of official capacity on a starship, and I won't allow it."

Now it was Picard who was beginning to get angry at Jellico's digs, but Nechayev stepped in before the meeting could escalate in hostility. "Captain, I must agree with the Admiral. Lord Si Cwan . . . I must respectfully reject your request. I am sorry."

Si Cwan rose from his chair and loomed over them. "No," he said. "You are not sorry. But you will be."

He headed for the door and Nechayev called after him, "Is that a threat, Lord Cwan?"

He walked out without slowing as he called over his shoulder. "No. A prediction."

III

"*Calhoun?!*"

In Picard's office, Jellico was making no attempt to hide his astonishment. He said again, "Calhoun? You don't mean Mackenzie Calhoun?"

"I most certainly do," said Picard, unflappably sipping his tea.

Jellico looked to Nechayev for some sort of confirmation that he was hearing a notion that was clearly insane. Nechayev was also surprised, but she hid it better. "I must admit, Captain, that I was under the impression you were going to recommend Riker for the position. That's the reason I didn't ask him to be here for this meeting."

"If Riker were interested, he would have let me know," Picard said reasonably. "Besides, I think Calhoun would be far more appropriate for the assignment."

"Picard, in case you haven't noticed, the man *resigned.* Calhoun is no longer a member of Starfleet. He hasn't been for . . . what, five years? Six?"

"Officially, he took leave."

"Officially? The man told me to go to hell! He stormed out of my office! He's floated from one job to another, some of them exceedingly shady! Do those sound like the actions of a man who has any intention of, or interest in, coming back to Starfleet?''

'' 'Shady?' '' asked Picard.

"There have been rumors," Jellico said. "I've heard dabbling in slave trade . . . gun running . . .''

"That's absurd. We can't be guided by rumors and innuendo."

"True enough," Nechayev said, "but we must be cautious."

"Face it, Picard, he was a troublemaker even when he was in the Academy. The fact that he was your protégé . . .''

"He was *not* my 'protégé,' " Picard replied. "He was simply a damned fine officer. One of the best we ever turned out." He put down his cup and began to tick off reasons on his fingers. "He knows that region of space. His homeworld, Xenex, is right up against the Thallonian frontier, and he did some exploration of the territory after he left Xenex, but before he came to the Academy. Furthermore, he knows the Danteri, in case they are involved somehow with the fall of the Thallonian Empire . . . and, Ryjaan's indignation aside, I believe that may very well be the case. Above all, Admirals, let us not delude ourselves. If the Thallonian Empire is falling apart, you're talking about planets at war with each other. Angry factions at every turn. You need someone who can pull worlds together. Calhoun has done that. He was doing it when he was still in his late teens. We need that strength and skill now, more than ever before.''

"He's unpredictable," Jellico said.

"So are the circumstances. They'll be well suited."

"He's a maverick. He's a troublemaker, he's—"

"Admiral," said Nechayev, "instead of complaining, may I ask whom you recommend?''

"The first officer of the *Excalibur,*" Jellico replied promptly. "Commander Elizabeth Paula Shelby."

"Shelby?" said Picard.

"You are familiar with her, as I recall."

"Oh yes," Picard said with a thin smile. "It is probably fortunate that Commander Riker isn't here; he'd be chewing neutronium about now. They did not exactly hit it off when she served aboard the *Enterprise* . . . particularly when he was busy trying to clean her footprints off his back.''

"Shelby is a solid, aggressive officer," continued Jellico. "She learned a good deal from Korsmo. She deserves her own command."

"She very likely does, but I do not feel that this is it," said Picard. "The unique situation, the challenges it presents . . . Calhoun is simply better suited."

"You're trying to put a cowboy in the captain's chair," Jellico told him.

"Absolutely," Picard replied. "This is a new frontier. Who better to send in to try and ride herd on it than a cowboy?"

"All right, gentlemen," said Nechayev. "I'd like formal proposals on my desk back at Starfleet within forty-eight hours. I'll review the specifics of your candidates' records, and consider other options as well. I'll render a decision as quickly as I can."

The meeting clearly over, Jellico began to head for the door, but then he slowed when he realized that Nechayev wasn't following him. He turned and looked at her questioningly.

"I need to talk with Captain Picard regarding another matter," she said. "If you wouldn't mind, Edward . . . ?"

Jellico tried to look indifferent as he shrugged and walked out, but Picard could tell that Jellico was annoyed. Then again, Riker had once observed that it was easy to tell when Jellico was annoyed: he was awake.

Nechayev turned to face Picard, her arms folded, and she said, "Regarding Calhoun . . ."

"I would hope, Admiral, that you haven't permitted Admiral Jellico's antipathy to prompt a hasty decision. . . ."

"Picard," Nechayev said slowly, "you have to understand that I'm about to tell you matters of a delicate nature."

The change in her tone puzzled Picard. "Delicate in what respect?"

She began to pace Picard's office. "There have been rumors, as Jellico mentioned, of Calhoun engaging in some shady dealings."

"As I said before, I would hope rumors wouldn't—"

"They're not rumors, Jean-Luc."

He raised an eyebrow. "Pardon?"

"Oh, the exact nature of Calhoun's activities may have been exaggerated in the retelling. These things always are. But Calhoun has engaged in some extremely questionable activities. I know because I assigned them."

"You—?"

"There are certain departments in Starfleet that prefer to keep a low profile, Captain. Offices that attend to matters which require a—how shall we say it—a subtle touch. Matters where general knowledge of Federation or Starfleet involvement would be counterproductive."

Picard couldn't quite believe it. "Are you saying that Calhoun has been acting as some sort of . . . of spy?"

" 'Spy' is such an ugly word, Captain," Nechayev said, sounding a bit amused. "We prefer the term 'specialist.' Mackenzie Calhoun has managed to establish a reputation for himself among certain quarters as a renegade Starfleet officer who will take on any assignment if the price is right. In doing so, he has both rooted out brewing problems and served our needs on certain occasions. You might say he is 'deep undercover.' "

"So he didn't leave Starfleet . . ."

"Oh, he left, all right. The incident involving the *Grissom* which prompted his departure was entirely genuine. But then he wound up getting himself into some trouble, and my office stepped in with a proposition that he couldn't exactly turn down. In short, we bailed him out of a situation from which he likely wouldn't have gotten out in one piece, and in return . . ."

"He's worked for you clandestinely. I see."

"It served both our needs, really. Mackenzie Calhoun is a man who needs challenges. He thrives on them."

"I know that all too well," acknowledged Picard.

"Well, we were able to provide him with that. It served the needs of all concerned."

"So what you're telling me is that Calhoun is out of the running. That you wish to reserve him for your . . . 'special needs.' "

Nechayev gazed out the window, her hands draped behind her back. "Not . . . necessarily," she said slowly. "I agree with you that Calhoun may be one of the best that the Academy ever turned out. Part of the reason for my recruiting him—under duress, I admit—was that I didn't want to lose him. I'm concerned that we may be on the verge of losing him now. He's been 'under' for too long, I think. Moving through disreputable, unsavory circles for so long that it's getting to him, bringing him down. Poisoning the essential goodness that is within him."

"He gazes into the abyss, and it gazes back."

"Exactly. For the purpose of achieving our own ends, doing what needs to be done . . . I'm beginning to fear that we may have damaged the man's soul. If we don't do something about it soon, the damage may be irreparable. If I simply 'fire' him from the department, though . . . God knows what will happen to him. He needs a purpose in life, Picard. He needs Starfleet, even if he doesn't fully accept that."

"With that in mind, do you feel he's still capable of resuming a place of command in Starfleet?"

She turned and looked back at Picard. "At this moment, yes. This would be the ideal time. A year from now, perhaps even six months . . . it might be too late. He might be dead . . . or worse."

"Can you bring him in to Starfleet Headquarters? Talk with him?"

"I'm not entirely certain he would listen to me," she said. "Not about the subject of coming back to Starfleet. And as for bringing him in, well . . . I think, in this instance, it might be easier for the mountain to go to Mohammed . . . if you catch my drift."

IV

Krassus stared appraisingly at the cards in his hand, and then across the table at the insufferably smug face of the Xenexian who was his main opponent. Moments before, a Tellarite and an Andorian had also been in the game of Six-Card Warhoon, but they had folded their hands and were watching the duel of wills between Krassus and the Xenexian with some interest.

The Xenexian wasn't giving the slightest indication of what he had in his hand. His hair was long, and there was a fierce scar down the right side of his face. His purple eyes were dark as storm clouds, yet they looked at Krassus with a sort of bland disinterest. As if there weren't a fortune in latinum currently sitting in the pot.

Krassus knew little about the Xenexian beyond that he apparently had some involvement in the slave trade. It was something that Krassus was comfortable with, what with slavery being his stock-in-trade as well. Krassus was an Orion, though, and had never had the opportunity to wander all that close to Xenexian space. But he'd heard through sources that Xenexians could be fairly tough customers, and this one seemed to be filling that bill admirably.

Krassus stroked his green chin thoughtfully. From nearby he heard a low chuckle. Zina was looking over his shoulder. "Stop breathing on me," he told her.

The scantily clad Orion slave girl took a step back, but she grinned in a manner that bordered on savage pleasure. Krassus had acquired Zina the previous year and had intended her for a quick resale, but he had taken a fancy to her. Even though he'd had a buyer lined up, he decided to keep her. The buyer had lodged a protest with Krassus. Krassus had, in response, lodged a dagger between the third and fourth ribs of the buyer, and that had put an end to the protest (and, for that matter, the buyer).

The reaction of the girl had not gone unnoticed by the Xenexian. "Seems to me like you've got a fairly good hand," said the Xenexian, "judging by your girlfriend's reaction. Perhaps I should fold right now."

In response, Krassus turned and cuffed Zina, knocking her back. She fell to the floor but landed like a panther, and she hissed fiercely at Krassus.

"Or perhaps," the Xenexian continued, "the two of you are working together to try and make me doubt myself. In which case . . ." He considered it, then nodded. "Yes. Yes, I believe that's probably it." He reached down into a case at his feet and pulled out two more bars of gold-pressed latinum, and dropped them onto the table. The table legs creaked slightly from the weight.

The card game had caught the attention by this point of all the rather seedy denizens of the equally seedy bar. Mojov Station was a way station convenient to several frontiers, a place where various types who might otherwise be questioned in more "civilized" establishments on more "civilized" worlds could come to relax, meet, greet, and try to parlay a few extra credits for themselves whenever possible.

Krassus looked at the bet, and felt the blood drain slightly from his face. "I can't cover that," he blustered.

"Seems to me like you're in trouble, then," replied the Xenexian.

Krassus' eyes flickered from his hand (which was a very solid one) to the bet on the table, and his greed was becoming overwhelming . . . to say nothing of his pride over the thought of losing to this pasty-faced Xenexian. Then his eyes caught Zina and he looked back at the Xenexian. "How about her?"

Zina was shocked to hear herself being put up as a bet, but the

Xenexian didn't seem the least bit surprised. It was as if he was expecting it. "She worth two bars of latinum? I don't think so."

"What she can provide in straight-up resale would be far less. What Zina can provide in the way of . . . physical gratification . . . she's worth ten times that. I speak from personal experience." Krassus chortled.

"Krassus!" she snarled.

The Xenexian regarded her thoughtfully. "If I won you, Zina . . . would you try to kill me as payback? Or would you show gratitude for one who would treat you far better than a man who'd put you up for a stake in a game of Six-Card Warhoon?"

Zina appeared to consider the point. Then a look of contempt crossed her face as she said to the Xenexian, "Clearly I have no more reason to be loyal to Krassus than he has to be loyal to me. Do what you will, Xenexian . . . and if it falls your way, I'll do what you will, as well."

"Fair enough," said the Xenexian. "It's a bet, Orion."

"Excellent!" crowed Krassus. "We finally have a game for true men, Xenexian! And now let us see which of us is the better!"

The back rooms in the bar were available for rent for just this sort of occasion, as the Xenexian strode into the room, pivoting quickly on his heel make sure that the Orion girl wasn't behind his back. Zina stood framed into the door, grinning ferally, her eyes sparkling. The room wasn't elaborately furnished; then again, the sturdy bed in the corner wasn't really much more than the room really required.

"I guess Krassus learned who was the better," she purred. "The great fool."

"More fool he," agreed the Xenexian.

"And what shall I call you?" She slinked across the floor, her hips swaying, the scraps of cloth that served as her clothing barely clinging to her.

"Mac," he said.

"And will you sell me, Mac? You own me now. Will you sell me, or keep me?"

"I thought I'd reserve judgment on that," said Mac.

"Until when?"

"An hour or two from now."

She sprang toward him, and his first reflex was to try and shove her away. But she wrapped herself around him in a rather unthreatening manner, her arms behind his back, her legs straddling his hips. "Merely an hour?" she said challengingly with a raised brow. "I think we can make up your mind faster than that."

And then her lips were against his, hungrily, and it seemed as if she weren't a woman so much as she was a force of nature. She practically stole Mac's breath away as she pulled at his clothing, trying to yank his loose shirt off him. He staggered back toward the bed, hit the mattress, and fell back onto it. She literally ripped off his shirt and started to do things down his bare chest.

He pulled her up to face him, looked into her eyes, and felt as if he were being sucked into a maelstrom. Her lips were drawn back, her teeth glittering and white, and he rolled her over so that he was atop her. Somewhere in all of that her clothes fell away, his chest pressed against her, and the heat was overwhelming. Her hands reached below his waist as his own arms extended up toward the pillow that lay at the far end of the bed.

The door to the room opened in complete silence. The Xenexian named Mac did not see Krassus enter, moving with stealth that seemed unnatural in one so large. Zina spotted him, though, but she said nothing . . . merely hissed more loudly to cover his entrance. Krassus carried a large knife, which glittered in the dim lighting of the room. He kept it highly polished, incredibly sharp. Keeping it clean was something of a challenge considering the number of times that he had shed blood with it.

He took two quick, silent steps and was across the room, the knife brought up over his head as he prepared to bring it slamming down. The Xenexian was oblivious, his back glistening with sweat, his right hand under the pillow. . . .

And suddenly there was a shriek of energy which tore through the pillow, blasting it apart, slicing through the air, slicing through Krassus. The energy bolt hit him dead square in the stomach, knocking him off his feet. He dropped the knife and, at that same instant, Mac suddenly arched his back and shoved Zina out from under him. She hit the floor, stunned and confused, as Mac snagged the falling knife from midair with his left hand. In his right hand he was holding the blaster he'd stashed under the pillow.

All of this happened before Krassus had even had time to hit the floor. The momentum of the energy bolt had slammed him back against the door, and he now slid to the floor with obvious confusion in his eyes.

Mac eased himself off the bed. From the floor, Zina looked at the fallen Krassus in shock and then back at the Xenexian. "You . . . you shot him . . . and you . . . you didn't even see him . . ."

"Practice," Mac said evenly. His voice, his demeanor, seemed to have changed. He seemed more in command, more formidable than before. If Zina were a fanciful type, she would have imagined that thunderclouds were massing over his head.

He walked slowly over toward Krassus, who was lying on the floor, clutching his belly. Blood was fountaining out, and Krassus was clutching things that he didn't even want to think about touching, trying to shove them back into his body. Mac crouched down, and his eyes were dead and cold. "Gut shot," he said, almost as if commiserating. "Takes a while to die of those. Painful as hell. And the damage is too extreme for any nearby med facility. You're dead. Of course"—he twirled the knife in his hand with surprising expertise; it seemed to come alive in his long fingers—"if you wish, I can end it for you faster."

"You . . . you bastard . . ." stammered out Krassus.

Mac nodded slowly. "Yes. I imagine so. But even bastards have friends. I've had a few, including one who saved my life once. His name was Barsamis. Name seem familiar?" At first Krassus shook his head, and then his eyes went wide in realization. "Ah. You remember him. Good," said Mac. "Barsamis had his faults, certainly. Something of a lowlife, really. But, as I said, he saved my life on one occasion, and that made me beholden to him. I owed him, and then some Orion slave trader violated an agreement and wound up killing him. Shoved a knife between his ribs." He looked speculatively at the blade in his hand. "This one, perhaps? Was this the knife?"

Wordlessly, Krassus nodded.

"Well, then," said Mac. "I'd say this falls into the realm of poetic justice, wouldn't you?"

And suddenly the warning tingled in the base of Mac's skull.

There was nothing psychic about the knack he had, nor anything mystical. The Xenexian simply had a knack for knowing when danger was imminent, and was able to react with speed and aim that seemed—to anyone else—supernatural. In the case of Krassus, of course, it had been easy. He'd been expecting just such a tactic as Krassus had pulled, and was prepared for it.

The attack of the Orion girl, Zina, on the other hand, was a bit more ill-timed.

Zina leaped at him, and Mac—still from a crouched position—slammed out with his right foot. It caught Zina squarely in the gut while she was still in midair and sent her falling to the floor. It did not, however, slow her down significantly. With an animal roar she was upon him, her fingers outstretched, her nails bared.

And out of the corner of his eye, Mac saw Krassus starting to reach into the folds of his shirt. It was possible that Krassus was simply trying to stop the bleeding. On the other hand, it was also possible that he was about to pull a weapon.

Mac took no chance. He yanked the blaster from his belt and swung it around with his left hand, the barrel hitting the Orion girl full in the face. He heard a crack which told him that he'd likely broken her lower jaw as she went down, screeching. His right hand, meantime, swept in an arc, slicing through Krassus's throat, severing his vocal cords, cutting through major arteries. Dark blood poured out from Krassus's throat and he slumped back, his eyes rolling up into the top of his head.

Mac scrambled to his feet as Zina backed against the far wall. There was the look of the wild, wounded animal in her face. Her damaged jaw fed pain into her that fueled her rage, and Mac brought the blaster up and even with her. "This has one setting, and it's a fatal one," Mac warned her. "I don't want to have to kill you . . . but I will."

Zina, with a bestial roar, leaped at him.

And a split second before he could squeeze the trigger, he sensed someone else behind him, but he couldn't fire in two directions at the same time. And then there was a blast from behind him, accompanied by the familiar whine of a phaser. The stun blast struck Zina and flipped her backward over the bed. She hit the floor and lay there, unmoving.

Mac spun, his blaster still leveled since he had no idea what to expect. But even if he had known . . . he would still have been surprised.

"I'll be damned," he said.

Jean-Luc Picard stood in the doorway, his phaser in his hand. He was dressed in civilian clothes of dark black. He was looking down at the bloody corpse of Krassus, and then slowly he shifted his gaze to Mac. "What the hell happened in here? Tell me it was self-defense."

"It was self-defense."

"Would you lie if it were otherwise?"

Calhoun's eyes flashed. "To others, yes. To you, no." He paused. "Did you come in a ship?"

"Of course."

"Let's get in it and I'll tell you." He started for the door, then paused and said, "Leave first. I'll follow a minute or so later. I don't want to be seen with you."

"Why not?"

"You know what you look like, Picard?"

Despite the goriness of the situation, the violence that had infested the room mere moments before, Picard couldn't help but smile inwardly. Reverence was never one of Mackenzie Calhoun's strong suits. "What do I look like, Calhoun?"

"You look like a Starfleet officer dressed in civilian clothes. If I'm spotted with you, I'll be ruining my reputation."

As the runabout hurtled away from Mojov Station, Picard turned from the controls to study Calhoun's face. He felt as if he were trying to find, somewhere within, the young man he had met twenty years ago. Calhoun, for his part, was calmly wiping away the last traces of Krassus' blood from his hands.

"You had to kill him, didn't you?" Picard asked after a time.

Calhoun looked up. "Yes. It was self-defense."

"That's how you arranged it. You allowed yourself to be pulled into a situation where you knew that you would be attacked . . . and then could defend yourself with lethal force."

Calhoun put down the towel he was using to dry himself. "He killed a man to whom I owed my life," he said. "Honor demanded that the score be evened. But I'm not an assassin. I couldn't just walk in and kill him."

"You're splitting hairs, M'k'n'zy."

"At least, unlike you, I still have hairs to split," replied Calhoun with a lopsided grin. He sat back. "Gods . . . 'M'k'n'zy.' It's been ages since I went by that. Hurt my ears to listen to people muck up the gutturals. Closest Terran tongues came was 'Mackenzie.' "

"Yes, I know. You officially changed your name on your records. M'k'n'zy of Calhoun became Mackenzie Calhoun."

" 'Mac,' to my friends." He eyed Picard with open curiosity. "Do you fall into that category, Picard?"

"I would like to think so." He paused. "You're trying to drag me off topic, which is something in which you've often excelled. The point is . . . if you have a grievance, you could have . . ."

"Could have what? Arrested him? Tried to bring him in for Federation justice? Picard," and he leaned forward, staring out into space, "it's different when you're out there. When you're on your own. When you don't have the power of the Federation at your beck and call. I work best outside the system, Picard . . . and since you've made a surprise visit, I take it you're aware of just how outside the system I am."

"And did it bring you personal satisfaction? Killing that Orion?"

He blew air impatiently between his lips. "Yes. Is that what you want to hear, Picard? Yes, it did." He sat there for a moment and then turned to gaze steadily at Picard. And in that dark stare, Picard saw a hint, just a hint, of a soul that had terrified armed men twenty years ago. Saw the fires that burned within Calhoun. "Don't you get it, Picard? I'm a savage. I always have been. I've created this . . . this cloak of civilization that I wrap around myself as need be. But I've kept this to remind me." He ran a finger down the scar on his face. "As much as I've tried to leave behind my roots, I've still felt it necessary to keep this with me so I never forget."

"Calhoun . . . Mac . . ."

"Do you know why I did it, Picard?"

"You told me. You killed him because—"

"Not that." He waved dismissively as if the Orion were unimportant. "Why I followed your suggestions. Why, when you eventually told me you thought I was destined for greatness. I—in my naïveté— believed you."

"You've never gone into specifics. I thought—"

"I had a vision of you, Picard. As absurd as it sounds . . . before we met. I had a vision of you. I believed that you would be important in my life."

"A vision? You mean a dream?"

"I mean I saw you as clearly, as plainly, as I see you here and now. I saw you and . . ." His voice trailed off.

"And—?"

"And . . . someone else. Someone with whom I was . . . involved. We kept our affair rather discreet."

"It did not end well, I take it."

"Nothing ends well, Picard. Happy endings are an invention of fantasists and fools."

"Oh, stop it!" Picard said so sharply that it caught Calhoun's attention. "Self-pity does not become you. It doesn't become anyone in Starfleet."

Calhoun got up and strode toward the back of the runabout. Setting the computer on autoguide, Picard followed him. Calhoun turned and leaned against the back wall, facing Picard.

"You should never have resigned, Mac. That's the simple fact of the matter. I know you blamed yourself for what happened on your previous assignment, the *Grissom.*"

"Don't bring it up."

"But Starfleet cleared you. . . ."

"I said don't bring it up!" said Calhoun furiously. The scar seemed to stand out against his face and, bubbling with anger, he shoved Picard out of the way as he started to head back to the helm of the runabout.

And to Calhoun's astonishment, Picard grabbed Calhoun by the wrist and swung him back around. Calhoun banged into the wall and, as much from surprise as anything else, slid to the ground. He looked up at Picard in astonishment. "Trying your hand at savagery yourself, Picard?" he asked.

Picard stabbed a finger at him. "Dammit, Calhoun, I believed in you! I looked into your eyes twenty years ago and I saw greatness! Greatness that did not deserve to be confined on Xenex."

"You should have left me the hell alone. Just as you should now."

"That is not an option. You're a Starfleet officer. No matter what you are now . . . that is what you will always be. You cannot turn away from that. You have a *destiny.* Don't you dare let it slide away. Now get up. Get up, if you're a man."

There was something about the words . . . something that stirred in Calhoun's memory. He automatically relegated what Picard was saying now—something about the Thallonians—to some dim and less important portion of his mind as he tried to dredge up the phrasing.

". . . and it is my belief that no one could be more suited—" Picard was saying.

"Jean-Luc, please, just . . . give me a moment," and the sincerity in Calhoun's tone stopped Picard cold. Calhoun pulled himself to standing and he was eye-to-eye with Picard. He was lost in thought, and Picard—sensing something was up—said nothing. Then Calhoun snapped his fingers. "Of course. You said that to me then. Gods, I haven't thought about it in years. . . ."

"I said what?"

"About my being a Starfleet officer. About destiny."

Suddenly looking much older, Calhoun walked across the runabout and dropped back into the helm chair. "That's the problem, Picard. That's always been the problem. I could see the future so clearly, even when I was a young man. I saw my people free, and it was so clear, so pure a vision, that I couldn't help but believe that I was destined to bring them to that freedom. And then I saw you . . . don't ask me how. And again I felt destiny tapping me on the shoulder, pointing me, guiding me. I guess . . . I had it easy."

"Easy?" Picard looked stunned. "You had an upbringing more brutal than anyone who wasn't raised a Klingon. Easy, you say?"

"Yes, easy. Because I never doubted myself, Picard. Not ever. I never doubted that I was destined for something. And I . . ." he smiled grimly. "I never lost. Oh, I had setbacks. I had obstacles thrown in my way. But in the end, I always triumphed. Moreover, I knew I would. And when I worked my way up to first officer on the *Grissom* . . ." He shook his head. "Dammit, Jean-Luc, no one guides a planet to freedom unless he feels that he was born to win. That feeling never left me."

"Until the *Grissom* disaster."

"Yes."

Picard sighed deeply. "Mac . . . I've been where you are now. I've suffered . . . personal disaster. Indignities. Torment, psychological and physical. And I'd be lying if I said there weren't times I nearly walked away from it all. When my body, my soul screamed, 'Enough. Enough.' But destiny doesn't simply call to Xenexian rebel leaders, Mackenzie. In a way, it calls to anyone who aspires to command of a starship."

"Anyone such as you," said Calhoun.

"And you. It called to you once, and it summons you now. You cannot, you must not, turn a deaf ear."

Calhoun shook his head. "It's crazy. You're not actually suggesting I get back on the bridge of a starship, are you?"

"That is exactly what I am suggesting. In fact, that's what I recommended, both to Admiral Nechayev and Admiral Jellico."

"Jellico?" Calhoun looked up and made no effort to hide his disdain. "He's an admiral now? Good lord, Jean-Luc, you want me to re-up with an organization so blind to talent that it would elevate someone like Jellico?"

"Jellico accomplishes that which he is assigned," Picard replied evenly. "We all of us work to the limits of our individual gifts. Except for a handful of us who walk away from those gifts."

"This is guilt. You're trying to guilt me."

"I'm trying to remind you that you're capable of greater things than skulking around the galaxy, accomplishing clandestine missions. Yes, you're doing the jobs assigned you. I take nothing away from your small achievements. But a Mackenzie Calhoun is not meant for small achievements. That is a waste of potential." He leaned forward, rested a hand on Calhoun's arm. "Twenty years ago I met a young man with more raw talent than any I'd ever encountered before . . . and quite possibly since. That talent has been shaped and honed and focused. Your service record was exemplary, and you cannot—must not—allow what happened with the *Grissom* to destroy you. Think of it this way: The *Grissom* disaster, and the subsequent court-martial . . . your resignation, your guilt . . . these are scars which you carry on the inside. But they are merely scars, not mortal wounds, and you must use them to propel you forward as much as the scar you carry on the outside does. The fact is, there is a starship that needs a captain, and a mission that would seem to call for your . . . particular talents. Do not let Starfleet, or yourself, down."

Calhoun leaned back in his chair, stroked his chin thoughtfully, and gazed out once more at the passing stars. Picard wondered what was going through his head.

He was a savage at heart, that much Picard knew. In some ways, he reminded Picard of Worf. But there were differences, though. Worf always seemed about as relaxed as a dormant volcano. His ferocity was a perpetual and prominent part of his nature. But Calhoun had gone much further. He had virtually created an entire persona for himself. As he'd said himself, a sort of cloak that he could wrap around himself, and use to keep the world at bay and his inward, tempestuous nature away from the world. As a consequence, he was uniquely focused, uniquely adept at problem solving, and one of the most dedicated individuals Picard had ever encountered.

What was he thinking? What great moral issues was he considering as he contemplated the thought of reentering Starfleet openly, to pursue his first, best destiny? What soul-searching, gut-wrenching contemplation was—?

Calhoun looked at Picard with a clear, mischievous air. "If I take command of a starship, Jellico will have a fit, won't he?"

Picard considered the matter. "Yes. He probably will."

Calhoun leaned forward, and there was a sparkle of sadistic amusement in his eye. "So tell me about this ship you want to put me on. . . ."

V

The light was blinking on Soleta's computer when she entered her apartment. As she removed her jacket, she looked at the flashing light with a distant curiosity. Outside it appeared that a storm front was moving in. It was clearly visible hanging in the distance over Starfleet Academy. It had already obscured her normally excellent view of the Golden Gate Bridge.

Soleta shrugged off her jacket and hung it carefully in her closet. She made several quick mental notes regarding lesson plans for tomorrow's class, and—since she was eminently capable of accomplishing more than one task at a time—she said briskly. "Computer. Messages."

"Two messages," replied the computer. "Playing first message."

The screen wavered for a moment, and then the image of Commander Seth Goddard from Starfleet Central appeared. His hair graying at the temples, Goddard was all business. "Lieutenant Soleta, this message has a callback command built in. Wait for live transmission, please."

Soleta sat down in front of the screen, folding her hands neatly in front of her. She wondered what Central could possibly want with her. She'd been fairly low-profile since taking on the teaching duties at Starfleet Academy. It was not precisely the life that she had anticipated for herself, but it was one that gave her satisfaction. Her journey of personal discovery as she endeavored to deal with her mixed heritage had been a long and rocky one. But that was far behind her now. She was at peace with herself.

At least, she liked to tell herself that.

The screen flickered to life and Goddard's image appeared on it. "Ah. Lieutenant. I appreciate your prompt response."

"How may I help you, sir?"

"You can help me by packing."

She looked at him blankly. " 'Packing,' sir? I don't . . . ?"

"You're being reactivated, Lieutenant. You're shipping out next week on the *Excalibur.*"

"Sir . . . no," she said with as much surprise as she ever allowed herself. "I do not . . . I am not seeking a shipboard position. I had thought that was clear to all concerned. That my place was here on Earth."

"It's called 'Starfleet,' Lieutenant, not 'Earthfleet.' I'm afraid you can't hide here forever."

"With all respect, sir, I am not hiding. I am doing a job, and a valuable one at that."

"You're doing a job that can be filled by at least a hundred people currently in the pipeline, all equally as capable as you. You're needed on the *Excalibur* as science officer, and you are the person singly suited to the job. Besides, you came highly recommended."

"Science officer . . . ? Recommended . . . ?" She was becoming frustrated by her communication skills, or apparent sudden lack thereof. "Recommended by whom?"

"Ambassador Spock."

If she had not become as skilled as she was at covering her surprise, she would have had to pick up her jaw off the ground in front of her. "Ambassador . . . Spock."

"I presume the name is familiar to you."

"Oh yes. Most familiar. And we have met. But I am still unclear as to . . . as to why he would recommend me for anything. Science officer, sir?"

"That's correct, Lieutenant."

"On the *Excalibur.*" Despite her hesitation, she was annoyed to find a tingle of anticipation. It wasn't as if they had abruptly decided to stick her on a science vessel and send her into the middle of nowhere. This was the *Excalibur,* a starship with a long and illustrious history. But then she tried, with determination, to shake off her momentary anticipation of the new assignment. "But sir, I still do not understand why, of all individuals, I am being assigned to this vessel. It has been three years, five months, and eighteen days since I logged any space time at all."

"You'll get your space legs back in no time," Goddard told her. "But you're probably wondering why we've zeroed in on you. Why the ambassador singled you out."

"Yes, sir, I believe I have asked that repeatedly."

The faint tone of criticism didn't appear to register on him. "The *Excalibur* is going to have a very specific assignment, Lieutenant. Sector 221-G."

Soleta did not even have to search her memory to pull that very familiar number up. "Thallonian space," she said slowly.

"That's right, Lieutenant."

"I had heard that there were difficulties. There were stories of refugees . . . civil war . . ."

"All that and more. And we're sending the *Excalibur* into the heart of it. It's going to be one hell of an adventure. I wish I could go with you."

"If the commander wishes. I would most happily step aside from my new post in deference to his own desires."

"Very funny, Lieutenant," said Goddard. "Let's not forget, you're still in Starfleet. The powers that be feel that, considering you're one of a bare handful of people who spent any time there, that your presence is essential."

Her instinct was to protest, to go over Goddard's head. Spock's recommendation aside, she was happy teaching. She had no desire to thrust herself once more into the rigors and dangers of space.

But still . . .

She couldn't help but feel that the mystery of Thallon remained an open door to her. There was something about that planet, something that intrigued her, and she'd never been able to investigate it. It had nagged at the back of her mind on and off for years, and the pronouncement from the commander catapulted it straight to the forefront.

"Very well, sir. I'll be ready."

"Good. Goddard out."

His image vanished, to be replaced by a blank screen and the computer voice saying, "Second message. Visual only."

She stared at the screen in confusion. There was just blackness; surely it was a mistake. But then, slowly, letters began to appear on the screen. Two words formed.

And the words were, *Don't move.*

"Don't move?" said Soleta in confusion. "What kind of message is that?"

And then she felt the blunt end of some sort of blaster weapon lodge itself securely in her neck. She couldn't believe it. Whoever was behind her, either they had entered the apartment while she was speaking to Goddard, or else they had actually been present the entire time and Soleta—despite her keen hearing—had been utterly oblivious.

"It is the kind of message," a soft but threatening voice said, "that you should pay attention to, if you know what is best for you. Now . . . you shall do exactly what I say . . . and may God help you if you do not, because no one else will be able to help you. That, I can assure you."

To Be Continued

INTO
THE
VOID

THE
EXCALIBUR

Captain's Personal Log, Stardate 50923.1. "Captain." Captain Mackenzie Calhoun. I thought I had left the Fleet forever behind me, and yet now I find myself not only back in the Fleet, but commanding a starship.

The Excalibur is currently a hive of activity. She's an Ambassador-class ship, registry number 26517. Funny. I've only been on her for a few hours, and I'm already taking pride in her. Not all crew members have yet reported in, but the final work is even now approaching its completion. I have spoken extensively with Chief Engineer Burgoyne 172, and s/he assures me that we will be ready to launch for Sector 221-G on the expected date. Burgoyne is the first Hermat I've ever met, and frankly, s/he's odd even for a Hermat. But s/he definitely knows engines, and that's what counts.

I still can't believe I'm here. When I was a young "rebel" on my native Xenex—battling the Danteri to try and drive those damned oppressors off my planet—I never dreamed of anything beyond the confines of my homeworld. It was Jean-Luc Picard who came to me when we were on the cusp of winning our long battle with the Danteri. He saw something in me, something that he felt should be shaped and honed *into a Starfleet officer. I will never forget when he told me of the noted Earthman, the Great Alexander, who supposedly wept when he realized that he had no new worlds to conquer. There I was, having accomplished the liberation of my people before I was twenty years old. Picard realized that if I allowed that to be the pinnacle of my life, that it would not go well for me in later years. He is the one responsible for my seeking out my true destiny.*

Damn the man.

I try to live my life without regrets. I did not regret resigning from Starfleet, for it was what I had to do at the time. And now I am determined not to regret rejoining. If nothing else, Picard was correct about the reaction of Admiral Jellico. Upon learning that I had been given command of the Excalibur, *with the mandate to explore the fallen Thallonian Empire of Sector 221-G and provide humanitarian effort whenever possible, Jellico looked angry enough to shred a Borg with his teeth. He's going to have to deal with it, however. That's his problem, not mine. My problem is to focus my attention on the job at hand, and not let my core impatience with the rigmarole and high-mindedness of Starfleet interfere with my job.*

Several major bits of business need to be attended to. I am still awaiting the arrival of Lieutenant Soleta, my science officer. She's had experience in Thallonian space. Even though Xenex is on the Thallonian/Danterian border, I possess only a smattering of knowledge about the territory. Soleta has actually been into the heart of that notoriously xenophobic realm and lived to tell of it. Her view of things will be invaluable. She is currently in San Francisco, teaching at the Starfleet Academy, but she should have received her orders by now and should be preparing to join us as soon as possible. Of the rest of my command staff, Dr. Selar is in the process of getting sickbay in fully operating condition. It's strange. I've worked with Vulcans before, and I'm well aware of their notorious reserve, but Selar is remote even for a Vulcan. So cold, so icy, so distant. I cannot help but wonder if she is simply overly dedicated to her Vulcan teachings, or if there is not something more going on in her head that I don't know about. Her medical performance is spotless and she came well recommended from Picard, who in turn heard nothing but good things about her from his own CMO. Picard's word is generally good enough for me, but to be blunt, Selar seems as if she'll have the bedside manner of a black hole, and I hope her presence here is not an error on my part.

Security Chief Zak Kebron is a Brikar, and certainly provides a feeling of security. I constantly have to request that he walk rather than run, since his running tends to make an entire deck vibrate. I've seen mountain ranges that are smaller. And yet he has astounding agility for someone who's got a hide tougher than twenty Hortas.

Astronavigator Mark McHenry comes highly recommended for helmsman, but he brings with him major caveats. I have very quickly learned that, during any conversation with Lieutenant McHenry, it seems as if he is either not listening at all, or listening to a conversation between two other people . . . neither of whom are in proximity. Yet he never seems to miss out on anything that's being said; how his mind is able to multitask in that way is a complete mystery to me.

Operations Officer Robin Lefler is recently promoted from Engineering. She seems very sociable . . . perhaps overly so, as if she's trying to compensate for something. "Desperately outgoing" would be the term I'd use. I'm having trouble getting a "read" on her, and will be keeping a weather eye on her for the time being.

The position of first officer remains open. I am finding the filling of that slot to be the most problematic area with which I have to deal. I have a number of worthy candidates, and have already interviewed several. Every single one has been eminently competent, knowledgeable, polite . . . and yet each of them seems a bit nervous around me. Intimidated, perhaps. They focus on my scar, the one I acquired in my youth when a Danterian laid open half my face. They seem to have trouble making eye contact. And they act as if at any moment I might start carving my initials in my desktop with the dagger I keep handy for sentimental reasons. I don't see why. It's my desk and my dagger, and if I happen to want to carve it into kindling, I damn well will.

Hmmm.

Clearly I will need a first officer whom I can not only tolerate, but who will also be able to tolerate me.

SHELBY

I

Elizabeth Paula Shelby gaped at Admiral Edward Jellico. He could not have gotten a more stunned reaction out of her if he'd suddenly ripped off his own face and revealed himself to be a Gorn wearing an exceptionally clever disguise.

Jellico was seated behind his desk, his fingers steepled in front of him. He watched Shelby pace his office with a mixture of amusement and awe. As always, the woman seemed like a barely contained dynamo of energy. When she was this upset, her face tended to darken and provide such a contrast to her strawberry blond hair that it looked as if her head were on fire. Her ire, her astonishment, were so inflamed that it took her several moments to regain her composure sufficiently to articulate her thoughts. "Calhoun?" was all she could get out. "Mackenzie Calhoun? *My* Mackenzie Calhoun?"

"*Your* Mackenzie Calhoun?" Jellico made no effort to keep the surprise out of his voice. "Commander, I'm well aware of the rumors regarding a history between you and Calhoun. Still, it's been my impression that it's been many years since he was *your* Mackenzie Calhoun."

"Yes, yes, God yes," she said quickly, having regretted the slip the moment she'd said it. "There's no feelings in that regard. None. There had been a . . . brief flirtation, I admit . . .''

"How brief?"

She drew herself up stiffly. "I don't believe that is necessarily your business, sir."

"Agreed. How brief?"

With a sigh she said, "Three years."

"That's not what I'd call brief, Commander," Jellico said doubtfully. Then he shrugged. "Well, it's not as if you were engaged. . . ." And then he saw her look. "You . . . weren't engaged to be married, were you? Well?"

Endeavoring to rally herself, Shelby said firmly, "Admiral, I am asking you to take my word for it that the past is squarely in the past. Furthermore, I feel I must inquire as to . . . that is, I'm curious as to the thinking behind . . ." She cleared her throat, and then forced herself to remember her place and station in life. "Permission to—"

"Yes, yes, speak freely," said Jellico impatiently.

At which point Shelby promptly tossed aside any attempt to speak in a diplomatic or tactful manner. *"Dammit, Admiral, what the hell is going* on *in Starfleet?"* demanded Shelby, the fury practically exploding out of every pore.

"I didn't quite mean *that* freely. . . ."

She didn't hear his dry response. She was too angry, waving her arms so vigorously that she looked as if she might go airborne any moment. "Putting aside that the *Excalibur* should be my ship . . . putting aside that I should have received my own command ages ago . . . putting aside all that . . . I find it personally infuriating that preference is being given to a man who walked away from Starfleet over an officer who has served unwaveringly and unstintingly!"

"I see you're determined to make this about you."

"Frankly, sir, since I'm the only one here aside from you, I think it's a thing for me to do." She shook her head. "May I ask whose decision this was? I know perfectly well it wasn't yours."

"Picard suggested it. . . ."

She rolled her eyes. "I might have known. Payback. Payback because I gave Riker a rough time."

Even though he knew it wasn't exactly the appropriate time, Jellico couldn't help but smile slightly. "Believe it or not, Commander, the galaxy doesn't revolve around you. Situations occur, decisions are made, people are born, grow old, and die, all without having anything to do with Elizabeth Shelby.''

"I'm sorry, sir."

"Don't apologize. At the rate you're going, someday maybe it *will* all revolve around you. The point is, although Picard suggested Calhoun, it was Admiral Nechayev who sealed the deal."

"Nechayev?" She was clearly surprised. "I thought there was no love lost between Nechayev and Picard."

"The last time I checked, there wasn't. There's something else going on, though. Something I haven't been able to completely find out about." He drummed his fingers on the desk thoughtfully. "There've been rumors floating around."

"What kind of rumors?"

"Stories, really. For instance, shortly after he resigned from Starfleet, Calhoun was alleged to have gotten into a serious drinking match with some admiral, and made a wager involving the world of Zantos."

"Zantos." Shelby made a face. "Wasn't that the world where a survey party got caught by the natives years ago, and they took the leader of the party and cut off his, uhm . . ." She shifted uncomfortably. ". . . his . . ."

"Privileges," Jellico said judiciously. "That's the place, all right. Never let it be said that Starfleet can't take a hint. We've steered clear of Zantos since then. However, Zantos apparently also produces the best ale in the quadrant. Better than Romulan ale, and tougher to get. Apparently, on a bet, Calhoun snuck onto Zantos, acquired a case of ale, and hotfooted it off the planet with half the Zantos fleet on his ass."

In spite of herself, Shelby smiled. "That sounds like Calhoun, all right." Then she shook her head. "But I don't understand what that has to do with anything."

"Perhaps nothing." Jellico shrugged. "Perhaps everything. Someone with that sort of attitude and resourcefulness might have been of interest to Nechayev. She has her fingers in a variety of 'unofficial,' 'behind the scenes' pies." He saw that Shelby was looking at him blankly and he sighed impatiently. "Do I have to spell it out for you, Commander?"

"Are you saying that Calhoun may have been involved in some sort of . . . of under-the-table information gathering, sir?"

"It's possible, Commander. We live in a universe of possibilities. What it all boils down to," and he leaned forward on his desk, "is that Calhoun apparently has powerful backers. And those backers are inclined to give him the *Excalibur* and turn him loose in the former Thallonian Empire."

By this point Shelby had sat in a chair across from Jellico. But Jellico's final statement seemed, to her, to more or less finish off the meeting. She slapped her legs, rose, and said, "Well, Admiral . . . I appreciate your candor." Trying to keep her voice even, to battle back the disappointment, she continued, "I hope you will keep my service record in mind for potential future assignments in—"

"Sit down, Commander, we're not done."

"We're not?" She was genuinely confused, even as she obediently sat again. "With all due respect, I'm not certain what else there is to say."

"I may have been overruled in the matter of the captaincy," said Jellico, "but I can pull enough strings to jump you to the top of the list for first officer."

She stared at him for a long moment. Then a short, disbelieving laugh jumped out of her throat, followed by longer, sustained laughter. Jellico displayed remarkable patience as he waited for the mirth to subside. It didn't happen quickly. Finally she managed to compose herself enough to say, "You're joking. You're not serious."

"Commander," he said evenly, "I have a reputation for many things, but it has come to my attention that 'comedian' is not one of them. Do I *look* not serious?"

"It's ridiculous."

"Ridiculous why?"

"For starters, I'm not interested in the post. Second, Calhoun would never accept me. Third . . ."

"Not interested in the post? Commander, I shouldn't have to do a selling job here," said Jellico impatiently. "It's a first-officer post on a ship with which you already have some familiarity. A ship that is about to embark on a very high-profile mission which offers excellent opportunities. As first officer, you'd be taking point on any away mission . . ."

She snorted. "You don't know Mackenzie Calhoun very well, Admiral. If you think he's going to sit around on the bridge while I spearhead away teams . . ."

"It's the first officer's job to make damned sure that the CO doesn't thrust himself into those types of high-risk situations." He leaned back in his chair and looked at her with what seemed to be faint disappointment. "Are you telling me, Commander, that you would be incapable of riding herd on Mackenzie Calhoun? That his bootprints would be all over you every time you tried to do your duty as you see fit? Well. Well well well," and he shook his head. "I guess I overestimated you."

Jellico could practically feel the waves of barely contained anger radiating from Shelby. "I did not say that, Admiral."

"I beg your pardon, Commander, but you most certainly did. . . ."

"I said Calhoun wouldn't sit still for it. That doesn't mean that I would just knuckle under." She smiled thinly. "To a certain extent, that's why we broke it off years ago. I wasn't his image of what he wanted in an ideal woman. I didn't jump to his tune, and I wasn't willing to make my career secondary to his."

"What a very old-fashioned attitude."

"He can't help it. It's part of his upbringing. When all is said and done, Xenexians aren't the most socially advanced of races."

"That is exactly my concern, Commander. Calhoun is a tricky devil. Very resourceful and very sneaky. I think he's going to need a first officer who knows all his tricks. Someone he can't pull any fast ones on, or try to steamroll over. Someone who can stand up to him." He permitted a small smile. "I'm not stupid, Shelby, nor am I completely disconnected. I knew damned well before you set foot in here that you and Calhoun had history together. In my opinion, that's exactly what he needs. And you have other . . . positives . . . that I think contribute to your viability as candidate for first officer."

"Those positives being that I'm ambitious," said Shelby. "That I want my own command. That if Calhoun screws up, I'm going to be there to note down the screwup in every detail so that, with any luck, we can get him out of the captain's chair and replace him with someone who deserves the position."

Jellico nodded. "I'm glad to see we're on the same wavelength, Commander. With your permission, then, I will put forward your application with my strongest recommendation."

She considered it for a long moment. "You do realize that he'll never go for it."

"Perhaps. Perhaps not. If I need to narrow the options available to him, I can pull a few strings in that department. I wouldn't do that immediately, of course; only if he proves 'reluctant.' ''

''Ah. Well.'' She folded her arms and looked squarely at Jellico. ''There's two other things that I think I should clarify, Admiral. The first is, reverse psychology is a fairly obvious tactic, and I wish you had not had to resort to it.''

''Mmm-hmm,'' he said noncommittally. ''And the second . . . ?''

''The second is,'' and she leaned forward with her knuckles on the desk, ''if I should get the assignment, understand: My loyalty as first officer will be to my captain. It doesn't matter if we were once lovers. It doesn't matter if I think he's pigheaded, or stubborn, or a first-rate pain in the ass. If I sign on, I sign on for the entire package. I accept it and I deal with it. And if you think that I'm going to weasel my way on board and then turn around and be some sort of snitch, spy, quisling, rat, or in some other way, shape, or form search out means by which I can undercut or disenfranchise my superior officer, all for the purpose of advancement, then you, Admiral, with all due respect, can go screw yourself.'' And with that she turned on her heel and walked out the door.

Jellico sat there, staring at the space which she'd just vacated with undisguised amazement. And then, to no one in particular, he said, ''Just once I'd like it if someone coupled the phrase 'with all due respect' with some sort of sentiment that was genuinely respectful.''

SI CWAN

II

Soleta had been caught completely flat-footed . . . a condition that was, to her, extremely annoying.

She was standing in her apartment in San Francisco. Her marvelous view of Starfleet Academy out the window had always provided a curious comfort for the Vulcan woman. Now it seemed to serve only as a sort of ironic counterpoint; out there would be possible rescue for her current odd situation, but it might as well have been on Venus.

On her computer screen, the words "Don't Move" . . . a message which had seemed very odd indeed when she first read it . . . still glowed at her in dark letters. "What kind of message is that?" she had demanded of the empty room.

That was when she had learned that the room was, in fact, anything but empty. From directly behind her, she'd felt the gentle but disturbing firm prodding of a weapon, and coldly spoken words: "It is the kind of message," a soft but threatening voice said, "that you should pay attention to, if you know what is best for you. Now . . . you shall do exactly what I say . . . and may God help you if you do not, because no one else will be able to help you. That, I can assure you."

Soleta was too well trained to let her astonishment show in either

her voice or her demeanor. She acted, in fact, as if the identity of her unknown visitor were of no interest to her at all. "I am impressed," she said. "My hearing has always been rather keen. That you were able to gain access to this apartment and hide in here without my detecting you is, as noted, impressive. That you were able to then get close enough to me to threaten me with a weapon, again without my hearing your movement, is nothing short of amazing," and then, as an afterthought, she added, "which would have more impact, of course, were I capable of being amazed."

"You are unafraid," said the voice. "You have not changed."

The voice struck a cord in Soleta's memory. She frowned almost imperceptibly. "We have met, have we not."

"Think of an opulent corridor," the voice told her, almost seeming to relish prolonging the moment. "Think of an escape attempt gone awry . . ."

"On Thallon," she said slowly.

"Correct."

"Si Cwan."

As if saying the name somehow released her from the threat of impending violence, Soleta turned to face him. Towering over her was indeed the formidable Lord Si Cwan, late of the Thallonian Empire. He had taken two steps back, clearly a respectful distance. "Stay where you are," he said firmly. "I am not interested in leaving myself vulnerable to the assorted Vulcan tricks at your disposal."

"Nor am I interested in utilizing them," replied Soleta, eyeing him with undisguised curiosity. "I still do not understand how I was unable to hear you come up behind me."

He shrugged as if it were an insignificant matter. "It is a technique I once learned. It is convenient for one who is as conspicuous as I to be able to blend in when such is required. I had a good teacher."

"I should say so." She gestured to a nearby chair. "Would you care to sit?"

Waving the barrel of his weapon slightly, he indicated another chair a few feet away. "After you," he said with exaggerated cordiality.

She nodded slightly and sat. A moment later he followed suit.

"The last time I saw you," said Si Cwan as casually as if they'd run into each other at a local pub, "you and Ambassador Spock were endeavoring to escape from Thallon. You'd staged a rather impressive breakout from your cell and were hoping to flee the palace when we happened to run into each other. Do you recall what happened?''

"Of course," she said. "You allowed the ambassador and myself to depart . . . after returning this to me," and she tapped the IDIC pin she wore in her hair.

He nodded. "All this time and you still wear it. It is comforting to know that some things in this ever-evolving universe remain unchanging.''

"What happened after our escape?"

"Guards were disciplined. Palace security was improved. Drills were held.''

"Nothing more . . . severe?''

"If what you are asking is if anyone was executed over their inability to keep you prisoner, no,'' Si Cwan assured her. "After all, the fundamental truth is that I allowed you to escape. Had I not done so, you would not have done so. It was a private decision I made, and one that I elected to keep private even as the investigation of your breakout was held.''

"Why? You were a nobleman. Certainly you weren't afraid of retribution.''

"Even noblemen have no desire to appear weak to their subordinates. It increases the difficulty of maintaining control.''

"And yet,'' Soleta said evenly, "you lost control anyway. Your family lost control of the Thallonian Empire.''

"A valid point,'' he admitted. "And, in fact, the reason that I am here.'' He seemed to regard her with intense interest for a moment, and then abruptly he holstered his blaster and placed his hands in his lap. The meaning of the gesture was unmistakable: It was time to put threats and attempts at intimidation aside. To be candid with, and trusting of, one another, if such a thing was possible.

"There are other things in this ever-evolving universe that should also remain unchanging, I should think,'' Si Cwan told her. "One of those is gratitude. Gratitude and appreciation for services provided, particularly when those services result in prolonging one's life.''

"I would assume you are referring to the fact that I am indebted to you for having allowed me to escape Thallon.''

"I am indeed.''

She looked down for a moment, and there was a slightly rueful expression on her face. "Were I fully Vulcan," she said, "my attitude would be that, in allowing my departure, you acted in a most illogical manner. Behaving illogically would have been your prerogative as a non-Vulcan. Once you had decided to behave in an illogical manner, however, my attitude toward you would have been one of . . ." She paused, searching for the right word. "Contempt, I should think. Contempt and even a bit of fascination that one could achieve a position of power while pursuing such illogical thought patterns. 'Gratitude' would never enter into it."

He nodded grimly. "That would explain Ambassador Spock's attitude. I appealed to his sense of gratitude during a private meeting, asking him to do my bidding. He refused, and even seemed puzzled as to what I was talking about when it came to feeling obligated to me."

"Ambassador Spock is likewise not fully Vulcan. However, he has had far more time to come to terms with that fact and compensate for it. Out of curiosity, did you threaten him with a weapon as you did me?"

"No," he admitted. "I decided to utilize it this time around for the purpose of emphasis." He considered the situation a moment. "May I take it from what you just said that you are *not* fully Vulcan? What are you?"

She fixed him with a level gaze and then said, with a softness that almost hinted at vulnerability, "I would prefer not to discuss it." There was silence for a moment, and then she said, "What did you want of Spock? For that matter, what do you want of me?"

"I need to get aboard the *Excalibur*. I need to be brought along, back into Thallonian space. It is important to me and, furthermore, I can be of use to you."

"You have already put in this request with Starfleet, I take it."

"Yes, and I was denied. They denied . . . *me,*" and it was clear that the thought still rankled him.

"Why?"

"Because they are fools. Because I am not a member of Starfleet. One man, a man named Jellico, forbade it, and the others would not gainsay him. They united against me."

"And what would you have me do?"

"Get me onto the ship."

She stroked her chin thoughtfully. "I do not know the captain," she said, "but I can certainly speak with him once I am there. Arrange a meeting between the two of you . . ."

"I am tired of meetings," Si Cwan said angrily. He rose from the chair, pacing furiously. "I am tired of groveling, tired of begging over matters that should be accorded to me out of a sense of correctness, of respect."

"Are you expecting me to sneak you on board somehow?" she asked skeptically.

And Soleta was completely unable to hide her astonishment when he replied, "Yes. That is exactly what I expect you to do."

"How? You're not exactly a Nanite, Si Cwan. You're over six feet tall. How would you suggest I smuggle you aboard? Fold you in half and put you in my suitcase?"

"I leave that to you and your resourcefulness."

"But if we speak to the captain . . ."

"He could say no. He very likely will. I expect that he will march in lockstep with his Starfleet associates."

"Even if I could somehow get you on board without anyone knowing," she said doubtfully, "you couldn't hide indefinitely."

"I'm aware of that. Once we're in Thallonian space, I'd make my presence known to your captain. By that point, it will be too late."

"Ship captains are historically not especially generous when it comes to stowaways, Si Cwan. In extreme cases, the captain would be authorized to punt you out of the ship in an escape pod with a homing beacon and no further obligation to see to your welfare. And since the captain is the one who defines what constitutes 'extreme,' he'd have a lot of latitude."

"I would deal with it."

"This is not a logical plan, Si Cwan. If you truly wish to go back into Thallonian space, you can hire a private vessel. As you well know, Sector 221-G is no longer forbidden territory."

"It is to some."

She raised an eyebrow. "Meaning?"

He dropped back into the chair opposite her, and with barely controlled anger, he said, "Understand me, Soleta. I still have followers. Many followers. At the risk of sounding self-aggrandizing . . ."

"A risk I'm sure you'll take," Soleta said dryly.

If he picked up on the sarcasm, he didn't let it show. ". . . I was one of the most popular members of the royal family. The mercy I showed you and Spock was not an isolated case. I helped out others from time to time, when such judicious displays could be performed without undue attention. In certain quarters, I was known as compassionate and fair, a reputation that was, quite frankly, deserved.''

"My congratulations."

"By the same token, I also had enemies. One in particular, a man named Zoran, was almost insane in his hatred for me. I never knew quite why; only that Zoran would have done anything to see myself and the rest of my family wiped out. In any event . . . there were supporters who helped me and other members of my family to escape when the empire collapsed. And we were . . .''

His voice trailed off, as if he was recalling matters that he would rather not be thinking about. Soleta waited patiently.

"We were supposed to meet at a rendezvous point," he continued moments later, as if he hadn't lapsed into silence. "Meet there and get out together. I was the only one to make it to the rendezvous point. I heard secondhand that most of the others were caught and executed."

"Most?"

The entire time she had been watching him, he had maintained an imperious demeanor. But now it almost seemed as if he were deflating slightly. A great sailing ship, becalmed, its mighty canvas sagging. "I have heard nothing of Kallinda."

She was about to ask who that was, but then she remembered something. She remembered when she first met Si Cwan, seen him sitting on his mount, proud and regal. And next to him was a young girl, laughing, clearly adoring the man next to her.

"The little girl who was with you?" she asked. "When I was first caught?"

"Yes. My sister. My little sister, who never did harm to anyone. Who was filled with joy and laughter." He looked at Soleta, his dark eyes twin pools of sadness. "Kallinda. I called her Kally. I have been unable to determine what happened to her. I don't know whether she is alive and in hiding, or . . .''

As if he was suddenly aware of, and self-conscious over, his emotional vulnerability, he pulled himself together quickly. He drew his regal bearing around him like a cloak. "It is galling to admit, but I need the protection that only a starship can provide. Protection from enemies such as Zoran. The influence such a vessel could provide. And a means through which I can search for my sister. None of these could be garnered through the hiring of some small, one- or two-man ship.''

"Lord Si Cwan, I wish I could help you, but . . .''

"No,'' he said sharply. "There will be no 'but's in this matter. I have need of your help, and you will help me. Once we are in Thallonian space I will more than prove my worth, but I need your assistance in getting me there. You owe me your life, Soleta. Not all the logical arguments, all the rationalizations in the world, are going to change that simple fact. If it were not for me, you would be dead; some rotting corpse in an unmarked Thallonian grave. If you have a shred of honor, you will acknowledge your indebtedness to me and do as I ask.''

"I would be putting everything at risk, Si Cwan,'' she warned him. "If my complicity in such an endeavor were discovered . . .''

"It would not be discovered through me,'' he told her in no uncertain terms. "That much, at the very least, I can promise you. Do not take this wrong, but you would be merely a means to an end. But you are a means I must take advantage of, for I see no other way at this point. I cannot command you to help me, obviously. But I ask you now, for the sake of your own life, which you owe me . . . for the sake of my sister's life, which might possibly yet be saved . . . help me.'' And then he added a word that he could not recall using at any time in his life.

"Please.''

And from the depths of her soul, Soleta let out a long, unsteady sigh, and wondered just who she should get to represent her at her court-martial.

III

Calhoun glanced up from the computer screen as the door to his ready room slid open. Dr. Selar entered and, with no preamble whatsoever, said, "Dr. Maxwell's performance is unacceptable. Please dismiss him from the crew complement immediately."

"Computer off," said Calhoun as he rose from behind his desk. He gestured for Selar to sit. The Vulcan doctor merely stood there and, with a mental shrug, Calhoun sat back down again. "His performance is unacceptable?"

"That is correct."

"Did you have sex with him?"

Selar seemed taken aback, although naturally she did not let her surprise become reflected in anything more than a raised eyebrow. "I beg your pardon?"

"Did you have sex with Dr. Maxwell?"

"No, of course not. Nor do I—"

"Is Dr. Maxwell an actor? Does he tend to burst into monologues or soliloquies?"

Selar was completely lost. "Not to my knowledge. I do not see how—"

"Does he play a musical instrument?"

Giving up trying to understand where her captain was going with the conversation, Selar said simply, "It does not appear on his resume. If he does, he has not done so in my presence."

"Well, I was wondering. You see, you come in here complaining about his performance, and since I know perfectly well that no patients have come through sickbay yet, I assumed you couldn't possibly have evaluated his performance as a doctor . . . which is, last time I checked, the reason he was here."

She tilted her head slightly. "Captain Calhoun, are you always this circumloquacious?"

"No, not really. Generally I simply tell people whom I feel are wasting my time to get the hell out of my office. But we haven't even left drydock yet, so I'm trying to be generous." He came around the desk. "Look, Selar . . ."

"I prefer *Doctor* Selar."

He smiled. "I heard a joke once. What do you call the person who graduates at the bottom of their medical class?" Without waiting for her to respond, he answered, " '*Doctor.*' "

She stared at him.

"Do you get what I'm saying?" he asked.

"I believe so. You seek to diminish the title to which I am due, based upon years of study and work, by implying that quality of scholarship may not be reflected in that title."

He rubbed his temple with his fingers and tried to remember why in God's name he'd let Picard talk him into this. "Look, Dr. Selar, it's your sickbay. If you want Maxwell out, he's out. I'm not going to argue. Perhaps you've perceived some potential trouble spots, or perhaps it's simply a personality clash. . . ."

"Vulcans do not 'clash,' " she informed him.

Keeping his voice even and calm, Calhoun said, "All I'm saying is that *you* are in charge of sickbay. The lineup for everyone working under you came from the Starfleet surgeon general's office. I okayed it based upon their recommendation, and I leave it to you to fine-tune it. Maxwell works under you. Use him, don't use him, blow him out a photon-torpedo tube for all I care. But I'll tell you right now, any changes in personnel have to be followed up with a formal report. I cannot put sufficient emphasis on this: I care very much about reports and following procedure. And you damned well better be ready to give concrete explanations for Maxwell's termination, because I think you should know that 'I felt like it' doesn't fly with Starfleet Central.''

"I see."

"Now, if you want my recommendation—and the joy of being captain is that you get my recommendation whether you want it or not—I suggest you sit down and speak with Maxwell about those areas in which you find him lacking. See if you can come to some sort of accord. That would be something that I'd very much like to see.''

"Are you offering your services as mediator, Captain, in order to facilitate matters?''

"Good God, no. I'd sooner stick my head in a warp coil. To be blunt, it sounds to me as if you're reacting out of some sort of core irrationality . . . which would be, to say the least, disturbing, considering who you are. Now, do your damn job and I'll do mine, and we'll both be happy. Or at least I'll be happy and you'll be,'' he gestured vaguely, "you'll be whatever Vulcans are. Now get the hell out of my office.''

She headed for the door, stopping only to say, "You use more profanity than any other Starfleet officer I have encountered.''

And with a wry smile, Calhoun replied, "I'm an officer. I'm just not a gentleman.''

Burgoyne 172 was working with Ensign Yates, overseeing the recalibrating of the Heisenberg compensators in Transporter Room D when the signal beeped on hish comm badge. S/he rose quickly, narrowly avoiding bumping hish head on the underside of the control.

The Hermat was of medium build, quite slender and small-busted. S/he had a high forehead, pale blond eyebrows, and two-toned pale blond hair that s/he wore in a buzz cut, but that was long in the back. S/he tapped hish comm badge and said, "This is Burgoyne. Go ahead.''

"Burgoyne? This is Shelby.''

"Commander!'' Burgoyne was genuinely pleased. S/he'd always gotten on well with Shelby, having worked with her on the *Excalibur* during the captaincy of the late, lamented Captain Korsmo. "How are you? For that matter, where are you?''

"I'm on a shuttle approaching drydock. They were kind enough to route this message through from the bridge. Tell me, Burgy, how long would it take you to get to a transporter room?''

Burgoyne smiled, displaying hish slightly extended canine teeth. "Well, let's see . . . allowing for the size of the ship, the measurement of my stride, the—"

"Burgoyne . . ."

"I'm *in* a transporter room, Commander, as it so happens."

"Perfect. I was hoping you could beam me aboard."

"That's against regulations." Burgoyne frowned. "Why not just dock in the shuttlebay? I'll inform the captain to meet you and—"

"That's what I was hoping to avoid."

"Avoid? I'm not following, Commander."

"I wanted to meet with the captain privately before I met with him publicly, if you catch my drift."

"I guess I do. You want to surprise him."

"In a manner of speaking. It'll be on my authority. Any problems with that?"

"None whatsoever, Commander. You're still technically my first officer until we leave port. If it's what you want, that's good enough for me. Just give me a moment to lock on to your signal," and hish long, tapered fingers fairly flew over the transporter controls, "and we'll bring you right on board."

Moments later the transporter beams flared to life, and Shelby appeared on the pad. She stepped down and stuck out a hand, which Burgoyne shook in hish customary extremely firm manner . . . so firm, in fact, that Shelby had to quietly move her fingers around in hopes of restoring circulation. "Good to see you, Commander."

"And you too, Lieutenant Commander."

"Shall I have Yates escort you to the bridge?"

"Oh, I think I can find the way."

And as she headed for the door, Burgoyne asked, "Are you going to be staying with us awhile, Commander?"

"That," said Shelby, "is what I'm going to try and find out."

Shelby stepped out onto the bridge and nearly walked straight into a mountain range.

At least, that's what it seemed like. She stopped dead in her tracks. She didn't really have much choice in the matter; her path was blocked. She looked up, and up.

The being who faced her was powerful and muscled, his skin a dusky brown with ebony highlights. Either one of his arms was bigger than both of hers put together, and he had three fingers on each hand: Two of the fingers in a [V]-shape, rounded out with an opposable thumb. His (assuming it was a he) head was squared off, like a rough diamond, and he had small earholes on either side of his skull. His nose consisted of nothing more than two vertical, parallel slits between his eyes that ran to just above his mouth.

"You've *got* to be a Brikar." She'd never seen one of the gargantuan beings before, but she'd heard them described. If what she'd learned about them was true, this behemoth could withstand phaser blasts that would kill a human . . . hell, kill a squad of humans.

He was wearing a Starfleet uniform that seemed stretched to its maximum, and all she could think was *Thank God he's on our side.*

"And you are?" he rumbled. His voice seemed to originate from somewhere around his boots.

"Commander Shelby. I'm here to see Captain Calhoun."

"I was not aware of your arrival, Commander."

"It's," and she bobbed her head from side to side slightly, "it's a bit of a surprise."

"I, with all due respect, sir, don't like surprises."

"Let me guess. You're in charge of security."

His eyes glittered down at her. She had a feeling he was eyeballing her quickly to see if she had weapons hidden on her. Apparently satisfied, at least for the moment, he said, "Wait here, Commander." The Brikar moved off toward the captain's ready room and entered. Shelby mused that it was fortunate the door opened fast enough. Otherwise the Brikar would likely have just walked right through it.

"Commander Shelby?" Shelby turned to see a pert young woman with a round face and dark blond hair, piled high on her head, standing near her. She had her hand extended and Shelby shook it firmly. "Lieutenant Robin Lefler. Ops. Burgoyne told me you were on your way up."

"I wish s/he'd told the walking landmass over there." She chucked a thumb in the direction that the Brikar had just gone.

"Wouldn't have mattered even if s/he had," said Lefler. "Zak is pretty single-minded. If the word doesn't come down from the captain, then as far as he's concerned, the word isn't given."

"Zak?"

"Zak Kebron. He's quite a piece of work, Zak is. I helped outfit him with a small gravity compensator he wears on his belt. The Brikar are such a heavy-gravity race that, if he doesn't wear the compensator, it makes it almost impossible for him to move. As it is, if he's in a hurry, you can hear him running from three decks away."

"I'd believe it."

"We have a few holdovers from when Captain Korsmo was in charge," continued Lefler. "They all had nothing but good things to say about you."

With a slightly mischievous air, Shelby said, "Well, they know better than to say anything bad."

Then Shelby heard a soft, rhythmic snoring noise. She looked for the source . . . and couldn't quite believe it. There was a lieutenant sitting at navigation, his feet propped up on the controls. His arms were folded across his chest, his head rising and falling with the rhythm of his snoring. He had short-cropped red hair and—curiously—freckles. Curious because Starfleet officers, not being exposed to tremendous amounts of sunlight in their insular adult lives, tended to be fairly freckle-free. Shelby turned to Lefler, an unspoken question on her face.

"He knows his stuff," Lefler said optimistically. "Really."

The door to the ready room slid open and Zak Kebron was standing there. "The captain will see you, sir," he said in a voice that sounded like the beginnings of an avalanche.

Shelby nodded briskly and headed into the ready room. Kebron stepped aside, allowing her to pass. The door slid shut behind him and Zak walked over to his station. Robin sidled over to Kebron and leaned over the railing. "Did the captain have any kind of reaction?"

" 'Reaction?' " He looked at her blankly.

"When he found out that the commander was here."

"Should he have?"

"I'm not sure. I was getting the impression that she was expecting . . ." Her voice trailed off. "I'm not sure what she was expecting. That's why I was asking you."

His face was immobile.

"Come on, Kebron. Did he smile? Frown? Did he seem tense, curious, excited, tepid . . . stop me when I hit a word that's accurate."

Nothing. Zak Kebron simply stared at her.

Lefler grunted in annoyance. "Lefler's newest law: Getting information out of you is like interrogating a statue." She turned away from him.

"Good," muttered Kebron.

Dr. Selar entered sickbay and went straight to her office. But she quickly became aware that Dr. Maxwell was following her with his gaze. He'd known fully well that Selar had been dissatisfied with his prep work in sickbay, and he had been perfectly candid about the fact that he thought Selar was being too hard on him. He had suspected, correctly, that Selar had gone to the captain to discuss the situation.

Unaccustomed to subterfuge, Selar turned and met his look squarely. And, in some ways, she felt as if she was looking at him—really looking at him—for the first time.

And she had never realized before how, with his dark hair, his squared-off jaw, his serious demeanor, Maxwell bore a passing resemblance to her late husband. To Voltak, who had died of a heart attack in the throes of *Pon farr.* Died while Selar had lain there helplessly, unable to aid him.

And the rational part of Selar's mind said, *No. That is ridiculous. Pop psychology, pat and unsatisfying. Having a negative reaction to a coworker because of a passing resemblance to Voltak? It is absurd. It is not logical. That cannot be it. There must be . . . other concerns.*

Except at that moment she couldn't think of any.

Deciding to break the uneasy silence, Maxwell stepped forward and said, "Dr. Selar . . . I'd like to know if you'll still be requiring my services."

"Do you have duties to attend to?" she asked him.

"Well . . . yes . . . but . . ."

"Then I suggest you attend to them. Our intended departure time has not been altered, and it behooves you to be prepared." And she turned and walked away to her office, leaving a confused but happy Maxwell behind.

The first thing that Shelby noticed was the short sword mounted on the wall. She stopped and stared at it. Calhoun seemed entranced by his computer screen, more than content to have Shelby speak first. She didn't let him down. "You still have it?"

He didn't even have to look up to see what she was referring to. "Of course."

"Mac, that sword laid your face open. It almost killed you. I'd hoped you'd outgrow the need to hold on to such things."

"It reminds me of the importance of keeping my guard up. As does this," and he tapped the scar. Then he turned in his chair to face her for the first time. "I can't say I'm surprised to see you, Commander."

"We're being formal, are we, Mac?"

"Yes."

Without missing a beat, she said, "Very well. Captain, I hope you will excuse my unannounced appearance, but I wish to discuss a matter of some urgency."

"You want to apply for the position of first officer."

"That is correct." She noticed her own picture staring out from the computer screen. Calhoun was reading up on her latest stats. "Since you are already in the process of reviewing my service rec—"

"Jellico told me not to use you."

She shook her head slightly as if trying to clear water from her ears. "Pardon?"

"I received a communiqué from Admiral Jellico. He told me you would be applying, and that he could not, in good conscience, recommend you for the post."

"I see." Shelby had assumed that Jellico would be backing her up. All right . . . if he wasn't going to, then fine. Calhoun couldn't possibly be aware of all the dynamics involved in—

"I assume one of two scenarios to be the case," said Calhoun, tilting his chair slightly back. "Either Jellico wanted you to spy on me, and you told him to go to hell, so that in a fit of pique he's trying to block the assignment. Or else he's hoping that you will, at the very least, make my life miserable . . . and by telling me not to use you, he hoped to employ a sort of reverse psychology. Like in the old Earth story you once mentioned to me, about the rabbit begging not to be thrown into the briar patch, he figured that by telling me not to use you, I would then turn around and do so." He gazed at her blandly. "How would you assess the situation, Commander?"

She did everything she could to fight down her astonishment. For a moment she felt as if she were clutching on to a roller coaster, and couldn't quite understand why the sensation had a familiar feeling to it.

Then she realized: She'd oftentimes felt like that during her relationship with Calhoun. *Why am I letting myself in for this again? I must be insane!* Those were the thoughts that went through her head. All she said, however, was "I would . . . concur with your assessment, Captain."

"Good."

She cleared her throat. "Captain," she began, "there are some things you should know. . . ."

"I don't need to hear it, Commander."

"Sir, with all respect, I believe you do. My record has been exemplary, I have served as first officer on the *Excalibur,* on the *Enterprise,* on the—"

"I said I don't need to hear it."

"I'm the right person for this job and, to be blunt, I'm the right person for *your* job, but at the very least I can provide a valuable—"

"Commander," he said, his voice icy.

"If you'll just listen to me—!"

"Eppy, will you shut the hell up!"

Her back stiffened. "Yes, *sir.*"

"Much obliged, Eppy."

"However, I should point out that if I am not addressing you by your first name, it would likewise be appropriate if you were not to call me by that . . . annoying . . . nickname."

"Elizabeth Paul. E.P. Eppy."

"I remember the derivation, sir. I would just appreciate your not employing it."

"You didn't used to consider it annoying. You thought it affectionate."

"No, it always annoyed me. I was just reticent about saying so because of our . . . involvement . . . at the time."

He gave her a skeptical look. "You? Reticent?" He sighed and turned his back to her, swiveling his chair so that he was gazing out at the narrow sliver of starscape which was visible through the sides of drydock. "It was good seeing you again, Commander."

"And you, Captain. And I guess I should say . . . putting aside our history . . . that I wish you the best of luck in the reassumption of your career."

"I appreciate that. Where's your stuff?"

She stared in confusion at the back of his chair. "Stuff?"

"Possessions. Equipment. Gear. Did you bring it with you or are you sending for it? Don't tell me you're going to waste time going back for it."

"I don't understand . . ."

He sighed. "Commander, we have to be out of here in forty-eight hours. I need to know if we're going to be required to sit around and wait for you to retrieve your gear, or whether you can be ready to go by the time we're prepared to shove off."

"Are you saying you want me aboard the *Excalibur?*"

"Yes, that it what I am saying."

"In what capacity?"

He turned to face her with a disbelieving expression. "Chief cook and bottle washer. Good God, Shelby, are you going to make me spell it out for you?"

"I think so, yes, sir."

"Very well." He stood and extended a hand. "Congratulations, Commander. You are the new first officer of the *Excalibur,* presuming you still want the job."

"Yes, I still want the job." She shook his hand firmly, but then a cloud crossed her face. "We might face a problem, however."

"That being—?"

"Well, the paperwork for my appointment has to be run past Admiral Jellico. If he was genuinely trying to block me because of—for whatever reason—that could be a problem. Procedures do have to be followed, reports must be made, and—"

"Shelby, I cannot put sufficient emphasis on this: I don't give a damn about reports and following procedure. The decision is mine, and the decision is made."

"Very well, sir."

She paused, as if wanting to say something else, and it was fairly obvious to Calhoun. "Well? Something else on your mind, Commander?"

"Captain." She shifted uncomfortably in place. "Our relationship . . . it was a long time ago. I'm over you. Way over you. I need to know if you're over me. I need to know if you took me on because of our past involvement."

"No, Commander. I took you on in spite of it. Dismissed."

"I just wanted to say—"

"Dismissed."

She nodded curtly, satisfied with the response, and walked out of the ready room. Calhoun turned back to his viewing port and stared out.

There had been any number of times when there had been people who thought he was crazy. The Danteri, for one, when he had led his people in revolt against them, thrusting himself into one dangerous situation after another with an abandon that many mistook for recklessness.

There had been fellow Starfleet cadets who were openly horrified, and secretly amused, by Calhoun's willingness to go toe-to-toe with the most formidable professors at the Academy, never hesitating to voice his opinion, never backing down if he was convinced that he was right.

In his sojourn on the *Grissom* he had learned the game of poker and quickly established a reputation as being capable of bluffing his way through any hand. Once they'd even brought in an empath as a ringer, and even the empath hadn't been able to get a bead on him.

The chances he had taken in subsequent years while performing the missions that Nechayev had liked to refer to as his "little adventures" on her behalf . . . well, Nechayev herself had said she thought he was out of his mind on more than one occasion, although that never stopped her from tapping him or his "peculiar skills" (as she termed them) whenever she needed something low-key handled.

But in all those times, in all those years of people thinking that he was crazy . . . never once had Mackenzie Calhoun himself shared that opinion about himself.

Until now.

"I just took on my former fiancée as my first officer," said Calhoun out loud. "I must be out of my mind."

"I assume she is qualified, sir."

The voice startled Calhoun, who swiveled around in his chair quickly to see a young Vulcan woman standing just inside the doorway. He mentally chided himself; he had been unforgivably sloppy. He'd actually been so lost in thought that he hadn't heard someone enter his ready room. In the old days back on Xenex, such carelessness could very likely have earned him a dagger lodged squarely in his back.

"Yes. She is eminently qualified, and that is all that matters," said Calhoun quickly. He stared at the Vulcan for a moment, her face familiar to him. Then it clicked: he'd seen it in computer personnel files. "You're Lieutenant Soleta."

"Yes, sir."

"Welcome aboard. We've been waiting for you."

"I encountered some . . . delays."

"I'd like to sit down with you and get a full picture of what you know of Thallonian space."

"As you wish, Captain. But first . . . there is a matter of some urgency that I need to discuss with you."

"Relating to . . . ?"

"My luggage."

He considered that for a moment. "Your luggage."

"Yes, sir."

He leaned forward, fingers interlaced, and said, "This should be good."

RYJAAN

IV

"This is not good."

Ryjaan, the Danteri ambassador, had only recently returned to his homeworld. Now he stood in his opulent office, high above the capital city, looking out at his most impressive view. Far below him the people of Danter went about their business, unknowing and uncaring of the efforts to which Ryjaan and other government officials went for the purpose of preserving their safety.

"No, not good at all," he continued, and he turned to look at the person who was seated in his office. It was a Xenexian who bore a passing resemblance to another Xenexian once known as M'k'n'zy of Calhoun. The difference was that he was taller, and wider, and also considerably more well fed, to put it delicately. To put it indelicately, he was terribly out of shape. However, his hair was neatly trimmed, as were his fingernails. His clothes were extremely fancy, far more so than was common for any Xenexian. He was clad in deep purples, with high black boots and a sword dangling off his right hip. The sword was largely for ornamental purposes; the only time he drew it was to show it off for a young lady whom he might be trying to seduce. It was indeed impressive-looking; the fact that it had never been used in combat didn't detract from that.

"Your brother," Ryjaan continued, "could cause us serious problems, D'ndai."

D'ndai shook his head in slow disbelief. "They actually put him in charge of a starship?"

"I was unhappy about this starship business to begin with," Ryjaan said. "When I was at the meeting aboard the *Enterprise,* I hoped to head this matter off. It would have served our purposes quite well to have the Danteri be the most significant starfaring presence in . . . what did they call it . . . ?" He quickly consulted a report that he had produced after the meeting. "Ah, yes. On their charts, it's called Sector 221-G. My, the Federation has always had a knack for creative names, haven't they."

D'ndai said nothing. Somehow he didn't feel that his input was being urged. He was correct.

"So our interests have been preempted. Oh, certainly we can come and go as we please. But we will have to move stealthily. Subtly. We cannot make any overt moves at this time."

"That might be fortunate," D'ndai finally offered. "At a time when there is confusion and chaos, no one is certain whom to trust. The larger the presence, why . . . the larger the target."

"Indeed."

"Yes." He shrugged expansively. "Let the Federation come in with their huge vessel. Let them parade around and draw fire and attention from all quarters. And once they are gone . . ."

And then D'ndai was nearly startled out of his chair by the abrupt thud of a dagger slammed down into the desk. It had been driven into it with significant force by Ryjaan, and now it quivered there, a trembling metal representation of Ryjaan's anger. Yet his expression was extremely placid in contrast.

"That sounds very much to me, D'ndai, like some sort of contrived rationalization for a very unfortunate situation," said Ryjaan, his voice having taken on a dangerously silky tone. "As I mentioned before, your brother is the captain of the vessel."

"I don't understand how they could possibly have put him in charge."

"Nor do I. Nor am I interested in understanding, because ultimately whether we understand or not, it's not going to make a damned bit of difference. The question is, how do we deal with it. And the answer is simple: You are to talk him out of it.''

''Me?''

''Who better? You're his big brother.''

D'ndai shook his head. ''You do not understand. It is rather ... complicated.''

Ryjaan studied him for a moment, and then said slowly, ''D'ndai ... we have had a long, healthy and mutually beneficial association these many years. I have helped you, you have helped me. We have taken a situation that could very easily have deteriorated into chaos and fashioned it into an equitable, beneficial situation for all concerned. Need I remind you that the continued growth and strength of the Danteri government is not only beneficial for Danter, but it also benefits your homeworld of Xenex? That being the case, I think you'd best explain to me just how, precisely, it is an overly complicated situation.''

D'ndai slowly rose from his chair and began to circle the office. ''You don't know what he's like,'' D'ndai told him. ''You just don't.''

''I don't follow. Are you saying—''

''I'm saying that he's incorruptible. That he has a strong sense of how things should be. And that he will pay little to no attention to my feelings on particular matters.''

''But why? You were freedom fighters together. Fought side by side, won the liberation of your people from my government. Certainly he must feel some degree of indebtedness. Some sense of what the old days were like for you. It can't be that he simply doesn't give a damn about you.''

''You don't know, you don't—''

D'ndai leaned against the glass of the window, his palms flat against it. He was struck by how cold the pane of glass was. ''We fought for ... ideals, Ryjaan. We fought for a certain view of how we wanted Xenex to be. And more than anything else, we fought for how we wanted to be. But once the basic freedoms for which we had fought so long and fiercely were finally won, things ... changed.''

''Changed how?''

''You know perfectly well how,'' D'ndai shot back, making no effort to hide the anger in his voice. ''Once we won our freedom, we had to get down to the business of governing. M'k'n'zy, he discovered he had no taste for it. No interest in it. He left it to me to pull our fractured world together, went off on his damned fool career path toward Starfleet. And then he came back and he . . . he judged me.'' D'ndai felt his blood boiling with the humiliating recollection of it. ''He came back to Xenex, all dressed up in that crisp new Starfleet uniform, and he looked down his nose at us. Like he was so much better than we. So much smarter, so much . . .'' He fought to regain control of himself and only partly succeeded. ''Nothing we had done was good enough for him. The government we had set up, the lives we had created for ourselves. He accused us of selling out our people to Danteri interests. He saw the lands we had garnered, the wealth we accrued that came as a result of doing business with your people . . . and it infuriated him.''

''You did what you felt was right,'' Ryjaan said, not unsympathetically. ''You did what *was* right. Treaties were signed, deals were made, understandings were entered into. Xenex is free, and everyone prospers.''

''Not everyone. I prosper. Some of my peers and associates prosper. Others . . .''

''Others eke out livings, I grant you. But they didn't take the risks you did. You're a leader, D'ndai. You and your peers, all leaders.'' He walked around his desk and intercepted D'ndai, who was still pacing furiously. He clapped a hand on his shoulder. ''Leaders earn more consideration, more rewards. Why else become a leader except to garner some special consideration?''

''That was always the difference with M'k'n'zy,'' said D'ndai bitterly. ''He became a leader because the people needed a leader. The concept of accruing anything aside from danger and risk . . . it never occurred to him.''

''And he's angry because it occurred to others.'' Ryjaan made a dismissive wave. ''It is far more his problem than it is yours.''

D'ndai heard the words, but somehow they did nothing to take the sting out of the recollections . . . recollections that he had thought he had long since managed to bury. M'k'n'zy, tall and straight and proud, looking contemptuously at D'ndai. Accusing him of selling out his people's interests, of becoming that which they had fought against. Telling him that Xenex was free in name only; that Danter had managed to sink its interests into Xenex in a far more insidious manner. And that this time, those who had fought for Xenex's freedom had virtually given it away again.

And all during that confrontation, D'ndai had barely said anything. He had withstood M'k'n'zy's tirade because, deep down, he had known it to be true. It had only been after his brother's departure that D'ndai had allowed his anger to build, had thought of everything he could have, or should have, said.

Ryjaan was silent for a brief time, and then he said, "However . . . even though it is his problem . . . it now becomes mine. I had hoped that I could count on you to control him."

"Ryjaan . . . if the entire Danterian government was not able to control him . . . what hope would I have?"

Ryjaan nodded thoughtfully. "A good point. But let us be blunt here, D'ndai," and his tone grew harsh. "We Danteri have, for the most part, been rather generous with you. We have asked little in return. As of this point, however, our interests are such that we need to ask a great deal. We need to ask you to exert whatever influence you have to convince your brother that our interests are his as well."

"And if I may be as equally blunt," replied D'ndai, "I don't think I have a prayer in hell of accomplishing that. I am curious, though, as to just what those Danterian interests might be. It would certainly help bring the larger picture into better perspective."

Ryjaan looked up toward the stars, as if he were capable of picking out the exact location of the Thallonian homeworld and fixing it with a gaze. "I have been candid with you thus far, D'ndai. I have no reason not to continue to be . . . do I?" He watched D'ndai's reaction, which amounted to nothing more than a strongly held poker face. "The planet Thallon," he continued, "in all of our most holy books, is a source of great power. The most learned and mystic of the Danteri elders call it the Rest World."

"Rest World? Why?"

"The reasons are somewhat lost to obscurity. It is our guess, however, that centuries ago, great fleets may have used the Thallon homeworld as some sort of a resting and refueling point. Why, we don't know. As I noted, it is merely conjecture. The point is, however, that we have waited a long, long time to have the opportunity to explore the secrets that Thallon possesses, whatever they might be. Perhaps some new source of limitless energy. Perhaps weaponry left behind by tremendously advanced races which could be of use to us. The possibilities are infinite . . . provided that the Danteri need not worry about interference from the Federation.''

"From my understanding, it is the Starfleet mandate that there be no interference.''

"Mandates are one thing. However, the simple fact is that we have to deal with a starship being captained by a Xenexian. A Xenexian, moreover, who was key in disrupting Danterian interests in the past, even when he was a know-nothing teenager. And he is quite far removed from that relatively lowly status. Now he is a knowledgeable adult with the power of a starship at his fingertips and the authority of the Federation covering his backside. If he desires to make life difficult for us, he can do so very, very easily. We will have to skulk about and proceed with extreme caution as it is, and that will be a major inconvenience. We wish to make certain that our inconveniences are limited to their current status. The fall of the Thallonian government is the ideal time for the Danteri to consolidate power. Your brother should not—*must not*—get in the way of that, both for his good and for our own. Are we clear on that?''

"Perfectly clear, Ryjaan. But I do not, as of yet, know exactly how to proceed.''

"Then I suggest you find a way, D'ndai.'' He returned to his desk, sat behind it, and then in a great show of confidence which he didn't exactly feel, he brought his feet up and placed them on the desktop. "Because if you do not find a way, then we shall have to. And that would be most unfortunate for all concerned.'' He paused and then repeated for emphasis, *"Most* unfortunate.''

Captain's Log, Stardate 50924.6. *We have launched from drydock and are on course as ordered.*

First Officer's Log, Stardate 50924.7. *We have achieved launch from drydock with a minimum of difficulty, and are proceeding toward Sector 221-G at warp six. I noticed in the captain's public log that he did not, as is Starfleet custom, enter the text of his launch speech. The launch speech is a long-standing Starfleet tradition. Some ship commanders read a prepared text, and some even read the same text on whatever ship they helm. Captain Calhoun chose to speak extemporaneously. In the interest of historical completeness, I am hereby entering it into the official log of the* Excalibur *via this entry. The speech was delivered via intraship audio at precisely 1120 hours on Stardate 50924.5:*

"Gentlemen . . . ladies . . . this is Captain Calhoun. I welcome you all aboard the Excalibur, *and look forward to the adventure in which we have been . . . thrown together, for want of a better phrase.*

"For many of you, this is your first time aboard a starship. It may seem vast, even intimidating to you at first. It is not. I would wager that

our little populace of six hundred and three, in comparison to the cities in which you likely grew up, is rather small. Furthermore, when we are measured against the vastness of the void we are about to hurl ourselves into . . . we are barely more than a speck.

"I have followed a rather . . . roundabout path to becoming your captain. I'm sure you all have your own stories, your own histories, your own reasons for joining Starfleet. I'm telling you now: They are all irrelevant to the job at hand. In the days of old Earth, I am told, there was an organization called the Foreign Legion, which men of questionable backgrounds could join in hopes of starting new lives for themselves. In a way . . . you are starting new lives here. Who you are, what you may have accomplished before . . . these are the elements that led you here. But from now on, anything you do will be, first and foremost, as crewmen of the Excalibur. *It is to that ship, to that name, and to your fellow crewmen, that I expect you to give your first allegiance.*

"We are all we have. There are no families, no 'civilians' aboard the Excalibur. *That is a luxury that I am afraid is left to larger vessels. Those of you who do not have families back home—and even those of you who do—look around you. The people to your left and right, behind you and in front of you . . . they are your family now. You will confide in them, depend on them, laugh with them, love them, hate them, and be willing to put your lives on the line for them. Nothing less than that level of dedication will do, because only under those circumstances will we be able to survive . . . and more . . . to triumph.*

"All right. What are you all doing standing around, listening to your captain chatter on as if he is saying something you didn't already know. Back to work."

Captain's Personal Log, Stardate 50924.7. Our launch was proceeding perfectly well until my first officer insisted I get on the loudspeaker and make a fool of myself to the crew. I don't even remember what I said: some sort of over-the-top, cloying, "Go get them, boys and girls" oration. Damnation, is this what modern-day Starfleet members need to bring them together? It was much easier on Xenex. All I needed to do was raise my sword over my head, shout "Death to the Danteri!" and the huzzahs would roll. Had I been wise, I would have informed Eppy that if she wanted a speech, she could damned well make it. But everyone looked to me as she stood on the bridge and suggested it; I didn't wish to seem a coward. It has been many years since I cared overmuch how I seemed in the eyes of others, and it is a disconcerting feeling. At the very least, I must take care to make certain that Eppy not put me in that sort of position again.

First Officer's Personal Log, Stardate 50924.7. The captain made a stirring and moving speech upon launch, which he would not have done had I not urged him into it. Although Calhoun's strategic skills and starship knowledge are indisputable, his people skills are in need of honing. It is my belief that, although Captain Calhoun has some rough spots to him, with my guidance he will develop into a thoroughly adequate leader. However, I do feel I need to discuss the contents of his off-the-cuff remarks, for the purpose of making certain that mixed messages are not sent to the crew.

V

Si Cwan floated in a point of consciousness between wakefulness and sleep. As he attained this state, his heart rate had slowed down to a point where it was almost undetectable. His breathing was incredibly shallow. He could have stayed that way indefinitely.

The darkness in the storage container was complete. But it did not bother him. He wasn't even aware of it.

In his semiconscious state, images floated in front of him. Images of his father, mother, uncles, all floated past him. All dead or missing, and even in his dreamlike haze, he didn't care overmuch. He had never liked most of them, had never gotten on with any of them. For they had tended to think of the Thallonian people as far beneath them, not only in their social status, but in their rights as sentient creatures. It was a philosophy that Si Cwan had never shared, and as a result he had gotten into any number of angry disputes over it. Although to the public they presented a united front, behind closed doors it was a very different story. Si Cwan had worked behind the scenes to get every consideration for the outlying regions of the Thallonian Empire.

And slowly, word had spread throughout the channels that such things always did. If there was a grievance to be filed, if there was a request to be made, it gradually became known that Lord Si Cwan was the one to make it through. For a time this had a beneficial effect, but soon word of Si Cwan's growing reputation reached the wrong ears in the palace. As a result, Si Cwan found every suggestion of his meeting with greater resistance than ever.

In the floating darkness of his semiconsciousness, Si Cwan saw himself arguing, warning, threatening. The fall of the Thallonian Empire was coming, any fool could see that. Why would they not open their eyes? Why would they not listen? But he could see the answer to that question in their faces. See the arrogance, the overwhelming self-confidence which would cost them dearly in the long run.

And there *she* was. There was Kallinda. Her arms outstretched, her face pleading, and in his mind's eyes she was mouthing the words *Help me*. Damn him for being off-planet when the trouble started. He, who had seen it coming, was in the wrong place at the wrong time. Of course, some would say that when an empire is collapsing, not being in the thick of it was the best position for someone at risk. But Si Cwan had precisely the opposite sentiment. If he had been there, he might have saved those close to him. Or, worst came to worst, he would have died with them.

Instead he now felt as if he were in limbo, floating, floating . . .

. . . floating . . .

And suddenly, brutally, Si Cwan was dragged back to reality.

He was jolted out of his meditative haze, light flooding him from everywhere. Caught completely off guard, he had no time to mount a defense as he was lifted bodily out of his hiding place.

His "hiding place," in this instance, consisted of a shining silver crate which was situated in one of the secondary cargo bays of the *Starship Excalibur*. It was relatively small, the ostensible contents being "Foodstuffs." Because of its limited space, Si Cwan was practically forced to fold himself in half in order to fit.

Under ordinary circumstances, it should have been many minutes, if not hours, before Si Cwan could possibly offer any sort of physical protest. He had brought minimal food and water into the container with him, since space had been at a premium and he wasn't exactly able to pack bathroom facilities in with him; furthermore, he had been exceptionally judicious in its use since he had not been entirely certain when he was going to be getting out of his hiding place. He had spent most of the time carefully regulating his bodily requirements, and as a result all the muscles in his body should have been completely slack. Furthermore his heartbeat had been slowed almost to nonexistence, and so getting adrenaline pumping so that he could attack should have been flatly impossible.

But circumstances, when it came to Si Cwan, were never ordinary.

As Si Cwan was being hauled out of the container, he barely had time to register the nature of his assailant. Whatever it was, it was a race unlike any that Si Cwan had ever seen before. His skin looked like thick, dark leather, and he was clutching Si Cwan with a massive three-fingered hand. He didn't know what this creature was capable of, and he didn't want to take the time to find out. Furthermore, despite the fact that he had stashed himself away in a very humble manner, he still possessed enough of his dignity to take umbrage at such treatment.

"I am *Excalibur* security chief Zak Kebron, and you are under—" Kebron began to say. And then Si Cwan's legs, which by all rights should have been immobile, lashed out. He drove both heels squarely into Kebron's face, staggering him by a grand total of an inch and a half. Kebron shook it off so quickly and easily that the blow might as well not have landed at all. "—arrest," he finished. There were several crewmen standing nearby, but all of them were general-maintenance crew. None of them were Security. Apparently Kebron considered himself all that was required to handle the present situation.

"Put me down," snarled Si Cwan, his feet dangling a meter above the ground.

"You are hardly in a position to bark orders," Kebron replied evenly. He seemed like someone who never lost his temper. It was entirely possible he never needed to.

Si Cwan, however, was not of similar temperament . . . particularly so considering the present situation. His body should have been unable to respond to the orders his brain was conveying, but through sheer force of will, Si Cwan struck back much faster than Kebron would have thought feasible.

His long legs scissored upward, and Si Cwan snagged Kebron's head firmly between his knees. Kebron staggered slightly, apparently more from confusion than from actual pain or even discomfort. And then, in an astounding display of physical control, Si Cwan twisted at the hip while in midair, achieving enough leverage to send Zak Kebron tumbling to the floor. At the last second Si Cwan leaped clear and Zak hit the ground with a sound and vibration not unlike that of an avalanche.

"I demand to see your captain!" Si Cwan announced as he scrambled to his feet.

Kebron did not seem in the mood for bargaining. "All you're going to see is the inside of the brig," he shot back as he clambered to his feet.

Si Cwan opted for discretion being the traditional better part of valor. For all he knew, the process of "due trial" on the *Excalibur* might be nothing more involved than this monstrous security guard unilaterally stashing him in a cell until he rotted. He had to find the captain. Certainly a man who lived his life in a position of command would be able to understand Si Cwan's predicament and accord him the courtesy to which his station in life entitled him.

It would have been impossible for any observer to guess that Si Cwan had been nearly paralyzed mere seconds before. He spun on his left heel, his right leg lashing out, and it squarely connected with the lower part of Kebron's face. A shuddering impact ran the length of his leg. It didn't manage to hurt Kebron any more than the first blow had, but it at least served to knock him off balance and send him down to the floor again. Si Cwan came to the quick and dismaying realization that, at least with matters the way they currently were, there was absolutely no way he was going to be able to defeat Kebron for any length of time. Kebron could afford to hit the floor. He could be knocked down a dozen times or more; it didn't matter. Because he would keep getting back up, as strong as ever and probably angrier each time.

Si Cwan bolted.

Two of the crewmen who had been watching the altercation tried to get in the way. Si Cwan leaped high, slammed out with both feet, and knocked them both flat. He landed lightly and was about to get out the door when it slid open moments before he got there. Someone else was about to enter.

Si Cwan didn't slow down, driving a fist forward so quickly that—to any onlooker—it would have been a blur.

And that was to be the last thing that Si Cwan remembered. That and a shouted word which sounded like, *"Later!"*

*   *   *

"Captain, a moment of your time, please," Shelby said as she spotted Calhoun exiting his quarters and heading toward the turbolift.

"Walk with me, Commander," he said briskly as he stepped into the lift. She followed him in, fully expecting that he was going to tell the lift to take them to the bridge. Instead he said, "Deck twelve."

"Deck twelve?" she said in mild surprise.

"Luggage problem," he replied. Her blank expression made clear that she had no idea what he was referring to, but before she could pursue it, he continued, "You have the moment of my time, Commander. What is it?"

"It's about your speech, sir. The 'welcome aboard' launch speech."

He nodded. "Brilliant oration, I thought."

"Yes, absolutely, there's just—"

"Just?" He eyed her skeptically. "Is there a problem?"

"Well, it was the part about the crew's first loyalty being to the ship and the ship's name and to each other."

"You disagree?"

"I don't dispute that those are important elements. But don't you agree that, first and foremost, loyalty should be to Starfleet and the ideals it teaches?"

He studied her levelly. "Of course," he said in a neutral manner. "Well-phrased. I agree, of course. Excuse me." The turbolift door slid open and Calhoun strode out, leaving Shelby behind. She was about to let the door slide closed when, with a frown, she ordered it to remain open and followed Calhoun out. He was walking with a brisk pace down the corridor and Shelby was hard-pressed to keep up, but she'd be damned if she asked him to slow down.

"With all respect, Captain, I believe I recognize that tone of voice."

"Do you?"

"Yes, I do. That's your I-don't-agree-but-I'll-say-anything-to-avoid-an-argument-I'll-probably-lose tone."

He didn't slow his stride, but a small smile did flicker across his lips. "I don't know that I'd concur with the 'probably lose' part, but the sentiment has merit."

"Captain, we are not going to be able to function if you do not tell me your state of mind at any given moment."

"Not my style, Commander."

"I'm sorry . . . what? Your *style?*"

Calhoun had stopped walking directly in front of the entrance to a cargo bay. He seemed to be listening carefully for something.

"Your style?" Shelby said again.

"Commander, later."

"Captain, I believe this indicates a larger issue that should be—"

The door suddenly slid open and a tall, dark red, and apparently very angry Thallonian intruder was barreling through it.

"I said later!" shouted Calhoun.

Calhoun seemed to register on the Thallonian's personal radar as nothing more than obstruction, something to be cleared out of the way as quickly and expeditiously as possible. Shelby, reacting in the proper procedure for such an emergency, slapped her comm unit and managed to get out, *"Shelby to Secur—!"* just as the Thallonian charged.

The captain moved so quickly that it seemed as if he weren't even hurrying. A quick step took him to the side of the Thallonian's path, and then Calhoun's right arm was a blur. His fist slammed into the side of the Thallonian's temple, striking a pressure point with such precision that the Thallonian was unconscious before he even fully realized it. His eyes disfocused and his hands clutched spasmodically at thin air. And then the Thallonian pitched forward and hit the floor. It seemed as if Calhoun were in a position to catch him, but the captain's arms remained securely at his sides as the Thallonian thudded to the floor.

The entire thing—the attack, the defense, and the dispatching of the opponent—had all occurred so rapidly that Shelby had barely finished the word with *"—ity . . ."* before the Thallonian was laid out in front of her.

Calhoun was staring down at the Thallonian with cool dispassion, and then Zak Kebron emerged from the cargo hold. "You called, Commander?" he rumbled.

"Quick response, Lieutenant," Calhoun said without missing a beat. "Well done."

"Thank you, sir," said Zak.

"If I am not mistaken," Calhoun continued, staring down at the prostrate form, "we are graced with the presence of Lord Si Cwan of the former Thallonian Empire. Lieutenant," and he gestured in Si Cwan's general direction.

Kebron reached down with one hand and picked the insensate Si Cwan off the ground. "Brig or sickbay, sir?"

"If we put him in sickbay, under the careful ministrations of Dr. Selar, he will likely wake up with no headache. In the brig, he'll wake up feeling like his head's going to fall off." He gave it a moment's thought. "Brig."

Kebron seemed to smile almost imperceptibly. "Good." And he proceeded to cart Si Cwan off down the corridor.

As he did so, Calhoun turned to face Shelby and smiled. "Now . . . you were saying?"

She looked at Kebron's departing form and then back to Calhoun. "You knew he was down here. You weren't coming here by coincidence. You knew perfectly well that that man, Si Cwan, was in the cargo hold."

"Yes."

Calhoun could see rage starting to build within Shelby, her body trembling in barely restrained fury. The door was just closing to the cargo bay when Shelby stormed through it. Calhoun followed her in, more out of curiosity than anything else.

The workers looked up as Shelby entered, but before any of them could say anything, Shelby snarled with barely contained fury, "All of you, out! Now!" Even under ordinary conditions they would not have been inclined to question an order, but considering Shelby's demeanor they were practically tripping over each other to evacuate the area. Shelby turned on her heel, smoldering, as Calhoun entered the cargo bay, the doors hissing shut behind him. Before he could get a word out, she turned and said with unbridled ire, *"How dare you? How* dare *you!"*

"Shouldn't you be asking for permission to speak freely?" he said, unperturbable.

"To Hell with that and to Hell with you, Mac! How *dare* you not inform me that you were aware we had an intruder on board! I'm your second-in-command! If I learn anything of importance then I inform you immediately, and I expect the same courtesy from you!"

"I'm afraid I can't agree. There will be times, Elizabeth," he replied in a formal tone, "when information will be on a need-to-know basis. And if, in my judgment, you don't need to know, then I can and will exercise discretion to keep that to myself."

Her flat hands swept the air in an impatient gesture. "Understood, of course, understood. But there is a line, Mac, between keeping things to yourself on the basis of Starfleet security, and keeping things to yourself out of some sort of misplaced need to prove yourself.''

''I have no such need, Elizabeth, I assure you.''

''Oh, bullshit,'' she snapped. He raised an eye at the profanity, but she steamrolled on. ''You have plenty to prove. You walked out on Starfleet, carrying guilt with you for years, and now you're back with more responsibility than you've ever known, and you're out to prove that you can do it all. Captain Mackenzie Calhoun, the one-man band of the *Starship Excalibur.* Well, it doesn't work that way, Captain. Not on any ship that I've ever been on. You think you're Atlas, carrying the entire universe on your shoulders, and if anything on this ship goes wrong, it's your fault. It wasn't true on the *Grissom,* and it's not true here.''

His face clouded. ''Leave the *Grissom* out of this, Elizabeth. If you have something to say, say it and be done with it.''

She looked down, the initial force of her fury spent, and then, still studying the floor, she told him, ''All I'm saying is that part of being a team means that everyone has responsibility, even though you have the ultimate responsibility. But even though you have that ultimate responsibility, your priority still has to be functioning as part of that team. That's where your priority has to lie. That's where your first allegiance has to be. To the *Excalibur* and the people on . . . her . . .''

Her voice trailed off. He stared at her, a carefully maintained deadpan firmly in place, as he said, ''Funny. I was saying that earlier and you were arguing with me about it. I'm glad you've come around to my way of thinking. If you'd care to join me at the brig . . . ?'' And as he headed out of the cargo bay, the doors slid open to reveal the assorted crewmen who had vacated the bay moments earlier. They were trying to look nonchalant or otherwise occupied; in short, like anything except people who were eavesdropping. They quickly dispersed, leaving Shelby alone.

''I hate that man,'' she sighed.

HUFMIN

VI

The captain of the *Cambon* didn't realize the danger until it was too late.

His name was Hufmin, he was a veteran star pilot and occasional smuggler from Comar IV, one of the worlds in the outer rim of the former Thallonian Empire. With many of his usual customers and routes in disarray, he was nevertheless turning a nice profit by offering his services to some of the more well-to-do refugees of the collapsing Sector 221-G. At least, that had been his intention. But somewhere along the way, as he had lent his aid for what had been intended as a mercenary endeavor, he had discovered—much to his annoyance—that he had a heretofore unknown streak of sentimentality. Perhaps it had been the desperate look of some of the women, or, even worse, the grateful faces of the children looking up at him. The *Cambon*'s comfortable complement was twenty-nine passengers; Hufmin crammed on forty-seven, many of them at less than the going rate and some of them— God help him—gratis. He considered it nothing short of a major weakness on his part. He could only hope for two things: that when this immediate crisis was over he would come to his senses, and that he did not suffer any misfortune, since he firmly believed that no good deed went unpunished.

With the *Cambon*'s facilities stretched beyond capacity, Hufmin decided to take a chance and cut through an area that was off his usual routes. On his starmaps it was listed as the Gauntlet, a holdover from more than a century ago when fleets from two neighboring worlds would take to the space between the worlds and blast away at each other. But that was long ago, and the area hadn't been a shooting gallery for ages. Granted, it had been the firm grip of the Thallonian Empire—to say nothing of the Thallonian's summary execution of the warring planetary heads as a warning to all concerned—that had brought a nominal peace to the area. And granted that, with the fall of the Thallonian Empire, anything could happen. But Hufmin couldn't believe that if the situation were to change, it could possibly happen fast enough to be a threat to his ship or its passengers.

He thought that for as long as it took for the first of the attack ships to drop out of warp.

He had gotten halfway through the Gauntlet when his sensors began screaming alarms at him from all sides. Frightened passengers began to call to him, asking what was going on, and all he could tell them to do was to shut up and buckle down. He couldn't believe what his sensors were telling him: attack vessels on both sides of him, all of them many times the size of Hufmin's modest transport, taking aim at each other. They didn't give a damn about him. They were only interested in blowing each other out of space.

Unfortunately, the *Cambon* was squarely in the way.

Hufmin banked furiously, slamming the controls forward, as the *Cambon* desperately tried to get clear of the area before the shooting started.

The vessels opened fire and suddenly the entire area of space was a hot zone. The ships fired with no particular grace or artistry, making no attempt to pinpoint respective targets and try for maximum damage with minimum fuss. Instead it was as if they were so overjoyed to have restraints removed from them that they simply let fly with everything they had. Blasts flew everywhere without regard for innocent bystanders. The attitude of the combatants was simple: Anyone who was within range should never have wandered in there in the first place.

The *Cambon* was hit twice amidships, and then a third time. The engines were blown completely off line, and only the laws of physics saved it, for the impact of the blasts sent the ship spiraling wildly. And since objects in motion tend to stay in motion, the *Cambon* was hurled out of immediate danger as the already existing speed of the ship carried it away from the firefight which had erupted in the Gauntlet.

Which did nothing to solve the *Cambon*'s long-term problems. Hufmin desperately tried to keep the ship on course, but failed completely. The ship was utterly out of control. Hufmin endeavored to concentrate on fixing the situation. But it was all he could do to focus on the problem at hand, for he had cracked his head fiercely on the control consoles when he was first hit. There was every likelihood that he was concussed. Indeed, he felt a distant blackness already trying to settle on him, and it was all he could do to fight it away.

He hit the autosend on the distress signal and prayed that someone would hear it. And then he vomited, uttered a quick prayer that they wouldn't fall into a sun, and slumped to the floor.

Out of control, unpiloted, and with apparently no hope in hell, the *Cambon* spiraled away into the void. Behind them two mighty fleets continued to shoot at each other, uncaring of the damage they had wrought. Without ten minutes the battle was over, as battles in space tend to end fairly quickly. The surviving ships limped back to their respective homes, and word was sent out that the Gauntlet was to be avoided at all costs.

Word that the *Cambon* would have been happy to spread . . . provided that anyone on it survived to spread it.

VII

Calhoun stood outside the brig, his arms folded. Si Cwan was standing inside, rather than sitting. Calhoun hated to admit that he was somewhat impressed by this; he could tell from the semiglazed look in Si Cwan's eyes that the Thallonian was fighting off ripples of pain and residual dizziness. He could just as easily have been seated, but something about him—pride, determination, arrogance, stubbornness—prompted him to be on his feet.

"Feel free to sit," Calhoun invited.

"I wish to remain taller than you," replied Si Cwan.

Inwardly, Calhoun smiled. Outwardly, all he did was glance at Shelby, who was standing at his side for a reaction. She rolled her eyes in a manner that simply said, *Men.* Of course, that might have applied equally to Calhoun.

"I am Lord Si Cwan," Cwan said archly.

"Captain Mackenzie Calhoun. Would you care to tell me why you stowed away on my vessel?"

"How did you know I had done so?"

"I ask the questions here," Calhoun said sharply.

Unperturbed, Si Cwan replied, "As do I."

Zak Kebron was standing nearby, his massive, three-fingered hands on his hips, watching the questioning. "Shall I break him in half, sir?" he asked. There was no eagerness in his voice, nor trepidation. It was merely a matter-of-fact query.

Calhoun gave it a moment's thought. "Go ahead, Lieutenant. If nothing else, it'll cure him of his annoying standing."

Kebron nodded and reached for the button to deactivate the field so that he could enter the brig and fold Si Cwan backward. Shelby looked from the expressionless Calhoun to Kebron to Si Cwan, who looked slightly disconcerted by the abrupt direction that matters were taking. She turned so that her back was to Cwan as she whispered to Calhoun, *"Captain!* With all due respect, you can't do that!"

"I'm not," Calhoun said reasonably, making no effort to keep his voice down. "Lieutenant Kebron is. Lieutenant, go ahead. Break him in half. Or a sixty-forty split would suffice. This isn't an exact science."

Shelby stared intently into Calhoun's eyes . . . and then understanding seemed to dawn. She turned back to Si Cwan and said, "I tried. I tried to talk him out of it. He won't listen to me. If it's of any consolation, I'll be sending a stern report to Starfleet in regards to this heinous treatment. If you'll excuse me," and she started to walk away.

Kebron shut off the forcefield and stepped in, immense fists flexing.

"Wait!" Si Cwan said, taking an unsteady step backward. Then he cleared his throat, trying to regain his composure. "Wait," he repeated, far more calmly this time. "I see no reason that we need to be adversarial about this. I . . . need passage back to my system. Back to Thallonian space."

In quick, carefully chosen phrases, he laid out his situation for them. Who he was, his desire to turn home, his need for protection that only a starship could provide.

"And you felt that sneaking on board was preferable to simply approaching the captain directly?" asked Shelby.

"I had already broached the notion to his superiors," Si Cwan said. "They had refused me. To encourage a subordinate officer to take actions counter to the sentiment of his superiors—even though they were sentiments that angered me—would have been dishonorable."

"But that's what you're doing now, isn't it?" Shelby countered. "You're asking him to countermand those orders."

"I am already here," replied Si Cwan. "It is a different situation.

I am giving him no choice *but* to countermand them and accept me as a passenger.''

"So it's all right to force someone to help you, but it's not all right to simply ask them,'' asked Shelby. Si Cwan made no reply, but merely gave a small shrug.

"What makes you think I won't toss you out of the ship right now? Leave you to fend for yourself? For that matter, what's to stop me from simply throwing you bodily out into space right now?'' Calhoun asked. Shelby knew damned well that, for starters, Starfleet regulations would stop him. But she said nothing since she didn't want to undercut her captain . . . and besides, one never knew with Mackenzie Calhoun. Shelby was ninety-nine percent sure that he wouldn't take such an action, but it was the remaining one percent that made her hold her tongue.

Unaware of what was going through Shelby's mind, Si Cwan replied, "Because to do so would be a tremendous waste of material. One does not become a leader of men by wasting material and opportunities when they present themselves.'' Si Cwan looked and sounded utterly confident. Whether he genuinely was or else was simply putting on the act of his life, Calhoun wasn't entirely sure.

"And what purpose would you serve on my ship, may I ask?''

"Goodwill ambassador. A connection to what once was in the hope of building that which will be. A guide through areas of space which are unfamiliar to you.''

Calhoun snorted skeptically. "A guide? Why don't I just make you ship's cook while I'm at it?''

"Captain,'' said Si Cwan, taking a step forward. Kebron growled warningly low in his throat, and it sounded like two asteroids crunching together. Si Cwan stopped where he was and wisely took a step back. "You are entering my home. My backyard, as you would call it. Quite simply, it would be the height of stupidity to toss aside any potential resource. The question becomes: Are you a stupid man?''

"Watch your tone,'' Zak Kebron warned him.

"Now, if you wouldn't mind, Captain, considering my candor . . . how *did* you know that I had smuggled myself aboard in that cargo?''

"Mislabeling, actually. Several bills of lading had been misplaced, and technicians were using tricorders to run quick scans on cargo contents. Saved us having to go through them box by box.''

"Clerical error. I see.''

"I'll be discussing this with my senior officers," Calhoun told Si Cwan. "You will remain here until the decision is made. Understood?"

"Your sentiments seem clear enough. And Captain . . ."

"Yes?"

"Thank you for your consideration. And thank you, Commander," he said to Shelby with a small smile, "for not permitting me to be broken in half."

"Don't mention it," she told him generously.

Zak Kebron stepped out and reactivated the forcefield as Shelby and Calhoun headed down the hall. As soon as they were out of earshot, Shelby told him with confidence, "I'm feeling a bit better."

"Are you."

"Yes. Because although our three years together gives us a degree of emotional baggage, it also means we can be in synch on some things without a lot of preplanning."

"Such as?"

"Well, just before. When we slipped into that 'tough cop, nice cop' routine."

He stopped and stared at her. "*What* are you talking about?"

" 'Cop.' Old Earth slang for a law-enforcement official. When they would question someone, two of the law officials would work in tandem, one being threatening, the other conciliatory, in order to manipulate the person being questioned. Tough cop, nice cop."

"Never heard of it." He started to walk away but she put a hand on his upper arm, stopping him.

For a moment she felt the hardness of his muscle and thought, *Well, he's certainly kept working out.* Out loud, though, she said, "You weren't *really* going to have Kebron break him in half."

Calhoun smiled in a manner so mysterious that even the Mona Lisa would have been hard-pressed to find fault with it, and then he walked away, leaving Shelby shaking her head before heading up to the bridge.

"So he 'covered' for me," Soleta said. It was not a question; it was as if she knew ahead of time.

"You don't sound surprised," Calhoun said.

"I try never to sound surprised. In this instance, though . . . I simply am not."

Soleta, Calhoun, and Shelby were in the captain's ready room. Calhoun was leaning slightly back, his feet up on his desk. "Why not?" asked Shelby.

"His desire was to get aboard the vessel. He accomplished that. There would have been no advantage at all in informing you of my duplicity. *Alleged* duplicity," she amended.

Shelby looked to Calhoun for an answer that she already knew. "So Soleta came to you with her dilemma, and you approved her 'sneaking' him aboard."

"That's correct. Problem with that?"

"Several, the most prominent being your not telling me beforehand. But putting that aside—I am going to make the educated guess that you intend to let him remain aboard."

"It is a logical assumption," Soleta agreed. Although the remark was addressed to Shelby, her gaze remained fixed on Calhoun. "After all, I warned the captain before we loaded the hidden Si Cwan onto the ship. We could just as easily have left him behind." Calhoun inclined his head slightly to indicate his concurrence with her astute observation.

"All right, then," Shelby said readily. "That being the case, why in the world did you go through all the subterfuge? Why did you act surprised? Why did you go through this entire song and dance?"

Calhoun draped his hands behind his head and leaned back in his chair. "I know Si Cwan's type, Commander. Hell, I've *fought* his type. The first and foremost consideration is ego. The second is pride. He's part of a ruling class, and is accustomed to doing things his way, even if that way is tremendously involved. In a way, Commander, you should be able to appreciate his point of view."

"How so?"

"Because he cared about two things: the chain of command, and settling a matter of honor. He did not wish to undercut superior officers, but he felt that Soleta owed him a debt since he helped save her life back on Thallon years ago. And you, Lieutenant, were correct to come to me with this situation."

"I saw no logical alternative. Basically, he was correct . . . I did owe him a debt of gratitude. By the same token, I owe my allegiance to Starfleet." She paused a moment. "Do you think that he knew I'd go to you and 'arrange' for him to sneak on, knowing all the time that it would be a setup?"

"Lieutenant, you can lose your mind if you try to think these things through too much."

"So what do we do, Captain? Do we let him stay?" asked Shelby.

"Of course we let him stay. As Soleta pointed out, I wouldn't have allowed him on, subterfuge or no, if I didn't intend to let him stay put."

"But why?"

He leaned back in his chair. "Because I've heard good things about him through the grapevine. Despite his position as part of the ruling family, he was—is—a man of compassion. One doesn't encounter many of those, and if nothing else, I'm intrigued enough to want to study him close up. I figure that he may give us some degree of insight into the Thallonian mind-set, if nothing else. The bottom line is, he may be an officious, arrogant ass, but he's a well-regarded officious, arrogant ass. So I reasoned that he might as well be *our* officious, arrogant ass."

"We can't have too many, I suppose," replied Shelby.

He opened his mouth to continue his train of thought, but the train was abruptly derailed as Shelby's comment sunk in. "Meaning?"

"Nothing, sir," deadpanned Shelby. "Simply an observation."

"Mm-hmm." He didn't appear convinced. But he allowed it to pass, and turned to Soleta. "All right, Lieutenant. Seeing as how he's your pal and all . . ."

"Pal?" She turned the odd word over in her mouth.

". . . go spring him from the brig, on my authority. Coordinate with Lefler and get him set up in quarters."

"Diplomatic?"

"Like hell. Crew quarters will suffice. We wouldn't want him to get any more of a swelled head than he's already got. Inform him, however, that he is on parole. We'll be keeping an eye on him. If he tries anything the least bit out of kilter, he's going to wind up as smear marks on Zak Kebron's boots. That will be all, Lieutenant. Oh, and Lieutenant," he added as an afterthought, "schedule some time for department heads to meet. I want a scientific overview of Thallon. I intend to make that our first stop."

"Straight to the homeworld?" Soleta raised an eyebrow. "Do you expect trouble with achieving that rather incendiary destination?"

"Expect it? No. Anticipate it? Always."

She nodded, an ever-so-brief smile playing on her lips and then quickly hidden by long practice, as she exited the ready room. When she was gone, Shelby folded her arms and half-sat on the edge of Calhoun's desk. "May I ask how you think Admiral Jellico will react to this development? He was the one who originally forbade Si Cwan from joining the mission."

"I imagine that he will be quite angry."

"And out of a sense of morbid curiosity, was this anticipated reaction part of your motivation in allowing Si Cwan to remain?"

"A part? Yes. A major part? No. The good admiral caused me grief in the past, and I certainly don't mind tossing some aggravation his way. But if I didn't think Si Cwan could be useful on this voyage, I wouldn't have allowed him on the ship just to annoy Jellico. That's simply . . ." He paused and then, for lack of a better word, he said, ". . . a bonus."

Si Cwan surveyed his quarters with a critical eye. Soleta and Zak Kebron stood just inside the doorway. After what seemed an infinity of consideration, Si Cwan turned to them and said, "I assume your captain did not give me diplomatic quarters because he did not wish to aggrandize my sense of self-importance."

"He didn't phrase it quite that way, but that is essentially correct."

Si Cwan nodded a moment, and then he looked at Kebron. "I would like a moment's privacy with Soleta." Kebron's gaze flickered between the two of them with suspicion. "Kebron, you'll have to leave me on my own sooner or later," Si Cwan reminded him. "Unless you were planning to make guarding me your life's work."

"It's my life," Kebron replied.

"We'll be fine, Zak," said Soleta, placing a reassuring hand on Kebron's arm. Kebron leaned slightly forward and Si Cwan realized that that was how Kebron nodded, since his neck wasn't the most maneuverable. The Brikar stepped back out of the room and the door closed.

"You and Kebron seem to share a certain familiarity with one another."

"We studied together at Starfleet Academy."

"And study was all you did?"

"No. We also saved one another's lives on occasion. You see the world rather oddly, Si Cwan. May I ask why you wished to speak privately?''

"I," and he cleared his throat. "I wanted to thank you for helping me."

"You're welcome."

"I hope I did not force you to compromise yourself in any way."

"It's a bit late now to be concerned about that," Soleta told him.

"That's valid enough, I suppose. Still I," and for a second time he cleared his throat. "I would like to think that perhaps the two of us could be . . . friends."

"Yes . . . I am sure you would like to think that." And she turned and left him alone in his quarters.

BURGOYNE

VIII

Burgoyne 172 prowled Engineering in a manner evocative of a cheetah. The *Excalibur* had only been out of drydock for a little over twenty-four hours, and Burgoyne had already established a reputation for perfection that kept hish engineering staff on their collective toes. Burgoyne stopped by the antimatter regulators and studied the readouts carefully. "Torelli!" s/he called. "Torelli, get your butt down here and bring the rest of you along for the ride!"

Engineer's Mate Torelli seemed to materialize almost by magic at Burgoyne's side.

"Yes, shir," said Torelli.

"I thought I gave you instructions that would improve the energy flow by five percent, and I asked for them to be implemented immediately."

"Yes, shir."

"Did you implement them?"

"Yes, shir."

"Then may I ask why I'm only seeing an improvement of three percent?"

"I don't know, shir."

"Then I suggest you find out." At that moment, Burgoyne's comm badge beeped. S/he tapped it and said, "Chief Engineer Burgoyne here."

"Chief, this is Maxwell down in sickbay. Dr. Selar would like a word with you."

"Can it wait?"

"It's been waiting for a while, shir. She was most emphatic." Maxwell sounded just a touch nervous.

"In other words, we're definitely in the realm of not taking no for an answer, correct?"

"A fair assessment, shir."

Burgoyne sighed. S/he'd been expecting this, really. S/he'd had hish head buried down in Engineering, overseeing every aspect of the refit. Burgoyne would have preferred another two weeks to complete the refit to hish satisfaction, but Starfleet had seemed bound and determined to get them out into space. It was Starfleet's call to make, of course, but Burgoyne couldn't say that s/he was happy about it.

And now the doctor, whom Burgoyne had barely had a chance to take note of in passing, wanted to see hir about some damned thing or other.

"On my way," said Burgoyne, who then glanced up at Torelli and said, "Be sure that's attended to by the time I get back."

"Yes, shir."

"By the way . . . first thing I'd do is make sure that the problem isn't in the readings rather than in the actual tech. If an object measures a meter long, and the meter stick is wrong, then that doesn't make the object a meter, now, does it."

"No, shir."

"Get on that, then," said Burgoyne. "And don't disappoint me. I don't take well to it. Last person who disappointed me, I ripped their throat out with my teeth."

"You certainly like to joke, Chief," Torelli said.

"That's true, Torelli, I do," Burgoyne agreed. S/he headed for the door and paused there only long enough to say, "Of course, that doesn't mean I was joking just now." And s/he flashed hish sharp canines and walked out.

*   *   *

Soleta and Zak Kebron stepped out onto the bridge to find that all attention was on navigator Mark McHenry.

He was leaning back in his chair, eyes half-closed. He didn't seem to be breathing. Lefler was staring at him, as was Shelby. Calhoun was just emerging from his ready room and he looked to see where everyone else's attention was. He blinked in mild surprise. "Is he dead?" he inquired in a low voice.

"We're trying to determine that," said Lefler.

Shelby looked extremely steamed, but then Calhoun waggled his finger to his senior officers, indicating that they should convene in his office. Within moments Robin Lefler found herself alone on the bridge, staring in wonderment at the apparently insensate astronavigator.

Calhoun, for his part, was wondering if he was ever going to get the hell out of his ready room and onto the bridge. Just to be different, he leaned on the armrest of his couch as Shelby said impatiently, "This is insane. We can't have a navigator who falls asleep at his station . . . if that's what he's doing . . ."

"He's not asleep," Soleta told Shelby with authority. "He's just thinking. He's very focused."

"Thinking?" Shelby couldn't believe it. She looked to Calhoun as if she needed verification for what she was hearing. "Captain, it's absurd . . . !"

"I was warned McHenry was somewhat unusual," admitted Calhoun. "I thought he'd fit right in on that basis. But even I'm not sure now . . ."

"Lieutenant Soleta is right," Kebron said, backing her up. "McHenry was like this back in the Academy. Actually, he was even more extreme. It's nothing to be concerned about. As the lieutenant said, McHenry's just thinking."

"About what?" demanded Shelby.

"Anything," said Soleta. "Everything. McHenry devotes exactly as much of his brain power as is required for routine duties. If there's an emergency, he'll devote that much more. And he devotes the rest of his brain to other things. Most humans can only concentrate on one thing at a time. McHenry is multifaceted. What you perceive as aberrant behavior is nothing more than what I would term an . . . eccentricity."

"His eyes are half-closed! We can't have a man at helm who's not alert!"

"He's alert, Commander," Soleta said confidently. "He's one hundred percent alert. If you walked over to him and spoke his name, he'd snap to instantly."

"Responding to his name isn't what concerns me," Shelby replied.

"Nor I," admitted Calhoun. "We need someone at that post who can respond to developing situations on his own, not a man who has to wait for someone to tell him what to do."

"May I suggest a simple test?" asked Soleta. When Calhoun gestured for her to continue, she said, "I can have Lefler reroute guidance through the ops station. Then we'll have her make a change in course. Nothing major. A simple alteration."

"What will that prove?" Shelby asked.

"A great deal, if I am correct," Soleta replied.

"You're not saying that he'll detect, without instruments, a deviation in ship's heading."

"That is precisely what I'm saying, Commander."

"That's impossible," Shelby said flatly. "That is completely impossible."

"Captain," Kebron spoke up, "Commander . . . I fully admit that I had the same initial reactions to McHenry when I met him years ago as you are currently having. I recommend you do as Lieutenant Soleta suggests."

Calhoun shrugged. "Sounds like a plan."

"Captain—?!"

"Calm down, Shelby. Soleta has something to prove. Let's let her try and prove it."

Soleta exited the captain's ready room and went straight over to Lefler. The others emerged and watched, fascinated in spite of themselves. Soleta bent in close to a puzzled Lefler and whispered in her ear. There was no sign of comprehension on Lefler's face, but she wasn't about to dispute a straightforward instruction. Within moments she had rerouted the navigations systems, and then made a course adjustment that would take the *Excalibur* eighteen degrees off course.

The moment the ship began to move in the new direction, the reaction from McHenry was instantaneous and stunning. He snapped forward, his attention completely focused—not on his instrumentation, but on the starfield in front of him on the screen. He then looked to his instruments, but clearly it was only to confirm that which he already knew. All business, he demanded, "Lieutenant, did you take us off course?"

Shelby was thunderstruck. "I don't believe it," she said. McHenry looked over to her, clearly not sure what Shelby was talking about.

"She changed headings at my direction, Lieutenant McHenry," Soleta informed him.

He switched his focus to Soleta, his eyebrows knit in puzzlement. "Why?"

"Why do you think?"

He considered the question a moment. "Because there was concern that I had zoned out and you decided to prove otherwise?"

"Correct."

"Ah. Okay."

"Without looking at your instruments, Lieutenant," Calhoun said, descending down the ramp to the command chair, "would you mind telling me how far off course we are?"

"I don't know, sir. Ballpark . . . nineteen degrees."

"Eighteen," Robin Lefler acknowledged in wonderment.

"Fairly close ballpark, I'd say," Calhoun said. "Would you agree, Commander?"

Shelby sighed. "Damned close."

"Lieutenant McHenry, bring us back on course."

"Aye, sir."

Shelby sank into her chair. Calhoun sat next to her. "You all right, Commander?"

"Fine," she sighed. "I'm fine. I swear, though, this is like no other ship I've ever served on."

"I'll take that as a compliment," Calhoun said.

"You are, of course, always free to exercise your discretion as commanding officer," Shelby replied, as she wondered what other oddities would surface about the crew during their voyage.

Burgoyne 172 strode into sickbay with an impatient look on hish face. S/he turned to Dr. Maxwell and said, "Well?"

"Well what, Lieutenant Commander?"

"Dr. Selar said she wanted to see me. Here I am. I have things to do, so if the doctor could please tell me what she wants, I might be able to get back to my duties."

Selar emerged from her office and said, "In here, Mister Burgoyne, if it is not too much trouble." She stood there as Burgoyne appeared to be studying her. "Is there a problem, Mister Burgoyne?"

"No. No problem at all," Burgoyne said as s/he entered Selar's office. "You know, I don't think we've actually had a chance to meet."

"You have not attended any of the initial department-head meetings," replied Selar. "That would have been the logical place."

"I had a lot to do to get things ready," Burgoyne said, not sounding particularly apologetic. It seemed to Selar that s/he was looking over the Vulcan doctor in a startlingly appraising manner. "It always comes down to the chief engineer having to pull everything together during the last minute. So . . . what can I do to help you, Doctor?"

"Your most recent medical examination is over two years old. By putting out to space without a more recent exam, we are technically already in breach of Starfleet regulations."

"Can't have that," Burgoyne said agreeably. "Do you wish to conduct it right now? Because I'm free now."

"Dr. Maxwell will attend to the actual examination."

Burgoyne made no effort to hide hish disappointment. "I would prefer you do it. Have the top woman attend to it, and all that."

She glanced at him with eyebrow cocked in mild curiosity. "Do you have an unusual condition which would require my direct attention?"

"Well . . . no . . ."

"Then I assure you, Dr. Maxwell will prove more than sufficient for your needs." She turned and became immediately engrossed in her computer screen, familiarizing herself with other medical profiles. It took her a few moments to realize that Burgoyne was still there, and looking at her with a very strange lopsided grin. "Is there something else, Lieutenant Commander?"

Burgoyne dropped into a chair opposite Selar, giving her the impression that s/he wasn't about to leave anytime soon. "Well, I admit if nothing else I'm disappointed in you, Doctor."

"How so?"

"There aren't very many Hermats in Starfleet, and none at command level aside from me. The Vulcans I know have always had a great inquisitiveness about the galaxy they live in and the people therein. I would be surprised if you, a woman of science, did not share that famed Vulcan drive to satisfy curiosity.''

She gave a brief acknowledging nod. "A small amount, I admit. Hermats, as a race, tend to keep to themselves. The tendency toward segregation from the rest of the Federation is well known . . . right down to your tendency to refer to yourselves with a unique set of pronouns to accommodate your dual-sex status. 'Hir' rather than 'him' or 'her' . . . 'hish' for the possessive forms of 'his' or 'hers' . . . 's/he,' '' and she punched a bit harder than usual on the separately accented *h,* "rather than 'she' or 'he.' ''

"We developed those actually to simplify direct communication with UFP representatives, and also to maintain our uniqueness as a race. Actually, we were originally going to combine 'she,' 'he,' and 'it' in order to cover all possibilities, but the term we developed—'sheeit'— caused Terrans to laugh whenever we would use it, so we surmised that it had some other, inappropriate meaning and discarded it.''

"That was probably wise.'' She paused a moment. "Is there a significant distinction between the Hermat and the J'naii?''

"The J'naii?!'' Burgoyne made an annoyed sound. "Those asexual, passionless creatures? No, no. They're neuters, denying all orientation. We celebrate the duality that makes us unique. They are neither. We are both. Fully functioning male and female capabilities.'' S/he leaned forward and grinned, displaying hish sharpened canines. S/he seemed to be someone who smiled a great deal and enjoyed it while doing so, as s/he repeated, *"Fully* functioning.''

"I comprehend the adverb,'' Selar said evenly. "However, I am quite certain my curiosity about the medical uniqueness of Hermats will be more than satisfied by my scrutiny of Dr. Maxwell's no-doubt detailed examination. For my part, I have a good deal that remains to which I must attend, and a routine exam which could be handled by any first-year resident does not fall into that category. Good day, Lieutenant Commander.''

Burgoyne's smile widened as s/he got up from the chair. Hish voice was light and musical as s/he said, "There's one thing you should know about me, Doctor.''

"Only one thing. Very well.'' Selar looked up with poorly veiled disinterest.

"I can sense when I'm going to get on well with someone," Burgoyne informed her. "There's something about the two of us . . . some chemistry . . . that I can't quite discern yet. But it's there all the same."

Folding her fingers, Selar said, "I am unclear as to your implication, Lieutenant Commander."

"Would you like me to clarify it?"

She considered for a moment and then said, "No. Actually, upon reflection, I prefer the vagueness. Good day, Lieutenant Commander."

"But—"

"I said . . . good day."

S/he stabbed a finger at Selar and said, "You're a challenge. I like a challenge."

"If that is what you desire, I understand surviving in a vacuum can be most challenging. If you wish, I can arrange to have you try that right now, and we can combine your examination with an autopsy."

Burgoyne laughed that delighted musical laugh and coquettishly ran hish fingers through hish close-cut blond hair. "Why, Dr. Selar . . . was that a threat?"

"Not at all. Merely that famed Vulcan drive to satisfy curiosity."

And with one final, lilting laugh and a toss of hish head, Burgoyne sashayed out of Selar's office, leaving the Vulcan doctor shaking her head and wondering two things:

What could she have possibly said or done that would have led Burgoyne 172 to think that there was a fragment of interest on Selar's part in hir?

And why was it that, as Burgoyne walked, Selar found herself watching the sway of hish hips?

IX

Calhoun looked around the conference lounge and nodded in approval. "Commander Shelby . . . Lieutenants Soleta and McHenry . . . Ambassador Si Cwan . . . Lieutenant Kebron . . . thank you all for coming . . ." He paused. "Although frankly, Mr. Kebron, I'm not entirely sure if your presence is required here."

"This will be the ambassador's first meeting with you, Captain, without a protective barrier between you. I feel it best if I be here to supervise."

"Yes, your Mr. Kebron has become somewhat attached to me as of late," Si Cwan said dryly. "I would have liked to think that he is fascinated by my sterling company. In point of fact, he's likely concerned I'll disassemble the ship bolt by bolt while his back is turned."

"Merely exercising reasonable caution in the presence of a party with questionable security clearance," Kebron replied.

Calhoun had the distinct feeling that Kebron's comment was a veiled jab at Calhoun himself. Kebron had made no secret that he was unhappy over Si Cwan's unorthodox (to say the least) means of joining the crew, even in a limited, semiofficial capacity. Nor was he any happier over Calhoun's condoning it. However, the Brikar was not one to question his captain's decisions, and so he endeavored to keep his doubts and criticisms to himself. He wasn't terribly good at it—his body language was generally a dead giveaway, as was his tendency to grind his large fingers into his palm with a scrape like rock on rock whenever he was particularly annoyed about something.

"Very wise, Mr. Kebron," Calhoun said diplomatically.

"I do appreciate the title of 'Ambassador,' Captain," Si Cwan commented. "Will quarters appropriate to the title likewise be issued me?"

Calhoun leaned forward and, keeping that same polite, diplomatic tone, said, "That cook job is still open."

"Understood," Si Cwan said in a neutral tone.

With a satisfied nod, Calhoun turned his attention to Soleta. "All right, science officer. You and Mr. McHenry have been working tandem, I understand?"

"Yes, sir. I've been talking extensively with Si Cwan to supplement my own knowledge of Thallon . . ."

"And I've always been something of a history buff," McHenry put in. "So I volunteered to help out with some separate research."

"Good to see, Mr. McHenry," Shelby said approvingly. She wasn't simply being flattering, either. McHenry's clear focus and relatively normal behavior ever since the earlier incident had mollified her concerns to some degree. "What have we got?"

Soleta and McHenry exchanged glances, and she nodded to him that he should begin. He ran his fingers through his shock of red hair, a slight nervous habit, and then said, "Thallon has achieved a nearly mythic status, from everything that I've been able to determine. For starters, the Thallonians were not native to the region. Thallon gained its start as a populated world in much the same way that Australia began."

"You mean criminals?" Kebron said. He made no effort to hide his distaste. In truth, he couldn't have hidden it even if he'd been so inclined.

"That's right. There was another race, a sort of *Uber* race, which had a variety of names as they were known by assorted worlds which were under their influence. The name they had for themselves is lost to history. They were a star-spanning empire who were, if we judge by their conduct, big believers in conquest but also tended to preserve life rather than destroy it, even if it was of no use to them. They used the planet we now call Thallon as a sort of dumping ground for criminals, unsavory types, political exiles . . . assorted refuse from throughout their system.''

''It was, at the time, a small, cold, and not especially fertile world,'' Soleta added. ''It may very well be that they did not expect any of the residents there to survive. Mr. McHenry has chosen to give a somewhat humanitarian spin to this *Uber* race's motivations, but for all we know, they simply regarded Thallon as an experiment in endurance. They may have wanted to see how long individuals could survive there before expiring from the harsh conditions.''

''So they simply kept dumping criminals onto this inhospitable world?'' asked Shelby.

Soleta shook her head. ''Not precisely. From archaeological records and the myths put forward by Si Cwan's people, the first of the Thallonians arrived in what we would call space arks. They were given provisions enough to last them a few months, plus materials to seed the ground and try to make a life for themselves there.''

''Seed unfertile ground,'' Calhoun mused. ''The parent race was all heart.''

''Yeah, but apparently they weren't all-knowing.'' McHenry picked up the story. ''The exiles were sent to a planet that had been described to them as inhospitable. But that's not what they discovered when they arrived there. The climate was fairly temperate, the world almost paradisiacal.''

''Could they have arrived at the wrong planet?'' asked Shelby.

''A logical conclusion,'' Soleta replied. ''However, the coordinates for the intended homeworld of the criminals had been preset and locked into the ark's guidance systems. After all, the race didn't want to have their exiles taking control of the ship and heading off to whatever destination they chose. There do remain several possibilities. One is that the planet underwent some sort of atmospheric change. A shift in its axis, for example, causing alterations in the climate.''

''Wouldn't that have changed the orbit and made the locating coordinates incorrect, though?'' Shelby said.

''Yes,'' admitted Soleta. ''Another possibility is that the present coordinates were simply wrong and they did not arrive at the intended world. Or perhaps someone within their race simply took pity on them and secretly made the change. It is frustrating to admit, but we simply do not know to a scientific certainty.''

''What we do know,'' McHenry stepped in, ''is that Thallon itself was an almost limitless supply of pure energy.''

''Pure energy? I don't follow,'' Kebron said.

''Think of it as an entire world made of dilithium crystals,'' explained Soleta. ''Not that it was dilithium per se, but that's the closest comparison. The ground is an energy-rich mineral unique to the world, all-purpose and versatile beyond anything that has ever been discovered elsewhere. The nutrients in it are such that anything planted in it grows. *Anything*. Pieces of the planet, when refined, were used to harness great tools of peace and growth . . .''

''And then, eventually, great tools of war,'' McHenry said.

The tenor of the meeting seemed to change slightly, and when the mention of war came up, eyes seemed to shift to Si Cwan. He shrugged, almost as if indifferent. ''It was before my time,'' he reminded them.

''With Thallon as their power base, they were able to launch conquest of neighboring worlds,'' McHenry said. ''And then, once they had those worlds consolidated under their rule, they spread their influence and power to other nearby systems. In essence, they imitated the race which had deposited them there in the first place.''

''What about this race you mentioned,'' asked Calhoun. ''Was there a conflict with them? Did they ever return to Thallon and discover what they had wrought? Or did the Thallonians ever go looking for them?''

''No to the first, yes to the second,'' McHenry replied. ''But they never found them. It's one of the great mysteries of Thallonian history.''

''And great frustrations,'' Si Cwan put in.

''Understandable,'' Kebron rumbled. ''Your ancestors wished to pay them back for the initial indignity of being dumped like refuse on another world.''

''You see, Lieutenant Kebron,'' Si Cwan said with mild amusement, ''you understand the Thallonians all too well. Perhaps we shall be fast friends, you and I.''

Kebron simply stared at him from the depths of his dark, hardened skin.

''The Thallonian homeworld has always been the source of the Thallonian strength, both physical and spiritual,'' said Soleta. ''The events of the last weeks, including the collapse of their empire, may have been presaged by the change in the planet's own makeup. In recent decades, the planet seemed to lose much of its energy richness.''

"Why?'' asked Calhoun.

"Since the Thallonians were never able to fully explain how their world acquired its properties in the first place, there's understandably confusion as to why it would be deserting them now,'' said Soleta. "Still, the Thallonians might have been able to withstand those difficulties, if there had not been problems with various worlds within the Thallonian Empire.''

"It was the Danteri,'' Si Cwan said darkly.

Calhoun seemed to stiffen upon the mention of the name. "You claimed that at the *Enterprise* meeting, I understand. Do you have any basis for that?''

"The Danteri have always hungered to make inroads into our empire. They've made no secret of that, nor of their boastfulness. I believe that they instigated rebellion through carefully selected agents. If not for them, we could have—''

"Could have retained your power?''

"Perhaps, Captain. Perhaps.''

"By the same token, isn't it possible,'' Calhoun said, leaning forward, fingers interlaced, "that the Danteri simply serve as a convenient excuse for the deficiencies in your own rule. That it was as a result of ineptitude among the rulers of the Thallonian Empire that the entire thing fell apart. That, in short . . . it was your own damned fault?''

There was dead silence in the room for a moment, and then, imperturbably, Si Cwan said once again, "Perhaps, Captain. Perhaps. We all have our limitations . . . and we all have beliefs which get us through the day. In that, I assume we are no different.''

"Perhaps, Si Cwan. Perhaps,'' said Calhoun with a small smile.

Then Calhoun's comm unit beeped at him. He tapped it. "Calhoun here.''

"Captain, this is Lefler. We're picking up a distress signal from a transport called the *Cambon*.''

"Pipe it down here, Lieutenant.''

There was a momentary pause, and then it came through the speaker. "This is the *Cambon*,'' came a rough, hard-edged and angry voice, "Hufmin, Captain. We've sustained major damage in passing through the Lemax system. Engines out, life-support damaged. We have nearly four dozen passengers aboard—civilians, women and children—we need help.'' His voice seemed to choke on the word, as if it were an obscenity to them. ''Repeating, to anyone who can hear . . . this is . . .'' And then the signal ceased.

''Lefler, can we get them back?''

''We never had them, sir. We picked it up on an all-band frequency. He threw a note in a bottle and hoped someone would pick it up.''

''Have we got a fix on their location?''

''I can track it back and get an approximate. If their engines are out, I can't pinpoint it precisely. On the other hand, they wouldn't have gone too far with no engine power.''

''Our orders are to head straight for Thallon,'' Shelby pointed out.

Calhoun glanced at her. ''Are you going to suggest that we ignore a ship in distress, Commander?''

There was only the briefest of pauses, and then Shelby replied, ''Not for an instant, Captain. We're here for humanitarian efforts. It would be nothing short of barbaric to then ignore the first opportunity to deploy those efforts.''

''Well said. McHenry, get up to the bridge and work with Lefler to find that ship. Get us there at fastest possible speed. Shelby—''

But she was already nodding, one step ahead of him as she tapped her comm unit. ''Shelby to engine room.''

''Engine room. Burgoyne here.''

''Burgy, we're going to be firing up to maximum warp. You have everything ready to go?''

''For you, Commander? Anything. We're fully up to spec. Even I'm satisfied with it.''

''If it meets your standards, Burgy, then it must measure up. Shelby out.''

McHenry was already on his way, and Calhoun was half-standing. ''If there's nothing else . . .''

But Si Cwan was shaking his head, as if discouraged about something. The gesture caught Calhoun's attention, and he said, ''Si Cwan?''

''The Lemax system. I know the area. He must have tried to run the Gauntlet. It shouldn't have been a problem.'' He sighed.

''The Gauntlet?''

''It's a shooting gallery. Two planets that used to be at war, until we imposed peace upon them. The Gauntlet was a hazard of the past, except apparently the danger has been renewed. Just another example of the breakdown occurring all around us.'' He shook his head again, and then looked around at the silent faces watching him. And then, without another word, he rose and walked out of the room.

Si Cwan stared at the wall of his quarters. Then he heard the sound of the chime. He ignored it, but it sounded again. "Come," he said with a sigh.

Calhoun entered and just stood there, arms folded. "You left rather abruptly."

"I felt the meeting was over."

"Generally it's good form for the captain to make that judgment."

"I am somewhat out of practice in terms of having others make judgments on my behalf."

Calhoun walked across the room, pacing out the interior much as Si Cwan had earlier. "How do you wish to be viewed aboard this ship, Cwan? As an object of pity?"

"Of course not," Si Cwan said sharply.

"Contempt, then? Confusion, perhaps?" He stopped and turned to face him. "Your title, accorded out of courtesy more than anything else, is 'Ambassador.' Not prince. Not lord. 'Ambassador.' I will hope you find that satisfactory. And by the same token, I hope you understand and acknowledge my authority on this ship. I do not want my decision to allow you to remain with us to be viewed by you as lack of strength on my part."

"No. I don't view it that way at all."

"I'm pleased to hear that."

Si Cwan regarded him thoughtfully for a moment. "May I ask how you got that scar?"

Calhoun touched it reflexively. "This one?"

"It is the most prominent, yes."

"To be blunt . . . I got it while killing someone like you."

"I see. And should I consider that a warning?"

"I don't have to kill anymore . . . I hope," he added as an afterthought.

They sat in silence for a moment, and then Si Cwan said, "It is important to me that you understand my situation, Captain. We oversaw an empire, yes. In many ways, in your terms, we might have been considered tyrannical. But it was my life, Captain. It was my life, and the life of those around me who worked to maintain it and help it prosper. Whether you agree with our methods or not, there was peace. There was *peace,*'' and he slapped his legs and rose. He turned his back to Calhoun and leaned against the wall, palms spread wide. "Peace built by my ancestors, maintained by my generation. We had a birthright given to us, an obligation . . . and we failed. And now I'm seeing the work of my ancestors, and of my family, dismantled. In a hundred years . . . in ten years, for all I know . . . it will be as if everything we accomplished, for good or ill, will be washed away. Gone. As traceable as a tower of sand on the edge of a beach, consumed by the rising tide. What we did will have made no difference. It was all for nothing. Every difficult decision, every hard choice, ultimately amounted to nothing whatsoever. We have no legacy for our future generations. Indeed, we'll probably have no future generations. I have no royal consort with whom I can perpetuate our line. No royal lineage to pass on."

"And you're hoping to use this vessel to rebuild your power base. Aren't you."

Si Cwan turned and stared at him. "Is that what you think?"

"It's crossed my mind."

"I admit it crossed mine as well. But I give you my word, Captain, that I will do nothing to endanger this ship's mission, nor any of its personnel. My ultimate goal is the same as yours: to serve as needed."

Slowly Calhoun nodded, apparently satisfied. "All right. I can accept that . . . for now."

"Captain . . . ?"

"Yes."

Si Cwan smiled thinly. "You were aware the entire time, weren't you. Aware that I had stowed away on your vessel."

For a moment Calhoun considered lying, a course that he would not hesitate to indulge in if he felt that it would serve his purposes. But his instinct told him that candor was the way to go in this matter. "Yes."

"Good."

"Good?"

"Yes. It is something of a relief, really. The notion that I was aboard a ship where the commanding officer had so little awareness of what was happening around him . . . it was unsettling to me."

"I'm relieved that I was able to put your mind at ease. And Si Cwan . . ."

"Yes?"

"Believe it or not . . . I can sympathize. I've had my own moments where I felt that my life had been wasted."

"And may I ask how you dealt with such times of despair?"

And Mackenzie Calhoun laughed softly and said, "I took command of a starship." But then he held up a warning finger. "Don't get any ideas from that."

"I shall try not to, Captain. I shall try very hard."

X

Hufmin stared out at the stars and, focusing on one at a time, uttered a profanity for every one he picked out.

Cramped in the helm pit of the *Cambon,* he still couldn't believe that he had gotten himself into this fix. He scratched at his grizzled chin and dwelt for the umpteenth time on the old Earth saying that no good deed goes unpunished.

He glanced at his instrumentation once more, his lungs feeling heavier and heavier. He knew that the last thing you were supposed to do upon receiving a head injury was let yourself fall asleep. And so he had kept himself awake through walking around in the cramped quarters, through stimulants, recitation, biting himself—anything and everything he could think of. None of which was going to do him a damned bit of good because, just to make things absolutely perfect, he wasn't going to be able to breathe for all that much longer. The life-support systems were tied into his engines. When they went down, the support systems switched to backup power supply, but that was in the process of running out. Hufmin was positive it was getting tougher to breathe, although he wasn't altogether certain how much of that was genuine and how much was just his imagination running away with him. But if it wasn't happening now, it was going to be happening soon enough as the systems became incapable of cleansing the atmosphere within the craft and everybody within suffocated.

Everybody . . .

Every . . . body . . .

. . . lots of bodies.

Not for the first time, he dwelt on the fact that this was a case where the more was most definitely not the merrier. Every single body on the ship was another person who was taking up space, another person breathing oxygen and taking up air that would be better served to keep him, Hufmin, alive.

What had possessed him? What in God's name had possessed him to take on this useless, unprofitable detail? If he'd been a Ferengi he would have been drummed out of . . . well, whatever it was that Ferengi were drummed out of when they made unbelievably bad business decisions. The problem was that this was no longer simply a case of costing him money. Now it was going to cost him his life.

. . . lots of bodies . . .

"Dump 'em," he said, giving voice finally to the thought that had bounced around in his head for the last several hours. It was a perfectly reasonable idea. All he had to do was get rid of the passengers and he could probably survive days, maybe even weeks, instead of the mere hours that his instruments seemed to indicate remained to him.

It wouldn't be easy. There were, after all, forty-seven of them and only one of him. It wasn't likely that they would simply and cheerfully hurl themselves into the void so that he, Hufmin, had a better chance at survival. No, the only way to get rid of them would be by force. Again, though, he was slightly outnumbered . . . by about forty-seven to one.

He had a couple of disruptors in a hidden compartment under his feet. He could remove those, go into the aft section where all the passengers were situated, and just start firing away. Blow them all to hell and gone and then eject the bodies. But then he pictured himself standing there, shooting, body after body going down, seeing the fear of death in their eyes, hearing the death rattles not once, not twice, but forty-seven times. Because it was going to have to be all of them. All or nothing, he knew that with absolute certainty. He couldn't pick and choose. All or nothing. But he was no murderer. He'd never killed anyone in his life; the disruptors were just for protection, a last resort, and he'd never fired them. Never had to. Kill them and then blast them into space . . . how could he . . . ?

Then he realized. He didn't have to kill them. Just blast them into space, into the void. Sure, they'd die agonizingly, suffering in space, but it wasn't as if death by disruptor was all that much better.

The *Cambon* was divided into three sections: The helm pit, which was where he was. The midsection, used for equipment storage mostly, and his private quarters as well. And the aft section . . . the largest section, used for cargo . . .

. . . which was where all his passengers were. They were cramped, they were uncomfortable, but they were alive.

Hufmin's eyes scanned his equipment board. And there, just as he knew it would be, was the control for the aft loading doors. There were controls in back as well, but they were redundant and—if necessary—could be overridden from the helm pit. The helm pit, which was, for that matter, self-contained and secured, a heavy door sealing it off from the rest of the vessel.

All he had to do was blow the loading-bay doors. The passengers back there probably wouldn't even have time to realize that their lives were ended before they were sucked out into the vacuum of space. Granted he'd lose some air as well. With power so low, the onboard systems would never be able to replenish what he lost to the vacuum. On the other hand, he'd have the remaining air in the helm pit and in the midsection. Not a lot, but at least it would be all his. All his.

. . . lots of bodies . . .

The bay-door switch beckoned to him and he reached over and tapped it, determined to do what had to be done for survival before he thought better of it. Immediately a yellow caution light came on, and the operations computer came on in its flat, monotone masculine voice. "Warning. This vessel is not within a planetary atmosphere. Opening of loading-bay doors will cause loss of air in aft section and loss of any objects not properly secured. Do you wish to continue with procedure? Signify by saying, 'Continue with procedure.' "

"Con—" The words caught in his throat.

. . . lots of bodies . . .

"Con . . . contin—"

There was a rapping at the door behind him. It reverberated through the helm pit, like a summons from hell. *"What is it?!"* he shouted at the unseen intruder.

"Mr. Hufmin?" came a thin, reedy voice. A child's voice, a small girl. One of the soon-to-be corpses.

"Yeah? What?"

"I was . . . I was wondering if anyone heard our call for help."

"I don't know. I wish I did, but I don't. Go back and sit with your parents now, okay?"

"They're dead."

That caught him off-guard for a moment, but then he remembered; one of the kids had lost her parents to some rather aggressive scavengers. She was traveling with an uncle who looked to be around ninety-something. "Oh, right, well . . . go back with your uncle, then."

There was a pause and he thought for a moment that she'd done as he asked. He started to address the computer again when he heard, "Mr. Hufmin?"

"What is it, damn you!"

"I just . . . I wanted to say thank you." When he said nothing in response, she continued, "I know you tried your best, and that I know you'll keep trying, and I . . . I believe in you. Thank you for everything."

He stared at the blinking yellow light. "Why are you saying this? Who told you to say this?" he asked tonelessly.

"The gods. I prayed to them for help, and I was starting to fall asleep while I was praying . . . and I heard them in my head telling me to say thank you. So I . . . I did."

Hufmin's mouth moved, but nothing came out. "That's . . . that's fine. You're, uh . . . you're welcome. Okay? You're welcome."

He listened closely and heard the sound of her feet pattering away. He was all alone once more. Alone to do what had to be done.

"Computer."

"Waiting for instructions," the computer told him. The computer wouldn't care, of course. It simply waited to be told. It was a machine, incapable of making value judgments. Nor was it capable of taking any actions that would insure its own survival. Hufmin, on the other hand, most definitely was.

"Computer . . ."

He thought of the child. He thought of the bodies floating in space.

So many bodies. And he would survive, or at least have a better chance, and that was the important thing. "Computer, continue with . . ."

What was one child, more or less? One life, or forty-seven lives? What did any of it matter? The only important thing was that he lived. Wasn't that true? Wasn't it?

He envisioned them floating past his viewer, their bodies destroyed by the vacuum, their faces etched in the horror of final realization. And he would still be alive . . .

. . . and he might as well be dead.

With the trembling sigh of one who knows he has just completely screwed himself, Hufmin said, "Computer, cancel program."

"Canceling," replied the computer. Naturally, whether he continued the program or not was of no consequence to the computer. As noted, it was just a machine. But Hufmin liked to think he was something more, and reluctantly had to admit that—if that was the case—it bore with it certain responsibilities.

He leaned back in his pilot's seat, looked out at the stars, and said, "Okay, gods. Whisper something to *me* now. Tell me what an idiot I am. Tell me I'm a jerk. Go ahead. Let me have it, square between the eyes."

And the gods answered.

At least, that's what it appeared they were doing, because the darkness of space was shimmering dead ahead, fluctuating ribbons of color undulating in circular formation.

Slowly he sat forward, his mind not entirely taking in what he was witnessing, and then the gods exploded from the shadows.

These gods, however, had chosen a very distinctive and blessed conveyance. They were in a vessel that Hufmin instantly recognized as a Federation starship. It had dropped out of warp space, still moving so quickly that it had been a hundred thousand kilometers away and then, an eyeblink later, it was virtually right on top of him. He'd never seen such a vessel in person before, and he couldn't believe the size of the thing. The ship had course-corrected on a dime, angling upward and slowing so that it passed slowly over him rather than smashing him to pieces. He saw the name of the ship painted on the underside: *U.S.S. Excalibur.* The ship was so vast that it blotted out the light provided by a nearby sun, casting the *Cambon* into shadow, but Hufmin could not have cared less.

Hufmin had never been a religious man. The concept of unseen, unknowable deities had been of no interest to him at all in his rather pragmatic life. And as he began to deliriously cheer, and wave his hands as if they could see him, he decided that he did indeed believe in gods after all. Not the unknowable ones, though. His gods were whoever those wonderful individuals were who loomed above him. They had come from wherever it was gods came from, and had arrived in this desperate environment currently inhabited by one Captain Hufmin and his cargo of forty-seven frightened souls.

Thereby answering, finally, a very old question, namely:

What does God need with a starship?

And the answer, of course, was one of the oldest answers in the known universe:

To get to the other side.

Robin Lefler looked up from Ops and said, "Captain, everyone from the vessel has been beamed aboard: the ship's commander and forty-seven passengers."

Shelby whistled in amazement as Calhoun said, clearly surprised, "Forty-seven? His ship's not tiny, but it's not *that* big. He must have had people plastered to the ceiling. Shelby, arrange to have the passengers brought, in shifts, to sickbay, so Dr. Selar can check them over. Make sure they're not suffering from exposure, dehydration, et cetera."

"Shall we take his ship in tow, sir?" asked Kebron.

"And to where do you suggest we tow it, Mr. Kebron?" asked Calhoun reasonably. "It's not as if we've got a convenient starbase nearby. Bridge to Engineering."

"Engineering, Burgoyne here," came the quick response over the intercom.

"Chief, we have a transport ship to port with an engine that needs your magic touch."

"My wand is at the ready, sir."

"How many times have I heard *that* line," murmured Robin Lefler

. . . just a bit louder than she had intended. The comment drew a quick chuckle from McHenry, and a disapproving glance from Shelby . . . who, in point of fact, thought it was funny but felt that it behooved her to keep a straight face.

"Get a team together, beam over, and give me an estimate on repair time."

"Aye, sir."

He turned to Shelby and said briskly, "Commander, talk to the pilot. Find out precisely what happened, what he saw. I want to know what we're dealing with. Also, see if you can find Si Cwan. He's supposed to be our ambassador. Let's see how his people react to him. If they throw things at him or run screaming, that will be a tip off that he might not be as useful as we'd hoped. Damn, we should have given him a comm badge to facilitate—"

"Bridge to Si Cwan," Shelby said promptly.

"Yes," came Si Cwan's voice.

"Meet me in sickbay, please. We have some refugees there whom we'd like you to speak with."

"On my way."

Shelby turned to Calhoun. "I took the liberty of issuing him a comm badge. He's not Starfleet, of course, but it seemed the simplest way to reach him."

"Good thinking, Commander."

She smiled. "I have my moments," and headed to the turbolift.

The moment she was gone, though, Kebron stepped over to Calhoun and said, "Captain, shall I go as well?"

"You, Kebron? Why?"

"To keep an eye on Cwan."

"What do you think he's going to do?"

"I don't know," Kebron said darkly. He seemed to want to say something more, but he kept his mouth tightly closed.

"Lieutenant, if you've got something on your mind, out with it."

"Very well. I feel that you have made a vast mistake allowing Si Cwan aboard this vessel. He could jeopardize our mission."

"If I believed he could, I would never have allowed him to remain."

"I'm aware of that, sir. Nevertheless, I feel it was an error."

"I generally have a good instinct about people, Lieutenant. I've learned to trust it; it's saved my life any number of times. If you wish to disagree with me, that is your prerogative."

"Then I'm afraid that's how it's going to remain, Captain, until such time as I'm convinced otherwise."

"And when do you think that will be?"

Zak Kebron considered the question. "In Earth years, or in Brikar years?"

"Earth years."

"In Earth years?" He paused only a moment, and then responded, "Never."

Shelby entered sickbay and looked around at the haggard faces of the patients in the medlab. Immediately her heart went out to them. They were a mixture of races, with such variations of skin colors between them that they looked like a rainbow. But there was unity in the fact that they were clearly frightened, dispossessed, with no clear idea of what lay ahead for them. Dr. Selar was going about her duties with efficiency and speed. Shelby noticed that Selar and her people already seemed to be working smoothly and in unison. She felt some relief at that; Calhoun had mentioned that there'd been some difficulty between Selar and one of her doctors, but Shelby wouldn't have known from watching them in action.

"I'm looking for the commander of the vessel," she said to the room at large.

One of the scruffier individuals stepped forward. "That would be me." He stuck out a hand. "Name's Hufmin."

"Commander Shelby, second-in-command."

"You people saved our butts."

"That's what we're here for," she told him, even as she thought, *Did I just say that? I sound like something out of the Starfleet Cliché Handbook.*

And then Shelby saw the attitude of the people in sickbay change instantly, as if electrified. A number who were on diagnostic tables immediately jumped off. One even pushed Dr. Selar aside so he could scramble to his feet. They were all looking past Shelby's shoulder. She turned to see that, standing behind her, was Si Cwan.

There was dead silence for what seemed an infinity to her, and then a young woman, who appeared to be in her early twenties by Earth standards, seemed to fly across the room. She threw her arms around Si Cwan so tightly that it looked as if she'd snap him like a twig, even though she came up barely to his chest.

"You're alive, thank the gods, you're alive," she whispered.

And now the others followed suit. Most of them did not possess the total lack of inhibition of the first woman. They approached him tentatively, reverently, with varying forms of intimidation or respect. Si Cwan, for his part, stroked the young woman's thick blue hair as gently as a father cradling his newborn child. He looked to the others, stretching out his free hand as if summoning them. They seemed to draw strength from his mere presence, many of them genuflecting, a few had their heads bowed.

"Please. Please, that's not necessary," said Si Cwan. "Please . . . get up. Don't bow. Don't . . . please don't," and he gestured for them to rise. "Sometimes I feel that such ceremonies helped create the divide between us that led to . . . to our present state. Up . . . yes, you in the back, up."

They followed his instructions out of long habit. "This ship is bringing you back to power, Lord Cwan?" asked one of the men. "They'll use their weapons on your behalf?"

Shelby began to state that that was uncategorically not the case, but with a voice filled with surprising gentleness, Si Cwan said, "This is a mission of peace, my friends. I am merely here to lend help wherever I can." And then he glanced briefly at Shelby as if to say, *A satisfactory answer?* She nodded in silent affirmation.

Then Shelby turned back to the refugees and said, "What were you all fleeing from?"

A dozen different answers poured out, all at the same time. The specifics varied from one individual or one group to the next, but there were common themes to all. Governments in disarray, marauders from an assortment of races, wars breaking out all over for reasons ranging from newly disputed boundaries to attempted genocide. A world of order sliding into a world of chaos.

"We just want to be safe," said the young woman who had so precipitously hugged Si Cwan. "Is that too much to ask?"

"Unfortunately," sighed Si Cwan, "sometimes the answer to that is yes."

"The rest of the royal family . . . are they . . . ?"

He nodded and there were a few choked sobs . . . and also, Shelby noted, a few sighs of relief.

"What's going to happen to us now?" asked one of them.

"First, we're going to repair Captain Hufmin's vessel. We have a team there right now," Shelby told them. At this, Hufmin moaned softly and shook his head, which piqued Shelby's curiosity. "Problem, Captain?"

"Well, don't think I'm not grateful for the rescue and repair. I am. More than you can believe. But I have to ask . . . how much is the repair job going to cost? Because I'm not making the kind of money off this job that you'd probably think I am—"

"Captain Hufmin," Shelby began.

"—and you've got your experts who, I'm sure, are the best that money can buy, but my credit level is so low that unless we set up some sort of payment schedule . . ."

"Captain, there's no charge," Shelby interrupted him.

This brought him up short. "No charge?"

"None."

"Well then . . . what do you get out of this?"

"We get nothing more from it than the awareness that we're fulfilling the mandates of Starfleet. That, and simply the knowledge of a job well done," Shelby told him, and this time she thought, *Dammit, I know I've mostly specialized in fighting the Borg, and have far more strategic bridge experience than I do with one-to-one diplomacy, but I have got to drop the homilies before someone beats me to death with a baseball bat.*

"And then what?" asked another of the refugees.

"Then we'll make sure that you get where you're going. Where are you going, by the way?"

"Intended destination is Sigma Tau Ceti," Hufmin told her. "Not the greatest planet on the rim, but it's within range considering what they were able to pay. Although if you've got other suggestions, I'm sure they'd be happy to discuss it. . . ."

At that moment, Si Cwan's comm badge beeped. He seemed slightly startled by it since he was, naturally, unused to wearing it. He tapped it tentatively and said, "Yes?"

"Si Cwan, this is Soleta," came the Vulcan's voice. "We've received a communiqué I think you should be aware of."

"What is it?"

"It's another vessel. They not only sent out a distress call, but they included a passenger roster. If I'm recalling correctly, didn't you say your sister's name was Kallinda?"

For a moment Si Cwan felt as if his heart had stopped. "Yes. Yes, I did."

"Well, her name's on it."

"I'm on my way," he said without hesitation. He paused and said to the refugees, "Trust these people. They will take care of you," and then he was out the door, his long legs carrying him so rapidly that Shelby felt as if he'd vanished between eyeblinks.

Hufmin took a step forward and, clearing his throat, said, "Uhm, Commander . . . as long as your people are over there . . . you know, the phase converter's never worked really up to what I'd like. Also I could use a replacement of the dilithium charger, and a full cleaning of the—"

"Hufmin . . ."

"Yes, Commander Shelby?"

She smiled wanly. "Don't push it, okay?"

Inside the midship area of the *Cambon,* Burgoyne shook hish head in annoyance as s/he looked over the damage report. "Interior and exterior damage to the impulse rods, as well as the primary warp stabilizer. And look at the age of some of these parts; I hope we can match it. To say nothing of the fact that we'll have to do EVA repairs." S/he sighed. "This'll take forever."

"Can we bring this ship into the shuttlebay and work on it there?" asked Yates.

Burgoyne shook hish head. "Too big. If we were in a Galaxy-class ship, yes, it'd fit. But in the Ambassador-class size? Not near enough room. Although I suppose if we could bring it close enough in to the *Excalibur,* we could raise shields and encompass it within the shield sphere. Then all we'd need is some floaters to move around it, rather than have to put up with clunky EVA suits. You'd think after four centuries of a space program, we'd have come up with better EVA suits than what we've got." Burgoyne tapped hish comm badge. "Burgoyne to bridge."

"Bridge, Kebron here."

"Zak? Tell the captain we're talking at least a nine-hour repair job here."

"Nine hours?" Kebron sounded skeptical. "You could disassemble the *Excalibur*'s engines and put them back together in nine hours."

"If you think you can do better, Kebron, you're welcome to try. Burgoyne out."

Si Cwan studied the passenger roster with a rapidly growing sense of urgency. "What's the ship's name again?" he asked.

"The *Kayven Ryin*," Soleta said, coming around from the science station. Si Cwan was at the tactical station, looking over the incoming transmission. Kebron had at first stood firm, but ultimately backed off a few feet and simply glowered with arms folded. "It's not a Federation ship, but it's in the registry nonetheless. It's a freelance science and exploration vessel."

"Why would a science vessel be carrying any passengers at all, much less Si Cwan's sister?" asked Kebron.

"It makes sense," Si Cwan said with more excitement than Soleta had ever heard in his voice. "You're absolutely right, Kebron, it's not the type of vessel that would be used for transport. Secondly, unless I'm mistaken, it's big."

"Quite big," affirmed Soleta. "Such vessels usually are. Science and exploration vessels generally tend to be prepared for anything. It can easily accommodate a scientific team of up to one hundred people, transporting sufficient life-support equipment to sustain them for—"

"We get the idea, Lieutenant," Calhoun said, rising from his chair and standing on the lower level of the bridge in front of the tactical station. "But according to the manifest, how many passengers in this instance on the *Kayven Ryin?*"

"Only nine, actually."

"I see. How long ago was the message sent?"

"It's still being sent, Captain," Kebron said. "It's on live feed, a steady pulse."

"Try to raise them."

Kebron made that slight bow that passed for a nod and stepped up to tactical. He took a small amount of pleasure in hip-checking Si Cwan out of the way as he sent an autohail back through subspace. While he waited for a response, he watched Si Cwan's reactions carefully. And he could see that Si Cwan was ...

... afraid.

This struck Kebron as unusual, to say the least. He wasn't quite sure what to expect from Si Cwan, but fear hadn't quite been it. Kebron immediately started to become annoyed with himself as he realized he was feeling something for Si Cwan that he didn't want to feel: sympathy. He pushed such annoying thoughts as far away as he could as he reported briskly, "No response."

"How far away are they?"

"Approximately two hours at warp two."

"Captain, we have to go get her," Si Cwan said urgently. "She can't be that close and we don't do anything."

"We're already working on one rescue effort, Ambassador," replied Calhoun. "We finish one before we move on to the next. We can't go running helter-skelter throughout the sector."

"Captain, please," began Si Cwan.

But Calhoun cut him off emphatically. "We have four dozen frightened and shaken-up people on this vessel. I'm not about to start dragging them on side trips."

"A side trip? Captain, there are *lives* involved."

"My decision is final, Ambassador. I'm sorry." He hesitated. "Unless ..."

"Unless?" demanded Si Cwan with obvious urgency.

Calhoun turned to Lefler and said, "Refresh my memory, Lefler. We have a runabout down in the hangar bay?"

"Aye, sir. The *Marquand*."

"Can it make warp two?"

"That and a bit more in a pinch."

He nodded and looked back to Si Cwan. "Ambassador ... we're remaining on station until such time that repairs are completed and we can send our passengers on their way. But if you want to grab a runabout and rendezvous with the *Kayven Ryin*, I'll authorize it."

"That is more than generous, Captain," Si Cwan said. "I'll prepare to leave immediately. ..."

"Captain!" exclaimed an alarmed Zak Kebron.

"Problem, Mr. Kebron?"

"Sir, as head of security, I must register a formal protest."

"Formal. And me without my dress uniform."

"Sending a non-Starfleet individual out in a runabout . . ." Kebron couldn't find the words.

"On second thought, Mr. Kebron, you're absolutely right."

Zak let out a sigh of relief. "I'm pleased that you—"

"You'll be accompanying him."

"Captain! No, you can't—"

And Calhoun stepped in close to Kebron, and when he spoke his voice was low and angry, and his scar seemed to be standing out against his skin. "I can, and I am. I ask nothing of my crew members but the best they have to offer, and if the best you can offer is insubordination, then I'm going to get a new crew member and you can damn well walk home. Understood?"

"Yes, sir," said Kebron tightly.

"Good." Calhoun stepped back and then his gaze transfixed Si Cwan. "Do you have any problems with Mr. Kebron accompanying you?"

Si Cwan seemed ready to make one response, and clearly thought better of it, and said instead, "None whatsoever."

"Just what I wanted to hear: nothing. Lefler, have the shuttlebay prepare the *Marquand* for departure. Gentlemen . . . have a pleasant flight. And stay in touch. You know how I worry."

XII

Shelby stared incredulously at Calhoun. "You must be out of your mind."

Calhoun looked up from his desk. "I assume you're referring to the errand on which I sent Mr. Kebron and Ambassador Cwan."

"Of course I am! Kebron's made no secret of the fact that he doesn't like Si Cwan. How could you stick the two of them in a runabout together and send them out on a jaunt? We could have broken off from our repairs on the *Cambon*. If we'd left it sitting in space for a few hours while we checked out this other distress signal . . ."

"Nothing would have happened, yes, I know. That wasn't the point."

"Then what was?"

"You've checked out Mr. Kebron's psych profile, I take it?"

"I read over his career highlights, yes. A solid officer . . . no pun intended. Diligent. Thorough."

"Yes, but sometimes he has difficulty . . . oh, what's the old phrase . . . working and playing well with others. Particularly when it comes to races with whom he has little to no familiarity."

"The fact that he's extremely suspicious makes him well suited to being head of Security. You don't want someone who trusts everyone."

"Granted. But you don't want someone who is so distrustful that it impedes his ability to function . . . particularly when it comes to interaction with other crewmen."

"Point taken," said Shelby reluctantly. "Do you have any reason to believe such would be the case with Kebron?"

"There was an incident—a series of incidents, really—during his first year at Starfleet Academy. He apparently wasn't at the Academy for more than five minutes before he got into a brawl with another cadet, who happened to be the first Klingon at the Academy . . ."

"Worf?" asked Shelby in surprise.

"You know him?"

"I've worked with him. He's a . . . unique individual."

"Most individuals are," he observed. "In any event, it appears that Mr. Kebron's tendency to be judgmental and suspicious proved a hindrance, and friction continued between him and Worf. In order to alleviate the problem, the Academy heads forced Mr. Kebron and Mr. Worf to be roommates. The close proximity prompted an airing out of difficulties and, eventually, a smoothly operating relationship."

"I see. And you decided that pushing Kebron and Si Cwan together for a period of time might smooth out the hostilities in this instance."

"That is my plan, yes. What do you think?"

"Risky and unnecessary. Simply order Kebron to cooperate with Si Cwan and let it go at that."

"I've found that human nature . . . or, for that matter, Brikar or Thallonian nature . . . doesn't generally respond well to . . ."

And then his voice trailed off, and he frowned.

Shelby watched in confusion. "Mac?" she said after a long moment. "What—?"

"We're in trouble," he said.

"What do you mean? What kind of—"

"*Captain!*" It was Lefler's voice, and there wasn't panic in it, but there was extreme concern. "We've got company!"

Instantly Calhoun was out on the bridge, his attention on the screen. Soleta had moved to the tactical station to cover for the absent Kebron, and she said, "It just dropped out of warp."

The vessel on the screen was approaching them rapidly. It was large and black with silver markings. As a result it almost seemed to be one with the starry background behind it.

"Go to yellow alert. Beam the repair crew off the *Cambon* this instant and then raise shields. Scan it for weaponry," said Calhoun.

"Scanning," she confirmed as the yellow-alert klaxon sounded.

In a low voice, Shelby asked Calhoun, "How the hell did you know?"

"I usually know. It's a knack."

Before she could inquire further, Soleta said, "Scan complete. They possess front- and rear-mounted phase/plasma cannons. Primitive but effective. If we get into a pitched battle, we could be hurt."

"Captain," said Shelby, "They've made no hostile move. With all respect, you can't go into any situation assuming that every vessel you're going to encounter may open fire . . ."

And Lefler suddenly called out, *"Captain, they've opened fire!"*

The silence was thick in the runabout *Marquand.* Kebron was taking great pains not to look in Si Cwan's direction.

"Lieutenant," Si Cwan finally said, "would you mind telling me what your problem is?"

"Problem? I have no problem," said Kebron with exaggerated formality.

"Lieutenant, dissembling ill suits you."

"Are you calling me a liar?" inquired Kebron.

Si Cwan studied him a moment more, and then unstrapped himself from his seat and moved to the aft section of the ship. "All right," he said. "Let's go. Come on."

"What are you talking about?"

"I know what this is about. This is about the fact that, in your very first assignment as security chief of the *Excalibur,* you were beaten up."

"I was not beaten up."

"Yes, you were. I should know. I was the one who did it."

Kebron tried to get up so quickly that he almost knocked his chair backward . . . which was a formidable feat, considering that it was bolted down. "Knocking me off balance is hardly the same as 'beating me up.' "

"Well, now you'll have the opportunity to prove it." Si Cwan stood in a limber, prepared fashion, his arms poised, his legs slightly bent. "Come on. Take a shot at me. Let's settle this once and for all."

"We're on a mission," Kebron told him angrily. "This is not the time for pointless displays of combat."

"I see. Perhaps you're afraid, then."

"Of you?" Kebron laughed contemptuously. "In a true, honorable fight, you would not stand a chance against me."

"Then let's find out right now."

"No." And Kebron sat back down again.

Si Cwan strode forward. "Why not?"

"Because," he said reasonably, "if your sister is aboard the vessel, do you wish to greet her with your face bruised and battered? I would think she would be frightened to see you in such a state."

Si Cwan laughed curtly. "My being disfigured would not be a factor."

"Your confidence is misplaced."

"As is your hostility. We're on the same side, Kebron."

Keeping his gaze fixed resolutely on the stars streaking past them, Kebron said, "I dislike dictators. I dislike stowaways. And I dislike those who feel they are superior to others. You fall into all three categories. As I'm sure you can surmise, then . . . I dislike you."

For a time, Si Cwan said nothing. And then he drew very close to Kebron and said in a quiet voice that seemed filled with pain, "I've noticed that those who are the most confident that they know another person are the most likely to know the least."

And with that, he sat back down in his seat in the cockpit, and said nothing more for a full hour. Until their sensors told them that the science vessel *Kayven Ryin* was just ahead. Immediately, Kebron began hailing on the subspace radio again, and as he did so, Si Cwan said nothing. Kebron became aware that Si Cwan was holding his breath, and it was an awareness that annoyed him tremendously. For Si Cwan's concern over his sister was going a long way toward "humanizing" Cwan in Kebron's eyes, and it was so much easier to dislike someone when you could find nothing redeemable in their character.

And then a voice came over the radio. Si Cwan jumped so unexpectedly at the sound that he banged his head on the ceiling of the runabout as a voice said, "Incoming vessel . . . this is the *Kayven Ryin.* Are you here to aid us?"

"This is the *Marquand,* dispatched by the *Starship Excalibur,*" Kebron responded. "We are here to provide whatever temporary aid we can, and then report back to the *Excalibur*. In a short time, however, we'll be able to offer you the full services of our main ship.''

''Kallinda,'' Si Cwan was whispering urgently. ''Ask them about . . .''

''Your passenger manifest listed a Thallonian named Kallinda,'' Kebron said. ''Is that Kallinda of the deposed royal family of Thallon?''

There was a hesitation on the other end. ''We don't generally discuss private matters of our passengers, *Marquand* . . .''

''You have nothing to fear from us, *Kayven Ryin*. We're from Starfleet. We're here for humanitarian aid and,'' he glanced at the agonizingly eager Si Cwan, ''if she is the Kallinda in question . . . I have her brother here.''

There was the briefest of pauses. ''Si Cwan is there?''

''That is correct, yes.''

''Tell him . . . tell him his sister never stops talking about him, and is looking forward to seeing him.''

It was all Si Cwan could do to steady himself. Kebron gestured toward the console, silently indicating that if Si Cwan wanted to say something, he could. And Kebron was surprised to see that Cwan clearly could not do so because apparently he didn't trust himself to speak, so choked was he with emotion. ''Consider the message passed along. We'll be there within five minutes. . . .''

''We'll be ready for you, *Marquand*. . . .''

. . . and aboard the *Kayven Ryin,* several Thallonians were grouped around the communications board. ''We'll be ready for you, *Marquand*,'' one of them said. Then he snapped off the comm unit, and turned to the most powerfully built of the group, who was sliding a fresh energy clip into the barrel of his plasma blaster. ''We will be ready for them . . . won't we, Zoran.''

''Oh, yes,'' said Zoran. ''And finally I'll have that reunion with Si Cwan I've so been looking forward to.''

And he slammed the clip tightly into place. . . .

To Be Continued

THE
TWO-FRONT
WAR

MACKENZIE

Captain's Log, Stardate 50926.1—The Excalibur *has been endeavoring to provide humanitarian aid to the stranded vessel* Cambon *and its four dozen passengers presently in sickbay. However, we now find ourselves face-to-face with an unexpected intruder, who has opened fire on us.*

First Officer's Log, Stardate 50926.1—Our attempt to effect repairs on a stranded private crew ship, the Cambon, *populated by refugees from the fallen Thallonian government, has been interrupted by the appearance of an unknown vessel, which is reacting in a hostile manner to what is undoubtedly perceived as our trespass. Ideally, Captain Calhoun should be able to handle this matter in a calm and reasonable manner.*

I

"I want to blow those bastards out of space."

The *Excalibur* had just been rocked by the opening salvo from the black-and-silver ship that hung 100,000 kilometers to starboard. The phase/plasma cannons had pounded against the starship's shields, firing specially created "phaser/plasma" essentially designed not to smash shields apart, but instead to determine the wave harmonics of the shielding and basically eat through them with violent force. The first of the blasts went a long way toward cracking through the primary shields, and the *Excalibur* was jolted by the impact.

Nonetheless, even though the starship had been subjected to this most undignified and unprovoked attack, Captain Calhoun's angry order prompted a startled gasp from Commander Shelby. "Captain—!"

"Save the indignation, Commander. I didn't say I *would* . . . merely that I wanted to. Still, the day's young," and Calhoun rose from his chair, looking energized and confident. "Lefler, damage report."

"Some damage on primary shields," Robin Lefler reported from ops. "No structural damage. Forward shields at eighty percent and holding."

"McHenry . . ." began Calhoun.

And to his surprise, the normally laid-back helmsman said in staccato fashion, "I've angled the ship to protect the damaged shields, sir. Taking evasive action." He caught Lefler's look from the corner of his eye and turned to glance at the captain. "Was that jumping the gun, sir?"

"Yes, but I'll let it go this time," replied Calhoun, who had in fact been about to issue exactly those orders. "Mr. Boyajian, have you raised them yet?"

"Not yet, sir." Boyajian, a tall, black-haired tactical specialist, had stepped in to cover for Zak Kebron while the security chief was off-ship.

Calhoun spoke briskly and forcefully, yet in a manner so unhurried that it gave the impression he felt fairly unthreatened by the present situation. Whether that was truly the case or not was impossible to tell. "Keep trying, but meantime see if you can determine where their key points of vulnerability are and target them."

"Trying, Captain. Tough to scan them through their shields."

"Do your best." He turned toward the science station. "Lieutenant Soleta, any thoughts on the ship's pedigree?"

"Although the vessel bears passing similarities with Kreel vessels, it is not of that race," she said as she checked her scanners. "It will take time to make a full analysis."

"Fine, you've got twenty seconds."

"I appreciate the leisure time, sir."

"They're coming around again," warned Shelby.

"Firing again!" Boyajian warned.

Two phase/plasma bolts streaked out from the underside of the black-and-silver ship. Mark McHenry's eyes seemed to glitter with an almost demented glee as his fingers flew over the controls with such speed that Lefler, sitting not ten feet away, couldn't even see them.

The twin blasts arced right for the front of the saucer section, and would have struck it cleanly had not the *Excalibur* suddenly—with alacrity and grace—executed a forty-five-degree roll on her horizontal axis. Terms such as "sideways" had no meaning in the depth of space when there was no other body, such as a planet, to relate it to. Nonetheless, "sideways" was what the *Excalibur* suddenly was as the plasma blasts shot past her, bracketing her on either side.

"Excellent!" Shelby called out. McHenry had had no more vocal critic or detractor than Shelby when she had first seen him at his post, apparently unfocused and uninterested. But faced with a crisis, McHenry had reacted with ingenuity and full capability.

McHenry's response to Shelby's spontaneous praise was to turn and grin at her.

Soleta, who appeared oblivious to McHenry's maneuvering, glanced up from her science station. "Sir, I believe that bulge to their aft section is the key to their propulsion system . . . some sort of a concentrated ion glide."

"Mr. Boyajian, target it, ready phasers for a three-second shot at full strength. Then put me on ship-to-ship."

"Aye, sir, but I can't promise they're listening."

"I'll take that chance. Oh, and the moment I get to five, fire."

"You're on intership, Captain," said Boyajian, "but what did you mean by—?"

Calhoun didn't give him the opportunity to finish the question. Instead, in a no-nonsense tone, he said, "Attention alien vessel. This is Captain Calhoun of the Federation starship *Excalibur.* Your attack is unprovoked. We will give you to the count of five to back off, or we will open fire."

Understanding the earlier order, Boyajian's finger hovered over the firing control.

And Calhoun, without hesitation, said, "One . . . two . . . *five.*"

Boyajian fired the phaser reflexively upon hearing the command, acting so automatically that the phasers had already been unleashed before he realized that a few numbers had been missing in the countdown.

The phasers lashed out, striking the attacking vessel directly in the section that Soleta had suggested. The attacker rocked wildly, the phasers coruscating off the shields.

"Direct hit," Boyajian reported. "Their shields held, but I don't think they were particularly thrilled."

"I didn't expect to damage them," said Calhoun. "Not with a three-second burst."

"A warning shot," Shelby realized. "To let them know that we've targeted a vulnerable area."

Calhoun nodded, and that was when Boyajian said, "We're getting an incoming hail, sir."

"Good. Let them sweat a few moments before putting them on."

In a low voice so as not to sound openly questioning of her superior officer in front of the rest of the bridge crew, Shelby murmured, "If you wanted to warn them, you could have fired at half-strength. Perhaps even fired across their path rather than an invasive direct strike."

"If I have a bow and arrow, Commander, I don't shoot a padded shaft to my target's left in order to express my annoyance. I fire a steel-tipped arrow into his leg. That's my idea of a warning shot."

"You're the Gandhi of the spaceways, Captain."

He smiled and then said, "Put me on with them, Boyajian."

"You're on, sir."

"This is Captain Calhoun of the *Excalibur*," he said. "Identify yourselves and prepare to stand down from hostilities. Otherwise I can assure you that you will not leave this confrontation in one piece."

The screen shimmered for a moment, and the commander (presumably) of the opposing vessel appeared.

Although distinguishing gender was frequently a bit problematic in any first encounter, the *Excalibur*'s opponent looked distinctly female. Moreover, by Earth standards she appeared almost angelic. She was hairless, her skin golden, her brow slightly distended in a manner that was—amazingly enough—still attractive. It was difficult to make out the color of her eyes, but when she tilted her head they seemed to glow with an almost purple sheen. When she spoke, her voice had a vibrato to it that gave it a somewhat musical quality.

"I am Laheera of Nelkar," she replied. "Do you wish to discuss terms of your surrender?"

"Surrender?" Calhoun cast a skeptical glance at Shelby as if to say, *Do you hear this?* He looked back to Laheera. "You expect me—a Starfleet captain—to surrender my vessel on our maiden voyage to the first opponent who looks to pose a challenge? Sorry. That's not my style."

"And is your style trespass, then? We know your type, Calhoun," said Laheera. Her voice was such that, even when annoyed, she had a tone of amusement to her. "Our once-orderly sector is now subject to the attentions of scavengers and pirates. People who will take every opportunity to ravage us, to feed on helplessness. We must protect ourselves."

"I can appreciate that," replied Calhoun, "but you've misjudged us. We're here only to help."

"How do we know? Why, there is a transport vessel right next to you that is empty and damaged. How do we know you haven't picked it clean of whatever it might have had to offer?"

"The transport vessel's crew is aboard this ship. We were lending humanitarian aid. If you wish, I can have you speak to its captain and a delegation of its crew."

Laheera glanced to the side of the screen and murmured something, as if consulting with someone unseen. Then she looked back and said, "That would be acceptable."

"Give us five minutes. Calhoun out." He didn't even wait for the screen to blink off as he said, "Bridge to sickbay."

"Sickbay, Dr. Selar here," came the crisp response.

"Doctor, I'd like you to get Captain Hufmin and a couple of representatives of the *Cambon* passengers up here immediately. Whoever is healthiest and is qualified to speak on their behalf. And make it fast."

"Will three minutes suffice?"

"Make it two. Calhoun out." He promptly turned to Boyajian and said, "Can you raise the *Marquand?*"

"Aye, sir."

"Good. Get me Si Cwan on subspace. I want to see what he knows about these 'Nelkar' people."

He looked to Shelby and he knew what she was thinking. She was musing that if Calhoun hadn't let Si Cwan and Zak Kebron head out in the runabout for the purpose of rendezvous with the ship *Kayven Ryin,* then he would be aboard the *Excalibur* now, in a position to be of some use. Shelby, however, was far too good an officer to voice those thoughts . . . at least, while other crewmen were around. So instead she nodded noncommittally and simply said, "Good plan, sir."

"Zoran, it's slowing down!"

Aboard the *Kayven Ryin,* a group of Thallonians had been watching the approach of the *Marquand* with tremendous interest and smug excitement. For what seemed the hundredth time, Zoran had checked over his disruptor, making certain that the energy cartridge was fully charged. But with the alarmed shout from one of his associates, Rojam, Zoran tore himself away from his preoccupation with his weapon.

Rojam was correct. The *Marquand,* dispatched by the *Excalibur* and bearing the unknowing target of Zoran's interest—named Lord Si Cwan, former prince of the Thallonian Empire—had been proceeding at a brisk pace toward the *Kayven Ryin.*

"They suspect," muttered Rojam.

"Do something, then," snapped Zoran. "We can't be this close to having Si Cwan in our hands, only to let him slip through our fingers now! I must have his throat in my hands, so that I can squeeze the life from him myself!" The other Thallonians nodded in agreement, which was hardly surprising. Whenever Zoran spoke, the others had a tendency to concur.

Reactivating the comm channel, Rojam hailed the oncoming runabout. He tried not to sound nervous, apprehensive, or all that eager, although a little of any of that would have been understandable. After all, they were representing themselves as frightened, stranded passengers aboard a crippled science vessel. A degree of nervousness under the circumstances would be right in line with the scenario they were presenting. "Shuttle craft *Marquand,* is there a problem? You seem to be slowing." He paused and then added, "Aren't you going to help us?"

There was no reply at first and another of the Thallonians, a shorter and more aggressive man named Juif, whispered, "Target them! Target them! Use exterior weapons and blast them into atoms! Hurry, before it's too late!"

"They're at the outer edge of the firing range," Zoran noted angrily. "We likely couldn't do them any significant damage, and they'd still be in a position to get away. Hell, their instruments would probably inform them we're locking on to them. They'd leap into warp space and be gone before we got a shot off." The edge to his voice became more pronounced as he said in a threatening manner, "Rojam . . ."

"They're not responding."

"That is unacceptable. Get them on the line."

"But if they won't respon—"

Zoran's large hand clamped down on the back of Rojam's neck, and the latter felt as if his head was about to be torn from his shoulders. "Providence has delivered Si Cwan to us," snarled Zoran, "and I will not have him escape. Now get them on the line!"

Never had Rojam been more convinced that his demise was imminent. And then, as if in answer to unvoiced prayers, a gravelly voice came over the speaker. "This is Lieutenant Kebron of the *Marquand*. Sit tight, *Kayven Ryin*. We're just dealing with a communiqué from our main vessel. Kebron out."

"Raise them again!" urged Zoran.

"I can't. The channel's gone dead."

"If they get away," Zoran said meaningfully, "that channel won't be the only thing around here that's dead."

Si Cwan stroked his chin thoughtfully. "The Nelkarites, eh?"

"You know them?" Calhoun's voice came over the subspace radio. "Are they trustworthy?"

"Nowadays, there are few in Sector 221-G whom I would consider absolutely trustworthy," Si Cwan told him. "Relatively speaking, the Nelkar had been fairly harmless. Never started any wars, more than happy to accept Thallonian rule. However . . ."

"However?" prompted Calhoun when the word seemed simply to dangle there.

"Well . . . they're a scavenger race, by and large. Fairly limited in their design and potential. They tend to cobble their vessels together from whatever they can find, using technology that they don't always understand."

Soleta's voice was audible over the link as she commented, "That would explain the somewhat haphazard design of their vessel."

"Does that answer your questions, Captain?" asked Si Cwan, not quite able to keep the urgency out of his voice. "Because if it's all the same to you—"

"Stay on station. Do not proceed to the *Kayven Ryin* until you hear back from us."

"But Captain—!"

"I want to get matters sorted out on this end before you board that vessel, and I want to know I can get in touch with you. If the comm system on the *Kayven Ryin* goes out, you'll be incommunicado."

"Captain—!" Si Cwan tried to protest.

But Calhoun wouldn't hear any of it. Instead he said preemptively, "Did you copy those orders, Lieutenant Kebron?"

Without hesitation, Kebron said, "Understood, Captain."

"*Excalibur* out."

Making no attempt to cover his anger, Si Cwan sprang to his feet and slammed his fists into the ceiling of the shuttle craft. Kebron watched him impassively. "What do you think you're doing?"

"I'm getting angry!" snapped Si Cwan. He began to pace the interior of the shuttle craft like a tiger. "Why, don't you ever get angry?"

"I try not to," said Kebron evenly. "If I lose control, things tend to get broken."

"Things. What kinds of things," demanded Si Cwan without much interest.

"Oh . . . heads . . . backs . . . necks . . ."

Captain Hufmin of the damaged vessel *Cambon,* along with two of the refugees—a husband and wife named Boretskee and Cary, who had developed into a kind of leaders-by-default—sat in the conference lounge with Calhoun and Shelby. On the screen was Laheera of Nelkar, and it was quite apparent to Calhoun that Hufmin and company were spellbound by her.

"You understand that we were only concerned about the welfare of your passengers," Laheera said to Calhoun in that wonderfully musical voice of hers. "Let us not lose sight of one simple truth: This is our sector of space. You are merely a visitor here. It is to our interest to watch out for one another. It is difficult to know whom to trust."

"Understood," Calhoun said neutrally.

"Captain Hufmin . . . I extend to you and your . . . *cargo,*" she seemed amused by the notion, "sanctuary on Nelkar. We welcome you with open arms."

Boretskee and Cary looked at each other with undisguised joy and relief. "We accept your offer," they said.

"Excellent. I shall inform my homeworld." The screen shimmered and she was gone.

"Now, wait a minute," said Shelby. "Are you quite certain about this?"

"Commander, we are not pioneers," Cary replied. "We are not intrepid adventurers like yourselves. We're just trying to survive, that's all. Whether we survive on their world or somewhere outside of the Thallonian Empire, what difference does it make?"

"Isn't there an old Earth saying about any port in a storm?" Hufmin reminded them.

"Yes, and there's also one about fools rushing in," said Calhoun.

Boretskee bristled a bit. "I can't say I appreciate being considered a 'fool,' Captain."

"I didn't say that—"

Cary cut in. "We are grateful to you for all you've done for us. You saved our lives. For that our next generation of children will be named for you. But, Captain," and Cary gestured as if trying to encompass the whole of the galaxy, "this environment you sail through— space—you're comfortable in it. You've made your peace with it. But myself, Boretskee, the others in our group . . . we're not spacefaring types. This vacuum . . . it presses on us. Intimidates us. We almost died in it. If the Nelkarites offer us safe escort and a life on their world, we'll happily embrace it."

Hufmin took in both Shelby and Calhoun with a bland shrug. "Look . . . I'm just a hired gun here. They're the passengers. Barring desires that run contrary to the safety of my vessel, I'm obligated to take them where they want to go."

"Perhaps. But I'm not," Calhoun said.

They looked at him, a bit appalled. "Captain . . . you wouldn't," said Boretskee.

"I have to do what I think is right. And I'm loath to thrust you into a potentially dangerous situation . . ."

"We're already in a potentially dangerous situation," Cary pointed out. "We're in the depths of space. That's dangerous enough as far as we're concerned. It almost killed us once. We have no desire to give it a second opportunity."

"With all respect, Captain, this shouldn't be your decision," Boretskee said.

"With all respect, sir . . . that is precisely what it is," replied Calhoun. He rose from his seat and turned away from them, his hands draped behind his back. "I'll let you know what I decide presently. That will be all."

"Now wait one minute—"

"I believe, sir, that the captain said that would be all," Shelby said calmly, her fingers interlaced on the table in front of her. "Temporary quarters have been set up to house you and your fellow passengers. Perhaps the time could be well spent discussing your options with them . . . just in the event that you're not all of the same mind."

"Apparently what we decide is irrelevant," said Boretskee challengingly. His fists were tightly clenched; it was clear that he was a bit of a scrapper, just waiting for Calhoun to react in some aggressive manner. When Calhoun did not even turn, however, Boretskee continued angrily, "Wouldn't you say so, Captain?"

Calhoun turned to look at him, and his purple eyes were as sympathetic as a black hole. "Yes. I would." The air turned more frigid with each word.

To his credit, Boretskee didn't seem inclined to back down. But Cary headed off any continuing hostility as she tugged on Boretskee's arm and he allowed himself to be led out of the room. Captain Hufmin paused at the door long enough to say, "Look, Captain . . . I don't give a damn either way. I'm making almost no money on this job as it is. But for what it's worth, these are people who have lost everything. Be a shame if they lost their self-respect, too."

Shelby waited until the moment that Hufmin was gone and out of earshot, and then she said to Calhoun, "It's not your choice, you know."

He raised an eyebrow. "Pardon?"

"Regs are clear on this. These people know where they want to go. You don't have any conceivable grounds upon which to overrule their desire."

"Yes, I do."

"That being?"

"My gut."

She leaned back, arms folded. "Your gut," she said, unenthused. "Funny. I don't remember reading about that in my Intro to Regs class back at the Academy. Guts, I mean."

"Nelkar smells wrong."

"First your stomach, now your nose. Are you a Starfleet captain or a gourmet?"

And to her utter surprise, he slammed the conference table with an iron fist. The noise startled her and she jumped slightly, but quickly composed herself. And just as quickly as she reined herself in, so did Calhoun. "I'm dealing with subtleties, Commander. Regulations aren't created for subtleties. They're created as sweeping generalizations to handle all situations. But not every situation."

"And it can't be that every situation, you do whatever the hell you want. Nor can it be that you let your frustration get to you so quickly and so easily."

"I'm not frustrated," Calhoun said. "I simply know what I know. And what I know is that Nelkar seems off. I don't trust Laheera."

"Be that as it may, Mac . . . do you want to be a dictator? With your history, do you feel comfortable with that label?"

He smiled thinly. "You always know just what to say."

"Long practice." She sauntered toward him, stopping several feet away. "Look, Mac . . . for what it's worth, I respect your gut, your nose . . . all your instincts. But that has to be balanced against conducting ourselves in an orderly fashion. We're the only Starfleet vessel out here. We're here at a time of disarray. We have to stand for something, and we can't simply come in and throw our weight around. It's patronizing; don't you see that?"

"Yes, I see that. By the same token, should I deliberately allow people to go into a dangerous situation when I can prevent them from doing so?"

She was silent for a long moment. "You mean like with the captain of the *Grissom?*"

With a deep sigh, Calhoun told her, "Eppy . . . you know I admire you. Respect you. Still have deep feelings for you, as much as I hate to admit it . . . although certainly not romantic, God knows . . ."

"Of course not," she quickly agreed.

"But so help me, if you bring up the *Grissom* again, I may become violent."

"Really. Try it and I'll kick your ass. Sir."

And he laughed. "You know . . . I'll bet you could, at that." But then he became serious again. "Very well, Commander. But this will be done on my terms."

"Your terms being . . . ?"

For reply, he tapped his comm unit. "Bridge . . . open a hailing frequency to the Nelkar ship. Pipe it down here."

Within moments Laheera was smiling at them in that beatific manner she had. "Greetings," she said. "Are you preparing to transport your charges over to our ship?"

"Actually," replied Calhoun, "I was anticipating that we would transport them ourselves, if it is all the same to you."

Shelby looked from Calhoun to Laheera, trying to get some hint of her state of mind. But if Laheera seemed at all disconcerted by Calhoun's statement, she did not give the slightest sign. "That would be perfectly acceptable. I will send you the coordinates for our homeworld. Laheera out."

When she blinked out, Shelby asked, "What about the *Cambon?* We can't haul it along at warp speed."

"We'll cut her loose and leave her here to drift until we come back for her," he said after a moment's thought. "Considering the condition she's in, I hardly think we have to worry about scavengers."

"Bridge to Captain Calhoun," came McHenry's voice.

"Calhoun here."

"Captain, we've gotten coordinates for Nelkar." He paused. "Were we expecting them?"

"Yes, we were. Warp five would get us there when, Mr. McHenry?"

"At warp five? Two hours, ten minutes, sir. They're not all that far."

Shelby commented, "Considering their own vessel isn't exactly the most advanced I've seen, I can't say I'm surprised. That still leaves us with one outstanding problem."

"Yes, I'm quite aware of that. McHenry, set course for Nelkar, warp five. Then have Mr. Boyajian patch me through to the *Marquand.* Let's make sure we're not leaving them in the lurch."

"You're making the right decision, sir," said Shelby.

"I'm so relieved that you approve, Commander." He grimaced. "My only problem is . . . you know that unpleasant feeling I've got about the Nelkarites?"

"Yes?"

"Well . . . now I'm starting to get it about the *Marquand* and its rendezvous with the *Kayven Ryin.* I hope that wasn't a mistake as well."

"Captain, if you keep second-guessing your judgments, you're going to make yourself insane."

"Why, Commander . . . I thought you decided I was insane the day I broke off our engagement."

And with a contemptuous chuckle, she said, "Captain . . . I hate to inform you . . . but I broke it off. Not you." She strode out of the conference lounge, leaving an amused Calhoun shaking his head. But then the amusement slowly evaporated as the reality set in.

He didn't like the situation. Not at all.

For years he had basically been his own boss. He had answered to no one except, in a very distant manner, Admiral Nechayev. He had been bound by no rules except those of common sense, and made decisions that were answerable only to himself. It had been an extremely free manner in which to operate.

But now . . . now he had rules hanging over him whichever way he turned. He had operated under rules before, yes . . . but he had been the one making the rules. Back when he'd been a freedom fighter on his native Xenex, his wiles and craftiness had earned him the respect of those around him and they obeyed him. They obeyed him unthinkingly, unhesitatingly. Had he told them to throw themselves on their swords, they would have done so with the firm conviction that there was a damned good reason for it.

But that wasn't the case here. Yes, he was captain. Yes, he was obeyed. But that obedience came as a result of a long tradition and history that dictated that obedience. They answered to the rank, not to him. When it came to he himself, he could sense that there were still double-takes or second thoughts. His crew—Shelby in particular—gave thought to his orders, questioned him, challenged him. It irked him, angered him.

And yet . . . and yet . . .

Shouldn't that really please him? Shouldn't that be something that made him happy rather than disconcerted him? After all, he had lived in an environment where blind obedience was expected as a matter of course, and punished if not given. The Xenexians had lived under the thumb of the Danterians, and during that time the Danterians had not been exactly reluctant to show who was boss at any given moment. They had unhesitatingly used the Xenexians as their objects, their toys, their playthings to dispose of at a whim or exploit as they saw fit. Young M'k'n'zy of Calhoun had seen those activities and a cold fury had built within him. Built and built until it had exploded into rebellion, and through sheer force of will he had brought an entire race with him.

Yes, he had indeed seen firsthand the dangers of requiring unquestioned obedience. At the same time, he was frustrated that the same rules under which he oftentimes felt constricted were what guaranteed that his own people would do what he told them to. He wanted more than that.

Time, a voice in his head consoled him. These things required time. He had always been impatient, always wanted everything at whatever moment he wanted it. It was an attitude that had, in the past, stood him in good stead. When tribal elders had told him that someday, someday in the far future, the Xenexians would be free, young M'k'n'zy had not settled for that. "Someday" was too ephemeral, too useless a concept for him. He wanted "someday" to be right then and there. He would make his own "somedays."

He smiled at the absurdity of it all. Despite everything he'd gone through, everything he'd seen, there was still an impatient young Xenexian within him who did not understand the need for patience. A young Xenexian who wanted everything immediately, and who had no use whatsoever for "someday."

He tapped his comm badge. "Calhoun to Shelby."

"Shelby here," came the prompt reply.

"Have we been in communication with Kebron and Si Cwan?"

"Yes, sir. They, in turn, have spoken with the crew of the *Kayven Ryin.* Although they are in distress, there is no immediate danger to them. They report life-support systems are still on line. Kebron and Cwan intended to board the *Kayven Ryin* and lend whatever aid they can until we rendezvous with them."

"Very well. Best speed to Nelkar, then . . . on my order," he added as an afterthought.

"On your order, sir," she said. Then there was a pause. "Captain . . ."

"Yes, Commander?"

"We're waiting on your order."

He smiled to the empty room. "Yes. I know." He paused a moment longer, then said simply, "Now."

"Now it is, sir."

It was a small pleasure, making them wait in anticipation of the order. Childish, perhaps. A juvenile reminder of who was in charge, but he found that it gave him amusement. And lately he'd had very little of that.

"Oh, and Commander," he said as an afterthought.

"Yes, sir."

"Just for your information: *I* broke it off. Calhoun out."

On the bridge of the *Excalibur,* Lefler turned in her seat and looked quizzically at Shelby. She noted that it seemed as if Shelby's chest were shaking in amusement. "He 'broke it off,' Commander?"

"So he claims, Lieutenant," replied Shelby.

From the science station, Soleta inquired, "Will he be needing someone to reattach it?"

And then she stared at Shelby in confusion as Shelby, unable to contain it anymore, laughed out loud.

SI CWAN

II

Zoran thought that he was going to go out of his mind.

He felt as if the damned shuttle craft had been hanging there forever, tantalizingly, frustratingly just out of reach. He had wanted to send multiple messages to it, telling them to get over to the ship immediately, that help was desperately needed, that they were going to die within seconds if immediate aid were not provided. But Rojam had cautioned against it. "They have their own instrumentation," he advised Zoran. "If we try to trick them, if we tell them there's immediate danger when there isn't, they'll be able to see through it."

"Maybe we should take that chance," Zoran urged.

"Then again, maybe we should not," fired back Rojam. "What should we say? That our engines are in danger of exploding? That our life-support systems are failing? These are not possibilities, because their own onboard readings will tell them that we're lying. And if they know that we're lying, then they're going to start to wonder what the truth is. And if they do that, then we have a major problem."

"Damn them!" snarled Zoran, pacing the room. His long and powerful legs carried him quickly around the perimeter, and his blue body armor clacked as he moved. His red face was darker than usual as he mused on the frustration facing him. "Si Cwan wasn't part of the plan, but now that he's here . . . damn him and damn them all!"

"Damning them isn't going to do a bit of g—" Rojam began to say. But then he stopped as a blinking light on the control panel caught his attention. "Incoming hail from the *Marquand,*" he said.

"It's about time!" Zoran fairly shouted.

"Will you calm down?" Juif said in exasperation. "If we're in communication with them and Si Cwan hears your bellowing, that's going to be the end of that!"

With effort, Zoran brought himself under control as Rojam answered the hail. "We were beginning to wonder, *Marquand.*"

"We needed to speak with the *Excalibur,*" came the deep voice that they knew to be the passenger other than Si Cwan. "What is your present emergency status? How long can you survive aboard your vessel?"

Zoran was gesturing that Rojam should lie, but Rojam was quite certain that that was not the way to go. He believed in all the reasons that he'd put forward to Zoran, and there was one other element as well: If Si Cwan was aboard the *Marquand,* not all the hosts of hell would get him to depart without his sister at his side.

"Lie!" Zoran hissed in a very low voice. "They're going to *leave* if we don't!" And the way his fist was clenching and unclenching told Rojam a very disturbing truth: namely, that if answered the question from the *Marquand* accurately and then the shuttle craft turned and left for the mother ship, Rojam would very likely not live out the hour. Not given the mood that Zoran was presently in.

But he felt he had to trust his instincts, and on that basis, he said, "Life-support systems are presently holding together. Our main problem is in engineering; our propulsion systems are out. Our batteries are running down and we likely could not survive indefinitely, but for the very immediate future, the danger level is tolerable."

There was a silence that seemed infinitely long, and Rojam could practically hear his life span shortening. But then the voice said, "This is the *Marquand.* With your permission, we will come aboard and give what aid we can, while we wait for the *Excalibur* to rendezvous with us. Will that be acceptable?"

"Yes. Absolutely acceptable," said Rojam, relief flooding through him. Behind him he could sense Zoran nodding in approval.

"Just one thing . . . ?"

"Yes, *Marquand?*"

"Please put the passenger called Kalinda on with us. Her brother would like to speak with her."

"Uhm . . ." Suddenly sweat began to beat on Rojam's crimson fore-head, his grimacing white teeth standing out in stark relief to his face. "Just a moment, please." He switched off the comm channel and then turned to Zoran. "Now what?"

"Now?" Zoran smiled. "Now . . . we give them what they asked for."

Si Cwan stared in confusion at Zak Kebron. "Why did you ask them to put Kalinda on?"

"Because," Kebron said slowly and deliberately—which was more or less how he said everything—"I am being cautious. It's my job to watch out for everyone on board the *Excalibur.* That even includes those who have no business being there at all."

"I appreciate the thought."

"Don't. As noted: It's my job." He paused. "Would you know your sister's voice if you heard it?"

"Of course." He waited for a response, but none seemed to be immediately in evidence. Concern began to grow within him. "You don't think there's a problem."

"I always think there's a problem," replied Kebron. "It saves time. And lives." He checked his instruments. "Their life-support appears stable. Pity. If they had lied about that, I would have known that there was something wrong. Perhaps it is a more subtle trap."

"Or perhaps they're truly in distress. But then . . . why hasn't Kalinda come on—?" It was a disturbing thought. He had simply taken for granted that his sister was truly a passenger on the science vessel. The notion that she might not be was agonizing for him. To have his hopes raised and then dashed in such a manner . . .

But even more disturbing, he realized, was the concept that he had not questioned it for one moment. One did not acquire or maintain power by being easily duped. Had he let his love for his sister, his desire to try and reconstruct some semblance of his former life, completely blind him to all caution? That was a very, very dangerous mind-set to have.

And then a girlish voice came over the comm system. "Si Cwan?" it said.

Si Cwan came close to knocking Kebron aside—or as close as one can come to budging someone who is essentially a walking mountain of granite. "Kally?" he practically shouted.

"Si Cwan, is that you?"

"Yes . . . yes it is . . . Kally, everything is going to be all right . . ."

"I'm so glad to hear your voice, Si Cwan . . ."

Si Cwan felt himself choking with relief, but then Kebron said in a sharp whisper, "Ask her something only she would know."

"What?" He seemed to have trouble focusing, which of course bugged the hell out of Kebron.

"Something only she would know," he repeated.

Slowly, Si Cwan nodded. "Kally . . . remember that time? That time shortly before we had to leave? Remember that? When I said that I would always be there for you? Remember, when we spoke at our special place?"

There was a short hesitation, one that made Si Cwan wonder ever so briefly, and then her voice said, "You mean that time by the Fire Falls? That?"

He closed his eyes and nodded. Kalinda, meanwhile, naturally couldn't see him as she continued, "Si Cwan? Is that what you're talking about?"

"Yes, that's it."

"Why did you want to know about that?"

"Just being careful. You understand. These days, we can't be too careful." He looked triumphantly at Kebron, who merely grunted and edged the ship forward toward the *Kayven Ryin*.

"Okay, Si Cwan . . . whatever you say."

"We'll be there in a few minutes, Kally. Don't worry. We'll be right along."

"Okay, Si Cwan. I'll see you soon." And the connection broke off.

And the moment that happened, Kebron brought the ship to a dead halt in space. Si Cwan was immediately aware of it. "What are you doing?" he demanded.

Zak Kebron turned in his chair. "I don't like it."

"What?"

"I said I don't like it."

Si Cwan appeared ready to explode. His body was trembling with repressed fury. "Now, you listen to me," he said sharply. "I know what this is about."

"Do you," asked Kebron, unimpressed by Si Cwan's ire.

"It's not enough that you continue to resent me, or deny my right to be aboard the *Excalibur*. But now . . . now you'd hurt a young girl whom you've never met . . . who's never done anything to you . . ."

"It must be nice to be a prince," Kebron said evenly, "and know everything there is to know about everything." Then he glanced at the control board. "They're hailing us."

"Of course they are! They're wondering what's happening." Si Cwan came around his seat and confronted Kebron, fury building. "They have no idea that a resentful Brikar is endeavoring to make my life impossible!"

Kebron ignored him, instead bringing the hail on line. He began to say, *"Marquand* here," but he wasn't even able to get that much about before an upset voice said, with no preamble, "Why are you backing off?"

"We are returning to our vessel," Kebron said flatly. "A situation has come to our attention. *Marquand* out." And with that he severed the connection.

"What are you hoping to accomplish?" demanded Si Cwan.

"Merely being cautious."

"The hell you are. This is all part of your attempt to upset me, to interfere with—"

Unperturbed, the Brikar cut him off with a terse "This solar system, like all others, does not revolve around you. I do not like that she severed communications with us. If I were a young woman, connecting with my brother who might have been dead for all I knew, I would keep talking to him until he was aboard. I wouldn't shut down the connection, as if I were afraid he might figure out that I was an impostor."

"That is—"

And then a light began to flash on the control panel, a sharp warning beep catching their attention. Kebron immediately began to bring the ship around as Si Cwan demanded, "What's happening?"

"We're being targeted. They're going to fire on us."

"They're . . . what?"

Si Cwan looked out the main window, catching a glimpse of the *Kayven Ryin* as the shuttle craft started to angle away from it. A motion on the aft section caught his attention. Despite their distance, his eyesight was formidable and he zeroed in with impressive visual acuity. What he saw were two gunports opening, and twin heavy-duty phaser cannons snapped into view. And the last thing he saw before their view of the science ship was cut off was the muzzles of the cannons flaring to life.

"Brace yourself!" shouted Kebron. "I'm trying to bring the warp drive on line before—"

He didn't have time to complete the sentence before the *Marquand* was struck amidships by the phaser cannons. The runabout spiraled out of control as Kebron fought to regain command of the battered ship. To his credit, he never lost his cool. Indeed, it might not have been within his makeup to become disconcerted.

Si Cwan was not strapped into his chair. As a result, he was tossed around the interior of the cabin, reaching out desperately to try and grab hold of something, anything, to halt himself. He crashed against one wall and felt something in his shoulder give way.

Sparks flew out of the front console as Kebron tried to institute damage procedures. The shuttle craft was rocked again, and Kebron shouted, "We have to abandon ship!"

"What?" Si Cwan was on his back, looking around, stunned and confused.

There was a gash in Si Cwan's head which Kebron hoped wasn't as bad as it looked. It wasn't going to look good in his service record if he'd left with a live passenger and returned with a corpse. The notion that the status of his record might be utterly moot didn't enter into his considerations. He was not prepared to admit that as a possibility. "Warp engines are down. We're perfect targets out here. We have to assume that they're going to keep shooting until they blow us to pieces."

"Why are they doing this?"

"As a guess: because they want to kill you. I'm simply the lucky bystander." He grabbed Si Cwan by the arm and Si Cwan howled in such agony that Kebron quickly released him. He knew he hadn't pulled on Si Cwan with any force; the mere movement of the arm had been enough to elicit the screams, and he realized that Cwan's arm was injured. "Get up!" he said, urgency entering his voice for the first time. "We have to go."

"Go where?"

"There!" Kebron stabbed a finger in the general direction of the science vessel that they had come to aid. Si Cwan was staggering to his feet and Kebron grabbed him by the back of the neck, which somehow seemed a less injurious place to hold him. He propelled him toward the two-person transporter nestled in the cockpit of the shuttle craft.

Fire was beginning to consume the main console, smoke filling up the interior of the shuttle craft. Moving with surprising dexterity considering their size, the Brikar's fingers yanked out a small panel from the wall next to the transporter, revealing a red button which he immediately punched. It was a failsafe device, provided for a situation precisely like this one, where voice recognition circuitry was failing and setting coordinates through the main console was an impossibility.

The emergency evacuation procedure was activated, an automatic five-second delay kicking in, providing Kebron and Si Cwan that much time to step onto the transporter pads. Si Cwan was nursing his injured shoulder as Kebron half pushed, half pulled him onto the pads and hoped that they actually had five seconds remaining to them.

The transporter automatically surveyed their immediate environment and locked on to the first, nearest destination that would enable them to survive. And an instant later, Si Cwan's and Zak Kebron's bodies dissipated as the miraculous transporter beams kicked in, sending their molecules hurtling through the darkness of space to be reassembled in the place that was their only hope for survival: the science vessel *Kayven Ryin*. The vessel which had assaulted them, and now provided their one chance to live . . . if only for a few more minutes, at best.

When Zoran saw the *Marquand* backing away, he began to tremble with fury. "Where are they going? We gave them what they wanted. Si Cwan spoke to his sister. Get them back here!" And he cuffed Rojam on the side of the head. "Get them back!"

Rojam barely felt the physical abuse. He was too concerned with the *Marquand* suddenly moving away from the station, as if they had tumbled to the trick. More on point, he was concerned with how Zoran was going to react, and what precisely Zoran might do to vent his displeasure. Hailing the shuttle craft, he tried to control the growing franticness he was feeling as he asked, "Why are you backing off?"

From the shuttle craft there came nothing more than a brief, to-the-point response: "We are returning to our vessel. a situation has come to our attention. *Marquand* out."

"They know! *They know!*" roared Zoran.

Rojam's mind raced as he tried to determine the accuracy of the assessment. "I . . . I don't think they do. Suspect, perhaps, but they don't know. They want to see what we'll do. If we're just cautious . . ."

"If we're cautious, then they're gone!"

"We don't know that for sure! Zoran, listen to me—!"

But listening was the last thing that Zoran had in mind. Instead, with a full-throated roar of anger, the powerfully built Thallonian knocked Rojam out of his seat. Rojam hit the floor with a yelp as Zoran dropped down at the control console. "Get away from there, Zoran!" Rojam cried out.

"Shut up! You're afraid to do what has to be done!" Even as he spoke, Zoran quickly manipulated the controls.

"I'm not afraid! But this is unnecessary! It's a mistake!"

"It's my decision, not yours! You're lucky I haven't killed you already for your incompetence! And if the phaser cannons you rigged up don't perform as you promised . . ."

But the need to complete the threat didn't materialize, for the phaser cannons dropped obediently into position, even as their targeting sights locked onto the *Marquand.*

"In the name of all those whom you abused, Si Cwan . . . vengeance!" snarled Zoran as he triggered the firing command.

The phaser cannons let loose, both scoring direct hits, and the cries of triumph from the half-dozen Thallonians in the control room was deafening. Actually, only five of them cheered; Rojam pulled himself to sitting, rubbing the side of his head where Zoran had struck him. "This isn't necessary," he said again, but he might as well have been speaking to an empty room.

The shuttle craft was pounded by the phaser cannons, helpless before the onslaught. The Thallonians cheered every shot, overjoyed by Zoran's marksmanship. Even an annoyed Rojam had to admit that, for all his faults, Zoran was a good shot. Of course, having computers do all the work certainly helped.

"Hit them again!" crowed Dackow, the shortest and yet, when the mood suited him, loudest of the Thallonians. Dackow never voiced an opinion until he was absolutely positive about how a situation was going to go, at which point he supported the prevailing opinion with such forcefulness that it was easy to forget that he hadn't expressed a preference one way or the other until then. "You've got them cold, Zoran!"

Zoran fired again, this time missing the shuttle craft with one phaser cannon but striking it solidly with the other.

But as Zoran gleefully celebrated his marksmanship, Rojam commented dryly, "What happened to having Si Cwan's throat in your hands, enabling you to squeeze the life out of him?"

The observation brought Zoran up short for a moment. "If you had done your job better, I might have had that opportunity," he said, but it seemed a hollow comeback. The truth was that Rojam's statement had taken some of the joy out of Zoran's moment of triumph. Granted he had won, but it wasn't in the way he would have liked.

And then a flash consumed the screen as the shuttle craft erupted in a ball of flame. Automatically the Thallonians flinched, as if the explosion posed a threat to them. Within mere seconds the flame naturally burned itself out, having no air in the vacuum of space to feed it. The fragments of the vessel which had been the *Marquand* spun away harmlessly, the twisted scraps of duranium composites no longer recognizable as anything other than bits of metal.

"Burn in hell, Si Cwan," Zoran said after a long moment. The others, as always, nodded in agreement.

Only Rojam did not join in the self-congratulations. Instead he was busy checking the instrumentation on an adjoining console. "What are you doing?" asked Zoran after a moment.

"Scanning the debris," Rojam informed him.

"Why?" said Juif, making no effort to keep the sarcasm from his voice. "Are you concerned they still pose a threat?"

"Perhaps they do at that."

The pronouncement was greeted with contemptuous guffaws until Rojam added, "They weren't aboard the shuttle craft."

"What?" The comment immediately galvanized Zoran. "What are you talking about? Are you positive? It's impossible."

"It's not impossible, and they weren't there," Rojam said with growing confidence. "There's no sign of them among the debris. I wouldn't expect to find any bodies intact . . . not with the force of that explosion. But there should be *something* organic among the wreckage. I'm not detecting anything except pieces from the shuttle craft."

"Are you saying they were never aboard? That it was some sort of trick?" Zoran's anger was growing by the minute.

"That's a possibility, but I don't think so. If they were never at risk, then they went to a great deal of trouble to try and force our hand. But here is a thought: Some of those Federation shuttles come equipped with transporter pads."

"You think they may have evacuated before the ship blew up."

"Exactly."

"But the only place they could have gone to . . ." And then the growing realization brought a smile to his face. ". . . is here. Here, aboard the ship."

Rojam nodded.

Beaming with pleasure, Zoran clapped a hand on Rojam's back. "Excellent. Excellent work." Rojam let out a brief sigh of relief as Zoran turned to the others and said briskly, "All right, my friends. Somewhere in this vessel, Lord Si Cwan and his associate, Lieutenant Kebron, are hiding. Let's flush them out . . . and give our former prince the royal treatment he so richly deserves."

SELAR

III

Soleta glanced up from her science station as she became aware that McHenry was hovering over her. She glanced up at him, her eyebrows puckered in curiosity. "Yes?" she asked.

Glancing around the bridge in a great show of making certain that no one was paying attention to them, McHenry said to her in a lowered voice, "I just wanted to say thanks."

"You're welcome," replied Soleta reasonably, and tried to go back to her studies of mineral samples extracted from Thallon.

"Don't you want to know why?" he asked after a moment.

"Not particularly, Lieutenant. Your desire to say it is sufficient for me."

"I know I was 'spacing out' earlier, like I do sometimes, and I know that you were defending me. I just wanted to say I appreciate it."

"I was aware that your habits posed no threat to the *Excalibur*," she said reasonably. "I informed the captain and commander of that fact. Beyond that . . . what is there to say?"

"Why'd you leave, Soleta? Leave Starfleet, I mean."

The question caught her off guard. Now it was her turn to look around the bridge to make sure that no one was attempting to listen in.

She needn't have worried; eavesdropping was hardly a pastime in which Starfleet personnel habitually engaged. Still, she was surprised over how uncomfortable the question made her feel. "It doesn't matter. I came back."

"It does matter. We were friends, Soleta, back at the Academy. Classmates."

"Classmates, yes. I had no friends." She said it in such a matter-of-fact manner that there was no hint of self-pity in her tone.

"Oh, stop it. Of course you had friends. Worf, Kebron, me . . ."

"Mark, this really isn't necessary."

"I think it is."

"And I say it isn't!"

If they had been trying to make sure that their conversation did not draw any undue attention, the unexpected outburst by Soleta put an end to that plan. Everyone on the bridge looked at the two of them in unrestrained surprise, attention snagged by Soleta's unexpectedly passionate outburst. From the command chair, Calhoun asked, "Problem?"

"No, sir," said Soleta quickly, and McHenry echoed it.

"Are you certain?"

"Quite certain, yes."

"Because you seem to be having a rather strident dispute," he said, his gaze shifting suspiciously from one to the other.

"Mr. McHenry merely made a scientific observation, and I was disagreeing with it."

And now Shelby spoke up, observing, "It's rare one hears that sort of vehemence from anyone, much less a Vulcan."

"Lieutenant Soleta cares passionately about her work," McHenry said, not sounding particularly convincing.

"I see," said Calhoun, who didn't. "Mr. McHenry, time to Nelkar?"

"Twenty-seven minutes, sir," McHenry said without hesitation, as he turned away from Soleta and headed back to the conn.

Calhoun never failed to be impressed over how McHenry seemed to carry that knowledge in his head. Only Vulcans seemed nearly as capable of such rapid-fire calculations, and McHenry seemed even faster than the average Vulcan.

Which Soleta, for her part, did not seem to be. Her outburst had hardly been prompted by some sort of scientific disagreement. But Calhoun didn't feel it his place to probe too deeply into the reasons for it ... at least not as long as he felt that his ship's safety was not at issue.

If it did become an issue, though, he would not hesitate to question Soleta and find out just what exactly had caused her to raise her voice to McHenry despite her Vulcan upbringing.

"Vulcans," he muttered to himself.

Soleta turned in her chair and looked questioningly at Calhoun. "What about Vulcans, Captain?" she asked.

He stared at her tapered ears, which had naturally zeroed in on the mention of her race, and he said, "I was merely thinking how what we need on this ship is more Vulcans."

"Vulcans are always desirable, Captain," she readily agreed, and went back to her analyses.

The main lounge on the *Excalibur* was situated on Deck 7 in the rear of the saucer section, and was informally called the Team Room, after an old term left over from the early days of space exploration. It was to the Team Room that Burgoyne 172 had retired upon hish returning to the ship. S/he had felt a certain degree of frustration since s/he had not had the opportunity to complete hish work on the *Cambon*. If there was one thing that Burgoyne disliked, it was leaving a project unfinished.

And then s/he saw another potentially unfinished project enter the Team Room. Dr. Selar had just walked in and was looking around as if hoping to find someone. Burgoyne looked around as well and saw that all of the tables had at least one occupant. Then s/he looked back at Selar and saw an ever-so-brief look of annoyance cross the Vulcan's face. That there was any readable emotion at all displayed by the Vulcan was surprising enough, and then Burgoyne realized the problem. Selar wasn't looking for someone to sit with. She was trying to find an unoccupied table.

Her gaze surveyed the room and she caught sight of Burgoyne. Burgoyne, for hish part, endeavored to stay low-key. S/he gestured in a friendly, but not too aggressive manner, and waved at the empty seat opposite hir. Selar hesitated a moment and then, with what appeared to be a profound mental sigh, approached Burgoyne. Burgoyne could not help but admire her stride: she was tall, almost regal of bearing. When Selar sat down, she kept her entire upper body straight. Her posture was perfect, her attitude unflinching.

"I believe," Selar said in her careful, measured tone, "that our first encounter was not properly handled . . . by either of us."

"I think the fault was mostly mine," Burgoyne replied.

"As do I. You were, after all, the one who was rather aggressively propositioning me. Nonetheless, it would not be appropriate to place the blame entirely on you. Doubtlessly I was insufficiently clear in making clear to you my lack of interest."

"Well, now," Burgoyne shifted a bit in hish chair, "I wouldn't call it 'aggressively propositioning' exactly."

"No?" She raised a skeptical eyebrow.

Burgoyne leaned forward and said, "I would call it . . ." But then hish voice trailed off. S/he reconsidered hish next words and discarded them. Instead s/he said, "Can I get you a drink?"

"I am certain that whatever you are having will be more than sufficient."

Burgoyne nodded, rose, disappeared behind the bar, and returned a moment later with a glass containing the same dusky-colored liquid that was in hish glass. Selar lifted it, sniffed it experimentally, then downed half the glass. It was only her formidable Vulcan self-control that prevented her from coughing it back up through her nose. "This . . . is not synthehol," she said rather unnecessarily.

S/he shook hish head. "It's called 'Scotch.' Rather difficult to come by, actually."

"How did you develop a taste for it?"

"Well," said Burgoyne, and it was obvious from the way s/he was warming to the subject that s/he had discussed this topic a number of times in the past. "About two years ago, I was taking shore leave on Argelius Two . . . a charming world. Have you ever been there?" Selar shook her head slightly and Burgoyne continued, "I was at this one pub, and it was quite a lively place, I can tell you. It was a place where the women were so . . ."

Burgoyne was about to rhapsodize about them at length, but the look of quiet impatience on Selar's face quickly dissuaded hir. "In any event," continued Burgoyne, "I felt very much in my element. We Hermats are sometimes referred to as a rather hedonistic race. That's certainly a sweeping generalization, but not entirely without merit. In this pub, however, watching the Argelians and assorted visitors from other worlds engaging in assorted revelries and debaucheries, why . . . I felt that my humble leanings were dwarfed in comparison.

"And then my attention was drawn by one fellow seated over in a corner. A Terran, by the look of him, with hair silver as a crescent moon."

"You are attracted to him, no doubt," said Selar dryly.

"No, actually. He was a bit old for my tastes. But I was interested in him, for he seemed to be watching everything without any interest in participating. Furthermore he was wearing—believe it or not—a Starfleet uniform that hasn't been issued in years. A costume, I figured. I asked the bartender about him, and apparently he'd simply wandered in one day some weeks previously and just—I don't know—taken up residence there. He hardly ever left. So I went over and chatted with him. Asked him what he was doing there. He told me he was 'reliving old times,' as he put it. Remembering friends long gone, times left behind. He was reticent at first, but I got him talking. I have a knack for doing that."

"Indeed."

"Yes. And he seemed particularly intrigued when I told him I was an engineer. He claimed that he was as well. Claimed, in fact, that he wrote the book on engineering."

"A man with drinks in him will claim a great many things when he seeks the attention of a pretty face," observed Selar.

Burgoyne was about to continue when s/he paused a moment and, with a grin, said, "Are you saying you think I have a pretty face?"

"I am saying that, with sufficient intoxication, anyone may seem attractive," replied Selar. "You were saying—?"

"Yes, well . . . as I said, he boasted of a great many things. Sufficiently intoxicated, as you noted. Came up with the most insane boasts. Said he was over a hundred and fifty years old, that he served with Captain Kirk . . . all manner of absurd notions. And he also had no patience at all for—how did he put it—?" And Burgoyne made a passable attempt at imitating a Scots brogue as s/he growled, " 'The wretched brew what passes for a man's drink in this godforsaken century.' He was drinking this," and Burgoyne tapped the glass of brown liquid.

"That very drink?"

"Not this specific one, of course. It was two years ago, remember. But he seemed to have a somewhat endless supply of it. We seemed to communicate quite well with one another. At first, I believe, he took me for a standard-issue female, and he openly flirted with me. When I informed him of the Hermat race and our dual gender, at first he seemed amazed and then he just laughed and said," and again Burgoyne copied the brogue, " 'Ach, I would have loved to set up Captain Kirk with one of ye on a blind date. There would have been some tales to tell about that one.' " Burgoyne paused and then added, by way of explanation, "There are some who find our dual sex disturbing."

"Is that a fact," said Selar noncommittally.

"Yes." Burgoyne swirled hish drink around in the glass. "Tell me, Doctor . . . are you among them?"

"Not at all. I find *you* disturbing."

Burgoyne's smile displayed hish fangs. "I'll take that as a compliment," s/he said.

"As you wish."

"So anyway, the Terran offered me some of what he was drinking, and I tried it, and I swear to you I thought that it was going to peel the skin off the inside of my throat. I quickly realized that he was right: The stuff they've gotten us accustomed to in Starfleet is nothing compared to genuine Earth alcohol. Hell, even Hermat beverages pale in comparison to," and s/he rubbed the glass affectionately, "good ol' Scots whiskey. He told me if I had any intention of being a genuine engineer, that I should be able to drink him under the table. So I matched him drink for drink."

"And did you succeed? In drinking him under the table, I mean."

"Are you kidding?" Burgoyne laughed. "The last thing I remember was his smiling face turning at about a forty-five-degree angle . . . or at least that's what it seemed like before I hit the floor. But before that happened, I really let him have it."

" 'Have it'?"

"I told him that I thought he was being gutless. That he was sitting in this pub hiding from the rest of the galaxy, when he could be out accomplishing amazing things. That he might be telling himself that he was being nostalgic, but in fact he was just being gutless," and s/he tapped one long finger on the table three times to emphasize the last three words. Then s/he winced slightly and said, "At least I think that's what I told him. It got a little fuzzy there at the end. When I came to, I was in a back room at the pub with all sorts of debauchery and perversity going on all around me. Reminded me of home, actually. And I found that he'd left me something: a bottle of Scotch, and a message scribbled on the label of the bottle. And the message was exactly two words long: He'd written, 'You're right.' "

" 'You're right.' That was the message in its entirety."

"The whole thing, yes. Never saw him again, but I can only assume that he decided to get back out to where he belonged."

"And where would that be?"

"Damned if I know." Burgoyne leaned forward. "Do you understand what I'm saying to you, Doctor?"

"Oh. Well . . . not really, no. I had simply assumed that this was a long and fairly pointless narrative. Why? Is there something to this story beyond that?"

"What I'm saying, Selar, is that we shouldn't be afraid to try new things. We Hermats have our . . . unusual anatomical quirks. But—"

She put up a hand. "Lieutenant Commander . . ."

"An unwieldy title. I prefer Burgoyne from you."

"Very well. Commander Burgoyne . . . despite a valiant endeavor, this conversation is not proceeding in substantially different fashion than our previous one. I am not interested in you."

"Yes, you are. You simply don't know it yet."

"May I ask how you have come to this intriguing, albeit it entirely erroneous, conclusion?"

"All right . . . but only if you promise to keep it between us."

She pushed the drink of Scotch several inches away from her as she said, "I assure you, Chief Burgoyne . . . nothing will give me greater personal satisfaction than knowing that this conversation will go no further than this table."

S/he leaned forward conspiratorially and gestured that Selar should get closer to hir. With a soft sigh, Selar did as Burgoyne indicated, and the Hermat said in such a low voice that even the acute hearing of the Vulcan could barely hear hir:

"Pheromones," whispered Burgoyne.

"I beg your pardon?"

"Pheromones. Hermats can detect an elevated pheromone level in most races. It's a gift. It cues us to rising sexual interest and excitement."

"I see. And you're detecting an elevated pheromone level in me."

"That is precisely right," Burgoyne said with such confidence that even the unflappable Selar felt a bit disconcerted. "You're becoming sexually excited . . . more so when you're with me, I like to think, although that may simply be wishful thinking on my part. I have always been something of a romantic."

"Commander . . . I am certain that you are quite good at your job . . ."

"I am."

"But you are unfamiliar with Vulcan biology. It is . . ." And then she caught herself, surprise flooding through her mind. She had been about to discuss such delicate and personal matters as *Pon farr* with an offworlder. What was she thinking? Why was she having trouble prioritizing? ". . . it is impossible that I would be interested in you, in any event."

"Impossible why?"

"I cannot go into it."

Burgoyne leaned forward with a look of genuine curiosity on hish face. "Why can't you go into it?"

"I cannot," Selar said, her voice rising a bit more than she would have thought appropriate. The volume of her response didn't quite penetrate.

"Look, at the very least, I'd like to be your friend. If there's some problem that—"

And Selar was suddenly on her feet, and her response was a roar of fury. *"I said I cannot go into it! What part of 'cannot' did you not comprehend?!"*

The silence was instantaneous throughout the Team Room. Selar had managed, with no effort at all, to focus all attention in the room on herself. It was hardly a position that she desired to be in. Slowly her gaze surveyed the Team Room. Fighting to recapture her normal tone of voice, she asked, "May I assume you have something of greater importance on your minds than me?"

The crewmen needed no further urging to return to their respective conversations, although there were assorted quick glances in Selar's direction.

Automatically she put her hand to the underside of her throat. Her pulse was racing. The sounds of the room suddenly seemed magnified. Her temper had flared with Burgoyne, and although s/he might be one of the more irritating individuals that Selar had ever met, s/he was hardly enough to warrant the Vulcan tossing aside years of training and indulging in an emotional outburst.

"I have to go," she said, exerting her magnificent control over herself.

All flirtation, all smugness, was gone from Burgoyne. Instead s/he took Selar's hand firmly in hish own. Selar tried halfheartedly to pull clear, but Burgoyne's grip was surprisingly strong. Belatedly Selar remembered that Hermats had physical strength approximately two and a half times Earth norm. "Selar . . . if nothing else, we're fellow officers. If a fellow officer is in trouble, I'll do everything I can to alleviate that trouble. Whatever is wrong with you, I want to help."

"I do not need help. I merely need to be left alone. Thank you." And she exited as quickly as she could from the Team Room. This left everyone staring in confusion at Burgoyne. Burgoyne, for hish part, merely raised a glass. "May the Great Bird of the Galaxy roost on your planets," s/he said to the collective Team Room. S/he finished off the contents of hish glass and then, with a shrug, s/he reached over, picked up Selar's glass, and knocked that back, too.

Selar ran as quickly as she could down the *Excalibur* corridors. Twice she almost knocked over passing crewmen before she made it to sickbay. Upon seeing her return, Dr. Maxwell promptly proceeded to give her a quick precis on the status of the four dozen passengers from the *Cambon*. But before he could get out more than a sentence, she cut him off with a sharp gesture.

"Is there anything wrong, Doctor?" asked Maxwell, now clearly concerned about the condition of the chief medical officer. "Any problem that I can help with?"

"I am fine," she replied in a less-than-convincing manner.

"Are you sure? You seem rather flushed. Is there a—"

"Are you an expert on Vulcan physiology?" Selar demanded.

"No . . . no, not an expert per se, although I'm certainly well versed in—"

"Well, I am an expert, Doctor," she shot back. "I have been living inside my particular Vulcan physiology for quite some time now, and I assure you that I am in perfect health."

"With all due respect, Doctor, I don't know as I'd agree."

"With all due respect to *you*, Doctor, your agreement or lack thereof is of no relevance to me whatsoever." And with that she stalked quickly to her office, locking the door behind her to guarantee privacy.

She had no desire to subject herself to a medical scan in sickbay in full view of every one of her staff and technicians. She had no particular concern over the privacy of other crew members when it came to getting physicals or having problems attended to. But now that it was she herself who was in question, her right to privacy had assumed paramount importance. It was ironic, and yet an irony that she was not exactly in any condition to truly appreciate.

She opened an equipment compartment in the wall and extracted a medical tricorder. Adjusting it for herself, she began to take readings.

Pulse, heartbeat, respiration . . . everything was elevated. Moreover, she was having trouble focusing on anything.

Selar reached deep into herself. A calm, cool center of logic was drilled into Vulcans at such an early age that it became utterly ingrained into their nature. Yet Selar was having to relive that training, finding that cool center and tapping into it. Her body, her system, was entirely at the command of her mind and she would force it to obey her commands. Slowly she quieted her hurried breathing. She cleared away every noise, every distraction, until she could hear the accelerated beating of her own heart. She slowed it, bit by bit, replacing the dim red haze which seemed to have taken hold of her with a sedate, serene blue.

She thought back to her first days at the Academy, the first time that she had encountered the Academy pool. Such things were virtually unknown on Vulcan, an arid planet with a steady red sky and a sun so searing that Vulcans had even developed an inner eyelid to shield themselves against its effects. The pool might well have been an alien artifact; indeed, in many ways it was to her.

Clad in a bathing suit, she had stood on the edge of the pool, dipping a toe into it, unsure of what to do. Every logical bone in her body had told her that there was nothing to fear. That fear was besides the point, as it so often was. And yet she could not bring herself to ease herself into the water . . . until the decision had been taken out of her hands when a passing cadet named Finnegan had thought it the height of hilarity to shove her from behind into the pool. She had fallen feet-first into the deep end of the pool . . . and proceeded to drown, since naturally people who are born on a desert planet have absolutely no idea how to swim. The selfsame Finnegan, chagrined, had immediately leaped into the water and pulled out the sputtering Vulcan.

But Selar had taken that first unpleasant experience as a challenge, and every day found her at the pool until she was as good a swimmer as anyone at the Academy. Many was the time where she would simply float in the water, arms outstretched, bobbing with the gentle lapping of the water.

Now she was projecting herself back to that time. She imagined herself floating, floating ever so gently, buoyed as if by lapping waves. Bit by bit, she fashioned her recollections of the Academy pool into a place of escape. The rest of the world, her worries, her concerns, her uncharacteristic confusion, all melted away as she bobbed in the water with no distractions. She felt her composure returning to her, her ineffable logic controlling her actions once more. Whatever was happening to her, it was nothing that she couldn't control. Nothing that . . .

"Hi," said a voice. And there, swimming past her in a tight bathing suit that accentuated hish firm breasts, hish curvaceous hips, and also what seemed an impressive male endowment, was Burgoyne.

Selar snapped forward in her chair, the pool vanishing along with the Hermat intruder. She looked around and found herself, of course, still in her office. A quick scan with the medical tricorder told her that her bioreadings were back to normal. But the image of Burgoyne was solidly rooted in her mind.

She leaned forward toward her computer terminal and said, "Computer."

"Working."

"Personal medical log, Stardate 50926.2 . . ."

There was a pause, sufficiently long enough for the computer to prompt, "Waiting for entry."

Selar could only think of one thing to say, really. Five words that summarized her present situation with simple eloquence.

"I am in big trouble," she said.

KEBRON

IV

"How much trouble would you say we're in, precisely?" Si Cwan asked in a low, tense voice.

"A good deal," replied Zak Kebron.

Between them they had precisely one phaser, the sidearm that Kebron habitually carried whenever embarking on any sort of mission. They'd had no time to grab anything else off the shuttle before the unfortunate ship had blown up.

The science vessel was not terribly large—only eight decks deep—and it was one of the oldest models of such ships. Stairs or ladders between decks instead of turbolifts, and flooring made of grated metal that made a hellacious racket whenever Kebron, in particular, walked on it. Moreover the lighting was dim. Whether it was because they were on battery backup, or had deliberately made it that way just to throw off Kebron and Si Cwan, was impossible to say.

They hunched in a corner as best they could, considering Si Cwan's height and that Kebron wasn't exactly built for hunching. "This is insane," muttered Si Cwan. "Why did they shoot at us?"

"When you're trying to kill someone, that's usually a reliable method."

"But why were they trying to kill us?"

"Immaterial. The fact of it is all we need to deal with." From the shadows that surrounded them, he was surveying the area as thoroughly as he could.

"We need a plan," Si Cwan said urgently.

Kebron appeared to consider it a moment, and then he said simply, "Survival."

"That's *obvious*. Are you being deliberately obtuse, Kebron? Our lives are at stake . . ."

Kebron glared at him, and there was extreme danger in those eyes, glittering against the dusky brown skin. *"Our* lives are at stake because *you* insisted on trying to rescue your sister. Do not forget that."

"Of course not. Now that we've properly assigned the blame, can we deal with the problem at hand?" Si Cwan waited, but the only response he got was a grunt. Taking that to be a "yes," he considered the situation a moment and then said, "I say we should split up."

"And I say you're a fool," replied Kebron.

"Why? We're less of a target that way."

Kebron scowled at him. "Look at me. Look at you. Look at our size and build. Singly or together, we're targets. Individually, neither of us can watch each other's backs."

"As if you'd watch my back," Si Cwan snorted disdainfully. "Good luck to you, Kebron. I'll take my chances." He started to move out of the shadows, and suddenly he felt Kebron's powerful hand clamp on his shoulder. Before he could utter so much as a word of protest, Kebron had hauled him back and slammed him into the wall behind them. It shuddered slightly with the impact.

"You're not a prince here, Cwan," Kebron said tightly. "You're not a lord. You will do what I say, when I say it, or so help me I'll crush your head with my bare hands and save whoever's out to get us the trouble. Do we understand each other?"

There were a hundred responses that Si Cwan wanted to make, but he choked them all down . . . which wasn't especially difficult, since he was choking from the grip that Kebron had on him. So all he managed to get out was a very hoarse whisper of, "Perfectly."

Kebron released him and Si Cwan rubbed the base of his throat as he glared at Kebron. "You're supposed to be on *my* side?"

Zak Kebron didn't bother to dignify the question with an answer.

Instead he was listening. "Here they come," he said slowly, his voice dropping to nearly a whisper.

Si Cwan was listening as well. "Two of them. Do you think that's all there are?"

"Safer to assume it's not," observed Kebron, and this was a sentiment that Si Cwan couldn't disagree with.

Kebron pointed silently upward, indicating that he was hearing them from overhead. Si Cwan nodded, and then he looked behind them. Ten feet to the rear was a stairway angling to the upper floor, with spaces between the steps. Cwan chucked a thumb in the direction of the stairs, and Kebron immediately intuited what Si Cwan had in mind. They dropped back and tried to duck behind the stairs, but the space was too narrow for the both of them to fit. Kebron pointed a finger at Si Cwan and said, "Decoy."

Being a decoy was not exactly Si Cwan's first choice of responsibilities, but there was no time to argue the point. Besides, there was something in the challenging way that Kebron looked at him that angered him. As if Kebron was certain that Si Cwan would never present danger to himself and trust Kebron to bail him out of it.

Si Cwan took up a station directly in front of the stairs, standing about five feet back. Kebron took up a position behind the stairs. There was clattering from overhead and then two pairs of feet descended the stairs. Cwan gasped when he saw that they were two Thallonians. They slowed as they came within view of Si Cwan. Each of them was cradling a strange-looking weapon that Si Cwan didn't recognize at first, but then he did. They were plasma blasters, and there were few weapons in existence that were nastier.

The two of them stopped several steps above the floor. "Where's the other one, Si Cwan?" demanded one of the Thallonians. "The one with the voice like rumbling thunder."

"He died during the first bombardment of your ambush," replied Si Cwan. "He didn't make it off the ship."

"Now, why don't I believe you?" asked one of the Thallonians. "Are you trying to deceive us, Si Cwan?"

"Where is my sister? Who are you?" he demanded.

They hadn't budged from their place on the stairs. "You are in no position to ask quest—" one of them started to say.

"Where is my sister, and who are you?" There was a dark, fear-

some tone to his voice, and the Thallonians found themselves shuddering to hear it. Once upon a time, to hear such a tone would be tantamount to a death sentence. Even though the unarmed Si Cwan was staring down the barrels of weapons aimed squarely at him from point-blank distance, it seemed as if he was the one who was in charge.

"My name is Skarm," one of them finally said, and he indicated the Thallonian standing next to him with a nod of his head. "And this is Atol. It is only fitting, I imagine, that you know the name of the ones who are about to kill you. As for your sister," and Skarm smiled lop-sidedly, "that's for us to know."

He touched a small button on the side of the plasma blaster and took a step down. He aimed it squarely at Si Cwan, and the former prince merely stood there, dark eyes sparkling with cold fury.

And Zak Kebron's hands snaked out from underneath the steps, grabbing Skarm's ankles. Skarm, confused as to what was happening, let out an alarmed yelp, his arms pinwheeling as he tried to halt his forward plummet. He didn't succeed and he crashed forward, even as the one called Atol frantically tried to figure out what had just happened.

The blaster tumbled out of Skarm's hand and clattered to the floor. Si Cwan lunged for it and Atol immediately fired off a shot from his own blaster. It was like having a weapon that fired molten lava. The plasma blast stream blew directly in front of Si Cwan, and only Cwan's speed saved him as he ducked backward. The stream hit the fallen weapon, immediately rupturing the cartridge that contained the plasma field.

Si Cwan had a split second to react, and he did the only thing he could think to do. He leaped straight up, fingers desperately grabbing the grillework of the rampway directly above him, and he swung his body upward just as the crippled gun exploded. A stream of flame ripped right beneath him, and he could feel the back of his jacket catch on fire. Instantly he shucked the jacket, allowing it to drop into the flames beneath him, and he felt them licking at him hungrily.

Atol was blistered by the heat, but even so he tried to look down beneath the steps. He had only a split-second warning as he saw the terrible eyes of Zak Kebron, and then Kebron—disdaining the subtle approach—smashed upward, tearing the stairs out of their moorings and sending Atol pitching forward into the flames of the burning plasma.

Skarm rolled off the steps as Kebron shoved them upward, and it was clear from the lolling of his head that he was already dead. When he'd fallen, he'd snapped his neck.

Atol let out a truncated shriek as the flame consumed him. It had all happened within the space of a few seconds, and then the ship's automatic firefighting defenses kicked in. High-powered spray hissed out from hidden pipes lining the sides of the corridor, battling the flames and quickly extinguishing them.

Si Cwan dropped to the ground, landing in a crouch. Kebron tossed aside the twisted remains of the stairs as Cwan went immediately to the fallen Atol. Atol's body was a mass of burns: the plasma had done its work quickly, efficiently, and horribly. Clearly he was done for, but Si Cwan was not inclined to let him depart quite that easily. He grabbed Atol by the side of the head, yanking him upward. This did him no good, as the skin he was gripping peeled off in his hand, no more than a large, blackened, and charred fistful of flesh. With a grunt of disgust, Si Cwan tossed it aside and elected instead to snarl into Atol's face, "Where is my sister? Is she on this vessel? Who's behind this? If you have any hope of greeting your ancestors with a shred of integrity—the ancestors who swore fealty to my bloodline before the birth of your father's father's father—then answer my questions *now!*"

Atol's mouth moved, but no word emerged. However, Si Cwan could still make out what Atol was saying, even without sound. A two-syllable name that he'd hoped not to hear ever again. "Zoran?" he said with dread.

Atol managed, just barely, to nod, and then his body began to tremble. "Go to your ancestors," Si Cwan told him, and as if obeying a final order from his former liege, Atol's head shook—although whether in compliance or from final spasms, it was impossible to tell. And then his eyes rolled up into the top of his head.

Kebron stood over the two fallen Thallonians, looking at his handiwork. His phaser was still snugly in its holster, untouched. "I was under the impression," Si Cwan said, "that Starfleet security officers usually give people the option of surrendering."

The Brikar appeared to consider that a moment as he nudged Skarm's body with the toe of his boot. Then he replied, "Ugly rumors." He paused, and then asked, "Who is Zoran?"

"A very unusual man. He's someone who wants to kill me."

Kebron looked at him and, with the famed Brikar deadpan, said, "I hope you don't think that wanting to kill you makes him unusual."

Si Cwan grunted in a tone that almost indicated morbid amusement, and then he stepped past Kebron. Cwan was a natural leader, and his tendency was to take the point, to be in the forefront, during any situation.

This time it almost cost him his life.

Kebron only noticed at the last second that a shadow was separating from other shadows farther down the hallway. The two had been accompanied by a third, and he'd come down and around while the first two were engaging them by the stairway. Zak only had a moment to react. With a sweep of his massive arm he knocked Si Cwan to the floor, yanking his phaser clear and firing . . .

. . . not in time. The assailant at the far end of the hallway saw the phaser being brought to bear on him, and he dodged under the beam even as he fired off a shot with the plasma blaster. The blaster struck Kebron in the upper right shoulder, and the Brikar let out a pained grunt, which was the most he would do to acknowledge pain. With any other species, the plasma would have torn off the shoulder right down to the bone. The Brikar's hide was considerably tougher than that. Even so, the Brikar was clearly in pain, the plasma sizzling on his shoulder and the ghastly smell of burning flesh filling the air.

He dropped his phaser, and Si Cwan snatched it out of midair. He caught it, aimed, and fired in one smooth motion, and the phaser blasted the Thallonian assailant back. He smashed against the far wall, the plasma blaster spinning out of his hand, falling to his side. Clutching his chest, the Thallonian tried to lunge for the blaster, but then he saw that Si Cwan was targeting him again, and he leaped away in the other direction, disappearing down a cross corridor before Si Cwan could nail him with a phaser shot. Si Cwan charged after him, not even stopping to check on the condition of the fallen Brikar. His focus was entirely on catching up with this latest assailant and finding out whether or not Kalinda was anywhere on the ship. Even if he had to beat it out of him, he was going to find out.

He rounded the corner, not even stopping to pick up the plasma blaster, because he was in such a hurry to catch up with the Thallonian.

There was no sign of him, and Si Cwan moved around another corner and started down another corridor.

He never even saw the iron bar that lashed out. But he felt it as it slammed into the arm that was holding the phaser. To his credit he held on to it and he tried to bring it up to bear on his attacker, but another swing of the bar crunched his fingers and knocked the phaser out of his hand.

"Afraid to face me man-to-man, O great lord?" taunted the Thallonian. The bar he was holding was about three feet long, and he was gripping it firmly at the base.

"I know you. Dackow, isn't it," Si Cwan said slowly. One of his hands was throbbing, but the other was functioning just fine, and his fingers curled around the floor grating beneath him. He felt a bit of give in the flooring, and realized that it wasn't one solid piece, but instead fitted in sections, the edges of the crisscrossed metal fitting neatly into slots in the base of the hallway flooring.

Dackow paused, surprised. "I'm impressed that such a great man as yourself would remember a humble nothing such as me."

"It's difficult to forget someone quite as sycophantic as you. As I recall, you preferred to hover around the fringes of the great court, laughing at the right times when the right people spoke, scowling when others fell out of favor. And when the tide turned against my family, you were one of the first to switch to the side of those who wanted us out. You bend with the wind, Dackow, and doubtlessly congratulate yourself over your foresight, when the fact is that you're just a coward. A coward through and through."

With a roar of fury, Dackow drew the bar back over his head and swung it down in a fierce arc. Had it landed, it would have caved in Si Cwan's skull.

With a quick twist, Si Cwan ripped the metal flooring out from under himself and held it up as a shield. The bar crashed into the grating, the reverberation of the metal almost deafening. Dackow switched angles and tried to strike Si Cwan across the ribs. Again, no good. Si Cwan intercepted it, down on one knee. Again and again, fury building with every stroke, Dackow tried to slam his bar into the Thallonian prince. Left, right, up and down, and every time Si Cwan blocked it.

Dackow, with a roar of rage, reversed his grip on the bar and tried to drive it downward as if staking a vampire. Si Cwan backrolled, putting a short distance between himself and Dackow, and then he threw the flooring as if it were a discus. Dackow saw it coming, but there was no room in the narrow corridor to get out of the way. The grating lanced into him with tremendous force, the edges driving into his solar plexus. Dackow howled in pain and Si Cwan was on his feet, his powerful legs thrusting him forward, his hands outstretched. He caught the edges of the grating and shoved as hard as he could. The force of the lunge drove the edging of the grating right into Dackow, penetrating half a foot, and the charge lifted Dackow off his feet. His back crashed into the wall and there was an audible snap . . . the sound of his spine breaking, as if being impaled wasn't enough.

Blood poured from his mouth as Si Cwan stepped back, releasing his grip on the grating and allowing Dackow to fall to the ground. "Where is Kalinda? Where is my sister?" demanded Si Cwan.

Dackow gathered some of the blood that was pouring from his mouth, and managed to transform it into a contemptuous spit which he hurled at Si Cwan. It was the last thing he would ever do.

There was a heavy step behind Si Cwan and he whirled, his arms in a defensive position, but it was only Kebron standing behind him. The Brikar was massaging his damaged shoulder as he said, *"First* question . . . *then* kill. More productive."

"I'll try to keep that in mind," shot back Si Cwan. He stood, feeling momentarily shaky. The wear and tear of the running fight was beginning to take its toll. "How many more do you think there are?"

"I have no idea," replied Kebron. "That's what bothers me." He picked up the fallen phaser, returned it to its holster. He was cradling one of the plasma blasters and pointed out the other one, which had fallen. "Grab it and let's go."

Earlier, Si Cwan might have been annoyed at the commanding tone of Kebron's voice. But now he simply nodded and picked up the fallen plasma blaster. "I don't generally like weapons," he commented. "They can malfunction or be taken from you."

"Really. I'm the same way. Use them if I have to, though." He pointed with authority. "That way."

"Why that way?"

"Why not?"

Having no ready answer, Si Cwan shrugged and they headed off in the direction that Kebron had indicated. But then they heard a small, high-pitched sound from behind them. They stopped, turned . . .

. . . and realized that Dackow was beeping.

In the control center, Zoran was staring at Rojam in disbelief. "You can't raise *any* of them?"

Rojam shook his head. "I've lost contact with all three of them. They're not responding on the comm links at all."

"Three armed Thallonian ravagers against a single Starfleet fool and an effete snob," snarled Zoran. "How is it possible?"

And Rojam lost patience with Zoran, which was a very dangerous thing for him to do, but he no longer cared. "Because Starfleet is not composed of fools, Zoran, and because Si Cwan—for all that you dislike him, for all that any of us dislikes him—is anything but an effete snob. He's as formidable a warrior as they come, and you'd do well to remember that."

"I would do well to remember that? I would do well? And you would do well," snarled Zoran, his hands flexing in fury, "would do well to remember—"

He didn't have the chance to finish the sentence, however, because the comm panel beeped. Rojam punched the link-up, noting the identifier assigned to it, and said, "Dackow? Progress?"

There was a pause, and then a familiar voice said, "Dackow isn't making much progress at the moment." They could hear a soft chuckle, and then: "Hello, Zoran."

Low and angry, Zoran snarled, "Si Cwan."

"It has been a long time, hasn't it."

"I'll kill you for this."

"For this and for every other imagined insult." He'd sounded amused, but then he became deadly serious. "Where is Kalinda, Zoran? She has done nothing to you. And you are nothing but a sadistic pig." His tone became mocking. "I would have thought you'd release her so that this could be between us, Zoran. Between men, without the threat of a girl's welfare overshadowing it. You always held yourself up to such a 'high' standard. Always thought yourself so much better than I. And this is how low you have fallen, consumed by your jealousy and anger. Posturing and presenting yourself as some superior individual, when you don't have the courage to—"

"She's dead, you idiot!"

Rojam turned and looked in shocked disbelief at Zoran, and for once Zoran couldn't blame him. The phantom of Kalinda had been an upper hand that they would have been able to wield against Si Cwan. Perhaps force him into some situation where he couldn't possibly get away. But he had now tossed that aside.

Zoran turned away and Rojam suspended the transmission, crossing quickly over to Zoran. "Why did you do that? Why?" he demanded.

Zoran whirled to face him and hissed, "Because I want to hurt him. I want him to die inside first. You heard him! Heard his insults, his smugness—"

"He was baiting you and you fell for it! We had an advantage! We could have made demands on him! Instead you've removed that!"

"We have an advantage! We're armed! There's more of us! There's—"

But now Juif stepped forward and pointed out, "They're likely armed, too. We have to assume they took weapons off the others. They're roaming the ship, and they're very much in a position to hurt us."

Zoran, with apparent effort, focused on Juif. "What are you saying?"

"I'm saying we cut our losses, abandon the vessel, and blow it up from a safe distance."

"And let him get away?"

"We were never supposed to capture him! He was never part of the plan!" Juif said. "You've lost sight of that! You've lost sight of everything because Si Cwan wandered into the middle of all this, and suddenly your priorities changed! Well, my priorities are to get out of this insanity in one piece! And if that isn't yours, then there's something wrong with you."

"Wrong with me?"

"Yes!"

A calm seemed to descend upon Zoran, and truthfully the calm was more frightening than the anger. "Ten minutes," he said.

Rojam and Juif looked at each other. "What?" asked Rojam.

"Ten minutes. I want ten minutes to hunt the bastard down. If I don't have his head in ten minutes, we do as you suggest. How say you?"

The truth was that neither of them was especially enthused with the plan. But they saw the cold look in his eyes and realized that this was the best they were going to get. Slowly, and reluctantly, they nodded in agreement.

"Rojam," said Zoran, sounding almost supernaturally calm, "set a bomb for fifteen minutes. That will allow me the ten minutes to which we've agreed, and another five to get to our vessel and clear the area. More than enough."

More than enough for someone with a death wish... Rojam thought, but he didn't dare say it aloud. He had the feeling that he'd already gotten away with saying more than he would have thought possible.

"She's dead, you idiot!"
The words lanced through Si Cwan's heart, chilled his soul. He didn't even realize that he was wavering slightly until he felt Kebron's hand on his arm, steadying him. His red face became dark crimson, as it was wont to do when he was truly upset. He was gripping the comm unit they'd lifted off the fallen Thallonian, gripping it so tightly that he was on the verge of breaking it.

"Si Cwan... calm down," Kebron said forcefully. "I need you calm. They're trying to make you angry. Anger will put you at risk. At the very least, it will make you less useful to me."

It was impossible to tell whether Si Cwan heard him or not. He snarled into the comm unit, "You're lying! *You're lying!*"

There was no response and he shook the comm unit furiously until Kebron forcibly pried it out of his hands, even as he said, "You're wasting your time. He's not responding."

Si Cwan spun to face the Brikar, and there was murder in his eyes. Kebron had felt mostly disdain for Si Cwan since they'd met. Disdain, annoyance, anger. Never, however, had he felt the least bit intimidated. The Brikar, with their massive build and the confidence that came from having as sturdy hide as they did, tended to make them rather hard to scare. When Kebron looked into Si Cwan's eyes at that moment, however, he was not exactly scared. But he knew beyond any question that he would most definitely not want to be this Zoran individual.

"We're going to find him," Si Cwan said tightly. "We're going to find him and when I kill him, Kebron, understand: I cannot use this," and he indicated the plasma blaster. "He must die with my hands on his throat. No other means will be acceptable."

"There are alternatives to killing him," Kebron told him.

The temperature in the corridor dropped about twenty degrees from the chill of Cwan's voice alone. "No. There are not."

And suddenly the comm unit beeped. Kebron tapped it and they heard Zoran's voice say, "Hello, Si Cwan. I assume you can hear me."

Si Cwan was about to snap out a harsh response, but Kebron put a finger to his lips. At first Cwan was confused, but then he realized the wisdom in this course. Conversation with Zoran would only cause Si Cwan to become angrier, more inclined to lose his temper, and that would simply give Zoran even more confidence. Cwan had to forcibly bite down on his lower lip, and several drops of blackish blood dripped out.

"Si Cwan," Zoran was saying slowly, "you were so easy to fool. All I had to do was reprogram the computer to synthesize her voice. Only took thirty seconds. Thirty seconds to get your hopes up." His voice dropped. It sounded like an obscene purr. "She died crying your name, Si Cwan. Over and over, she called for you. I won't tell you how she died. I won't tell you what was done to her, or how long it took, or any details at all. Do you know why? Because you'll envision every worst-case possibility. I wouldn't want to take the chance of the truth being less severe than whatever you might conjure up in your imagination."

Si Cwan was visibly trembling. It was all he could do to contain himself.

"I'm looking for you, Si Cwan," came Zoran's taunting voice. "Come and find me . . . if you can." And he shut off the comm link.

"Si Cwan . . . Get a grip." Kebron saw that Si Cwan was inarticulate with fury, and he gripped him firmly by the shoulders.

His voice was a strangled whisper. "I'll kill him . . ."

"If I were you, I would, too. No question. But right now, in your state of mind, he'll kill you first. Again, no question. You're giving him exactly what he wants: a target who's out of control." But Si Cwan wasn't hearing him. He was completely internalized, muttering to himself, not at all relating to their environment. His head was filled with the imagined dying screams of his sister. Kebron shook him and said, "Cwan, I know how you feel."

With effort, Si Cwan focused on him. "No, you don't . . . you can't . . ."

"Oh yes I can," Kebron shot back. "My parents, on a mining colony . . . killed by Orion pirates who stripped the colony, looking for anything they could steal. They worked to send me to the Academy, and while I was there, their dedication was repaid with murder. And when I heard, I took leave from the Academy and tracked the pirates down. And you know what? I almost got killed. When Starfleet reps caught up with me, I was near death. I was in the hospital for two months while they put me back together. I never caught up again with the ones who destroyed my family, and I was lucky to survive the encounter, all because I was blinded by rage, just like you are now. Now snap out of it."

It was the longest speech Si Cwan could ever recall Kebron making. For that matter, it was the longest speech Kebron himself could recall making. And he had to keep on speaking quickly, while he had Si Cwan's attention. "This Zoran . . . tell me all about him. Tell me what to expect."

"Zoran . . ." Si Cwan took a deep breath. "Zoran . . . he'll probably have company, besides the ones we already disposed of. One named Rojam, the other named Juif. They're a trio."

"How do you know?"

"Because," Si Cwan said coldly, "we used to be a quartet." He paused a heartbeat. "Have you ever had to kill your best friend? Is that in our mutually shared experience as well?"

"No," admitted Kebron.

"Well . . . good," and Si Cwan gripped Zak Kebron by the elbow. "Come along, then. I'll show you how it's done."

V

"Isn't it amazing?" murmured Calhoun, as the planet Nelkar rotated below them. He gazed at it upon the screen. "One planet looks so much like another when you're up here. Sometimes you want to take planet-bound races who are at war with each other, bring them up here, show them their world. Make them realize that it's one world that they should all be sharing, rather than fighting over it."

From her position next to him on the bridge, Shelby asked, "And if someone had done that for young . . ." She hesitated over the pronunciation, as she always did, gargling it slightly, "M'k'n'zy of Calhoun . . . would he have stopped fighting?"

"No," he said with amused admission. He thought of the short sword mounted on the wall of his ready room. "Mr. Boyajian," he said in a slightly louder voice, deliberately changing subjects, "have you raised the planet's surface yet?"

"Not yet, sir. As of this point, I'm . . . Wait. Receiving transmission now."

"On screen."

The screen wavered ever so slightly, and then a male Nelkarite appeared. He had much the same angelic look as Laheera did . . . that same "too good to be true" appearance that Calhoun had felt so annoying when they'd first encountered the Nelkarites.

"Greetings," he said in a musical voice evocative of Laheera's. "I am Celter, governor of the capital city of Selinium. Welcome to Nelkar."

"Mackenzie Calhoun, captain of the *Excalibur*. Laheera informed us that you were willing to provide sanctuary for the passengers we have aboard."

"That is so. And she informed us," and clear amusement tinged his features, "that you did not trust us."

"It is my duty to be judicious when making first contacts," Calhoun said reasonably. "I would be remiss if I did not have at least some concerns with depositing four dozen people on an alien world."

"I remind you, Captain, that *you* are the aliens here. If anyone has the right to be concerned, it is we. Yet we welcome you, trust you. We would like to think that we should be accorded, at the very least, similar consideration."

"Point taken," said Calhoun. "Nonetheless, if it is all the same to you, we will send an escort down with our passengers. I'd prefer a firsthand report of the environment where we're dropping them off."

"As you wish, Captain," said Celter with polite indifference. "We have nothing to hide. We are merely doing our best to be altruistic. These are, after all, unusual times."

"All times are unusual, Governor. Some are just more unusual than others. Please send us the coordinates for an away team, and we will prepare your new residents for landfall. Calhoun out." The screen blinked off before Celter could say anything else.

And then, before Calhoun could give any order, make any pronouncement, Shelby said crisply, "Captain, request permission to head the away team, sir."

The request stopped Calhoun in midthought, and he turned to Shelby. One look into those deep purple eyes of his, and Shelby instantly knew that her surmise had been correct: Calhoun had intended to lead the away team himself, despite Starfleet's policies to the contrary. Had he voiced the composition of the away team before she'd said anything, she would have had to try and talk him into changing his mind after already speaking it. She had no desire to get into a contest of wills with him; by the same token, she had every intention of fulfilling her obligations as first officer of the *Excalibur*. And one of those obligations was to spearhead away teams so that the captain could remain safe within the confines of the bridge.

All this was conveyed by a silent look passing between the two. It was so subtle, so understated, that it went past everyone else on the bridge. Calhoun knew Shelby's mind, and she knew his. He knew precisely why she had jumped in, and he didn't seem particularly appreciative of it. By the same token, he was also aware that she was trying to be respectful of his position and feelings. She had volunteered in such a way that her presence on the away team could now come across as a snap command decision by Calhoun, rather than a point of order over which the two of them would have to argue.

Slowly he said, "Very well. Commander Shelby, you'll take an away team composed of yourself, Lieutenant Lefler, and Security Officer Meyer."

Robin Lefler looked up from her station. "Me, sir?"

"I want an assessment on their level of technology. Your engineering background makes you the appropriate choice. Plus you finished in the top three percentile of your class in First Contact Procedures at the Academy."

She blinked in surprise, clearly impressed by her captain's apparent command over the minutiae of her academic career. Even she didn't remember exactly where she'd ranked in that one particular class. "Uhm . . . yes, sir." She rose from her station, and Boyajian, a solid "utility player" on the bridge, stepped in to take her place. She headed out at Shelby's side.

"Captain," McHenry said the moment they were gone, "how did you know that Lefler scored so high in the F.C. Pro class?"

Calhoun smiled. "I didn't. But who's going to deny doing well in a class?"

"Captain."

He turned to face Soleta, who had just spoken. "Yes, Lieutenant?"

"Dr. Selar would like me to come down to sickbay."

"Are you ill, Lieutenant?"

"Not to my knowledge, sir. I'm not entirely certain why she wants to see me. She just now contacted me privately over my comm badge. I assume it is some sort of personal matter. Permission to leave the bridge?"

Calhoun considered it a moment, wondering whether he should go directly to Selar and ask after her. But something told him to keep a distance from the situation. "You're asking my permission for something as simple as leaving the bridge?"

"Regulations state, sir, that during a time of contact or in the midst of a mission, all hands are to remain on station and must request permission for any reason if—"

"I know the regs, Lieutenant, but the person who wrote them isn't here. You're a big girl, Soleta. Just tell me you're going and don't drop your comm badge down the commode or something so I can't reach you."

"Sir, leaving the bridge."

"Have a nice trip."

She headed into the turbolift and Calhoun sighed inwardly. What was going to be next? Shouting "Captain on the bridge!" whenever he set foot into the place? Part of him appreciated the endeavors to have respect for proper procedures. By the same token, he had seen people follow procedures so rigidly that others had died because of it. Died needlessly.

An inner voice warned him not to dwell on it excessively, for that way lay madness. And so he turned his attention back to the planet that was spinning below them.

He felt the hair on the back of his neck rising.

He didn't like the feel of this one bit.

The *Excalibur* didn't have the facilities to beam all four dozen passengers from the *Cambon* down at one time. So they were sent down in groups of six, with Shelby, Lefler, and Meyer in the first group. Meyer was slim but wiry, and he had piercing blue eyes that seemed to take in everything that was happening around them. He also had the fastest quick-draw on the ship.

Lefler immediately began studying the architecture of Selinium, as well as recording her observations on her tricorder. They had materialized in what appeared to be a main square of the city. They were standing on an upper walkway, constructed above roadways upon which traffic was moving at a brisk clip. Lefler noticed that the vehicles were strictly low-tech, moving on wheels rather than any sort of antigrav or mag-lev basis.

The city towered all around them. However, it was not a particularly large place, which was unusual considering it had been mentioned as the capital. In point of fact, the initial scans of Selinium didn't seem to indicate more than a hundred thousand people residing there, which was—relatively speaking—puny.

Still, there was something about the buildings that seemed . . . off a bit. Lefler promptly began scanning them. She was so involved in it that she didn't even see the welcome party approach the away team, and didn't look up until she heard Shelby say, "Hello. I'm Commander Shelby, *U.S.S. Excalibur.* Captain Laheera, as I recall."

Laheera, flanked by several other officials, bobbed her head in acknowledgment. " 'Captain' would be more your term than ours. The more accurate equivalent would a term along the lines of 'First Among Equals.' But 'Captain' will suffice, if you are comfortable with that."

Lefler was struck by the fact that Laheera was relatively short. Indeed, of the group of them, none of them was much above five feet tall. And yet there was something about them, some sort of inner light that made them appear—it was hard to say—bigger than they actually were. Bigger, more impressive . . . *some*thing.

Certainly her clothing did not leave much to the imagination. As opposed to the more "official" look of the outfit she'd worn when they first saw her, Laheera was now dressed completely in clinging white: a tight white top with a hem just below her hip, and white leggings under them. The cloth adhered so closely to the line of her figure that Shelby had to look twice to ascertain whether it was, in fact, body paint. It wasn't, but it certainly could have been.

Shelby made quick introductions, and then found that Captain Hufmin of the *Cambon* was hovering nearby. He had been one of the first to come down, concerned with making sure that his charges were being properly attended to. Although Shelby could tell, from the slightly panting way that he was looking at Laheera, that there had been more to Hufmin's cooperative attitude than merely wishing to honor the desires of his passengers. He was clearly taken by the indisputable beauty of their hosts. And considering Laheera's current ensemble, his interest was on the rise. Laheera could likely have asked him to stick a phaser in his mouth and pull the trigger, and he would gratefully have complied, with his last words being profound thanks for the honor of serving her.

Lefler, meantime, turned her attention back to her duties while the introductions were being made. Shelby sidled up to her as Laheera, along with her associates, moved beyond them to meet and greet the rest of the refugees, who were continuing to beam down.

"Opinions, Lieutenant?" asked Shelby.

"Commander . . . you're familiar with the Borg, as I recall."

"A bit," Shelby said dryly.

"Well . . . this place reminds me of them a little bit, in that the Borg have . . . what's the word . . . ?"

"Assimilated?" suggested Shelby . . . always a good word when discussing the Borg.

"Right. Assimilated technology from throughout the galaxy. The thing is, the Borg have integrated it smoothly into one, uniform whole. Here, it's . . . it's a hodgepodge. Look around you." She indicated the buildings. "Everything's just sort of strewn together, with no rhyme or reason. You can't get any sense for the character of the environment. Over there, for instance," and she pointed. "Look at the dome of that building."

"What about it?" said Shelby, but then she slowly started to answer her own question. "Wait a minute . . . isn't that . . . ?"

"Andorian, yes. You can tell by the markings along the lower rim."

"What's a dome from an Andorian building doing here?"

"There's an abandoned Andorian colony on the border of Sector 221-G. My guess is that at some point, the Nelkarites picked it clean. They took whatever caught their interest. That person over there, with Laheera? Wearing a cloak of Tellarite design. That gold iris-eye door fitted into that building over there? It's off an Orion slave ship. This place is like a giant jigsaw puzzle. It's like," and she tried to find the right comparison. "It's like walking into a cannibals' village and finding clothes or trinkets taken from previous . . . uh . . . meals."

"Are you saying we have to worry about becoming the Nelkarites' consuming interest?" Shelby said slowly. She noticed that Laheera and the others had finished greeting the refugees, and were now heading back toward herself and Lefler.

Lefler seemed to consider the notion for a moment, but then she discarded it. "No . . . no, I don't think so. They just seem interested in technology, that's all. I don't think there's anything particularly dangerous about them. They're just a small, scrappy race, trying to make use of whatever they happen to get their hands on, for the purpose of getting ahead. I'll wager they even cobbled together the ship we confronted."

"Yes, Soleta made the same observation. Not saying it was 'cobbled together,' but it seemed to be a patchwork of other technology, most conspicuously Kreel."

"It's possible that Kreel raiders tried to show up here to take advantage of them . . . and paid for it with their ship."

"Which means that the Nelkarites are fully capable of protecting themselves," Shelby mused. "Certainly that's good news for the refugees. They could use some protection."

"Commander," came Laheera's musical voice. "Did I hear you saying something about . . . protection?" She seemed almost amused by the notion. "Certainly you don't think we pose a threat to you?"

Captain Hufmin sauntered up on the tail end of the comment, and before Shelby could say anything, he announced confidently, "Oh, I doubt that Commander Shelby ever thought such a thing. Right, Commander?"

Shelby smiled noncommittally. "I'm rather curious, Laheera," she said. "We're depositing four dozen refugees on you. Where do you intend to put them?"

"Oh, that's not a problem at all. I'm glad you asked that, in fact," and indeed Laheera seemed more than glad. She seemed delighted out of all proportion to the question. "We have some wonderful facilities which we've prepared."

"Not some sort of camps or something equally uninviting, I trust?"

"Not at all, Commander." Laheera leaned forward, sounding almost conspiratorial. "They're so luxurious that you might want to stay on yourself instead of returning to the *Excalibur*."

Doing a fair impression of Laheera's almost giddy, singsong voice, Shelby replied with faux excitement, "That's a chance I'm willing to take." Lefler put a hand to her mouth to cover her own laughter, although the slight shaking of her shoulders betrayed her amusement.

"Come," said Laheera, and then she waved to the refugees who were congregating in the square, looking around in wonderment at their new home. "Come along, all of you. I'll show you to your residences." She turned back to Shelby and said, clearly pleased with herself, "And then you can return to your captain and let him know that your people are in safe hands." As she spoke, she hooked her arm through Hufmin's and together they sauntered off.

Shelby and Lefler exchanged looks.

"I think I'm going to be ill," said Lefler.

VI

"I believe I am ill. Mentally ill. And I require your services to ascertain that."

Dr. Selar and Lieutenant Soleta were in Selar's private quarters. Soleta had reported to sickbay as Selar had requested, but as soon as she was there the Vulcan doctor immediately decided that her office did not provide sufficient seclusion, and so she had requested that they relocate the meeting.

Soleta was impressed at how utterly stark Selar's quarters were. It was as if she didn't really live there; as if her entire life were sickbay, and her quarters was simply where she retired to in order to attend to the minimal requirements necessary to her perpetuation. There was her computer (standard issue), her bed (standard issue) . . .

. . . and a single light.

The fact that there was nothing else in the room to draw her attention naturally prompted Soleta to focus on it. It was tall, about a foot high, and cylindrical, and shimmered with a blue radiance. She found something unutterably sad about it, and she couldn't exactly figure out why. Why would a light have a sadness about it?

Selar saw what had drawn her attention. She didn't smile, of course, or frown, or in any way evince any emotion. "You have not seen a Shantzar? A Memory Lamp?"

"No, I . . . have not," Soleta said. "A tribute of sorts?"

"Of sorts, yes. To someone . . . long gone." Briskly, she turned to Soleta and said, "I am in a . . . somewhat difficult position. I must ask your indulgence, not only as a crew woman, but as a fellow Vulcan . . . indeed, the only other Vulcan on this vessel. I ask . . ." She cleared her throat. "I formally ask you to grant me Succor."

Soleta was not quite as skilled as Selar when it came to covering her surprise. "A formal request? You could not simply ask for my help, and assume that I would give it?"

She looked downward. It was surprising to Soleta that Selar was having trouble meeting her direct gaze. "We speak of delicate matters and uncertainties. I do not wish to impose on friendship."

"Are we friends?"

"Not to my knowledge," said Selar. "That is the point."

"I cannot say I understand, because that would be lying."

Selar looked around her cabin, looked anywhere except at Soleta. "I do not . . . interact well with others," she said after a time.

"A curious admission for a doctor to make," Soleta couldn't help but observe.

Another might have taken that as a criticism, but Selar merely nodded in acknowledgment. "As a doctor, I do not see myself interacting with individuals, but rather with their ailments. It is no more necessary to make an emotional investment in patients than it is for an engineer to bond with a power coupling. If it breaks, it is my job, my vocation, to repair it. That is all."

"But engineers do bond, do they not?" asked Selar. "Humans in particular. They tend to invest inanimate objects with a sense of life. They even ascribe genders to their vessels, calling them 'she.' "

"Granted. It gives them . . . comfort, I would imagine. Humans are frequently in need of comfort." She looked imperiously at Soleta. "Vulcans are not. That is one of the elements which has been our greatest strength."

And with a sigh, Soleta replied, "Or weakness."

Selar seemed inclined to reply to that, but clearly she changed her mind. "We have gotten off the subject," she said, and once again seemed intensely interested in looking anywhere but at Soleta. "I have formally requested Succor. Do you understand the parameters of such a petition?''

"I believe I do," Soleta said slowly. "You are asking that I oblige myself to help you with some matter without knowing the nature of it, or what that obligation binds me to. It gives me no option to state that the request is beyond my ability to help you. Gives me no opportunity simply to refuse, for whatever reason. It is generally an application made by a fairly wretched and frightened individual who feels that she has no one on whom she can count.''

"I would dispute the accuracy of the last statement . . .''

"Would you?" asked Soleta with such sudden intensity that it virtually forced Selar to look directly at her. "Would you really?''

"I . . .'' Her Vulcan discipline was most impressive. Her chin ever-so-slightly outthrust, she said, "Since I am presently in the process of asking you for Succor, it would not be appropriate for me to engage in a dispute over your opinions. Believe what you wish. But I would appreciate an answer to the question.''

"The answer is no.''

Soleta turned on her heel and headed for the door. She was almost there when Selar halted her with a word . . .

"Please.''

There was no more emotion, no more inflection in the one word than there had been in any of the words preceding it. And yet Soleta was sure that she could hear the desperation in Selar's voice. She turned back to the doctor and said flatly, the words in something of a rush, "I hereby, of my own free will, grant you Succor. In what way may I be of service.''

Selar took a step forward and said, "Mind-meld with me.''

"What?''

"I am concerned over my frame of mind. My concern is that my mental faculties are beginning to erode. I have been experiencing . . . feelings. Sensations. Confusions which can only be deemed inappropriate in light of my training and experience.''

Slowly, Soleta sank into a chair, not taking her eyes off Selar. "You want me to mind-meld with you.''

Selar paced the room, speaking in a clinically detached manner that made her feel far more comfortable than acknowledging the emotional turmoil she was straining to keep at bay. "I believe that I may be

suffering the earliest stages of Bendii Syndrome, causing the disintegration of my self-control.''

"If that is what you believe, then certainly there must be medical
tests . . .''

But Selar shook her head. "Bendii Syndrome, at this point, would
not be detectable through standard medical technologies. There are
physical symptoms, yes, changes in certain waves patterns. But these
are ascribable to a variety of possible ailments. It could also be Hibbs
Disease, or Telemioistis . . . it could **even be *Pon farr*, although that
is an impossibility**.''

"Impossible . . . why? Timing is wrong?''

Selar suddenly felt very uncomfortable. "Yes.''

"When was the last—?''

"It cannot be, believe me,'' Selar told her in no uncertain terms.
Clearly considering the subject closed, she continued briskly, "In this
situation, diagnosis via mind-meld would be the accepted and appropriate procedure to follow on Vulcan. There are doctors, psi-meds, who
specialize in the technique.''

"But we're not on Vulcan, and I'm not a doctor,'' Soleta reminded
her. "This is not a situation with which I am comfortable.''

"I fully understand that. However, it would not be required that
you have any medical training. During the mind-meld, I will be able to
use your 'outside' perspective as if it were a diagnostic tool. Were I not
a doctor myself, and were I not thoroughly trained in such procedures,
it would be impossible. As it stands, it is more cumbersome and inef-
ficient than simply to have a psi-med conduct the process. But I am
willing to make do.''

A long moment went by, during which Soleta said nothing. Selar
was no fool; Soleta's hesitation was evident. But she was not about to
back off. "You have granted me Succor,'' she reminded her, as if the
reminder were necessary. "You cannot refuse.''

"True. However,'' and Soleta stood, squaring her shoulders. She
seemed even more uncomfortable now than Selar had moments before,
and she did not have the self-discipline or control to cover it as skillfully
as Dr. Selar. ". . . however, I am within my rights to request that you
release me from my promise. I do so now.''

"I will not.''

"You would force me to mind-meld with you?'' Soleta made absolutely no effort to hide her surprise. "That is contrary to . . ." She couldn't even begin to articulate it. Mind-meld was a personal, private matter. To force someone to perform it upon you, or thrust your own mind into another . . . it was virtually unthinkable.

"Lieutenant, I understand your hesitation," Selar began.

"No, I do not think you do."

"We barely know one another, and you feel pressured," Selar began. "Such a mind-meld will require you to probe more deeply than one normally would. The sort of meld that is either performed between intimates, or by extremely well trained psi-meds who are capable of such private intrusions while still shielding the—"

But Soleta waved her off impatiently. "It's not about that. Not about that at all."

At this, Selar was bit surprised. "Well, then . . . perhaps you wish to explain it to me."

"I do not. Now release me from my promise."

"No."

The two women stared at each other, each unyielding in their resolve. It was Soleta who broke first. She looked away from Selar, and in a voice so soft that even Selar almost missed it, she murmured, "It is for your own good."

"My own good? Lieutenant, I need your help. That is where my 'own good' lies."

"You do not want my help."

"I believe I know what I want and—"

*"You do not **want** my **help**!"*

The outburst was so unexpected, so uncharacteristic, so un-Vulcan, that—had Selar been human—she would have gaped in undisguised astonishment. As it was she could barely contain her incredulity. Soleta looked as if someone had ripped out a piece of her soul. She was fighting to regain her composure and was only partly successful. Selar, in all her years, had never encountered a Vulcan whose emotionality was so close to the surface. All she knew was that she was beginning to feel less like a supplicant and more like a tormentor.

"I release you," she said slowly.

Soleta let out an unsteady sigh of relief. "Thank you," she said.

Clearly, now, she wanted to leave. She wanted to put as much distance between herself and Selar as she possibly could. But the reasons for her outburst, and Selar's open curiosity, were impossible to ignore. She could not pretend that it had not happened, and—despite the size of the *Excalibur*—it was, in the grand scheme of things, a small place to live when there was someone whose presence was going to make you uncomfortable. Particularly when it was someone such as the ship's CMO; not exactly the type of person one could hope never to have any interaction with.

Soleta leaned against the wall, her palms flat against it, as if requiring the support of it. She weighed all the possibilities, and came to what she realized was the only logical decision. Still, she had to protect herself. "If I tell you something relating to my medical history . . . will you treat it under the realm of doctor/patient confidentiality."

"Does it pose a threat to the health or safety of the crew of the *Excalibur?*"

The edges of Soleta's mouth, ever so slightly, turned upward. "No. No, not at all."

"Very well."

She took a deep breath. "I am . . . impure," she said. "You would not want me in your mind."

"How do you mean 'impure'? I do not understand."

"I am not . . . full Vulcan."

Selar blinked, the only outward indication of her surprise. "Your records do not indicate that." She paused, considered the information. "It is an unexpected revelation, but it is hardly cataclysmic. Your attitude, your demeanor, indicates you consider your background to be . . . shameful in some manner. Some of the greatest Vulcans in history do not have 'pure' parentage."

"I am aware of that. I am personally acquainted with Ambassador Spock."

"Personally." Selar was impressed, and made no effort to keep it out of her voice. "May I inquire as to the circumstances?"

"We were in prison together."

Selar found this curious, to say the least, but she decided that it was probably preferable not to investigate the background of that statement. Clearly there were greater problems to be dealt with. Selar was all too aware that bedside manner was not her strong suit. And her experiences since the death of her mate, Voltak, had done nothing to soften her disposition. She knew that she had become even more distant and remote than her training would require, but she had not cared overmuch. Truthfully, since Voltak had died those two long years ago, she had not cared about anything. Nonetheless it was clear that Selar had to put aside her own concerns and deal with those of Soleta.

She placed a hand on Soleta's shoulder. Soleta looked at it as if it were an alien artifact. "Neck pinch?" she asked.

"I am endeavoring to be of comfort," Selar said formally.

"Nice try." The words had a tint of humor to them, but Soleta did not say them in an amused manner.

Slowly Selar removed her hand from Soleta's shoulder. Then she straightened her uniform jacket and said, "I do not recall your service record indicating any mixed breeding. Although I will respect the bond of doctor/patient confidentiality, falsifying your record is frowned upon. In some instances, it could even result in court-martial in the unlikely event your parentage included a hostile race such as . . ."

Her voice trailed off as she saw Soleta's expression, anticipating the word. Selar barely dared speak it. "Romulan?" she whispered.

Soleta nodded.

"You . . . lied about one of your parents being Romulan?"

But at that Soleta shook her head. Slowly she sank back down into the couch.

"My mother was Vulcan," she said softly. "I thought my father was as well. They were colonists . . . scientific researchers. Several times, in the throes of *Pon farr,* they had endeavored to conceive a child, but each time the pregnancy had resulted in miscarriage. It was a tragic circumstance for them, but they dealt with it with typical Vulcan stoicism. Besides, they had their work to keep them occupied.

"And then there came a day when my mother was on a solo exploration, my father occupied with something else. To her surprise, she came upon a downed ship, a small, one-man vessel. Deciding that there might be someone in need of rescue, she investigated. She found someone. He was a Romulan, injured from the crash. He said he was a deserter."

"A deserter?"

"So he claimed. He begged my mother not to inform anyone of his presence. His concern was that the Federation would turn him back over to the Romulan government . . . or else put him in prison. She informed him that she could not make that promise. It would have been logical for her to lie, but my mother could not bring herself to do so. He was very angry with her, tried to stop her. She fought him and then she . . .'' Soleta lowered her voice. "She learned the true nature of his background. He was not a deserter. He was an escaped criminal. A violent, amoral individual, and he . . .''

Her voice trailed off. But there was no need to finish the sentence.

Selar said nothing. She did not trust herself to be able to speak without emotion.

"When my mother returned home, she was already pregnant," said Soleta. "She contemplated having an abortion . . . and rejected it. It was not a logical decision."

"Not logical." Selar, who prized logic no less than any Vulcan, couldn't quite believe what she'd heard. "Had she aborted the pregnancy, you would not be here."

"True enough. But considering the circumstances of my conception . . . the nature of my sire . . . making certain that I was not born would have been the logical choice. But my mother and . . . the man I thought of as my father . . . they felt it . . . illogical . . . to dismiss my existence simply because of who my true father was. They were willing to take the chance that I would not be some sort of violent criminal. That their care, their training, their guidance, would be more than enough to overcome whatever unfortunate tendencies my genetic makeup might carry with it. It was a foolish gamble, but one they were willing to make. Perhaps they were not thinking clearly because of their frustrated encounters with *Pon farr.* Or perhaps they were too . . . disoriented . . . by the recent events to come to a more sensible decision. Whatever the reason, they chose to let the pregnancy proceed. This time, she did not miscarry. There is a great irony in that, I suppose."

"And you did not know the nature of your true origins?"

"No. No, I was raised in the belief that I was a full Vulcan. Neither my father nor my mother told me the truth. They saw no point in it. They felt it was information that I did not need to possess. I was, after all, my mother's daughter, and my father could not have been more devoted to me had he been my genetic parent. So you see, Doctor, there was no attempt at deception on my part. When I enrolled in Starfleet Academy, the information I provided Starfleet was correct and true, to the best of my knowledge. You should have seen me back then, Doctor. I was as pure Vulcan as anyone could ask. Cool. Unflappable. My training was thorough, my mind-set absolutely ideal. I spoke in the formal English dialect favored by our people. You would never have known who my true father was. How could you? I never knew.''

"What happened to him? After he . . . after the incident with your mother, was he caught? Returned to the Romulans?''

It took an effort for Soleta to get the words out. "When my mother first returned to the colony city . . . after her violent encounter . . . my father sought out the Romulan who had abused her. But he had disappeared—repaired his ship sufficiently to escape. He eluded capture.''

"And he was never found?''

"Oh . . . he was found . . .'' And Soleta laughed. It was a most unusual sound, and it startled Selar profoundly. She had never heard a Vulcan laugh. "The fates, if such there be, do like their little pranks. He was caught many years after the 'incident,' as you call it. He had built up quite a reputation for himself; had a very impressive smuggling operation set up. A Starfleet vessel, the *Aldrin,* put an end to his illegal activities. And there was a junior-grade science officer aboard that vessel by the name of Soleta. She had heard about Romulans, you see, but had never had the opportunity to see one up close. She considered them to be of scientific interest, what with their being an offshoot of the Vulcan race. Her scientific curiosity drove her to walk past the brig, to observe him, to approach him and begin to ask him questions.

"And he noticed something. Something she had in her hair. A family heirloom which her mother had always worn, but had passed on to her daughter when Soleta went off to the Academy.''

Selar realized immediately, saw it glinting in Soleta's hair. "The IDIC.''

"Yes.'' Soleta tapped the IDIC pin she customarily wore in her hair. "Precisely. He was quite given to talking, the Romulan. He was rather proud of his achievements, particularly the more debased ones. I think he was, in his way, as interested in me as I was in him. I believe that he desired to see whether he could 'shock' me somehow. He proceeded to tell me the exact circumstances in which he had previously seen such a pin. The Vulcan woman who had worn one, and how he had knocked it out of her hair when he had . . . taken her forcibly. He went into intimate detail of the event. To shock me, as I said. And he did, but not in the way he had thought. For he simply believed that the recitation of the events of his brutality—his painting a vivid picture of how he had abused a Vulcan woman—would be disconcerting to me. He would have failed, for my training was too thorough. But he spoke of the world upon which he had crashed, spoke of when it happened, and there was the connection with the pin . . .'' Soleta took a deep, shaky breath. ''He had no idea. No idea to whom he was speaking. He thought it was simply an identical pin. A mere coincidence. And that's all it should have been, truly. I mean, the truth . . . the truth was too insane to contemplate, wasn't it. Father, all unknowing, telling his daughter the details of the rape that had led to her conception? It was . . .''

Her shoulders started to tremble, and her discipline began to crack. A single tear rolled down her cheek. Selar went to her then, tried to put a hand out, but Soleta shoved it away. Realizing the violence inherent in her move, she quickly wiped her face with the back of her hand as she said urgently, ''I'm sorry, I—''

But Selar waved dismissively. ''No apology necessary. Considering the circumstances . . .''

''After my encounter with my . . . with the Romulan . . . I informed Starfleet that there was an emergency of a personal nature which required my immediate attention. I had to speak to my parents in person. This was not something that could be dealt with over subspace. I returned home, returned to Vulcan, which was where my parents had relocated to in the interim. I confronted them and they . . . admitted to the true nature of my parentage. They even pointed out that they had never lied to me . . . and they had not, you know. What child, living in a normal environment, thinks to ask her father whether he is truly her father? No lie was required, for the question had never been posed. They told me that it should make no difference. That it did not diminish me, or make me less of a person than I was.'' Slowly she shook her head. ''No difference,'' she repeated in clear disbelief, and then she said it again, her voice barely above a whisper, ''No difference.''

Selar waited. When Soleta said nothing after a time, Selar asked gently, ''Did you return to Starfleet?''

''Not immediately. I could not. I felt . . . unworthy. Despite my parents' urging, I felt I was less than the woman I was. It affected the way I conducted myself, deported myself. The way I dressed, the way I spoke . . . even to this day. Habits that I'd learned, training I had had . . . it all seemed a sham to me, somehow. Things learned by another person who was not me, but had only pretended to be me. I extended my leave of absence, and I roamed. Roamed for so long that eventually Starfleet got word to me that if I did not return, I would simply be dropped from the service. They put me in a position where I was forced to decide what to do with my life.''

"Obviously you decided to return to Starfleet."

"Obviously, yes, considering that I am sitting here in a uniform. But it was not, to me, an obvious decision to make."

"What prompted you to make it, then?"

"It was my mother's dying wish."

Selar lowered her eyes. "I am . . . sorry . . . for your loss. She must have been quite young."

"All too young. Vulcans have a long life span under ideal circumstances, but that is no guarantee."

"I know that, I assure you," Selar said. Had Soleta been less self-involved, she would have detected the slight ruefulness in Selar's tone, but she did not.

Instead Soleta found herself staring at the Memory lamp which Selar had burning in her cabin. "I asked to be assigned as a teacher upon my return, and considering my lengthy departure, Starfleet saw no reason to deny my request. I was more comfortable with that situation than with the thought of continuing to wander the galaxy. However, circumstances arose so that my presence was required here."

"And you never told Starfleet of what you had learned, about your true parentage."

"No. Technically, it is withholding information. I imagine that they could make matters difficult for me, were they to learn of it. But . . . in the grand tradition of my family . . . they did not ask, and so I have had no need to lie. Convenient, is it not?"

"Very."

Soleta said nothing for a time, appearing to consider something. Finally Selar told her, "For what it is worth, Soleta . . . I do not consider you 'impure,' as the humans might say. A tortured soul, yes. But impure? No. I consider you a person of conscience and integrity. No matter what happens in the future of this vessel, I will always consider it an honor to serve with you."

"Thank you. I appreciate that. Truly, I do. And in your saying that, you've enabled me to make up my mind about something." She clapped her hands briskly and said, "Clear your mind."

"What?"

Soleta waggled her fingers and indicated that Selar should bring herself closer. "If you still desire that I probe your mind . . . that I meld with you . . . I will do so. After your sitting here patiently and listening to my life's story . . ."

"I do not wish your help out of some misplaced sense of gratitude," Selar told her.

Soleta looked at her skeptically. "Pardon me, but as I recall, a short time ago you were endeavoring to force me into aiding you through a binding blind promise, am I correct? And *now* you are concerned about the ethics involved in my helping you?"

"Matters are different now. You were," and clearly she hated to admit it, "you were correct before. I was . . . 'desperate,' if we must discuss the situation in human terms. I did not wish to depend on such relationships as friendship in order to accomplish what I felt needed to be done. But now that you have unburdened yourself . . ."

"You feel closer to me?"

"Not particularly, no. I simply feel that you have more problems than I do, and it is probably unjust to burden you with mine."

This once again prompted Soleta, in a most shocking manner, to laugh out loud. It was not something she had great experience in doing. It was a quick, awkward sound, closer to a seal bark than an actual laugh. "Your consideration is duly noted," she told her. "But I tell you honestly now, Doctor, that if you are comfortable with the situation— knowing about me what you now know—then I will assist you in your self-examination. If I say to you that it is the least I can do, I ask that you accept that in the spirit in which it's given."

Selar nodded briefly. "Very well."

She drew a chair over to the couch and sat down, facing Soleta. She cleared her thoughts, her breathing slow and steady, relaxing into the state of mind that would most facilitate the meld. Soleta did likewise, almost with a sense of relief.

Soleta did not have a tremendous amount of experience in the technique of the mind-meld, but she was certain that Selar's experience and superior training would more than make up for whatever Soleta might herself lack. Slow, methodical, unhurried, she waited until she sensed that her breathing was in complete rhythm with Selar's. Then, gently, she reached out, touching her fingers to Selar's temples.

"Our minds are merging, Selar," she said.

Their minds, their thoughts, their personas drew closer and closer to one another. The tendrils of their consciousness reached toward each other, gently probing at first . . .

. . . and then . . . contact was made . . .

. . . drawing closer still, and their thoughts began to overlap, and it was becoming hard to determine where one left off and the other began . . .

. . . and Soleta had a sense of herself, she did not lose it, it was still there, still vibrant and alive, but she had a sense of Selar as well, she was Selar, and Selar saw herself through the view of Soleta, outside her own consciousness, looking inward . . .

. . . and Selar felt uncertain and fearful, and she wasn't sure whether the insecurities rose from herself as Soleta and the knowledge of her true lineage or from herself and her concerns over her own state of mind, and she fought past it . . .

. . . and Soleta saw images flashing past her, images that were herself but not herself, images and sensations and experiences that were as real for her as they could possibly be, except none of them, absolutely none of them, had ever happened to her . . . and she began to scrutinize herself with an expertise that she had never before possessed, except it was not herself that she was scrutinizing, and yet it was, and it was with a facility that she had never had, except she did . . .

. . . and Selar felt herself slipping deeply into her own consciousness, gliding into Soleta's mind and using it as an ancient deep-sea explorer would use a bathysphere. Waves of her own thoughts and unconsciousness rippled around her as she descended further and further, moving through her psyche, and she felt waves of light pulsing around her. No, not light . . . life, her life, spread all around about her . . .

. . . and Soleta felt pain, waves of pain, and she heard voices crying out, and one of them was her own, her very own voice, and one of them was not, it was a male, it was someone she had never met in her life, and his name was Voltak, and she knew him with greater intimacy than she had ever known herself, and she could feel him moving within her . . .

. . . and Selar felt him slipping away, and Soleta called out his name, and Selar felt his loss ripping at her, and then Soleta was suddenly yanked downward, further downward, left looking upward at Voltak in the way that a swimmer trapped beneath a frozen lake sees the face of someone above, on the ice, staring down at them . . .

. . . and Selar's mind was left naked and exposed, Soleta probing with Selar's expertise, burrowing down to the core of her psychic makeup, seeking, searching, and buffeted with wave upon wave of heat, red heat that washed over her in delicious waves of agony that she could not ignore, that swept into every pore of her skin, enveloping her, caressing her, and she moaned for the exquisite torment of it all . . .

. . . and she felt something calling her, driving her, and it was voices, not just hers, not just Soleta's and Selar's, not just Voltak's, but Vulcans, hundreds, thousands, millions of them, driving her toward the heat, toward the red waves, as if they were trying to pound her into an inferno shore, and she welcomed it, she welcomed the heat and the waves, she could not, would not turn away from it, she embraced it, wanted it, wanted it more than she had ever wanted anything, and her breath was coming in short gasps, their minds slamming together . . .

My God . . .

The separation was violent. Soleta yanked away from her, and Selar tumbled backward, the chair overturning and spilling her onto her back. Soleta fell over, rolled off the couch and onto the floor. She lay there panting, gasping, her fingers still spasming as sensations shook her body. Sweat was dripping off her forehead, spattering onto the floor. With supreme effort she managed to look over at Selar, who didn't appear to be in much better shape. Selar was lying on her back, her arms outstretched, sucking in air gratefully, as if she had forgotten to breathe for however long they had been joined. It clearly took tremendous effort but slowly Selar turned her head and managed to look at Soleta. Soleta, for her part, felt embarrassed, like a voyeur, even though it had been Selar who had asked for the probe.

Selar was trying to mouth a word. Soleta propped herself up on one elbow and angled herself closer to Selar, just close enough to hear her say it:

"Impossible" was the low whisper. Selar had now actually managed to muster enough strength to shake her head, and again she murmured, "Impossible."

"Apparently . . . not." Soleta was surprised, even impressed, with the calm in her voice. Ever since learning the truth of her background, stoicism had not been something that she had always been able to maintain. Here, though, she was clearly capable of rising to the occasion. "Apparently it's not impossible at all."

"But it was . . . it was barely two years ago . . . I . . . I went through it . . . not time . . . not for years, it is not time . . ."

"Perhaps it's because of the way that it ended the first time," Soleta said reasonably. "The urge was never truly satisfied, but because you were mind-melded at the time . . . it sent you into a sort of psychic shock . . . numbed you . . . but it's finally worn off . . ."

"You . . . you do not know . . . what you are saying . . ." Selar's face had gone dead white.

"Maybe not," agreed Soleta. "Maybe I don't know what I'm saying at all. Maybe I'm completely crazy . . . except I know what I saw, Selar. I know what I felt and experienced. Whether you like it or not, whether you want to admit it or not . . . what you're going through right now is the first stages of *Pon farr.* Your bad experience the first time threw your system off, but now the mating frenzy is back with a vengeance. And I have absolutely no idea what you're going to do about it."

And Selar had the sick feeling that, somewhere in the ship, Burgoyne was sniffing the air and grinning. And she wasn't far wrong.

VII

Through the corridors of the *Kayven Ryin,* Si Cwan moved with the utmost care, flexing his arm to work out the kinks in his shoulder.

He was alone.

He had given Zak Kebron the slip, for Kebron had quickly made it clear he had no intention of letting Cwan handle matters the way he wanted to. The idea of not using any of the hand weapons, for starters, was intolerable to Kebron. In his arrogance—at least, arrogance the way Si Cwan saw it—Kebron felt that he himself did not have to depend on weapons. But he was of the forceful opinion that if Si Cwan had the opportunity to use a weapon on Zoran, he should take it. That nothing was going to be accomplished by treating the situation as a grudge match.

But this had gone far beyond grudges. Si Cwan knew, beyond any question, that he was going to kill Zoran. He simply had to. Honor would not allow anything less. And he had to do it with his bare hands. This was not a question of honor allowing anything less, but rather his simple determination to make Zoran's punishment as painful as possible.

So Si Cwan had, moving quickly, left the Brikar behind. He'd been subtle about it; give him some credit. He'd darted down a corridor at a faster clip than the Brikar could maintain, and then run off down a connector, slid through a maintenance tube, and next thing he knew, he was on his own. And if he should live long enough to be in a position where he need make excuses, he could always simply claim that they had become accidentally separated from one another. Accidents, after all, did happen.

He heard a noise.

It was definitely not Zak Kebron. He already knew that rock-steady footfall. No, it was quick, extremely light-footed. He would almost have thought it was the movement of a small animal, so fast and nearly insubstantial was it. But Si Cwan wasn't fooled, not for a moment.

He crouched down and moved like a giant spider, arms and legs operating in perfect synchronization. He presented as minimal a target as possible, should it come to that.

He moved past one room, the door to which was closed, and from within he thought he heard something. A quick footfall, or perhaps something on a table within that was slightly jolted and sent skidding. Something. He paused outside the door, crouching to one side, trying to determine whether or not he should burst into the room. It could very well be that someone was waiting for him to do precisely that, and had a vicious weapon aimed squarely at the door.

Or perhaps they had anticipated that he would think entry through the door was a trap . . . and were instead aimed at the ceiling, or at a vent, hoping that he would make his entry that way.

He still had the plasma blaster slung across his shoulders, and practicality began to rear its ugly head. He still had every reason to want to throttle Zoran . . . but by the same token, he had a few more reasons to want to continue to live.

Well . . . perhaps using the plasma blaster wouldn't be such a crime after all, as long as the killing blow was struck by hand. That was, after all, the important thing.

He unslung the blaster, aimed it squarely at the door, and fired. At such close range, the plasma blast plowed through the door like acid through paper, and Si Cwan leaped headlong through the door, shoulder rolled and came up to face . . .

. . . nothing.

He was inside a laboratory, and there was no evidence of anyone else there. There was a beaker rolling across a table. Other than that, nothing.

He muttered a curse as he slung the plasma blaster over his back. The noise of the plasma blaster would undoubtedly attract Zoran or his compatriots there. Or else Kebron himself, which would leave Si Cwan with explaining to do and an undesired ally at his back. Si Cwan felt that if there was one thing he did not need, it was someone watching out for him.

He thought that up until the moment that the ceiling crashed in on him.

It caught him completely by surprise as an overhead grating slammed down onto him, driving him to his knees. A split second later, Zoran dropped down from his hiding place overhead inside one of the engineering service ducts, and landed squarely on Si Cwan's back.

He drove a vicious blow to the base of Si Cwan's neck, to the hard cluster of muscles situated there, and by all rights it should have paralyzed Si Cwan from the neck down for approximately five minutes. In the short term, it did the job. Si Cwan thudded to the ground, unable to feel anything in the rest of his body. The fall spilled Zoran to the floor as well, but Zoran rolled away and came quickly to his feet. Si Cwan struggled furiously, trying to regain command over his movements, as a sneering Zoran approached him.

"Too easy. Much too easy," he said.

The humans had a phrase for it: mind over matter. The mind belonged to Cwan, and the matter was—in this instance—his own body. He refused to acknowledge the physical reality that he was helpless. He would not allow himself to die helplessly in a paralyzed condition. It simply could not, would not be done. His brain sent commands to the rest of his body to respond, sending synapses roaring through him like photon torpedoes.

Against all odds, against anything that Zoran would have deemed possible, Si Cwan's legs slammed upward. They did not do so with all the force that they usually possessed. But it was sufficient as his legs scissored around Zoran's at the knees. Before Zoran could move, Si Cwan forced himself to twist at the waist. He felt sluggish, torpid, but slow for Si Cwan was still lightning for most anyone else. The move was enough to collapse Zoran's leg, and Zoran went down to find himself on the floor, face-to-face with the enraged Si Cwan.

Si Cwan rolled over, half leaping and half lunging toward Zoran. He landed squarely on his opponent, grabbed him firmly by the ears, yanked upward and then down, slamming Zoran's head onto the grated floor. Zoran's head rang from the impact, and with a roar and an effort fueled by the explosion of pain behind his eyes, Zoran shoved Si Cwan off himself. Si Cwan rolled over toward a table, saw an opportunity, and quickly upended the table, sending it tumbling toward Zoran. Zoran barely managed to scramble out of the way, and by the time he was on his feet, so was Si Cwan.

They stood there for a moment, catching their respective breaths, their chests heaving, their hatred almost palpable.

"It's been ages, Si Cwan," snarled Zoran.

"Where are the other two? Rojam and Juif, they must be nearby."

"You don't think I'd give away our strategic position, do you?" In point of fact, they were nowhere nearby. The confrontation was strictly between Zoran and Si Cwan, which was how Zoran had wanted it.

Yet Si Cwan smiled with thinly veiled contempt and said, "Did you embark on this stupidity on your own? Or, even better . . . did they accompany you on this endeavor and then take the opportunity to abandon you? Is that it? Have your cheerfully domineering ways managed to grate on them after all these years? That would not surprise me. No, not in the least."

Rallying himself, Zoran said, "Tell me, Si Cwan, what it is like knowing that you are a complete and total failure?"

Si Cwan did not even deign to answer the question. He merely tossed a disdainful look at him.

"I see you have a weapon on your back," continued Zoran. "And yet you would not use it."

"I've known you too long, Zoran. I knew that you would desire to settle this hand-to-hand, between the two of us. In many ways, you're sadly predictable."

"In many ways, so are you. The difference between us is, I make use of that predictability . . . and you don't."

And Zoran snapped his arm forward in what seemed an oddly casual gesture, as if he were endeavoring to shake hands.

A short blade hurtled out from his sleeve, thudding deeply into Si Cwan's already injured upper shoulder. Si Cwan let out an angry roar and tried to pull it out, but the tip was barbed and it wasn't going to be easy to remove. Nor was Zoran giving him the time, for Zoran vaulted the distance between the two of them, grabbed the blade by the handle, and twisted it. Pain screamed through Si Cwan, and he howled in fury.

"Enjoying your vengeance, Si Cwan?" asked Zoran as he wrenched the dagger around in place. Blood fountained from the gaping wound in Si Cwan.

But in order to handle the dagger, Zoran had had to get close in to Si Cwan, giving him opportunity to strike back. The base of Si Cwan's hand slammed into the bridge of Zoran's nose, and the crack—like a ricochet—sounded in the room. The world hazed red to Zoran, and suddenly he felt Si Cwan's hands at his throat. Cwan's thumbs dug in and upward, seeking out the choke hold, cutting off Zoran's air.

"I don't care what happens to me," Si Cwan said hoarsely, his voice a growl, "and I don't care how I die, as long as you die first."

Zoran drove a knee up into Si Cwan's gut. Si Cwan grunted, ignoring the pain, beyond its ability to influence him. He was focused on one goal: choking the life from Zoran. His hands were locked securely on, all his strength dedicated to the effort. The rest of the world seemed to evaporate around him. There was just Zoran, and him, and the feel of Zoran's pulse beneath his fingers which Si Cwan was determined to extinguish.

He started to force Zoran down, down to his knees, and Zoran cried out in pain and fear. And in desperation, Zoran managed to slam his head forward against the hilt of the dagger, driving it in even deeper.

Si Cwan had no choice. The knife struck a muscle which, as a reflex, caused Si Cwan's hands to flex open just for a moment. It was all Zoran needed as he tore himself away, literally throwing his body the distance of the lab. He crashed to the floor just inside the door.

Dark liquid covered the entire front of Si Cwan's tunic, but he didn't care. Like an unswerving juggernaut, he lurched toward Zoran, fingers still opening and closing spasmodically as if he still had Zoran's throat between them. As if he was positive that it would only be a matter of moments before he once again had Zoran's life in his hands.

There was much that Zoran had fancied about Si Cwan, for it had been several years since he had actually set eyes on him. There was much that he had managed to convince himself of. Once upon a time, he had spent days hunting by Si Cwan's side. He had wrestled with him, sparred with him, confided in him, given Si Cwan his confidence and received it in return. For the purpose of rationalizing the split that had occurred between them, Zoran had indulged in that habit which most sentient beings engaged in when separating from old friends: demonizing. Zoran had told so many people that Si Cwan was a fake, a fraud, a lazy bastard who was more lucky than skilled, and of whom everyone had been afraid because of his station in life, that Zoran had more or less convinced himself of that as well.

So it was very disturbing for Zoran to find himself in combat with Si Cwan now and come to the stark realization that his memory had played tricks on him. He had convinced himself that, face-to-face, hand-to-hand, he could easily handle Si Cwan.

Now he realized that, at the very least, he could handle Si Cwan but with extreme difficulty. Extreme difficulty meant that a good deal of time was going to be occupied accomplishing it. And time was something he did not have in abundance.

He tapped the comm-link unit on his wrist even as he backpedaled into the corridor. "All right, enough! Beam me out!"

That was when Zoran felt the ground starting to tremble beneath him. He glanced off to his right and saw what appeared to be a walking landmass advancing on him. Zak Kebron charged forward, arms pumping.

Then Zoran heard a defiant war cry and his attention was yanked back to Si Cwan. Cwan had actually ripped the barbed dagger from his shoulder, which should have been impossible. At the very least, any normal person would have collapsed in agony by that point. But if there was any doubt in Zoran's mind that Si Cwan was far from normal, it would certainly have been settled by now.

The dagger was dripping with Si Cwan's blood. He could not have cared less. He tossed it aside, sending it clattering across the floor leaving a trail of red behind him. And then he lurched forward toward Zoran.

One hand was outstretched, his palm covered with thick, dark fluids; his own.

He didn't care.

He had a weapon still strapped to his back.

He didn't care.

He was injured, wounded, every muscle in his body aching, and weak from blood loss. And Si Cwan didn't care.

The only thing he cared about was getting his hands on Zoran. Which, ultimately, he was unable to do.

A sound filled the immediate area. Although it was of a different timbre than the noise produced by a regulation Starfleet transporter, nonetheless it was easily identifiable as a matter transporter sound.

"*No!*" howled Si Cwan in outrage, and in desperation he leaped at Zoran. His hope was that if he managed to leap into range of the transport effect in time, he would be brought along to wherever it was that Zoran was heading. But he was too late. Zoran's form became just insubstantial enough for Si Cwan to fall right through it. He hit the metal grating of the floor as Zoran—along with Si Cwan's chances for revenge—disappeared.

"Get back here, you bastard!" shouted Si Cwan, slamming his fists on the floor in frustration.

"I doubt he'll hear you," observed Kebron, who had chugged to a halt just short of running Si Cwan over.

Then the comm unit that Si Cwan had taken off of the fallen Thallonian beeped. There was no question in his mind who it was who was endeavoring to get in touch with him. He activated it and said angrily, "I call you coward, Zoran!"

"I call you dead, Si Cwan," Zoran replied with just a touch of regret. "But if you wish to discuss it further, I suggest you adjourn to a location two decks below you, aft section." And he clicked off.

Without hesitation, Si Cwan pivoted and started off in the direction that Zoran had indicated, but he was brought to an abrupt halt by Kebron, who had gotten a firm grip on his arm. "No you don't. Not again."

"I'm not going to let him get away!"

"You already did. If you mean you won't let him get away *again,* that's up for debate."

"Kebron, let go of me!" he said with angry imperiousness. And then, in a tone that was a bit more pleading, he added, "Please."

"We go together. On your honor. Say it."

Si Cwan gritted his teeth and nodded reluctantly. "Together. But you will not interfere in the outcome. On your honor. Say it. Say you will do nothing to interfere in the outcome of the battle between Zoran and myself.''

"If you insist. On my honor, I will not interfere in the outcome of the battle.''

"Very well. Let's go.'' And he charged off, but slowly enough that Kebron could keep up.

Zoran stared out at the depths of space which beckoned to them. Rojam and Juif stood on either side of him, fidgeting nervously, staring at the darkened navigation console of their escape vessel. It was not a particularly large ship; indeed, joined as it was to the airlock of the *Kayven Ryin,* it had actually avoided the *Marquand* detecting it. It had room enough for three people, and also a single transport pad, which Rojam had used to get Zoran off the science vessel to which they were still attached.

"Zoran, get us out of here,'' Juif said urgently.

It was difficult to tell whether Zoran had actually heard him. He simply sat there, jaw set, anger flickering in his eyes.

Rojam crouched down and said sharply, "Zoran . . . I wish, for your sake, you had defeated him in the manner you desired. But we had a deal. We gave you your ten minutes. The bomb is set. Further delay risks all our lives.''

In a faintly mocking tone, Juif added, "It is the province of Si Cwan and his ilk to make promises that they do not keep.''

Slowly Zoran turned to them, appearing to notice them for the first time since he'd been beamed aboard the escape vessel. "I am curious,'' he said. "If I had not rigged this vessel so that its flight systems would only respond to my voice commands . . . would you have left me on the ship? Left me behind to die with Si Cwan? Or did you only stick to our plan because you needed me in order to escape?''

"Don't be ridiculous,'' Rojam said flatly, and Juif echoed the sentiment.

Zoran looked into their eyes, tried to see the true feelings there. "You are afraid,'' he said after a moment.

"Of course we're afraid!'' Juif told him in mounting exasperation. "We're attached to a vessel that's going to be space dust in a few minutes, and you're quizzing us over our devotion as your friends! Cut us loose from here and let's be done with it! We can discuss this all you want later, but if we don't break off now, there's not going to be a later!''

Zoran stared at them for a moment that seemed to stretch out into forever, and then he said, "Nav computer, voice ID, Zoran Si Verdin."

"Voice ID confirmed," the computer replied indifferently.

"Nav systems on line. Detach vessel from airlock. Set heading to 183 on the Y-axis. Activate."

"Activating."

There was a slight jostling, the sound of huge metal clamps releasing, and a moment later they were free of their moorings. The escape vessel dropped away from the doomed science vessel *Kayven Ryin* and arced away into the blackness of space.

And they didn't even notice that, far in the distance, something was starting to ripple into existence . . .

Si Cwan crept forward, and then was very unnerved as Zak Kebron strode by, making no attempt at subtlety. "Kebron!" he hissed angrily. "Zoran is just ahead! A little stealth would be appreciated!"

Kebron looked at him blandly. "I'm Brikar," he informed him. "I don't do 'stealth.' "

Si Cwan rolled his eyes.

"Besides," continued Kebron, marching ahead, floor rattling beneath him, "I suspect that the question will be moot. I don't think Zoran is there."

"What?"

"It would be foolish to blithely give away a position or the advantage of surprise in that manner."

"You don't know Zoran as I do," said Si Cwan, moving just behind Kebron.

"No, I do not. As a result, I assess him calmly and coldly, rather than letting my opinion be clouded by hatred. I tell you that such a move on his part would be sheer foolishness, and nothing that you've told me about him indicates that level of stupidity."

"What do you think to expect, then?"

"A trap."

Si Cwan blew air impatiently out between his teeth. "I can handle any trap of Zoran's."

They rounded a corner and then Kebron came to such an abrupt halt that Si Cwan banged into his back, crunching his face into Kebron's spine. He stepped back, rubbing his nose, about to complain angrily . . . and then he saw it.

It was large and cylindrical, with moorings that had fused it to the floor, ceiling, and walls so that it was impossible to move. It beeped imperturbably, and it was counting down.

Si Cwan's face darkened as Kebron turned to face him. "All right, Cwan. All yours. Handle it."

Si Cwan approached it tentatively. There was a small display on the face of it, counting down. "I think it's a bomb," he said.

"Yes. A superheated thermite bomb, if I'm not mistaken. From the readings and the power escalation, I'd say it's going to detonate within two minutes. If I had to guess, I'd surmise that Zoran is long gone, and has left us to the bomb's nonexistent mercies."

Trying to fight down desperation, Si Cwan's fingers explored the outer casing. It was seamless. "Kebron, I'm no munitions expert. You have to disarm it."

"I have sworn I would not interfere in the outcome of the battle. The bomb was obviously left by Zoran; it's part of the battle. For me to take any action would be in violation of my oath. It would be dishonorable. I'm afraid I can't do that."

Si Cwan looked at him with undisguised incredulity. "Is this some Brikar idea of a joke?"

"I'm quite serious." He paused. "You could, of course, release me from my vow . . ."

"I release you! *I release you!*"

The moment he heard that, Kebron crossed quickly to the bomb and began to look it over. Putting his strength into it, he attempted to twist open the casing. When it resisted his efforts, he pulled experimentally at the moorings, and then with greater force. The metal bars held firm. He paused, contemplated the situation a moment, and then turned to Si Cwan and put a large hand on Cwan's shoulder. "May you have the eyes of the gods upon you, and success and glory in all future endeavors."

"Don't just yammer at me! *Do* something!"

"I *am* doing something," he said unflappably. "I'm wishing you well in the afterlife. Aside from that, my options are somewhat limited."

"Disarm the bomb!"

"With two hours to work on it and a Starfleet bomb squad backing me up, that might be an option. As it is . . ."

"You have a phaser. Shoot it! Disintegrate it!"

"Any attempt to do so will set it off. Furthermore, do you see this indicator?" and he pointed to one panel. "It's a motion sensor. Any attempt to move the bomb will also set it off."

Si Cwan was already in motion. "Let's go."

"Where?" asked Kebron curiously.

"To the far end of the ship!"

"Cwan, when this thing goes off in under a minute now, *every* part of the ship is going to be the far end. It's going to be scattered all over the system."

In helpless frustration, Si Cwan stared at the bomb and came to the same realization that Kebron had come to the moment he'd seen it.

There was a long silence, and then Si Cwan turned to Kebron and said, "I want you to understand: I am not afraid of death. In some ways, it's almost a blessing. But it angers me that I die while Zoran gets away. It angers me very much."

"Life is loose ends."

Si Cwan nodded, watching the bomb tick down, and then he patted Kebron on the shoulder. "You are a fine warrior, Kebron. I regret that we did not have more time to work out our differences. At least . . . at least I go to be with my sister, as you go to be with your parents."

"My parents." Kebron looked at him blankly.

"Yes. Your parents. Killed on the mining colony by Orion . . . pirates . . ."

"Oh, that," and Kebron's massive shoulders moved in something akin to a shrug. "It seemed like a convenient thing to tell you at the time. Actually, my parents live on Brikar. My mother is a politician, my father a salesman of motivational programs. They're alive and well. Thank you for your concern, though."

Si Cwan stared at him. "You made it up?"

"Of course I did. I wanted you to feel we had something in common so that you'd listen to me rather than run about like an idiot. So much for *that* plan."

The bomb ticked down to zero.

"I hate you," said Si Cwan.

And the ship blew up.

LAHEERA

VIII

Calhoun was on his way up to the bridge, anxious to speak with Shelby and Lefler, who had just returned from the surface of Nelkar. In heading to the turbolift, however, he met Selar in the corridor. "Doctor," he greeted her, his voice carefully neutral.

"Captain," she replied, inclining her head in return and continuing on her way.

Unable to resist, he turned and said, "Dr. Selar . . . is everything all right?"

She stopped and faced him, her arms folded across her chest. "That is a broad question, sir. Could you be more specific?"

"I could. Are you going to force me to be?"

She simply stood there, staring at him with feigned disinterest.

"All right." He took a step forward. "I—"

Then his comm badge beeped, and he tapped it. "Calhoun here."

"Captain, we're receiving a communication from the Nelkarites," came Shelby's voice.

"On my way," he said. "Doctor . . . we'll continue this later."

"I look forward to it, sir," she told him, and it was only after

Calhoun had walked off that she came to the startled realization that she'd just told her first lie.

Calhoun walked out onto the bridge, noting that Soleta was back at her science station, and reasoning that it would be pointless to pump her for information regarding Selar. From the tactical station, Boyajian said, "On screen, sir?"

"Not yet. Shelby, Lefler . . . report, please." He sat in the command chair and steepled his fingers.

"The facilities that we were shown for the refugees, although hardly luxurious, are far from spartan," Shelby informed him. "The Nelkarites seem genuinely interested in providing aid, and accepting the refugees into their society."

"And the refugees desire to remain there?"

"They have made that quite clear. I even suggested that they return to the *Excalibur* for a final debriefing; instead they voted amongst themselves, and it was unanimously requested that their possessions be sent down to Nelkar. They wish to stay. They seem happy there."

"I'm overjoyed," Calhoun said with what seemed a significant lack of enthusiasm. "Lefler?"

"Their society is not terribly advanced by our standards. They seem . . . 'lazy' doesn't seem the right word. 'Unmotivated,' perhaps. They have no major scientific research programs. They merely acquire things from other races and use those things to advance themselves. They sort of 'piggyback' on the accomplishments of others."

"All right. Recommendations?"

"There doesn't seem to be much to offer in that department, Captain," Shelby said. "The refugees have made their desires clear. They wish to stay on Nelkar. We cannot interfere in their stated wishes, nor should we. It would be contrary to the Prime Directive. More than that . . . it would border on the tyrannical."

Calhoun looked at her with mild surprise. "Commander . . . I may be many things. But 'tyrant' is hardly among them."

"I'm very aware of that, sir," she said reasonably. "That's why I'm afraid there really isn't much choice."

He drummed his fingers on the armrest for a moment. "It certainly appears that way. All right, Boyajian . . . put them on screen."

A moment later, an opulent room appeared on the monitor. There was Captain Hufmin, swathed in fine blue robes. There was a smile plastered on his face, and considering the drink in his hand and the manner in which he was swaying, the smile wasn't the only thing that was plastered. Next to him was Laheera, and the somewhat inebriated Hufmin was no longer making any attempt to hide his leering appraisal of her.

"Hello, Captain Calhoun," Laheera said, in that musical voice of hers.

"Greetings," Calhoun replied evenly. "From what my first officer tells me, you've made quite an impression on our passengers. And, if I might note, on Captain Hufmin as well."

"Yes, so it would appear," she commented. "And now we have matters to discuss, Captain."

"I'm told there isn't much to discuss, actually," Calhoun said with a subtle glance at Shelby. "We'll be beaming down our passengers' belongings, and be on our way. It is my hope that they'll be happy in their new home."

"I'm certain they will be, Captain Calhoun . . . once you cooperate."

Although her voice never lost its pleasant inflection, there was an undertone to the words that was not lost on anyone on the bridge. It was, however, lost on Hufmin, who was leaning against Laheera and grinning in a lopsided fashion.

"Cooperate?" Calhoun said slowly.

"Yes. You see, Captain, you have very advanced technology. Computer systems, weapons systems, warp drive capabilities that far exceed—"

"Not to be rude, Laheera, but . . . you might as well stop right there. Don't think that we're not grateful that you've opened your home and hearts to the refugees. But I simply cannot turn over technology to you." He rose from his chair and walked slowly to the monitor, sounding as reasonable as he could. "There are rules we live by, laws we follow, just as I'm sure you have your own laws. Your society is at a certain level, and it wouldn't be right or proper for us to aid you in jumping to the next. You have to reach that point yourselves."

"We have selflessly extended aid," Laheera said with a slight pout that made her look, frankly, just adorable. "Can't you do the same for us? It makes you seem a bit selfish."

"It sure does!" Hufmin agreed. Then again, in his condition and with the nearness of Laheera adding to his intoxication, he would have agreed that the sun was actually made of steamed cabbage.

"It does make us seem that way," Calhoun acknowledged. "But believe me, Laheera, it's for the best."

"I'm afraid I can't agree with that," said Laheera.

"That's right, Captain," Hufmin echoed, "she can't agree with th—"

It happened so quickly that Lefler, who happened to be blinking at that exact moment, didn't see it. But the others on the bridge did.

The knife was in Laheera's hand, and she grabbed the grinning Hufmin by the hair with her other hand, snapping his head backward. The most eerie thing was that her smile never wavered as she expertly yanked the knife across Hufmin's throat. Blood poured out and down, his blue robes turning deep crimson. Some of it spattered on Laheera's face, red speckling the gold. She didn't appear to notice or care. Hufmin did not even realize he'd been murdered. He reached up in a vague manner for the gash and he was grinning insipidly, probably feeling the warmth as it gushed all over him, and then he sank down and out of sight.

Shelby, horrified, looked to Calhoun.

His face looked dead. There was no expression at all—not anger, not revulsion—nothing. But then she saw it, saw it in his purple eyes: a deep, burning, savage fury that was barely contained.

In an almost absentminded fashion, Laheera reached down to wipe the blood off the blade. It was obvious, even though they couldn't see it, that she had cleaned it on the fallen Hufmin. "Now," Laheera said conversationally, "I did that in order to show you that we will not hesitate to do whatever is necessary to get what we want. We will kill the refugees. All of them. Men, women, children . . . makes no difference. We shall begin killing them shortly and continue to do so until you supply us with the technology we need. We will give you one hour to think about it and get back in touch with you at the end of that ti—"

"No."

The word sounded like a death knell. Calhoun had said it with no hesitation, no remorse, and no sense of pity whatsoever.

Laheera tilted her head slightly, like a dog trying to hear a high-pitched noise. "You mean you've already decided to cooperate with us?"

"No," said Calhoun. "I mean no, there will be no deals. No, there will not be a discussion. And no, you needn't wait. Kill them."

Lefler gasped upon hearing this. Soleta kept her composure, but McHenry paled, and even Shelby appeared shaken. Calhoun looked at her and she mouthed the word, *Negotiate.*

Laheera didn't quite seem to believe she'd heard or understood Calhoun correctly. "Captain . . . perhaps you don't appreciate the severity of the situation . . ."

"My first officer," Calhoun cut in, "appears to be of the opinion that I should negotiate."

"She is wise."

Calhoun walked up to the main screen, his back straight, his eyes now cold. "Laheera . . . the refugees made their own decision. I gave them advice. They ignored it. Whatever situation they're in now is of their own making. I have no sympathy for them that you can play upon. No guilt. No compunction about letting them die. They made their free choice, and they die as free beings. Nor do I wish to negotiate with terrorists. There is no point to it."

"My understanding, Captain, from what the late Captain Hufmin told me, is that you were something of a terrorist yourself once," Laheera said. It was frightening how the singsong tone of voice never wavered. "Who are you, then, to judge me?"

There was dead silence on the bridge for a long moment.

And when Calhoun spoke, there was something terrifying in his voice. No one on the bridge had ever heard anything like it. It was as if an approaching natural disaster, like a tornado or an ion storm, had been given voice to declare the dreadful damage it was about to inflict.

"You desire negotiation, Laheera? That I will not do. I don't negotiate. That is an immutable law of my universe. Another immutable law, however, is one of physics: that for every action, there is an equal and opposite reaction. Kill the refugees, Laheera. Kill them all. I don't care. I've seen too much death to let it be used as a club against me. But when you're done killing them, be aware that you've killed yourselves. Because I will order this ship to open fire on your capital city and blow you all to hell. Who am I to judge you, Laheera? I am someone who knows what it's like to deal with someone like me. Calhoun out."

TO BE CONTINUED

END
GAME

Captain's Log, Stardate 50927.2: A slight wrinkle has presented itself in our dealings with the Nelkarites. I am attempting to deal with the situation in a Starfleet-prescribed manner of diligence and patience.

First Officer's Personal Log, Stardate 50927.2: We are faced with a somewhat disastrous situation. We have brought four dozen refugees to the planet Nelkar, at the invitation of the Nelkarites, who agreed to give them shelter. However, the Nelkarites are now using the innocent refugees in a bizarre power play. This is a classic section C-5 hostage scenario which calls for careful handling, but Captain Calhoun has displayed nothing but intransigence. If Mackenzie Calhoun thinks he can simply write off the lives of four dozen hostages . . . and follow it up by bombarding a planet . . . I am simply going to have to set him straight on that. And if I fail, then God help me, I may have to try and assume leadership of the Excalibur *on the basis that Mac is simply not fit for command.*

LAHEERA

I

The refugees from the *Cambon* bleated in fear as they were herded into a large auditorium. Pacing the front of the room was the woman whom they knew to be Laheera . . . apparently a high muck-a-muck in the hierarchy of the world of Nelkar. She looked at them angrily, her fury seeming to radiate from her in such a manner that it was measurable by instrumentation. Standing next to her was Celter, the governor of the capital city of Selinium, which was their present location.

One of the group's leaders, an older, silver-haired man named Boretskee, took a step forward and said with slow uncertainty, "Is there . . . a problem? We were about to be moved into our new homes when—"

"Yes, you could say there's a problem," Laheera said, making no effort at all to contain her fury. It was rather an impressive combination: the golden, almost angelic hue of Laheera combined with unbridled fury. "We have asked that the *Excalibur* provide us with a simple form of 'payment,' as it were. Compensation for the trouble that we are going to provide you with a new home."

The refugees looked at each other uncertainly. Cary, who was standing next to Boretskee, said, " 'Payment'? We, uhm . . ." She shifted uncomfortably from one foot to the other. "We had not been under the impression that any sort of payment was going to be required. We would . . . I mean, obviously, we would like to cooperate. Anything that we can do . . ."

Celter now spoke up. "We do not desire payment from you. You are merely—to be blunt—a means to an end. We are not looking for monetary gain, but rather a simple barter situation. We have what you desire—a place for you to stay—and the *Excalibur* has advanced technology which we find desirable. We give you what you need, and we're given what we need. All benefit."

"The problem is that the *Excalibur* captain has refused to cooperate," Laheera cut in. "He has made it clear that he does not care what happens to any of you. He cares for his rules and regulations and for his own foolish pride. That is all."

"Happens . . . to us?" Boretskee was now profoundly confused, but he knew he didn't like the sound of that. "In what sense do you mean . . . 'happens' to us?"

But now Cary, Boretskee's slim, brunette wife, was looking around, and a terrible suspicion was beginning to dawn on her. "Where is Captain Hufmin?" she asked.

"Ah yes. The fearless leader of the good ship *Cambon*," said Laheera, dripping disdain. "I'm afraid that we had to make an example of him. Best solution, really. His incessant pawing of me was beginning to get tiresome."

"An . . . example," Cary said slowly. "You . . . you don't mean . . . you can't mean he's . . ."

"If the word you're searching for is 'dead,' yes, that's correct," Laheera said flatly.

There were gasps from among the hostages. One young girl, named Meggan, began to cry. The others were too much in shock to do much more than reel at the news.

Drawing himself up, Boretskee said sharply, "And now we're next, is that it? Is that how this goes? Unless the starship does what you tell it to do?"

"That is correct, yes," replied Celter. Laheera nodded in silent agreement as Celter continued, "Now listen carefully to me. You have one chance, and one chance only, to survive. Captain Calhoun has made it clear that he is perfectly willing to let you die. It is up to you to change his mind. If you do not, we shall kill you all. Is that clear?''

Boretskee took a step forward, his body trembling with rage. He was something of a scrapper, and his dearest wish was to tell Laheera and Celter and every member of the Nelkarite race to simply drop dead and do their worst. But then he saw the frightened look on his wife's face, and saw likewise the fear in the expressions of the other refugees, reduced to nothing more than pieces in a sick power struggle between the Nelkarites and the *Excalibur*. And he could not help but feel that his was the responsibility. Calhoun had voiced apprehension about the Nelkarites, but Boretskee and Cary had insisted that taking the Nelkarites up on their offer was the right way to go. And now look where everyone stood. No, if anyone was going to do something about this mess, by right it had to be Boretskee.

''All right,'' he said slowly. ''Let me talk to him.'' And, noticing the sobbing young girl, he nodded his head in her direction and said, ''And her, too. Calhoun would have to be one cold-hearted son of a bitch to ignore the pleadings of a child. Between the two of us we should be able to get him to do what you want,'' and silently he added, . . . *you bastards.*

You bastard, thought Commander Elizabeth Shelby, but she didn't say it.

In the captain's ready room, just off the bridge, it was entirely possible that she didn't have to say it. She stood there, facing Calhoun, who was looking thoughtfully out his observation window.

''You're not really going to do this thing,'' she said.

''Is that an order or a question?'' he asked, his purple eyes flickering in—damn him—amusement.

''You cannot simply abandon the refugees to the mercies of the Nelkarites. Furthermore, you cannot then exact some sort of vengeance by firing upon Nelkar.''

''Why?'' He seemed genuinely puzzled. ''Which part?''

''The whole thing!''

''Indeed.'' He frowned a moment, and then started ticking off examples on his fingers. ''If I had forced the refugees to remain on the ship against their will, that would have constituted kidnapping. Kidnapping is against regs. So, in accordance with regulation, I allowed them to settle on Nelkar. As such, they are now part of Nelkar society. If the Nelkarites decide that they want to obliterate the refugees, that falls under their prerogative, as per the Prime Directive. Correct?''

Her mouth opened for a moment, and then closed. Grimly, she nodded.

''That leaves the question of firing upon the Nelkarites. The Nelkarites are endeavoring to perform extortion. Attempting to perform extortion upon a Federation vessel is a violation of Federation law. As captain of the *Excalibur,* I am the authorized representative of Federation law for this sector. I consider the populace of Nelkar guilty of extortion. Would you argue that they're not?''

''No,'' she said quietly.

''No reasonable person would. So they're guilty as charged, tried and convicted in absentia. I also have broad latitude when it comes to deciding upon a sentence. So I sentence them to photon torpedo barrage.''

''There is no such sentence in Federation law,'' Shelby informed him.

''True, but that's the 'broad latitude' part.''

She slammed the table with her open palms, much as he had done the other day. It caused the objects on the surface to rattle. ''There's got to be another way,'' she said tightly. ''There's got to be. This isn't a word game. This isn't a puzzle. This isn't a joke—''

''I know it's not,'' replied Calhoun, and for just a moment he let the frustration he was feeling show in his voice. He ran his fingers through his dark hair in frustration. ''You don't understand, Elizabeth. I've faced this sort of situation before.''

She tilted her head slightly and looked at him in puzzlement. ''During your Starfleet career?''

He shook his head. ''No. On Xenex, when I was a teenager.'' He leaned against his viewing port, and for the first time Shelby noticed that he looked extremely tired. ''The Danteri captured the population of a small village, marched the people out, and announced that they were going to kill them all unless we, the leaders of the rebellion, surrendered ourselves.''

''And did you?'' she asked.

He grunted. ''Of course not. We weren't stupid. They would have killed us immediately. I wish you could have seen those people, those captives. Down to the smallest child, every one of them was filled with Xenexian pride. Their heads held high, their faces unflinching.''

"And you just . . . just stood by and let them all be slaughtered?''

"No,'' he said quietly. "We attacked. We attacked the Danteri while they were in the village. As we expected, they tried to use the citizens as shields. And there were the Xenexian hostages, shouting loudly, 'Shoot through us! Don't let them hide behind us! Don't inflict that shame on us!' ''

"But you didn't really shoot through them . . .'' But then she saw the look in his eyes, and her voice caught. "My God, you did. You killed them all.''

"No, not all. Most of them survived, a happenstance attributable to good aim on our part and the Danteri clearly being unprepared for their strategy not to work. To do otherwise would have been to bring dishonor among the Xenexians. They were willing to die for the cause.''

"Well, that's really great, Mac,'' said Shelby, beginning to pace. "That's just swell. But here's the problem: The people stuck on Nelkar aren't out to be martyrs. They're victims who just happen to be in the wrong place at the wrong time.''

"As were the villagers,'' replied Mackenzie Calhoun. "They didn't live their lives eagerly awaiting a violent death. But they were chosen by oppressors to be made pawns. If you let people with that mind-set bend you to their will . . . if you give in, even once . . . it encourages further such actions.''

"And it disempowers you, because you know you can be manipulated.''

He nodded. "Yes. I'm pleased you understand.''

Shelby stroked her chin for a moment, and then said, "If you don't mind my asking . . . who gave the order? To shoot through those hostages, I mean?''

She knew the answer even before he said it: "I did.''

"And how did that make you feel? Knowing that they might be killed when you opened fire?''

"I had no feelings about it one way or the other,'' he said quietly. "I couldn't afford to.''

"And you have no feeling about these hostages now? These people trapped below us on Nelkar?''

"None."

"I don't believe that," she said flatly. "The Mackenzie Calhoun I know wouldn't be uncaring. Wouldn't be writing them off."

He had looked away from her, but now he turned to face her and said, in a very quiet voice, "Then I guess you didn't know me all too well."

"That may have been why we broke up," she mused. Then, after a moment's further thought, she said, "Captain, there has to be some other way. Some middle ground. Some way to proceed between the extremes of simply writing off the hostages as lost, and giving in to the Nelkarites completely. Perhaps if you study precedents . . ."

"Precedents?" He had a slight touch of amusement in his voice, which for some reason she found remarkably annoying. "Such as . . . ?"

"I don't know specifically. Actions taken by other captains, other commanders. Some way that will enable you to find guidance. You have to find a way to work with these people on some sort of equitable basis."

"I understand what you're saying, Elizabeth. And there may very well be merit to it. Still, I—"

At that moment, his comm badge beeped. He tapped it and said, "Calhoun here. Speak to me."

"Captain," came Robin Lefler's voice, "we are receiving an incoming hail from the Nelkarites."

Calhoun cast a quick glance at Shelby, but she was poker-faced. "On my way" was all he said, and he moved quickly past Shelby out onto the bridge. His crew, although maintaining their professional demeanor, nonetheless looked a bit apprehensive. He knew that they had considered his pronouncement a short while ago to be somewhat disconcerting. The concept of sacrificing the hostages in the face of a greater concern . . . it was difficult for them to grasp. They were good people, a good crew . . . but, in this instance, perhaps a bit overcompassionate. It was not something that he could afford to let influence his decisions, however. "Put them on visual," he said crisply.

A moment later, the image of Laheera appeared, and with her was Boretskee.

"There are some people here who wish to speak with you, Captain," Laheera informed him. She nodded to Boretskee.

Boretskee looked as uncomfortable as a person possibly could. He cleared his throat loudly and said, "Captain, I understand that we . . . that is to say, that you . . . have been placed in a rather difficult position. I . . . we regret this inconvenience and—"

Laheera made an impatient noise. He tossed a look at her that could have cracked castrodinium, and then resumed what he was saying. "There are innocent people down here, Captain. People whose lives are depending upon what you will do next."

Laheera now spoke up. "And do not get any charming ideas about using your transporters to solve the difficulties, Captain. We've scattered the hostages throughout the city. They're at no one location from which you can rescue them. For that matter, if you attempt to lock on to our transmission and, say, beam me out so that I can be used as a hostage . . . they will be killed. You've said that, as far as you are concerned, they are dead, and you will act accordingly. We both know it is easy to say such things. I invite you, however, to look upon the face of the 'dead.' "

She reached out of range of the viewer and dragged someone else into the picture. It was Meggan, the little girl with her hair tied back in a large bun, her eyes as deep as the depths of space.

Calhoun looked neither right nor left, did not look at any of his people. Instead he kept his gaze leveled on the screen. When Laheera spoke it was with grim defiance—and yet that annoying voice of hers, with its musicality, made her life-and-death terms seem almost charming to hear. "Now then, Captain . . . your stubborn nature might be slightly more reasonable when the depths of your situation become apparent. You have said that you will open fire on us if we slay the hostages. My question to you is: Do you really have the nerve to stand there and let us kill them? You have said that the *Excalibur* is on a humanitarian mission. What sort of humanitarian would you be if you followed the course that you have set out for yourself, hmm? So, Captain . . . what will it be?"

Calhoun seemed to contemplate her with about as much passion as he would if he were peering through a microscope and watching an amoeba flutter around. And then, very quietly, he said, "Very well, Laheera. You are correct. This is a pointless exercise."

"I'm pleased you are listening to reason."

But Calhoun had now turned his back to Laheera. Instead he was facing Boyajian, who was standing at the tactical station, filling in for the absent Zak Kebron. "Mr. Boyajian," he said, and his tone was flat and unwavering. "Arm photon torpedoes one and two."

If Boyajian was surprised at the order, he was pro enough not to let it show. "Arming photon torpedoes, sir. Target?"

"Torpedo one should be locked on to the origin point of this transmission. Torpedo two . . ." He hesitated a moment, considering. "Run a quick sensor sweep on Selinium. Find a densely populated section of town."

"Populated?" Shelby spoke up, unable to keep the astonishment from her voice. "Sir, perhaps a technological target might be preferable? Some area of high energy discharge, indicating a power plant or—"

"Power plants can be rebuilt," Calhoun said reasonably. "People can't. Mr. Boyajian, have you got those targets locked in yet?"

"Yes, sir." Boyajian didn't sound happy about it.

"Projected casualty count from both torpedoes?"

Boyajian felt his mouth go very dry. He licked his lips, checked the estimates, and then said, "Ap . . ." His throat also felt like dust. "Approximately five . . . hundred thousand, sir."

All eyes were now on Calhoun. From her science station, Soleta's face was stoic and unreadable. At conn, Mark McHenry actually looked amused, as if he was certain that Calhoun would not do what he was preparing to do. Only Robin Lefler at ops was allowing her concern to show. She was biting her lower lip, a nervous habit that she'd been trying to break herself of for ten years. She wasn't having much success, and moments like this weren't making it easier on her.

And Shelby . . .

. . . Shelby was looking at him, not with anger, as he would have guessed, but with a vague sort of disappointment.

All of this, Calhoun took in in a second or two. "Half a million. Impressive. Mr. McHenry, how long until we're in range?" he asked.

"At present orbital speed, one minute, three seconds," said McHenry, without, Calhoun noticed, checking his navigation board. Below them the blue/gray sphere that was Nelkar turned beneath them as they circled it.

"And once we've fired the torpedoes, how long until they reach primary targets?"

"Forty-seven seconds."

He nodded and then said to Boyajian, "Engage safety locks on the torpedoes, Mr. Boyajian. Forty-four-second cut-off."

"Engaging safety locks, aye, sir."

On the screen, Laheera watched the activity on the bridge without fully understanding what was going on. "Captain, what are you playing at? May I remind you we have the fate of the hostages to consider."

"There's no need. What you don't understand is that I am determining their fate. Not you. Me. And I'm determining your fate as well. Your earlier point is well taken. There's no need for me to stand around waiting for you to murder the hostages. For that matter, you've already killed one: Captain Hufmin. For that alone, you should consider this your punishment. A pity that others have to die with you, but those are the fortunes of war." And with what seemed virtually no hesitation on his part, he turned back to Boyajian and said crisply, "Fire photon torpedoes, and then give me a countdown."

For the briefest of moments, Boyajian paused, and then in a firm voice, he replied, "Aye, sir." He punched a control and two photon torpedoes leaped from the underbelly of the *Excalibur* and hurtled downward toward the unprotected city. "Torpedoes away," he said. "Forty-seven . . . forty-six . . . forty-five . . ."

It sounded as if Laheera's voice had just gone up an octave. Boretskee and the small girl were looking around in confusion, not entirely grasping what had just occurred. "What have you done?!" demanded Laheera.

"I have just fired two photon torpedoes. They'll be slowed down a bit as they pass through your atmosphere, but they'll still have sufficient firepower to level whatever they hit."

". . . thirty-seven . . . thirty-six . . ." Boyajian was intoning.

"You'll kill them! You'll kill her!" and Laheera shook the young girl, who let out a squeal of alarm. "You wouldn't!"

"Yes, I would."

"They're blanks! You're bluffing!"

". . . thirty . . . twenty-nine . . ." came the steady count from Boyajian.

"They're running hot, I assure you," he said with quiet conviction. "But they're armed with safety locks. I can abort them during the first forty seconds. In the last seven seconds, however, nothing can turn them back. Agree to release the hostages, or within the next . . ."

"... twenty ..." supplied Boyajian.

"Thank you, twenty seconds ... you're dead. You, and about half a million Nelkarites. Gone, in one shot, because of the threats and strong-arming of you and Governor Celter for shortcuts. Decide now, Laheera."

For a moment she seemed to waver, and then she drew herself up and said firmly, "You are bluffing. I can smell it from here. Do your worst."

Calhoun's face was utterly inscrutable. "You're gambling half a million lives, including yours, on your sense of smell."

"Mine? No. No, I'm broadcasting from a deep enough shelter that I'll be safe. As for the rest, well ... as I said, I'm positive you're bluffing. I'll stake their lives on my instincts any day."

"If you care about your people, reconsider."

"No."

There was dead silence on the bridge, and through it reverberated Boyajian's voice as he began the final countdown. "Ten ... nine ... eight ..."

An infinity of thoughts tumbled through Shelby's mind. This was the time. This was the time to do it. For she knew now something that was previously unclear to her. Mackenzie Calhoun had spent his formative years as—simply put—a terrorist. It was easy to overlook that, because one tended to give him more flattering, even romantic labels such as "rebel leader" or "freedom fighter." But at core, he was indeed a terrorist, and he had fallen back on terrorist tactics. Proper procedures meant nothing to him. Life itself meant nothing to him. All that mattered was pounding his opponents until they could no longer resist.

"... seven ..."

Now, her mind screamed, *now! Take command, declare Calhoun unfit, and order Boyajian to abort! It's not mutiny! No one on this bridge wants to see this travesty happen! They're looking to me to take charge!*

"... six ..."

On the screen was Laheera, arms folded, smug, confident. The stunned, shocked faces of Boretskee and the young girl were evident.

"... five ..."

On the bridge was Calhoun, arms behind his back, staring levelly at the screen, and then, for no apparent reason, his gaze flickered to

Shelby. Her eyes locked with Calhoun's, seemed to bore directly into the back of his brain.

Boyajian's lips began to form the letter "f " for four. . . .

"Abort," said Calhoun.

Boyajian's finger, which had been poised a microcentimeter above the control panel, stabbed down, the reflex so quick that he didn't even have time to register a sense of relief.

Several thousand feet above Selinium, two photon torpedoes—which normally would have exploded on impact—received a detonation command. They blew up prematurely, creating a spectacular flash of light and rolling of sound in the blue skies overhead. The people of Selinium—who had no idea that a pair of torpedoes had been winging their way—looked up in confusion and fear. No one had a ready explanation for what had just happened. A number of people had to be treated for flash-blindness, having had the misfortune to be looking directly into the explosion when it occurred. Many others had a ringing in the ears from the noise. Even as the echo of the detonation died away, Nelkarites turned to one another for answers and found none.

But an explanation was not long in coming. For Governor Celter immediately went on citywide comm channels and, with that famed, calming presence of his, seemed to be looking into the hearts of anyone who watched as he announced, "No doubt most, if not all, of you were witness to the explosion overhead. I am pleased to announce that we have been testing a new weapons system which will—I assure you—give us a new, more secure Nelkar than ever before. This was, however, a secret test, as such things often are, and we were not able to announce the test beforehand. On that basis, I hope you will forgive us any concern that might have been caused on your part. We are, after all, working for a common goal: the best, safest Nelkar possible. No need to concern yourselves, and you can all go on about your business. Thank you for your attention."

And he smiled in that way he had.

Once again there was silence on the bridge . . . except this time it was broken by low, contemptuous laughter.

The laughter was coming from Laheera. She could see the entire scene on the bridge of the *Excalibur*. It looked as if that Shelby woman was sorry that she couldn't simply reach through the viewscreen and strangle her. Still, Shelby's state of mind was hardly a major concern to Laheera.

Calhoun, for his part, stood straight and tall . . . and yet, somehow, he seemed . . . smaller.

"Now then, Captain," Laheera said, "since we know where each of us stands . . . let's get down to business, shall we? We can be flexible in our demands. Advance, in our weapons systems, in our warp drive propulsion . . . oh, and matter transportation, of course. We know that you've mastered it. Our experiments in that realm have been somewhat less than satisfying. Our test subjects have not come through the process in—shall we say—presentable condition. We trust that you will be able to aid us in these matters?"

"Yes," said Calhoun, in a voice so soft that it was barely above a whisper.

Indeed, Laheera made a show of cupping her ear and saying, "Excuse me? I didn't quite hear that."

"I said yes," Calhoun repeated, more loudly but with no intensity. It was as if there had been fire in him that had been doused.

"That's good to hear. Very good."

"We would like to . . . review the information that you need," Calhoun said. "Understand, this is not an . . . an easy thing we're doing. We still feel that giving you what you request is fundamentally wrong and potentially harmful. Obviously we have to cooperate with you, under the circumstances. But we want to try and minimize what we perceive as the damage we may do you."

"That's very considerate of you, Captain," said Laheera, making no effort to keep the irony from her voice. "After all, we know that at this moment, the Nelkarites are likely your very favorite race in the entire galaxy. Naturally you would be placing our welfare at the very top of your list of concerns."

Calhoun said nothing. There didn't seem to be any point to it.

"You have twenty-four hours, Captain. That should be more than enough, I would think. More than enough."

"Thank you," said Calhoun. "That's very generous of you."

She smiled thinly. "I can afford to be generous in victory . . . just as you appear to be gracious in defeat."

She snapped off the viewscreen and turned to face Boretskee and Meggan. "There," she said in that charmingly musical voice. "That wasn't so difficult now, was it?"

Boretskee's mouth drew back in a snarl. He was so filled with fury that he couldn't even form words.

"Now then . . . the guards will escort you to your quarters," she continued. "And there you will remain until we've gotten what we wanted. And if, for some reason, the *Excalibur* does not come through as promised . . . well then, we'll get together again," and she smiled mercilessly, "for one last time. Now . . . off you go. Oh, and have the guards be sure to take you past the Main Worship Tower. It's very scenic, and I wouldn't want you to miss it."

Shelby was prepared to console Calhoun in whatever way she could. To tell him that he had acted correctly. That in displaying mercy, he had shown strength, not weakness. That anyone else on the bridge would have done the exact same thing. That she was not ashamed of him, but proud of him.

She didn't have time to say any of it, because the moment that the screen blinked out, Calhoun turned to face his crew, wearing a look of grim amusement.

" 'Gracious in defeat' my ass. I'm going to kick the crap out of them."

THALLON

III

Thallon was a dying world . . . of this, the leader was certain.

The leader was in his study when the ground rocked beneath his feet. This time around, nothing was thrown from the shelves, no artwork hurled off the walls. It wasn't that the quake was any gentler than the previous ones; it was just that the leader, having learned his lessons from previous difficulties, had had everything bolted in place.

Still, that wasn't enough to prevent structural damage. The quake seemed to go for an eternity before finally subsiding, and while he was clutching the floor, the leader noticed a thin crack that started around the middle of the room and went all the way to one of the corners. His own, red-skinned reflection grimaced back at him from the highly polished surface.

He drew himself up to a sitting position, but remained on the floor long after the trembling had stopped. This place, this "palace" once belonging to the imperial family . . . it was his now. His and his allies'.

It was what he had wanted, what they had all wanted. What they had deserved. The royal family had ruled, had dictated, had hoarded, had been moved by self-interest for more generations than anyone could count. It was high time that the people took back that which was rightfully theirs. And if it benefited the leader, so much the better.

In a way, the royal family had led a collectively charmed life. Their ascension to power had its roots in the earliest parts of the planet's history, when they had been among the first to devise the Great Machines which had tapped into the energy-rich ground of Thallon. The machines' power had been theirs, and as the world had thrived . . . and later the empire had expanded . . . so had the influence and strength of the royal family spread as well. Indeed, the early stories of both Thallon's origins and the origins of the royal family were so steeped in legend and oral tradition that the world itself seemed to smack of mythology. It was as if there was something bigger-than-life about the homeworld of the Thallonian Empire.

But in recent years, as everyone on Thallon knew, the Great Machines were finding less and less energy to draw for the purpose of supplying Thallon's energy needs. Like an oil well drying out, Thallon was becoming an energy-depleted world. There had been cutbacks, blackouts, entire cities gone dark for days, weeks at a time. The legend had acquired a coat of tarnish, and that general feeling of dissatisfaction had grown and grown until it had spiraled completely out of control.

When wealth and power were plentiful, it seemed that there was enough for all. When such things were reduced to a premium, then did the remaining mongrels fight over the scraps. And the royal family had been torn asunder in the battle.

Many had already abandoned Thallon, the stars calling to them, offering them safer haven. There were, after all, other worlds within the once-empire that could sustain them. In addition there were places outside the empire to which they could go.

But there were others who refused to run. The symbol of their achievements was right here on Thallon. Indeed, many of them firmly clutched on to the idea that somehow, by dint of the royal family being dismantled, matters would turn around—that Thallon would be entering a new era thanks to the ejection of the royals—and there were many who did not want to take the chance of missing out.

And, unfortunately, there were a few—a precious few—who wanted the royal family back.

"You look preoccupied."

The leader glanced over and saw Zoran standing in the doorway.

The tall, powerfully built Thallonian seemed to occupy the entire space as he stood there, staring in mild confusion and amusement. "Do you find it particularly comfortable on the floor?"

"In case you didn't notice, we just had another quake."

"Yes, I noticed. Nothing that any true Thallonian should be overly concerned about, though."

"You think not? Your confidence is most reassuring," muttered the leader, making no effort to hide his sarcasm. He rose to his feet and dusted himself off. "I am concerned that these quakes are going to continue to occur until . . ."

"Until what? The planet explodes?" Zoran made a dismissive noise. "Such things are the province of fantasy, not reality. This world is solid, and this world will thrive again. And you stand there and act as if it's going to crack open like a giant egg. You need to have a little more confidence."

"And you need to have a little less," said the leader. He began to pace, his hands draped behind his back. "I expected to hear from you via subspace radio. The lengthy silence was not anticipated."

"I felt it would be better to run silent," Zoran replied. "Transmissions can always be intercepted."

"Fine, fine," the leader said. "How did it go? Was the ambush successful? Was M'k'n'zy lured to the science station, as we anticipated?"

Zoran was mildly puzzled at the leader's attitude. He would have anticipated some degree of urgency in the questions, but instead the leader seemed barely interested. "No. The signal was sent out, as planned, and the *Excalibur* did receive it, but they did not show up."

The leader looked mildly surprised. "Odd. Ryjaan was positive that they would, as was D'ndai."

"Really." Zoran did not even try to suppress his smug grin. "And did either Ryjaan, the Danteri fool, or D'ndai, the idiot brother of M'k'n'zy Calhoun, tell you that Si Cwan was aboard the ship?"

The leader's face went a deeper shade of red as he stared in astonishment at Zoran. "Lord Si Cwan? He lives?" He seemed to gasp, his surprise apparently overwhelming.

"Not anymore. He and a Starfleet officer—a Brikar—flew out to the station on their own, in a runabout. Supposedly they were to provide temporary aid until the *Excalibur* could join them later, but what really caught Si Cwan's attention was that we listed his sister among the passengers.''

"Why did you do that?"

"We thought that listing a member of the former royal family would be an additional lure and incentive for the *Excalibur*. We didn't want to take any chances of failing to catch their attention. Kalinda was the only one who is officially still listed as missing." He smirked. "One might consider it 'divine inspiration,' I suppose. I plucked her name out of the ether, and as a consequence, got the brother."

"You mean Lord Si Cwan is dead."

"That is correct."

"I see." He scratched his chin thoughtfully. "And it never occurred to you that if we disposed of him in a more public forum . . . say, here on Thallon . . . that it might better serve our interests."

"My interest was in seeing him dead. Period." Zoran was beginning to bristle a bit. "I would have expected a bit of gratitude from you. Some thanks. I tell you I wiped out Si Cwan, the man whom you hated more than any, and all you can do is stand there and make snide comments."

"No. That is not all I can do." And then, with a move so quick that Zoran didn't even see it coming, the leader's fist swept around and caught Zoran on the point of his chin. Zoran, caught off guard, went down. He sat there for a moment, stunned, the world whirling about him. From above him the leader said mockingly, "Do you find it particularly comfortable on the floor?"

Zoran's anger, barely controlled even at the best of times, began to boil up within him. "Why . . . why did you . . ."

"He's not dead."

"Yes, he is," Zoran said forcefully as he staggered to his feet. "I blew him up! Blew up the station! Ask Rojam if you don't believe me! Ask Juif! They were there!"

"Yes, I know they were. And so was D'ndai."

Zoran gaped. He could barely get any words out, and the one word he was able to manage was "What?"

"You heard me."

"He wasn't! He was nowhere around!"

"He showed up just as you departed. He wanted to check on your progress, to see if the *Excalibur* had fallen for the bait. He had intended to leave as quickly as he had arrived, but when he saw your hurried departure and no sign of the starship anywhere, he scanned the science station and discovered that there were two individuals aboard . . . and an energy buildup that indicated a bomb set for detonation. Since you had clearly deviated from the plan, he opted to take no chances and beamed them aboard his own vessel.''

"They're safe?!" Zoran was trembling so violently one would have thought another quake had begun. "They're safe! I left them for dead, Si Cwan and the Brikar both! *They're safe?!*"

"No, they're merely alive. 'Safe' is a very subjective term. D'ndai has both of them in lockup on his vessel. He's bringing them here.''

"Here! Why here?''

"Because," said the leader, and his voice became deep and harsh, "we're going to hold a proper execution. His will not be a fine and private death. All of Thallon will see the execution of Si Cwan. They will see him writhe, and cry out, and soil himself. There are some, you see, who still hold him in esteem. Still have an image of him as being a protector of the people, someone who cares about them. But I know him, you see, as do you. Know him to be as arrogant and insufferable as any of his brethren. And when the people see him wallowing in his own misery, then finally—once and for all—they will put aside all thoughts of their previous leadership." He clapped a hand on the shoulder of Zoran and smiled. "It will be glorious.''

"Do you think that it will work out so easily?" asked Zoran. "Are people truly that easily manipulated?''

"The masses will believe what we want them to believe," replied the leader. "You would be amazed how easily people can be persuaded to accept whatever it is you want, particularly when you appeal to any of their four most basic motivations: Greed. Fear. A contempt for weakness. And self-preservation. When those are brought to the forefront of people's minds, governments topple, and the citizens congratulate each other and call themselves patriots.''

LAHEERA

III

Three hours before she was confronted by a bloodthirsty mob, Laheera first learned that she had a serious problem on her hands.

She was in her office in the main government building. As military head and right arm to Governor Celter, she was naturally entitled to rather impressive quarters . . . not only in the main wing, but also in the subterranean shelter from which she was capable of conducting subspace negotiations with relative assurance of her own safety. It had been barely two hours since the communiqué with the *Excalibur* wherein she had signed off by congratulating Calhoun on being a gracious loser. She was busy trying to calculate how best to profit through acquiring the technology that would provide near-instantaneous matter transmission, when Celter had come running into her office. He slammed open the doors with his shoulder, barely slowing down, and his gold skin had gone completely ashen. "Have you heard what they're doing? What those bastards are doing? Have you seen? Have you heard?"

She looked up at him in confusion. "What are you talking about? What—"

"It's all over the comms! All over everything! Everywhere! Everyone's heard about it! You've killed us, Laheera! You've killed us all!"

He was becoming hysterical, words tumbling over each other, becoming impossible to understand. She rose from behind her desk angrily, crossed the room, and stood before him, arms folded impatiently. What she really wanted to do was slap him but, aside from slitting the occasional throat or blowing an opponent out of space, Laheera tried to avoid violence whenever possible. "Would you calm down and tell me what you're talking about?"

For answer, Celter pulled a remote off his belt, aimed it at her viewscreen, and thumbed it to life. The screen snapped on . . .

. . . and Laheera was seeing the bridge of the *Excalibur.* The angle was from over Calhoun's shoulder as he was facing the viewscreen . . .

. . . and she was on the screen. She was sitting there, conversing with Calhoun, and she was wearing an insufferably smug expression, and Calhoun was saying with a deadpan expression, "You're gambling half a million lives, including yours, on your sense of smell."

"Mine?" Laheera was smirking. "No. No, I'm broadcasting from a deep enough shelter that I'll be safe. As for the rest, well . . . as I said, I'm positive you're bluffing. I'll stake their lives on my instincts any day."

"If you care about your people, reconsider."

"No."

Laheera watched, feeling the blood drain from her face until her tint matched Celter's. Her mouth moved, but no words emerged, as the entire scene played itself out. Then the screen wavered slightly and the entire scene began again.

"Do you have any idea how this makes us look!" Celter was nearly shrieking. "There's the noble captain of the *Excalibur,* trying to save the hostages that we're holding . . . and yet valuing Nelkarite lives so highly that he preserves the lives of our citizens while we ourselves are willing to throw them away!"

"They were never in danger," Laheera tried to stammer out.

"Well, they don't see it that way!"

"Shut the picture off," she said, and when Celter didn't respond quickly enough, she grabbed the remote out of his hand and did it herself. She whirled to face him. "It's originating from the *Excalibur,* isn't it?"

"Of course it is! Where else?!"

"Jam it," she said tightly. "Jam the transmission!"

"We tried! They kept overriding it!"

"Shut it down, then! Shut down the entire comm system! Take it off the air!"

"We did that, too!" said Celter in exasperation. "We went dark over an hour ago! It took them no more than ten minutes to wire it back to life!"

"From *orbit?* What are they, magicians?!"

"They're devils! Devils incarnate!" Celter was wringing his hands. "There's uprising everywhere! The people are going berserk! They're furious! They say we don't care about them! That we used them, just as we're using the hostages!"

"We were trying to act in their best interests. . . ."

"I know that! You know that!" He pointed out in the general direction of the city. "But they don't know that! They don't care about it! They say we've betrayed them, and they're out for blood!"

"All right," said Laheera after a moment's thought. "Get to your personal broadcast studio. Get out onto the comm. Tell the people that this is all a trick. That the Federation is playing them for fools."

"They won't believe it," and he gripped her upper arm so hard that she felt as if he were going to dislocate it. "You haven't heard the things they've been saying. The rioting, the fury . . . I can't even get their attention. . . ."

"Yes, you can," she said confidently. Delicately she disengaged his grip on her. "That's always been your strength. Speak to them. Get out over the comm and tell them . . ."

"Tell them what?"

For a moment her patience wavered and she said, *"Something!"* Then she reined herself in and said more calmly, "Something. Anything. Just do it. And stop nodding like that!" Whenever Celter was particularly anxious, his head tended to bob in an accelerated manner. "You look like your head's about to fall off!" Celter grimaced and immediately gained control of himself.

Then he patted her on the shoulders, as if he were drawing strength from her, and said, "Bless you, Laheera. I don't know what I'd do without you to help steady me." And then he hurried out of her office to prepare what he was determined would be the speech of his life. But he stopped just before he left and turned to Laheera, pointing a trembling finger. "And you . . . you get in touch with these *Excalibur* people.

With this Captain Calhoun. We've tried to hail him; he ignores us. Perhaps he'll respond to you. You tell him we'll obliterate the hostages, every one of them, immediately!''

"I have that very thought in mind." She raised her voice slightly and said, "Okur!"

Okur was the name of one of the two guards who stood directly outside her office at all times. Okur was half again as tall as any Nelkarite that Laheera had ever met, and twice as wide. He was also her lover on the side; a nice way, she felt, of commanding loyalty. He took a step into the door, moving aside as Celter bustled out. He nodded slightly and said, "Yes?"

"Ready my safe room. And bring me Meggan. No others: just Meggan. I don't need any of the men attempting heroics. This time I'll cut her from sternum to crotch while Calhoun watches."

There had been no excess chatter on the bridge of the *Excalibur* for some time. Calhoun merely sat there in his command chair, fingers steepled, gazing intently at the planet below. "Lefler," he would say every so often, "how is it going?"

And she would say the same thing: "Broadcast continuing as ordered, sir."

He would nod, looking mildly distracted, and then go back to studying Nelkar, as if he were capable of actually seeing what was happening on the surface.

Speaking in a low voice so that only he could hear, Shelby leaned forward and said, "Mac . . . are you sure about this?"

He looked at her without answering, his purple eyes appearing distracted for a moment before focusing on her. Then he gave an ever so slight shake of his head before smiling widely. "I guess we'll find out together if this is a good idea."

Boyajian looked up and said, "Incoming hail, sir."

"Still from Celter?"

"No, sir. This is from Laheera."

"Ah." He rose from his chair, as if he felt some degree of comfort or even confidence by speaking to her on his feet. "Finally the power behind the power speaks to me again." He tapped his comm badge. "Burgoyne. Speak to me."

"Burgoyne here," came the voice of the Hermat chief engineer.

"As we discussed, Burgy. Are you at your designated post?"

"Ready and waiting for your order for emergency beam-out, sir."

"I'm keeping this channel open. Listen to everything that goes on and wait for my signal." He glanced at Shelby, who nodded back. "All right, Boyajian," he ordered. "Put her on visual."

The screen shimmered and Laheera appeared. With her, just as Calhoun suspected would be the case, was Meggan. Laheera cut straight to the point: "What did you think you were doing, Captain?"

He affected a blank look. "I have no idea what you're talking about, Laheera. Is there a problem?"

"Don't be disingenuous with me, Captain."

He turned to Shelby with what appeared to be a puzzled expression. "Polite word for lying," she explained.

"Lying? Me?" He turned back to the screen. "I am shocked and appalled that you would imply such a thing, Laheera. Here we are, working to give you the best possible opportunities as we submit to your demands. And your response is to insult me. You have no idea how hurt I am."

"This is a charming little dance you have, Captain," she snapped at him. "I know what this is about. You seek to even out the status quo. You feel I undercut your authority in front of your people. So you decided that it would only be fair if you returned the favor. I will not bother to offer any thoughts as to your actions, since I see no reason to give you even more fodder to confuse the good people of Nelkar. I want you to cease the broadcast immediately."

"Broadcast?"

She rubbed the bridge of her nose, her exasperation mounting. "Do I have to threaten you once more, Captain? Do I have to threaten her?" and she inclined her head toward Meggan. "Our instruments show the broadcast is coming from your ship."

"From *our* ship? An unauthorized broadcast? I am shocked and appalled. Lieutenant," Calhoun said stiffly, turning to face Lefler, "do you know anything about some sort of . . . 'broadcast'?"

Lefler made a great show of checking the ops board, and then she let out a gasp so loud that one would have thought she'd just been tossed into a vacuum and all the air in her body was being expelled. "Captain! We seem to have a problem with the BVL," and then, by way of explanation, she said to Laheera on the screen, "Bridge Visual

Log,'' before continuing to Calhoun. ''Apparently the Visual Log detailing your communication with Laheera has been set into some sort of automatic broadcast into the communications web of Nelkar.''

''Good Lord!'' declared Calhoun. ''How could this have happened? This must be stopped immediately!''

''I'll get right on it, sir. I'll run a level-one diagnostic. I'll have this glitch tracked down in no time.''

''Laheera,'' Calhoun said, turning back to the screen. ''Please accept my most heartfelt apologies. This is a new vessel, and we're still working out many of the bugs. I must tell you that, having learned of this situation, I am, frankly, shocked.''

''And appalled?'' Laheera said dryly.

''Yes, absolutely, appalled. Far be it from me to risk stirring up the ire of your people.''

''Captain, perhaps you think you are charming, or clever. But I am fully aware of your Prime Directive that states there must be no interference in planetary affairs. You are doing so now, and I insist that you cease all such interference. Or to put it in simpler, one-syllable words: Hands off.''

''Interesting, Laheera,'' Calhoun said thoughtfully. ''You want us to abide strictly by the Prime Directive when information being disseminated is not to your liking . . . but want us to violate it when it serves your convenience. You can't have it both ways, Laheera. And I wouldn't ask you to choose.''

For a long moment the two of them simply stared at each other, challengingly, and then Laheera smiled. ''Very charming, Captain. You seem to think you have proven a point. Perhaps I am now supposed to break down, admit the error of my ways, and remove the terms I have that govern the fate of these people,'' and she touched Meggan on the shoulder. Meggan shrank from her hand. ''Captain, you are not in a position to try and enforce guilt on me, or make me bow to your desires.'' Something seemed to catch her attention, and then she said, ''Governor Celter is about to address the people. I think it would interest you to see how a beloved leader can calm the concerns of even the most fearful of people.''

She reached forward, apparently touching some sort of control, and then her image was replaced on the viewscreen by Celter. He was sitting in his office, looking quite relaxed in an overstuffed chair, his legs casually crossed. Calhoun could not help but be struck once more by the sheer golden beauty of these people. If only they weren't so contemptible and foul within.

"My good people of Nelkar," began Celter, spreading his hands wide.

That was as far as he got.

He jumped suddenly as the whine of a disruptor sounded outside the door of his office. He was on his feet, shouting out questions, demanding to know what was going on. It took absolutely no time for the answer to be supplied as the door was smashed open. Infuriated Nelkarites poured into the room, and if the faces of the Nelkarites looked nearly angelic when they were pleased, there was something incredibly terrifying to see those cherubic visages twisted into pure fury. They looked for all the world like a heavenly host, come to wreak a terrible vengeance.

"No, wait!" he shouted. "We were never going to hurt you! It's not that we didn't care! We can work this out, yes, we can!" and his head was bobbing furiously in that manner which Laheera had found so annoying.

But they were not listening to him. They had already heard all they needed to hear. One of the mob was wielding a phaser-like weapon, and he fired. His aim was not particularly good, however, as his pencil-thin beam shot past Celter's head, missing him by a good few inches.

Celter, however, didn't see it, so distracted was he by the shouting and anger which filled the room. A Nelkarite wielding a club swung at Celter, and Celter adroitly dodged to his left. It was a quick move, and had the beam from the weapon not been there, he would have managed to avoid—at least for a few seconds more—serious injury.

But the beam was there, and since Celter didn't see it, the force and direction of his jump carried him straight through the beam, which sliced through his neck as efficiently as piano wire through cheese. Celter hadn't fully comprehended what was happening, and he was still nodding with desperate agreeability when his head slid off his shoulders and thudded to the floor.

There was a stunned silence on the bridge, and Shelby looked to Calhoun to see grim satisfaction in his eyes.

The screen switched back to reveal a shocked Laheera, who had clearly seen the entire thing. She was looking upward and to her left, apparently having witnessed the entire scene on another screen. Meggan had seen it as well, and she'd gone dead white, putting her hand to her mouth as if she was worried that she was going to vomit . . . which she very well might have.

Laheera looked straight at Calhoun, and then back at the unseen screen. And then it was as if she forgot that she was on a live transmission with the *Excalibur.* Instead she shouted, "Okur! Okur! Get in here!"

But there was no immediate response from the person she was trying to summon. Instead what she heard, as did the rest of the crew, was more sounds of shouting. Of running feet, and weapons being fired, and howls of pain and terror.

"People want to believe in their leaders, Laheera," Calhoun said quietly. "You betrayed them, put them at risk, were willing to write off half a million lives on a whim. People don't take kindly to such betrayals."

The door to her inner sanctum began to buckle inward, and Laheera let out a shriek. Meggan saw it as well, and she tried to bolt for a far part of the room, but Laheera snagged her by the wrist and whipped her around, holding her in front of her body as a shield. The child struggled as Laheera yanked out a knife—the same one that she had used to kill Hufmin—and put it to the child's throat. "Don't come in here!" she was shouting, although it was doubtful she could be heard over the torrent of abuse and anger that was pouring through the door.

"Captain . . ." Shelby said nervously.

Calhoun looked carved from marble. "You still on line, Burgoyne?"

"Still here, sir."

"Get ready."

On the screen, they saw the door bend still further, and then it burst inward. They saw a quick glimpse of Okur, and he was fighting with such fierceness that Calhoun had a moment of sympathy for him. Whoever this behemoth was, he was clearly not going down without a fight. There were cuts and bruises all over him, looking like obscenities against the pure gold of his skin. And then he did indeed go down, driven to the ground by the infuriated Nelkarites stampeding through the door.

"Don't move!" Laheera was shouting at the crowd. She pressed the knife up and against the child's throat. "Don't move or this one's death will be on your heads!"

And that was when Calhoun, calm as you please, said, "Burgoyne . . . energize."

And everyone watched as, on the screen, the familiar hum and scintillation of the transporter beams began to take effect. Laheera looked around in confusion as she heard the sound. Then she recognized it for what it was and for a moment—just for one moment—she thought she was about to elude her attackers.

She thought this for precisely as long as it took for Meggan's molecular structure to dissolve and be spirited away to the *Excalibur*. And then Laheera found herself holding her knife to thin air.

Laheera spun, faced the screen, looked straight across the distance at Calhoun, and Laheera the blackmailer, the extorter, the murderer, screamed to Mackenzie Calhoun, *"Save me!"*

And it was M'k'n'zy of Calhoun, M'k'n'zy the savage, M'k'n'zy the warrior, who had crossed swords with an empire and lived to speak of it, who replied with icy calm, "You wanted hands off. You've got hands off."

The mob descended upon her, and just before she vanished beneath their number, she howled, *"You bastard!"*

He replied softly, as much to himself as to her, since she was otherwise distracted and unable to hear him. "You don't know the half of it. Good-bye, Laheera." He turned to Lefler and said, "Screen off."

Robin Lefler moved to switch off the transmission, but just before she could, she saw blood spatter on the picture. She jumped back slightly, as if concerned that it was going to spray on her. And then the potentially gory scene was replaced by their view of the planet below. It turned calmly, serenely, and from their godlike height it would have been impossible to tell that there was anything extraordinary going on.

"Commander," said Calhoun quietly, "give things an hour or so to calm down. Then contact the planet surface, find out who's in charge, and ascertain whether the safety of the refugees can be assured. Let's hope the new regime will be more reasonable. It's hard to believe they'd be less so." And he headed for the turbolift.

"If I may ask, sir, where are you going?" inquired Shelby.

He paused at the lift entrance and then said thoughtfully, "To Hell, probably." And he walked out.

The bridge crew looked after him, and then Mark McHenry opined, "Give him six months, he'd be running the place."

No one disagreed.

Calhoun sat in the Team Room, staring intently at the drink in his hand. Crew members were glancing his way and talking softly among themselves. Word had spread throughout the ship of how Calhoun had handled the blackmail and threats of the Nelkarite government . . . correction, the former Nelkarite government. A general consensus had already formed among the crew: This was a man you definitely wanted on your side rather than against you.

"Captain . . ."

Calhoun looked up and saw Burgoyne 172 standing there. To Calhoun's mild surprise, Burgoyne stuck out hish hand. "If it's not too forward, sir . . . I'd like to shake your hand."

"Very well." Calhoun took the proffered hand and was astounded. Burgoyne's hand seemed to swallow his and, despite its apparent delicacy, the fact was that Burgoyne had one hell of a grip.

"I've served with a lot of Starfleet officers," said Burgoyne. "And many of them wouldn't have had the nerve to make the kind of calls you did. I have a knack for seeing things from both sides . . ."

"Yes, I just bet you do."

". . . and I just want to say that it's going to be an honor serving with you. An honor. May the Great Bird of the Galaxy roost on your planet."

Calhoun stared blankly at hir. "The *what?*"

"You've never heard of the Great Bird of the Galaxy!" said Burgoyne in surprise. "Giant mythic bird. Considered good luck, although," s/he added thoughtfully, "some races consider it a bad omen. But there are always malcontents, I suppose."

"Well . . . I'll take your 'blessing' in the spirit it's intended, then."

Burgoyne released hish hold on Calhoun and then strode out of the Team Room, leaving Calhoun trying to restore circulation to his fingers.

Shelby entered the Team Room and saw him seated off in a corner by himself. She walked slowly over to the table, nodding silent greetings to crew members as she passed them. Standing in front of him at the table, she couldn't even tell whether he was aware that she was there.

"Captain?" she said softly.

He glanced up. She remembered the first time she had looked into those eyes of his. One would not have been able to tell from her outer demeanor, for Shelby had already constructed the tough, no-nonsense, get-ahead attitude which she had considered necessary for advancement in Starfleet. But somehow those eyes had seemed to see right through it, as if no amount of artifice was sufficient to withstand his piercing gaze. Part of her was frightened. Another part was challenged. And a third adored him for it. And she was annoyed to discover now that her basic reactions had not changed, although she was doing everything she could to tone down the adoration part.

"You have a report, Commander?" he replied.

She nodded and sat down opposite him. "I've been speaking to the new provisional governor. His name is Azizi. A little dour and down-beat, but basically a stand-up individual. He has given his personal assurance that the refugees are welcome to take up permanent residence on Nelkar. As a matter of fact, he's rather pleased with the notion. He considers them to be symbols of government folly. Of how people in charge can lose sight of truly important values."

"That's good to hear." He didn't sound particularly pleased. He didn't sound particularly anything, really. "And the refugees from the ship? From the *Cambon?* They're satisfied with this?"

"They've already met with the new leaders. They're convinced that they're sincere. The fact that Azizi and his comrades have not asked us for anything certainly seems to reinforce their sincerity. As a matter of fact, Azizi has stated that Nelkar has a large area of unsettled land to the north. That if we wind up with more refugees in some future situation, we should feel free to bring them back to Nelkar and they will be accommodated. They're most anxious to make you happy, Captain. It, uhm," she cleared her throat in mild amusement, "it seems they consider you something of a hero."

"Fancy that. Very well then. Good job, Commander. I knew I could count on you to handle the situation."

"It's comforting to get the rare vote of confidence."

He looked at her with a slightly quizzical air, but she suspected the puzzlement was feigned. He likely knew exactly what she was going to say. "Anything else?"

"You did it again," she said. "Developed a plan and weren't honest with me about it. I didn't gainsay you when you decided to feed our record of the conversation to the Nelkarites. I rationalized that that was simply dissemination of information regarding already existing planetary situations. But you only said you hoped that the citizens would bring pressure to bear. You didn't say anything about a governmental overthrow.''

"I didn't plan it."

"Oh, didn't you?"

"No," he said quietly. "I didn't."

"But you hoped for it."

"I hoped that the people would do what was right."

"What you felt was right, you mean?"

He smiled thinly. "That depends, I suppose, on whether you consider right and wrong to be universal absolutes, or hinging on one's perspective."

"You could have saved her. Saved Laheera."

"Yes, I could have."

"I thought that's what you had planned as a backup, just in case matters did go over the top," said Shelby.

"Would you like a drink?"

"Don't change the subject, and yes."

He nodded, got up, and went over to the bar. He poured her a shot of synthehol and returned to the table, sliding it in front of her. She took it without comment and downed half the contents, then put the glass back on the table. "Well?"

"Well what?"

"Are you going to answer my question?"

"You didn't ask a question. You made a statement."

"I hate when you do this," she said, stabbing a finger at him. "I hate when you split hairs when you're in a discussion that makes you uncomfortable."

"You know me too well." He shifted in his chair, and then leaned forward. "I know you thought that was my backup plan. I let you think that. But I arranged with Burgoyne that, on my order, s/he would lock on to the origin point of the signal and beam up any non-Nelkarite lifeforms."

"Leaving Laheera to face mob justice."

"At least it was some kind of justice," he shot back. "She committed crimes."

"We had no right to judge them."

"*We* didn't."

"Oh yes we did. Admit it, Mac. If we were in a similar situation, witnessing a violent governmental overthrow, and the person being overthrown was someone whose policies you agreed with, you wouldn't think twice about saving him or her. But with Laheera, you stood by and did nothing."

"Isn't that what the Prime Directive is all about?" he retorted. "Sitting around, doing nothing, tiptoeing around the galaxy and trying not to leave any footprints behind? I would have thought you'd be pleased with me, Elizabeth. I obeyed the Prime Directive."

"You obeyed the letter, but played fast and loose with the spirit. And dammit, you should have discussed it with me."

"I felt it would lead to an unnecessary argument."

"Maybe it would have led to a necessary argument." She leaned forward as well until they were almost nose to nose. "Level with me, Mac. Was her greatest crime that she murdered Hufmin and threatened the others? Or was it that she injured your pride? Called your bluff? Would you have let her live if you hadn't felt she made you look weak in front of the crew?"

He swirled the slight remains of his glass around in the bottom, and then said softly, "There has to be responsibility taken for actions. *That* is the galactic constant. There must be responsibility, and in this case, I forced it on Laheera."

"It wasn't your place to do so."

"Perhaps. Perhaps not. Sometimes you simply have to assess a situation and say, 'Dammit, it's me or no one.' And if you can't live with no one, then you have to take action."

"But . . ."

"Elizabeth . . . let me explain this with a visual aid."

She rolled her eyes. "Mac, don't patronize me."

"I'm not. I swear, I'm not. I just want to make a point." He picked up Shelby's glass and indicated the remaining contents. "Answer me: Half empty or half full?"

"Aw, Mac . . ."

"Half empty or half full?"

"All right," she sighed. "It's half—"

But before she could complete the sentence he tossed back the drink, then turned the empty glass over and put it on the table. And he said, "The correct answer is: It's gone. So why dwell on it?"

He handed her back the empty glass. She stared into it. "Thanks for the half a drink, Captain."

"My pleasure, Commander. We have to do this again sometime." He rose and said, "Have McHenry set course for the *Kayven Ryin* and take us there at warp four."

"Already done, sir. We're under way."

He blinked in surprise and glanced out the viewing port. Sure enough, the stars were hurtling past, space warping around them in a spiral of colors. "Ah. Nicely done."

"Clearly I'm going to have to read your mind, since you're being less than successful at communicating with me orally."

He nodded and started to walk past her, but she placed a hand on his chest, stopping him for a moment. "Mac," she said softly, "your self-reliance was always one of the things I lov—that I admired about you. It's probably your greatest strength. But you have to start trusting your officers. You have to start trusting me."

"I do trust you, Elizabeth."

"But you trust yourself more."

He shrugged. "What kind of captain would I be if I didn't?"

Shelby didn't hesitate. "The kind who would have saved Laheera."

For a long, long moment he was silent. Shelby was expecting some sort of smart-aleck reply, so she was surprised when he said, "Do you want to know what bothers me? Not this shadow dance or moralistic carping about justice versus compassion. Do you want to know what bothers me the most?"

"Sure."

He looked at her and there was something very terrible in those purple eyes. "I'm bothered that I turned off the screen. If I was going to refuse to save her, then I should have been strong enough to stand there and watch justice inflicted upon her. Instead I turned away. I let myself out. Oh, I tell myself that I was sparing my crew, but the truth is that I couldn't watch."

She wasn't entirely sure what to say. "Mac, I . . ."

"I used to be a strong man, Elizabeth. I keep this," and he traced the line of his scar, "to remind me of the man I was, because I was always concerned that life in Starfleet . . . life away from Xenex . . .

would soften me. Would cause me to lose touch with my roots. And that's exactly what has happened. I made a threat, I was prepared to carry it out . . . and then I wavered. Then I carried out a plan that left a murdering bitch to her deserved reward . . . but could not watch. I've always told myself that I'm still M'k'n'zy of Calhoun, the barely contained savage wearing a cloak of civility. But what if, when you remove the cloak . . . there's nothing there?''

"Mac . . ." and she rested a hand on his shoulder. "You grew up at a time when compassion was a liability. A weakness. Now . . . now compassion can be your greatest strength. Don't be ashamed of it. Embrace it."

His reply was a grunt. "Let's agree to table this discussion, Commander."

"But—"

"No, Commander," he said in a tone that she had come to recognize. She knew there was no point in pursuing the matter as he continued, "Right now, my greater concern is Lieutenant Kebron and Ambassador Si Cwan. Let's hope their enforced time together at the *Kayven Ryin* was enough to make them think more highly of one another."

SI CWAN

IV

"I hate you," said Si Cwan.

"Are you ever going to tire of saying that?" asked Kebron.

Deep in the bowels of the dungeons beneath the palace that was once Si Cwan's home, Cwan and Kebron were securely held. It had taken significantly more effort to keep Kebron in one place. While reinforced cable was enough to hold Si Cwan, Kebron was anchored with neural feedback inhibitors. The large electronic shackles amplified whatever energies he put into the cuffs that deadened all sensation in his arms and legs. Try as he might, he simply could not command his limbs to do what he wanted them to.

"I will tire of saying it when I tire of thinking it. First you fabricated that entire story about your parents in order to gain my sympathy. Then you were unable to help me overwhelm our captors . . . ."

"We were outnumbered thirty to one," said Kebron. "There seemed little point to fighting them."

"Little point?" said Si Cwan incredulously. "Clearly they want to kill us!"

"If they want to kill us, why did they rescue us in the first place?" said the Brikar reasonably.

"Isn't it obvious? They want to make an example of me."

"Example?"

"They want to torture me and force me into making all sorts of confessions. They want to humiliate me, drag me down in front of the people of Thallon. To them I'm a symbol of everything wrong with this world."

"And aren't you? Tell me, Si Cwan . . . did you rule on your behalf, or on behalf of the people?"

"It's not that simple, Kebron."

"Perhaps," rumbled Kebron, "it should be."

Si Cwan sighed impatiently, clearly not interested in continuing the conversation. He looked around the cell and said, "You know . . . the irony of this is sickening."

"Really."

"Years ago, I allowed Soleta to escape from a dungeon cell . . . for all I know, this very one. So now I convince her to aid me in returning to my home . . . and I wind up in the dungeons. It goes full circle."

"Life often does," Kebron said.

Si Cwan tested the strength of his bonds. He pulled on them as hard as he could, but they seemed disinclined to give in the least. Kebron watched him impassively as, for long minutes, Si Cwan struggled, snarling and cursing louder and louder. Finally with an exasperated moan, Si Cwan sank to the floor.

"A very impressive display," Kebron said.

"Save the sarcasm, Kebron. It doesn't matter." And then, in a surprisingly soft voice, he said, "I guess none of it matters."

"Now *that* sounds somewhat defeatist."

Si Cwan seemed to have developed an interest in staring at his feet. "Kebron . . . what if I succeeded?"

"I'm not following."

"Let's say that I triumphed over my enemies. That the people rose up and supported me. That those who destroyed my life were, in turn, destroyed. Let's say that, once again, I was in power."

"I would assume that you would be pleased by that turn of events."

Cwan looked at him balefully. "It occurs to me that it would be as futile as pulling at these chains. Even if I wielded that power once more, I could not make my life the way it was. I could not bring my sister or any of the others back to life. I could do no more than create a shadow resemblance of my previous existence. I have my admirers, my supporters . . . but so what? For any rational, thinking person, there has to be more to life than that. There used to be, for me. But now there isn't.''

"Si Cwan . . .''

"Besides, for every single supporter I may have, there are twenty who would just as soon see me torn to ribbons. People who, if handed a blaster, would aim it at me and pull the trigger themselves. I have spent my life trying to do my best, Kebron. And clearly it was not enough.'' He nodded slowly. "Let them torture me, I suppose. Let them do what they will. It doesn't matter anymore. None of it matters.''

"And what of your enemies? You said that you didn't mind dying, but you were upset that Zoran would outlive you. Has that changed?''

"If I die before he does, or he before me, eventually we both end up in the same place. That's the odd thing about life. No one gets out alive.''

Zak Kebron eyed him speculatively. "I must say, Cwan, I find this new attitude of yours rather annoying. You were more interesting when you were insufferable.''

"I contemplate a life where I survive but know nothing but loneliness and memories of lost loved ones . . . or a life where I die after a battery of nauseating tortures. If those two possibilities render me 'annoying,' that's your problem, Kebron, not mine. You are merely a bystander in all this. If and when your vessel arrives on Thallon, they will likely release you to it with no difficulty. But I will be long de—''

The ground rumbled beneath their feet. Although Si Cwan was already seated on the floor, the force of the seismic shock sent him sprawling. Kebron, for his part, did not seem rattled at all. He merely sat there, looking—at worst—mildly vexed.

As the vibrations subsided, Si Cwan shook his head. "Now there's something to hope for: Perhaps the ground will simply swallow me up.''

"Look, Cwan . . . you still grate on me,'' said Kebron. "Should we survive this, I doubt I will be any more inclined to feel friendship for you than I am now. Nonetheless, I dislike the notion of torture. So I promise you, you will not be tortured.''

Si Cwan looked at him with a smirk that was, ever so slightly, condescending. "That's very kind of you to promise, Kebron, but I hardly think you're in a position to do anything about it.''

At that moment they heard footsteps approach . . . a lot of them.

The door to the cell hissed open and Si Cwan blinked against the sudden flood of light. There was a brace of guards there. The highest-ranking officer stepped forward, and he was smirking in a rather insufferable manner.

"Ah," Si Cwan said. "Hello, Herz."

"Hello, Si Cwan," replied the ranking officer. His speaking of Si Cwan's name was done in such a manner that it was clear he was enjoying the absence of any preceding title, such as "lord." "I'm flattered that you remember me."

"Herz was dismissed from our service," Cwan mentioned in an offhand manner to Kebron, "after two Vulcan prisoners escaped. Since the revolution, I see you are once again gainfully employed."

"Yes, no thanks to you. We have immediate plans for you, Si Cwan, and I assure you I have waited a long time for this."

"If what you intend is to take him to be physically abused . . . you shall have to wait a while longer," Kebron said. "You will not take him out of here."

There was something in his voice . . . something very certain, and very unpleasant. So unpleasant, in fact, that the guards seemed disinclined to get any nearer than they currently were. Impatiently, Herz said to them, "What are you standing there for? He can't break those neural inhibitors. Ignore him and take Si Cwan."

The guards started forward, and that was when Kebron began to focus his energy. With a grunt that reverberated throughout the room, he began to put pressure on the large cuffs. Immediately power started to ricochet back through his rock-like hide, but the Brikar either seemed to ignore it or, even more, to be spurred on by it.

"Stop it! You're not impressing anyone!" shouted Herz, trying to make himself heard over the accelerated howling of the cuffs. The fact was, he was lying. All of them were tremendously impressed. They were also having trouble hearing themselves think. The power surge was incredible, earsplitting; the Thallonians put their hands to the sides of their heads, assaulted by the intensity.

Si Cwan watched, wide-eyed, astonished, at the display of unrelenting strength. Kebron doubled, tripled his efforts. His muscles strained against his dusky skin, standing out in stark relief, and he was vibrating so violently that there might well have been another ground quake shaking the cell. Power coruscated around his body in an eye-searing display.

And then he broke the cuffs.

"Break" would actually be an inadequate description. With a roar that sounded more suited to a primordial beast, he shattered them, the bonds snapping under the strain, metal flying everywhere. One piece lodged in the thigh of an unlucky guard and he howled, going down. Another flew straight and true and thudded squarely into Herz's forehead. As it so happened, he was wearing a helmet. This was fortunate. Had he not been clad in that manner, the metal would likely have gone straight through his head without slowing. As it was, his skull was ringing, and it would only be upon removing the helmet later that he would discover the metal had stopped short of piercing his forehead by less than a centimeter.

"Fall back! Fall back!" he shouted, and the others did so, dragging the wounded guard with them. They stumbled back into the hallway and Herz punched a button on the wall that slid the door shut. It closed just barely in time as Zak Kebron slammed into it at full charge. The door, made of pure Staiteium, shuddered but held firm.

The guards' breathing came in ragged, disoriented gasps. Kebron, for his part, sounded utterly calm. "Listen carefully," he said. "Are you listening? I will only say this once."

"You're . . . you're not in a position to—" Herz tried to say, hoping to make up in bluster for his seriously crippled confidence.

"Be quiet," Kebron said impatiently. "I'm in exactly a position to do whatever I wish. If I put my mind to it, and pound on it long enough, I can get through this door. Or straight through the wall if I have to."

"You're . . . you're bluffing . . ." Herz declared.

"Apparently you have me confused with someone who cares what you think," Kebron informed him. "Now, then: There will be no torture of Si Cwan. He is not simply a former, fallen noble. He is a Federation ambassador. As such, he is entitled to certain courtesies under Federation law, including full access to the Federation embassy."

"What," and Herz looked at the others. "What 'Federation embassy'? There's no Federation embassy on Thallon."

"Yes, there is. This is it."

"That's not an embassy! It's a cell!"

"We intend to redecorate," Kebron informed them. "Now then . . . what with this cell being an embassy, you shall not be allowed to trespass here. This door does not keep me in. It keeps you out. If you attempt to violate this embassy, I shall take defensive action which will consist of ripping trespassers apart."

"We're in charge here!" said Herz unconvincingly.

"Out there, yes. In here, I am."

"You can't stay in there forever!"

"True. But we've no desire to. We shall stay until such time that the *Starship Excalibur* arrives."

"They don't know you're here!"

"I have every confidence in my associates that they will figure out where we are," replied Kebron, and indeed if there was any doubt within him, one could not have told it from his voice. "Once they have arrived, you will take us to them. And we will negotiate from that point. Now, kindly leave. The ambassador wishes to rest. It has been a trying time for him."

Realizing that control of the situation had completely spiraled away from him, Herz rallied himself and declared once more, *"That isn't an embassy!"* trying to make up in volume what he lacked in conviction.

Utterly composed, Kebron replied, "If you continue to maintain that attitude, we are not going to invite you to our first formal dance. And that, sir, will be your loss."

The wounded guard was still bleeding from where the metal had penetrated his leg, and the guards had decided by this point that further conversation was getting them nowhere. With a quick and angry glare over their shoulders, they hustled off down the hallway. Herz shouted defiantly over his shoulder, "This isn't over! We'll be back!"

"I await the challenge," Kebron called back. He peered after them through narrow slits in the door, watched them go, and then walked over to Si Cwan. With almost no effort at all, he snapped the bonds that had been holding Cwan. Cwan rubbed his wrists as Kebron stepped back and said, "So you fired that guard a few years back. I can believe that."

"How did you do it?" Si Cwan said, barely able to disguise his awe. "How did you break those bonds?"

"By refusing to fail."

Si Cwan shook his head. "I am impressed. I hate to admit it, but I am impressed. Now . . . let's get out of here."

"No."

Cwan was already halfway toward the door when he was brought up short by Kebron's curt answer. "What?"

"I said no."

"But we can break out!" Si Cwan said. "Unless you think you can't break down this door . . ."

"I probably can."

"Then we can escape from this cell!"

"And go where? You are the single most identifiable Thallonian on the planet, and I'll only blend in if there's an avalanche rolling down the main street."

He felt the old anger and impatience with the Brikar welling up within him. "So you would give up."

"Not at all. We do exactly what I said we'd do. We stay here until the *Excalibur* shows up."

"This is the wrong way to go, Kebron. I'm telling you, we should leave! Now!"

"Very well," and Kebron gestured toward the door. "Go ahead and leave."

"But I can't get through the door!"

"That is not my problem."

With a roar of anger, Si Cwan waved his clenched fists in front of Kebron, until he realized the utter stupidity of such ire since Kebron was his only definite ally on the planet. And besides, hitting Zak Kebron was—at best—an exercise in futility. His fury spent, Si Cwan leaned against the door and murmured, "I hate you."

"Really. I saved you from being tortured."

"I know. That may be why I hate you most of all."

BURGOYNE

V

Burgoyne 172 was scrutinizing the isolinear chip array, trying to determine possible methods of rearranging the chips to more effectively process sensor data, when s/he became aware of someone standing behind hir. S/he craned hish neck around and saw, to hish surprise, Dr. Selar. The doctor was maintaining her customary resolve, but it seemed to Burgoyne as if it was something of a strain for her.

"Do you have a moment?" she asked.

Burgoyne rose and brushed off hish hands . . . an old habit from the days when s/he would be up to hish elbows in various engine parts and have lubricant all over hish body. S/he missed those days more than s/he liked to think about. "For you, Doctor . . . two moments. Perhaps even three."

"I need to speak with you. Privately." She paused. "Woman to woman."

"You sure know how to hurt a guy," said Burgoyne. S/he gestured toward hish office. "After you."

Selar nodded and walked briskly to the office, Burgoyne following. The door hissed shut behind them and Selar turned to face Burgoyne. "I need to speak with you—"

"Woman to woman, I know. Doctor, you better than anyone should know I'm as much man as I am woman. . . ."

"Yes, and you've made your 'manly' interest in me quite evident. And Hermats are renowned for their rather cavalier approach to sexuality. . . ."

"I don't think I'd say 'cavalier,' " replied Burgoyne. "We simply see the opportunities inherent in—"

"Lieutenant Commander." Selar raised a hand, palm up. "I am really not interested in discussing Hermat philosophies right now, as endlessly interesting as I am sure they are. I desire you—"

Burgoyne sat up straight, a grin on hish face. "You desire me?"

"No," Selar said quickly, "what I am trying to say is that I desire *that* you . . . cease your efforts to pursue me on an amorous basis. I am aware of . . . indeed, impressed by . . . your remarkable affinity for pheromones. That you sense my . . . my interests. But I am asking you, as one officer to another, as . . . ."

"One woman to another?" asked Burgoyne with just a touch of annoyance.

"Yes. I am asking you not to pursue me. There are . . ." Selar put a hand to her head to steady herself. "There are solid medical reasons why it would not be a wise idea."

"Even though I know we could be great together."

"Even though. I do not . . . desire a relationship. I have . . ." Selar cleared her throat, suddenly feeling as if she couldn't hear her own thoughts over the pounding of her pulse. "I have made a conscious decision to eliminate that part of my life. I am asking you to honor it."

"Eliminate it?" Burgoyne could hardly believe what s/he was hearing. S/he leaned forward and, to Selar's surprise, took the doctor's hand firmly between hirs. Burgoyne, for hish part, was surprised by the warmth. With the frosty, formal reserve of Vulcans, Burgoyne had somehow always just assumed that their skin would likewise be cold to the touch. Such was definitely not the case. "Selar . . ."

"*Doctor* Selar."

"*Doctor* Selar, putting my own considerations aside . . . that's no way to live. Even Vulcans have mates. Where else would little Vulcans come from? What happened to you? Something must have happened to make you like this. . . ."

Carefully Selar disengaged her hand from hish. "With all respect,

Lieutenant Commander, it is none of your business. Nor is it any of your business why I am taking the time to ask you, specifically, to cease whatever amorous interests you may have in me.''

Burgoyne took a deep, steady breath. And then, in an utterly formal tone, Burgoyne said, ''Of course, Doctor. You merely had to ask. As a suitor, you need not worry that I will pursue you, amorously or otherwise.'' S/he paused, and then added, ''As a friend, I'm going to make the observation that you seem a very sad and lost individual, and keeping the world at arm's length your entire life will just give you a long and lonely life, and tired arms.''

''Thank you for your astute psychological analysis, Lieutenant Commander,'' she said. ''Perhaps you missed your calling.''

Ensign Ronni Beth knocked on the door to the office and Burgoyne gestured for her to come in. Beth entered and immediately said, ''Sir, there's a problem with the ion flux. Also, Lieutenant McHenry is waiting outside. He says the ship is a little sluggish responding to the helm, and wanted to talk to you about it.''

''I'm on it,'' Burgoyne said briskly, coming around hish desk. As s/he did so, s/he said gamely to Selar, ''On the other hand, perhaps I didn't miss my calling at that.'' And, in a gesture that could only be considered friendly, s/he patted Selar on the shoulder.

The merest touch of Burgoyne's hand jolted Selar, filling her with a sense of electricity rampaging through her. It was all she could do to control herself. Burgoyne didn't notice Selar's fingers gripping the edge of the desk. ''Perhaps not,'' Selar said, fighting to keep her voice even. It seemed to her as if she had barely managed to get the words out, and then Burgoyne walked out of the office and Selar sagged with relief.

She rose from the chair and walked toward the door with unsteady legs. As she crossed the engine room, she saw Burgoyne chatting with McHenry. No . . . not just chatting. Laughing. Something had struck the two of them as amusing, and they were laughing over it.

And Selar felt jealous. She couldn't help it. She also couldn't believe it. Here she had come down to Engineering in order to put an end to Burgoyne's interest in her . . . and apparently she had succeeded, if one could take Burgoyne at hish word. Yet now, even seeing Burgoyne engaged in a casual conversation with someone else was enough to upset Selar.

''This is insane,'' she murmured, and she headed immediately to sickbay, hoping and praying that there would be someone sick up there to whom she could attend. When there wasn't, she felt like going out and breaking someone's leg so that she would have something to occupy her time and her mind.

Still, at least she was back in "her" place. Her home ground. Selar drew strength from sickbay. If she were prone to dwell on the irony of such things, she would have mused on the inappropriateness of garnering strength from a place of illness. But she wasn't feeling particularly philosophical at that moment.

What she was feeling was the drive of *Pon farr,* and it infuriated her that she could not get the image of Burgoyne out of her head.

At that moment her comm badge beeped. She tapped it and said, "Dr. Selar here."

"Doctor?" It was the captain, and he sounded momentarily puzzled. She couldn't blame him, really, because she realized that her own voice was deeper and throatier than usual, as if she had too much blood in her body.

"Yes, Captain," she said, reacquiring her customary tone of voice with effort.

"I just wanted to alert you to have sickbay ready. We'll be approaching the science ship *Kayven Ryin* shortly. Although at last report everyone there was fine, there may be some who need medical attention. At the very least, we'll want you to check them over and give them a clean bill of health."

"I shall be ready for them, sir."

"I expected no less. Calhoun out."

She leaned back and let out something that was very unusual for her: a sigh of relief. There would be something for her to do other than dwell on her own problems. Perhaps this would not be such a hideous day after all.

On the viewscreen before them, there was nothing but assorted scraps.

Calhoun rose from his chair, staring with sinking heart at the remains in front of them. "Are you quite sure we're in the right place, McHenry?"

McHenry nodded briskly. As was always the case with McHenry, while he seemed easily distracted or otherwise occupied mentally when matters were proceeding routinely, he was one hundred percent focused when there was any sort of problem. Indeed, one could almost take a cue as to the seriousness of a situation by how McHenry was reacting to it. Considering his no-nonsense demeanor at the moment, it was a serious situation indeed. "Yes, sir," he said. "Absolutely positive. This was the last point at which we heard from Kebron and Cwan."

"What the hell happened?" demanded Calhoun.

"Scanning remains," Soleta said from her science station.

"Remains. Remains of the *Kayven Ryin* . . . or of the *Marquand?*" asked Shelby.

It took Soleta a few moments, and then she said, "Both."

"Any signs of bodies?" Calhoun wanted to know.

"Yes. Mixed in with the wreckage, I am detecting two fingers . . . what appears to be a leg . . . a piece of bone . . . from the length, a thigh bone, I should th—"

"Soleta," Calhoun said sharply.

She looked up at him blandly. "I thought you'd want to know details."

"What I want to know is, is it our people?"

"Impossible to say at this time. I can have them brought aboard and analyzed . . ."

"Do it," Calhoun said briskly. "Lefler, oversee the operation. I want enough parts of the wreckage and the bodies brought aboard so that we know exactly what it is we're dealing with. Soleta, coordinate with Burgoyne. Go over the remains millimeter by millimeter if you have to, but I want to know what happened here. Bridge to sickbay."

"Sickbay, Dr. Selar here."

"Doctor, we're going to have need of your services."

"As per your request, Captain, I am prepared to handle whatever personnel are—"

"There's no personnel, Doctor," he said flatly. "I'm going to need you to perform autopsies. Actually, that might be too generous a word. I'm going to send you puzzle pieces and you're going to have to assemble them for me so I can get the entire picture."

Calhoun had a feeling that if he'd been face-to-face with Selar, she would not have blinked an eye. He would have been correct. "Very well, sir. I will be ready."

"Captain," Lefler suddenly said. "There was another ship here. I'm detecting an ion trail."

He came over quickly to her, leaning over her station. "You think it's whoever destroyed the science station and the shuttle?"

"Possibly. By the same token, if we're going to be optimistic about it, they might have saved the lives of whoever was on the science station and the runabout."

"That is definitely optimistic, I'll grant you that. Can you determine the type?"

"Not at this time."

"Can you track it?"

She nodded briskly. "That I can do."

"Do it, then." He rose and turned to face his crew. "I want answers, people. I want to know what happened, so that when we catch up with whoever was the last person here, we know whether we're dealing with a potential ally . . . or avenging the death of two crewmen."

In the conference lounge, Calhoun sat at the head of the table. Grouped around him were Shelby, Soleta, Burgoyne, McHenry, and Selar. "So the ships were destroyed in two different manners?" he asked.

Soleta nodded, glancing at the computer upon which her analyses were appearing on the screen. "Yes, sir. The scorch marks on the remains of the *Marquand* indicate that they were destroyed by high-intensity firepower, although it is impossible to determine whether the science station itself was the origin of the attack. Now the *Kayven Ryin,* Chief Burgoyne believes—and I concur, with eighty-nine percent certainty—that the ship was destroyed by a bomb."

"A bomb?" Calhoun couldn't quite believe it.

"Yes, sir," Burgoyne spoke up. "A superheated thermite bomb, if I'm not mistaken, judging by the blast radius and chemical traces. I saw what one of those things did once to a surveying ship that wandered into Gorn territory."

"So somebody fired on the *Marquand* and then blew up the *Kayven Ryin.* Any guesses as to why or wherefores?"

"I dislike the notion of 'guesses,'" said Soleta. "If I had to reconstruct a scenario, I would say that the *Marquand* was ambushed within range of the science station . . . and then the station was subsequently destroyed, either to leave no clues as to what happened . . . or to kill whatever survivors there might have been aboard the station.''

"Speaking of survivors," and Calhoun turned his attention to Selar, "what do the remains of the bodies tell us?"

"I have run DNA analysis. They are definitely Thallonian."

There was silence for a moment. "Si Cwan?" Shelby finally asked.

But Selar shook her head. "I do not believe so. Nor am I able to determine precisely what the cause of death was. Whether they were killed by the blast or before it is impossible to say."

"Any remains of a Brikar?"

"No, Captain. Not from what was presented to me."

Looks were exchanged around the room. Shelby asked, "Considering the density of Brikar hide . . . what are the odds that there would have been nothing detectable left of him?"

"If I had to estimate," and she considered it a moment, "seven thousand twenty-nine to one."

"That's impressive," Calhoun said slowly. "All right, McHenry," said Calhoun. "Have you got any bead on where we're heading? Where this 'mystery ship' has gone?"

"Well, obviously I don't know for sure where the trail ends until we get there," said McHenry. "But I tracked it ahead and, assuming that it didn't change course . . . we're heading straight toward Thallon."

"Thallon? Are you sure?"

McHenry nodded with conviction. "Yes, sir. I don't make mistakes."

"You don't?" Burgoyne said with amusement. "How very nice for you. I've never met anyone who doesn't make mistakes."

"I made a mistake once," McHenry said, but then he frowned and said, "No . . . wait. That time wasn't my fault. Sorry, my mistake. I was right the first time."

Wisely, no one commented.

"Well, we were supposed to go to Thallon," Shelby said after a moment. "Seems that we're getting there sooner rather than later."

"Indeed. Mr. Burgoyne, let's crank up the warp speed, shall we?"

"Ask and it's yours, sir."

"McHenry," said Calhoun, "best speed to Thallon."

"Yes, sir."

"And let's hope to Hell that Kebron and Cwan are there." He rose and clearly the meeting was over.

As they were heading out, Burgoyne said to McHenry, "By the way, I think I've got that little problem taken care of. Let me know how she handles."

"Great. Thanks," said McHenry.

Selar looked at the two of them, realized that there were more unwelcome thoughts going through her head, and said in a low voice to Soleta, "I need to speak with you. Alone."

Soleta looked at her with mild surprise, but then nodded. "At my first opportunity," she said.

"Thank you." Selar looked around the now-empty conference lounge, and then said, "Soleta . . . I have never needed a friend before. But I need one now. I hope you will . . . indulge me." And she walked out quickly before Soleta could respond.

THALLON

VI

In the main council chamber of the Thallonian palace, the leader gaped at Herz. "An . . . embassy?"

"Yes, sir," Herz said, shifting uncomfortably.

Also in the room were: Zoran; D'ndai of Calhoun, the brother of M'k'n'zy of Calhoun . . . who, in turn, had not gone by that name in some time; and a new arrival . . . Ryjaan of the Danteri Empire. Ryjaan was squat and bulky, with bronze skin glistening with an even greater sheen than was typical for the Danteri. He had a ready smile, which had an additional tint of the sinister about it as his perfect teeth were slightly sharp.

Ryjaan had his hands draped behind his back and said, "Well, well . . . we've certainly got a muddle of this, haven't we? D'ndai, I ask you to take your brother out of action. But you . . . you don't have the nerve to handle it yourself. So you ally yourself with Zoran here, who sets up a trap for the purpose of doing what I asked you to do . . . except he doesn't wind up snaring your brother. Instead he snags a security officer and a fallen prince." He turned to the leader and said, "This is one charming alliance we've forged between ourselves, Yoz. The Danteri and the Thallonians, working hand in hand, creating a coalition that could eventually rival the Federation. And what have we got? A Federation starship commanded by an extremely dangerous individual . . . and a prisoner who has taken over his cell.''

The leader, the one who had been addressed as Yoz, turned back to Herz and said angrily, ''Drag him up here. Go in there with guns blasting and take him out.''

''We, uhm . . . we tried that, sir.''

''You did? And what happened?''

The door had flown open, packed with guards who were heavily armed, and they opened fire.

With a roar the Brikar had charged them. The blasts had slowed him, staggered him . . . but they had not stopped him. Si Cwan had remained safely behind the Brikar, and then Zak Kebron got his hands on the foremost of the assailants.

Soon the hallway was thick with blood, and it was all Thallonian. The guards had retreated, screaming, slipping and sliding on blood that was spilling everywhere, and Zak Kebron—as calm as anything—closed the door.

It wasn't the Thallonians' fault. They had not known that there were few things more dangerous than a wounded Brikar. Unfortunately, they had found out the hard way.

Yoz, Ryjaan, D'ndai, and Zoran listened in quiet amazement. ''Gods,'' whispered Yoz. Then he drew himself up, his leadership qualities and conviction coming to the fore. ''All right. Gas them first. Don't even enter. Just gas them from outside. Knock them unconscious and haul Si Cwan out while the two of them are downed.''

''Uhm . . . we,'' and his voice sounded very faint. ''We tried that, too.''

''And . . . ?'' prompted Yoz.

The door had flown open and the guards hesitated, waiting for the thick clouds of gas to clear. They wore masks so that they could breathe. Now they peered carefully through the gas, trying to see where the insensate bodies of Kebron and Si Cwan might be.

They were able to make out, over in the corner, a fallen lump that seemed to have the general proportions of Cwan. But at first they couldn't see Kebron at all.

Then they did.

He had stepped forward from the mist, his mouth shut tightly. They didn't see his fist, obscured as it was by the mist.

Kebron's fist went straight into the lead guard, striking a fatal blow. Then he raised the still-twitching corpse over his head and hurled it into the crowd of guards, knocking several of them back. He ripped the masks off two of them, and then slammed the door once again. The guards, Herz in the lead, bolted down the corridor, not even waiting to hear the clang of the door as it slammed closed once more.

It wasn't the Thallonians' fault. They had not known that one of the only things more dangerous than a wounded Brikar is a wounded Brikar whom one has tried to gas into unconsciousness. Since Brikar can hold their breath for twenty minutes at a stretch, that was a useless maneuver. Unfortunately, they had found out the hard way.

Yoz turned to D'ndai and said, "I don't understand. If Kebron was such a formidable fighting machine, why didn't he do that on your ship? You said you had weapons leveled at him, and he simply raised his hands and didn't fight."

"It should be fairly obvious," said D'ndai. "He wanted to find out who was behind all of this. He wanted to get to the source of the situation. And now that he's accomplished that, he's making his stand, and waiting for my brother to come get him. And he will, make no mistake. M'k'n'zy and his people will show up. They won't believe that either Cwan or Kebron is dead unless they have corpses to prove it. And they will trace them here."

"Gentlemen," Yoz said slowly, "I am open to suggestions here."

"Who gives a damn about the Brikar?" said Zoran angrily. "Don't fiddle with gas to knock them out. Use poison gas. Even if it doesn't affect Kebron, it will be more than enough to obliterate Si Cwan. That's all that matters! We have to kill him!"

"And is that your opinion, as well?" D'ndai asked Yoz.

Yoz saw something in D'ndai's eyes. Something cool and calculating. "You feel that's not the case?"

D'ndai started to pace. "Yoz . . . my world fought a long war for freedom, against rather formidable odds. Every so often, the Danteri would foolishly . . . no offense,'' he interrupted himself as he addressed Ryjaan.

"None taken," said Ryjaan calmly.

"Every so often, the Danteri would capture a high-profile individual connected to our rebellion. They would make an example of him. They would execute him, usually in the most grisly fashion they could invent. Indeed, they'd try to outdo themselves every time. And all that happened was that they created martyr after martyr."

"What are you saying?"

"I'm saying, Yoz, that Si Cwan could be more dangerous to you dead than alive. You and your associates have thrown out the royal family, but you haven't consolidated your power. Chaos and rebellion are rife throughout what's left of the empire. Those who supported the rebellion may be starting to think that they were sold a dream, and the reality does not match the dream. If they see Si Cwan . . . if they see him die well, honorably, bravely . . . that could set forces into motion that you are not prepared for."

"So I was right," Zoran said sharply. "I should have killed him when he was out on the science station. For that matter, you should have killed him, D'ndai! You had the opportunity!"

"I'm not your hired assassin, Zoran. You were mine. If you bungle the job, it's not my responsibility to clean up after you."

"That's what you say," Zoran said in an accusatory tone. "Or perhaps you simply didn't have the stomach for it."

D'ndai smiled evenly. He bore a passing resemblance to his brother, even though the years had not worn well on him. "You are, of course, entitled to your opinion."

"What would you suggest, D'ndai?" said Yoz. "That we let him go?"

"No!" thundered Zoran, looking angry enough to leap across the room and rip out Yoz's throat with his teeth for even suggesting such a thing.

"No, I'm not suggesting that," said D'ndai. "I am suggesting he be tried, in an open court."

Yoz appeared to consider that, stroking his chin thoughtfully. "It has its advantages."

"Advantages!" Zoran clearly couldn't believe what he was hearing. "What advantages?"

"It puts us across as rational, compassionate beings," said Yoz. "If we beat him into submission and he agrees to whatever crimes we accuse him of, people are not stupid. It will reflect poorly on us. We do not want to appear simply as the greater bullies, the more merciless."

"But what crimes can we accuse him of?" asked Zoran. "There is no concrete proof of anything that he directly had his hand in."

"That much is true. But the activities of the others in his family, and in the generations preceding him, are public knowledge. Guilt by association."

"And there is . . . something else," D'ndai said slowly. "Something that I myself was witness to. I have been," and he looked around uncomfortably, "I have been reluctant to say anything until now, for I have no desire to disrupt the alliance between the Thallonians and the Danteri. Such a disruption could only cause difficulties for my people."

"Disruption?" Ryjaan seemed utterly confused. Nor did Yoz or Zoran comprehend either, as their blank looks indicated.

"There were," and D'ndai cleared his throat. "There were certain 'private' arrangements made. Certain allies that we Xenexians acquired when we were fighting for our freedom."

"What allies?" asked Ryjaan, and then slowly the significant look that D'ndai gave Yoz was enough to focus him on the Thallonian. "You?" he demanded. "The Thallonians allied with Xenex against us? *You!*"

Yoz threw up his hands defensively. "I knew nothing of it! You speak of matters twenty years ago! I was not even chancellor then!"

"Aye," agreed D'ndai. "Yoz speaks truly. He was not involved personally . . . not to my knowledge. But Si Cwan was."

"Si Cwan?" Ryjaan looked stunned. "But he was barely out of his teens at that time!"

"The same might be said of my brother," replied D'ndai. "And look at all that he accomplished."

"Zoran, did you know of this?" Ryjaan demanded.

Ryjaan looked to D'ndai, and for a long moment he was silent, wheels turning silently in his head.

"Well?" insisted Ryjaan. "At the time, you and Si Cwan were best friends. Did he mention anything of this to you?"

"No," said Zoran, sounding far more restrained than he usually did. "But there were any number of times that he left Thallon for lengthy periods. When he returned, he would never tell me where he'd been. He was rather fond of his secrets, Si Cwan was."

"So it's possible."

"Oh, yes. Eminently possible."

"Very well," said Ryjaan, and he turned back to D'ndai. "I appreciate your informing me of this situation."

"It's more than just a situation that I'm informing you of," replied D'ndai. "You see . . . I happen to know that Si Cwan, in his endeavors to undercut the authority of Danter, committed a variety of brutal acts. One, in particular, will be of interest to you."

"And that one is . . . ?"

He folded his arms and said, "He killed your father."

Ryjaan visibly staggered upon hearing this. "Wh—what?" he managed to stammer out.

"You heard me," said D'ndai with supernatural calm. "A high-ranking Danteri soldier named Falkar. Your father, I believe."

Numbly, Ryjaan nodded.

"You understand, I did not make the association immediately," D'ndai continued in that same, unperturbed voice. "But you and I have had continued meetings, and since our alliance was becoming more and more pronounced, I felt it helpful to—please pardon my intrusiveness—explore your background. I violated no secrets, I assure you. It was all information easily obtained through public records. But when I learned that Falkar was your father, well . . . please forgive me that it took me this long to tell you."

Slowly Ryjaan sank into a chair. "I was a child when he left," he said calmly. "When he said that he was going to Xenex to quell a rebellion, he made it sound as if there was no question that he'd return. And he never did. His body was eventually recovered. He'd been run through, and his sword was never found. The sword of our family, gone. And all this time, I thought it was in the hands of some . . . some heathen . . . no offense," he said to D'ndai, with no trace of irony.

"None taken," he replied.

"You have no idea, D'ndai, how this unclosed chapter in my life has hampered my ability to deal with the Xenexians. I do so because it is what my government requires of me. But after all this time, to be able to resolve the hurt that I've always carried . . . the unanswered call for justice.'' He squeezed D'ndai's shoulder firmly. ''Thank you . . . you, whom I, for the first time, truly call 'friend.' And when judgment is passed upon Si Cwan—when he is found guilty and is to be executed for his crimes—my hand will be the one that strikes him down.''

And Yoz nodded approvingly. ''We would have it no other way,'' he said. Then he considered a moment. ''What of Kebron? The Brikar? He slaughtered a number of our guards. Are we to simply release him?''

''He killed fools,'' Zoran said with no sympathy. ''Are we to publicly admit that a single, unarmed Federation representative obliterated squads of our armed guards? Rumors and legends of the might of the Federation are already rife throughout Thallon and the neighboring planets. Why provide them with even more fodder for discussion?''

''You're suggesting a cover-up then,'' said Yoz.

''I am suggesting mercy for the Brikar. After all, we have Si Cwan. We can afford to be . . .'' and Zoran smiled, ''. . . generous.''

And as the others nodded around him, he exchanged looks with D'ndai. A look that spoke volumes. A look that said, *All right. I've covered for you. And you'd best not let me down . . . or there will be hell to pay.*

SELAR

VII

Selar stood on the crest of Mount Tulleah, feeling the hot air of Vulcan sweeping over her. It steadied her, gave her a feeling of comfort. The sky was a deep and dusky red, and the sands of the Gondi desert stretched out into infinity. Selar had come to Mount Tulleah any number of times in her youth, finding it a source of peace and contemplation. Now, when her world seem to be spiraling out of control, she was pleased (inwardly, of course) to discover that Tulleah still offered her that same, steadying feeling.

She heard feet trudging up behind her and she turned to see the person she knew she would. "Thank you for coming, Soleta."

Soleta grunted in response. "You couldn't have been at the bottom of the hill?" she asked.

"One does not find spiritual comfort at the bottom of Mount Tulleah."

"No, but one does not run out of breath down there, either." She shook her head. "I have forgotten how arid the air is. I've rarely been to Vulcan."

"You do not know what you have missed."

"Actually," and she indicated the vista before them, "I suppose I do."

Selar shook her head. "This is an excellent reproduction, I don't dispute that. But in my heart, I know it is only that."

"In your heart. What an un-Vulcan-like way to put it."

"To court grammatical disaster . . . I have been feeling rather un-Vulcan-like lately."

"Selar," said Soleta, "you are in the early throes of *Pon farr*. If anything, you are a bit *too* Vulcan-like."

Selar stared out at the arid Vulcan plains for a time, and then she said, "I need to know what to do. I need to know what to do with these . . . these . . ."

"Feelings?"

"Yes, that is the word. Thank you. Feelings. I cannot," and she put her fingers to her temple, "I cannot get Burgoyne out of my mind. I do not know why. I do not know if the feelings are genuine or not, and it . . . it angers me. Angers me, and frightens me."

"Do you want to fight it, or do you want to give in to it?"

"Fight it," Selar said firmly. "I should be able to. I entered *Pon farr* two years ago. This is . . . this feeling I have now, I do not believe it to be genuine."

"Selar . . ."

"I know what you said to me. I know your assessment. But I do not think that what I am feeling is really *Pon farr*. Perhaps it is a . . . a delayed reaction to the death of Voltak. . . ."

"Delayed two years?" Soleta asked skeptically.

"Soleta . . . I profess to be an expert in many things. But emotions are not among them."

"Well," Soleta said thoughtfully. "I suppose it's possible. You were somewhat traumatized when you lost your husband. Perhaps, deep down, you desired to have that sort of connection once more."

"I resolved to divest myself of it," Selar said firmly.

"That may very well be the problem."

Selar stared out at the plains of Vulcan. "Burgoyne says s/he feels a connection between us. Says I am interested in hir. Perhaps s/he is right. Or perhaps my thoughts dwell on hir because s/he is the first individual who has ever shown that sort of interest in me. I do not know anymore. I do not know anything about anything."

"Admitting one's ignorance is the first step toward gaining knowledge."

"Thank you, Soleta. That still does not tell me what to do."

"I can't tell you that. No one can, except yourself."

Selar shook her head with as close an outward display of sadness as she ever came. "I have never felt any need to depend upon anyone except myself in my entire life. Perhaps . . . that has been part of the difficulty. I have been alone for much of my life . . . but until now, I have felt . . . lonely."

Far off in the distance, a flock of birds sailed through the sky on leathery wings. "I hope I have been of some help," said Soleta.

"Some. I still do not know precisely what action I will take. But at least I feel as if I am moving in some sort of a direction."

"That's all any of us can ask. I will be on the bridge if you need me."

Selar turned to her and said, "Thank you . . . my friend."

"You are most welcome."

Soleta turned and proceeded to climb down the mountain. Selar continued to look out over the Vulcan plains, but with half an ear she listened to Soleta's quiet litany of grunts, huffs, and muttered annoyance over the inconvenience of clambering up and down mountains. Within a few minutes, however, Soleta was gone, and Selar was struck by the fact that she missed her already.

She had so intensely desired to be alone, and yet she had to admit that she might have been craving a most unnatural state. Perhaps, even for Vulcans, loneliness was not a condition to which one should aspire. Perhaps there was more to life than isolating oneself, both intellectually and physically.

She found herself wishing that Vulcans truly were as many outsiders perceived them to be: emotionless. To have no emotions would be to simplify life tremendously. The problem was that Vulcans did indeed have emotions, but they had to be suppressed. Controlled. And perhaps she had gone too far in her effort to control all aspects of her life.

It was not surprising, she mused. After all, in addition to being a Vulcan, she had chosen medicine as her vocation. She was a doctor, and there was no breed who had to stay more in control, both of situations and themselves, than doctors. And so she never had any opportunity, nor any inclination, to relax and be herself with anyone. She always, first and foremost, had to be steering a situation. She could never give herself over to the natural movement of the event. In all likelihood, her aborted and awful experience with Voltak had soured her on that notion forever. After all, she had done that very thing, there in the joining place with Voltak. She had let herself be carried along by the currents of their emotionality, and the two of them had paid a terrible price for it.

And she had sworn that day never to let down her guard again, with anyone, for anything, under any circumstance.

But now it was finally beginning to dawn on Selar that there was a world of difference between being emotionally repressed and emotionally crippled.

Her natural inclination, as a healer, was to help those who were crippled, in any way she could. Now, looking to her own needs, she found herself reminded of an admonition from the Earth bible which one of the teachers had once mentioned to her. A saying that was particularly appropriate at this time:

Physician, heal thyself.

"Computer, end program."

The plains of Vulcan vanished, to be replaced by the glowing yellow grids of the holodeck wall.

"Physician, heal thyself," she said, and then left the holodeck, although just for a moment she had the oddest feeling that she felt a faint wisp of a Vulcan wind on the back of her neck.

"Thallon, dead ahead, sir," announced McHenry. "Looks like they have some company."

That did indeed appear to be the case. There were several vessels already in orbit around Thallon. But only one of them immediately seized Calhoun's attention as he rose from his chair. "Son of a bitch," murmured Calhoun.

Shelby looked up in surprise. "Problem, Captain?"

"That ship there . . ." and he walked over to the screen and actually tapped on it. "Lefler, full magnification."

The ship promptly filled the entire screen. It was green and triangular in shape, with powerful warp engines mounted on the back.

Stepping away from her science station, Soleta observed, "That is a Xenexian ship, is it not, Captain?"

He nodded slowly. "It goes to show how quickly things change. When I lived there, we had no starbound ships. Our experiments with space travel were rudimentary at best. We weren't a starfaring race. Once we broke free from the Danteri, however, we began to take quantum leaps forward in our development. Sometimes I think it was the worst thing that ever happened to my people."

"The worst thing? Why?" asked Shelby.

He turned to face her. "Because I knew that we were getting help, and I never knew from where. It was a . . . rather sore point on the rare occasions when I came home. One of the main reasons I stopped coming home, as a matter of fact. But that's not just any Xenexian ship," and he turned back to the screen. "I recognize the markings on her. That's my brother's ship."

"Sir," Soleta spoke up. "The ion trail we were pursuing . . . it ends here. Not only that, but I believe that that vessel was the source of it."

"Hail her, Mr. Boyajian."

"Actually, Captain, they're hailing us."

"I suspected they would. Put them on screen."

A face appeared on the screen then, and Shelby was struck by the resemblance to Calhoun . . . and yet, by the differences as well. He looked like Mackenzie, but with a more self-satisfied, even smug manner about him. He inclined his head slightly and said, "Hello . . . Mackenzie." He overpronounced the name with tremendous exaggeration, as if it were unfamiliar to him. "That is how you wish to be called these days, is it not?"

"Where are my people, D'ndai?" Calhoun demanded without preamble.

D'ndai seemed amused by the lack of formality. " 'Your' people. I can see you making that reference to the rather large fellow in the Starfleet uniform . . . but am I to understand that Lord Si Cwan, former High Lord of the Thallonian Empire . . . is also to be grouped in among 'your' people?"

"I don't want to shadow-dance with you, D'ndai. Do you have them or don't you?"

"Have a care with your tone, little brother," D'ndai said sharply. "If it weren't for me, 'your' people would be nothing but scattered atoms right now. Scraps for you to collect and keep in a jar. So I would have a bit more respect right now if I were you. Now," and he leaned back, looking utterly in control of the situation, "if you would like to come over here and discuss the matter of your missing crewmen . . . I would be more than happy to extend an invitation to you."

"Accepted," replied Calhoun without hesitation. "Calhoun to transporter room."

"Transporter room, Watson here."

"Watson, ready the transporter room. I'll be down in a moment and you'll be beaming me over to the vessel that we're currently in communication with."

"Aye, sir."

"Captain, I'd recommend a security escort," Shelby said immediately.

"Security?" Overhearing this on the screen, D'ndai actually seemed amused by it. "Are you overly concerned that I may harm you, Mackenzie? Has our relationship come to that?"

Calhoun was silent for a moment, and then he said to Shelby, "No security team will be necessary."

"But—" Then she saw his expression and simply said, "Aye, sir."

"I'll be there in a few minutes, D'ndai."

"We'll be certain to have out the good silver," replied D'ndai, and the screen faded out.

Before Shelby could say anything further, Calhoun turned quickly and said, "But before I'm going anywhere, we're going to find out what the hell is going on with our people. Soleta," and he turned to face her. "You said that the capital is called Thal?"

"Yes, sir. Last time I was there, in any event."

"Work with Boyajian and send out a message to them. I want to talk to whoever is in charge and find out if Kebron and Si Cwan are down there. If necessary, send an away team. I want to know what's going on with them, and I want to know now."

For the moment, matters were quiet at the Federation embassy, Thallon branch, Zak Kebron overseer and sergeant at arms.

The gas had cleared out and Kebron was sitting quietly, letting his body's impressive healing capabilities tend to the wounds that he had sustained. The fact was that Kebron was in more pain than he would have cared to admit, but the Brikar had a stoicism so renowned that they made Vulcans look like laughing hyenas in comparison.

It had been a while since Si Cwan had said anything as well. He sat on the far side of the cell from Kebron, his legs drawn up, his arms around his knees. Finally, he spoke up: "Kebron."

"What?" One could not have told from his reply that he was in any sort of physical discomfort.

"I . . ." He paused, and then continued, "I just . . . wished to say . . . thank you."

"You're welcome," replied Kebron.

After which point, nothing more was said. It didn't seem necessary.

Then they heard footsteps from the direction of the door of the cell. Slowly Kebron rose to his feet, a brief grunt being the only indication that he was starting to wear down. But from outside they heard a voice say, "Do not concern yourselves. There will be no battle. I am alone. No guards are with me."

Kebron noticed from the corner of his eye that something was wrong with Si Cwan. There was utter astonishment registering on his face. He looked at him questioningly, but it was as if Cwan had ceased noticing that there was anyone else in the "embassy."

"Do you recognize me, Si Cwan?" The voice came once again from outside the cell.

"You're dead," Si Cwan said, as if speaking from very far away.

"I was reported dead. One should never confuse reports with reality."

"Friend of yours?" Kebron asked.

Si Cwan looked at him with undisguised shock. "I had thought so, once upon a time." Then he called back, "Yoz? Chancellor Yoz?"

"Once Chancellor, yes. The tainted title given me by the oppressive royal family of Thallon, back before I saw the error of my ways and aided the people of the Thallonian Empire in throwing off the shackles of oppression."

"Save the rhetoric for the gullible," Si Cwan retorted. He was leaning against the wall, using it for support as he raised himself to standing. And as he spoke, his voice became increasingly louder and angrier. "Our trusted Chancellor Yoz. You helped organize the . . . the rebellion? You helped oversee the overthrow of the Thallonian Empire? You *helped destroy my family!? We trusted you!*"

"I was your flunky and you treated me with contempt. Don't endeavor to rewrite history now to suit your own purposes. I was always a second-class citizen to—''

And once more the ground beneath them shook.

This one was more violent than the previous occasions. Si Cwan stumbled back and fell onto Kebron, who managed to catch him at just the right angle so that he didn't injure himself against Kebron's rocky body. They could not see Yoz on the other side of the door, but Cwan took some bleak measure of satisfaction in the notion that Yoz was being flipped around helplessly. Kebron, unmovable, held on to Cwan and prevented him from rolling about more inside the cell.

And then something cracked.

They looked in astonishment as the cell floor shifted beneath them, and a large chunk of the ground actually cracked and thrust itself upward by about a foot. "I don't believe it," whispered Si Cwan. "What the devil is happening around here?"

Slowly the shuddering subsided. "Yoz," called Cwan. "Are you still with us?"

"Thank you for—" Yoz started to say, and then he coughed loudly. Dust was seeping in through the door; it was possible that a portion of the wall had crumbled outside, sending up waves of dust. "Thank you for your concern," he continued sarcastically. "I am here to inform you that your space vessel is here. An away team will be coming down to the People's Meeting Hall fairly shortly. You are invited to join us there. In order to do so, you will have to leave your 'embassy,' of course, but I guarantee you safe conduct."

"The 'People's Meeting Hall'?" inquired Si Cwan.

"What you used to call your throne room. All such artificial trappings are now in the possession of the good people of Thallon."

"It could easily be a trick," Kebron pointed out.

"Yes, your Commander Shelby said you might say that. She asked me to relay to you the following: Code Alpha Gamma Alpha. Does that have any significance to you?"

Kebron turned to Si Cwan and said, "It's no trick. We have regular security codes for identification purposes for just such situations."

"Situations such as this? That is impressively comprehensive planning."

"We are Starfleet. We endeavor to be prepared."

"So tell me, Yoz. Once I am brought to this People's Meeting place, what will happen to me there?"

"You will face your accusers," replied Yoz. "You will face the people of Thallon, and Thallonian justice."

"Very well. I accept your terms."

In a low voice, Kebron said, "I do not like this situation. You do not know what you are agreeing to. This could be some sort of setup."

"I agree," said Cwan. "But I do not see much choice in the matter, do you? I mean, as charming as these facilities are, and as pleasant as your company may be, I have no desire to spend the rest of my life in this 'embassy.' Do you?"

"I must admit that I had career and life plans which would be difficult to pursue from this location."

There seemed nothing more to say. Kebron walked slowly to the door and pulled on it slightly. It was not locked. He slid it open and, sure enough, there was only the Thallonian named Yoz standing there. Si Cwan came up behind Kebron and said slowly, "You know . . . I kept telling myself that if I encountered anyone from the happier days of my life, I would be overjoyed to see them. This simply goes to prove that nothing ever works out as one expected."

Rather than bothering to reply, Yoz instead made a sweeping gesture down the corridor. "It's this way," he said.

"I believe," Si Cwan replied icily, "that I know the way to the throne room . . . oh, I'm sorry. The People's Meeting Hall."

"How lovely that must be for you."

And as they started down the corridor, ex-Chancellor Yoz said, "Lieutenant Kebron . . . I apologize for your being dragged into all this. You are merely an innocent bystander in our planetary politics, and we do not hold you liable for any actions you may have taken as a result of our . . . disagreements. I trust we understand each other."

Kebron did not even look at him. He merely said, "Stay out of my way or I'll crush you like an egg."

Yoz stayed out of his way.

D'NDAI

VIII

D'ndai was waiting for his brother in his quarters. The classic term for it was "home field advantage." But if Calhoun was at all discomforted by being on someone else's "home turf," he did not let on.

He looked around and nodded in what appeared to be approval. D'ndai's quarters were opulently decorated, with furniture that was both sturdy and also intricately carved. A large portrait of D'ndai hung on a wall, and Calhoun immediately recognized the style as one of Xenex's master portrait painters. "Well, well, D'ndai . . . you've certainly done well for yourself, haven't you?"

"That was always the problem between us, wasn't it, M'k'n'zy?" said D'ndai. "The fact that I have done so well for myself." He reached into a cabinet and withdrew a large bottle of liquor. "Drink?" he asked. "Far more potent and useful than that pale synthehol which I know is the beverage of choice on your starships."

"No, thank you."

"Why not, M'k'n'zy? Do you not trust my food or drink? What," and he laughed, "do you think I'm going to poison you or something?"

Calhoun smiled thinly and made no reply.

The silence itself was damning, and D'ndai made a great show of taking umbrage over it. "You cut me to the quick, brother. Such lack of trust! Such lack of faith!"

Ignoring his brother's posturing, Calhoun walked slowly around the quarters, surveying it. He rapped on the furniture, ran a finger along the edges of one as if he were checking for dust. "Where are they, D'ndai?" he asked, sounding remarkably casual.

"Are you going to thank me for saving them first?"

"Thank you for saving them. Now where are they?"

D'ndai took a sip of his drink and then said, "You know . . . in a way, I'm glad that you are back in uniform. It suits you well."

Each word from Calhoun was dripping with ice. "Where . . . are . . . they?"

"As it happens, they're on the planet's surface. I was going to be going down there myself within a few minutes. You are welcome to join me. We can see them together. They are healthy and unharmed . . . although not for lack of trying."

Calhoun cocked an eyebrow. "What do you mean by that?"

"I mean that, as much as I hate to admit it, the Thallonians attempted some rather assaulting behavior on Messrs. Kebron and Cwan. These efforts were resisted, however. Your Mr. Kebron is a rather formidable individual."

"I will relay to him that you felt that way." He started to head for the door.

"M'k'n'zy! Don't leave so soon!" D'ndai called out. "There is much for us to discuss! Don't you think it about time that we did, in fact, discuss it?"

"And what would be the point?" demanded Calhoun angrily. Then he calmed himself and repeated, much more quietly, "What would be the point? You made your decisions. You know how I felt about them. What else is there to say?"

"I made decisions that benefited Xenex."

And this time Calhoun did not attempt to hold back his ire. Crossing the room quickly, his fists balled, he said tightly, "You made decisions that benefited you, D'ndai! *You!* You and the others!"

"Xenex has prospered under our guidance, M'k'n'zy. You know this. The people are happy."

"The people are miserable and simply don't know it!"

"And you do!" said D'ndai. He circled the room, speaking with his eyes thrown wide as if he were addressing the heavens. "You do! You know so much! You, M'k'n'zy, who went off to chart his own course and left us behind, know the state of Xenex's mind more than we do!"

"I left because I thought my job was done. Because I thought you could be trusted."

"And I could be."

"You sold out our people's spirit!" Calhoun said angrily. "We won our independence from Danter, and then the first thing you do is arrange alliances and trade agreements with them!"

"We became partners with them. It's called advancement."

"We became slaves to them all over again! Oh, we were better kept, better pampered, but once again we were under the thumb of Danter! And this time we accepted it willingly! After twenty years we're right back where we started, and no one realizes that or understands it!"

"You keep saying 'we' as if you were a part of Xenex," D'ndai said quietly. "In case you've forgotten what uniform you wear, it seems to me that you, as an individual, have no say at all in the direction that our people have gone."

"Oh, I saw the direction it was going early on. I saw you in your meetings, your private sessions with the Danteri. I saw what you were up to, you and your cronies. I objected at the time."

"The war was over, M'k'n'zy. We won. Had we listened to you, we would have kept on fighting even when the other side was giving up. We would have become isolationist, cut ourselves off from opportunities." His presence seemed to fill up the room as D'ndai continued angrily, "When you were offered the opportunity to leave Xenex and gallivant around the stars, I didn't see you turning down that opportunity. But you would have had us turn away from a hand outstretched in peace that, once upon a time, would only attempt to swat us down."

"Don't you understand, D'ndai?" Calhoun said urgently. "The triumph of Xenex was a triumph that came from within the souls of the Xenexians. We won our freedom without allies, depending only upon ourselves! Why was it then necessary to turn to our enemies for the purpose of maintaining that freedom . . . ?" But his voice trailed off as he saw something in D'ndai's expression. Partly it seemed like a self-satisfied smirk, as if D'ndai knew something that he wasn't telling. But there was also a hint of sadness in his expression. "D'ndai . . . ?"

"What makes you think we had no allies?" asked D'ndai.

"What?"

"M'k'n'zy, whether you're a Starfleet officer or not, you're still a fool. Of course we had allies."

"But . . ." Calhoun was confused, and for just a moment he felt as if he were no older than the nineteen summers he'd possessed when he'd first led his people to freedom. "I . . . I don't understand. What are you—?"

"Didn't you wonder where our supply of weapons came from? Our provisions when the Danteri cut off our supply lines? No . . . no, probably you didn't," said D'ndai contemptuously. "You were so busy planning strategies and anticipating the next move that the Danteri might make, you had no time to be concerned about any other matters. You were more than happy to leave them all to me. And I handled it."

"How?" And then, slowly, it dawned on him. "The Thallonians."

"That's right, M'k'n'zy. The Thallonians. There was no love lost between them and their neighbors, the Danteri. And when the Thallonians learned of our struggle against the Danteri, they were more than happy to supply us whatever we needed in order to keep that battle going. The matter was handled quietly; the Thallonians did not like to draw attention to themselves. But we had an alliance between us."

"And this happened without my knowing?" Calhoun couldn't believe it. "You should have discussed it with me! I had a right to know!"

"You were a teenager! An idealistic, battle-obsessed teenager, with more pride than the sky has stars. You would have fought to reject all offers of help. You would have disrupted everything, because you had a deep-seated need to handle everything yourself. I knew it would be the height of folly to tell you of our allies. I had no choice but to hide it from you. It would have led to unnecessary arguments."

"Or perhaps to necessary arguments!" shot back Calhoun. Then he paused a moment, wondering why those words sounded vaguely familiar to him.

Then he remembered. Remembered Elizabeth Shelby hurling practically the same sentiments at him. And he thought, *The irony of this is just sickening*. Rather than voice that sentiment, of course, he then asked, "But wait . . . how did we . . . you . . . become allies of the Danteri, then?"

"Because, with our being beholden to the Thallonians, we did not want to put ourselves into a position of weakness with them. By turning around and allying with the Danteri, it was a way of keeping the Thallonians in check. After all, we had no desire to have broken free of the Danteri Empire, only to find ourselves falling under the long arm of the Thallonian Empire. A sensible concern, wouldn't you say?"

"Very sensible. You always were the most sensible of men."

Calhoun stood there for a time after that, leaning against the ornate chest of drawers. D'ndai crossed the room, placing his drink down on the top of the chest, and he took Calhoun by the shoulders. "M'k'n'zy . . . come back to Xenex. You can do so much good there . . . more than you know. More than gallivanting around in a starship can accomplish. We of Xenex, we are your first, best destiny."

"Return for what purpose? So that I can fight you every step of the way? Or perhaps I'll simply get my throat cut one night in my sleep. That would not upset you too much, I'd wager."

"You wound me, brother."

"You'd do far worse to me and we both know it."

"I warn you . . ."

Calhoun stared at him, his eyes flat and deadly. "You're *warning* me? Warning me that my only chance is to become like you?"

Realizing that he was now treading on dangerous ground, D'ndai said quickly, "I know what you're thinking."

"No, you don't."

"Yes, I do. You're thinking that I've let down our people. That I, and the rest of the ruling council, sacrificed their interests for the various perks and privileges offered to me by the Danteri. That I am motivated by self-interest rather than general interest. I can do nothing to change your perceptions except to say that, in my own way, I care about Xenex as much as you do."

"You see . . . I was right. You don't know what I'm thinking."

"Well, then . . . perhaps you'd care to enlighten me."

Calhoun's arm moved so quickly that D'ndai never even saw it coming. The uppercut caught him on the tip of the jaw and D'ndai went down to the floor. He lay there for a moment, stunned and confused.

"I was thinking about how much I would like to do that," said Calhoun.

"Did that..." D'ndai tried to straighten out his jaw while lying on the floor. "Did that make you feel better?"

"No," said Calhoun.

"So...you see...perhaps you have grown up after al—"

Calhoun kicked him in the stomach. D'ndai, still on the floor, doubled up, gasping.

"*That* made me feel better," Calhoun told him.

Soleta and Lefler stood on the flatlands outside Thal, Soleta with her hands on her hips surveying the area. Her tricorder hung off her shoulder, and there were a variety of instruments in the pack on her shoulders. She pointed to one area and said, "It was right there."

"The sinkhole?"

"Yes." She unshouldered the tricorder and approached the area which had, ten years earlier, swallowed her shuttlecraft. "This has been an annoyance to me for a decade. I landed my ship on an area that I thought was stable...and then it wasn't."

"Is that possible?"

"I would have thought not. But it would seem that on the surface of this world, virtually anything is possible." Lefler helped pull the backpack off her shoulders and then knelt down, beginning to remove instruments from the back.

Soleta walked forward slowly, the tricorder in front of her, taking surface readings. Behind her, Lefler was glancing over her shoulder at Thal, even as she set up a complex array of detection devices. The spires of the city were tall and glistening, framed against the purple skies of Thallon. But it was purely reflection of the fading sunlight. She remembered that, last time she had been there, the city was lit up. Not now, though. The lights were dark, to conserve energy. Energy that had always been in plentiful supply before the wellspring of Thallon had dwindled. "How do you think Commander Shelby and McHenry are doing over in Thal?"

"I am quite certain that they are handling the situation as well as, if not better than, can be expected. My concern is completing the job that I began ten years ago—namely determining the reasons for this planet's instability. An instability, I believe, which has only become more accentuated over the years. I also need to learn the origin of the energy that seemed to radiate from this planet's very core.''

"My understanding is that they've been having a number of seismic disturbances as well," Lefler noted. She studied the sensor web array that she had assembled. "But what's odd is that initial sensor readings haven't detected any geological fault lines. So I'm not sure what could be causing them.''

Soleta walked carefully, tentatively, around the area that had swallowed her shuttlecraft. Even though her tricorder told her that it was solid, she still found herself reluctant to take any chances. Although it was hardly more scientific than the tricorder, she reached out carefully and touched the area with her toe. It seemed substantial enough. She walked out onto it, like a would-be ice skater testing the strength of a frozen lake.

Meantime, the sensor web was anchored into the ground, sending readings deep into the surface of Thallon. They were the sort of detailed readings that simply were not possible from orbit. Lefler looked over the energy wave readings and shook her head in confusion. "I'm reading some sort of seismic . . . pulse," Lefler called. "That might be responsible for these shifts.''

"A . . . 'pulse'? That's a rather vague term," Soleta informed her. "What's the cause of it?''

"Unknown. Don't worry, though. I'll get it figured out.''

"I have every confidence that you will, Lefler. Just as I am confident that I shall figure out this curiosity with the fluctuation of the planet's surface.''

"My my," said Lefler with amusement. "Nice to know you're so sure of yourself. It hasn't occurred to you, for instance, that maybe . . . just maybe . . . you accidentally parked your ship on a sinkhole and simply didn't realize it. And that the area you're looking over now is simply not the same place. You're asking me to believe that the ground out here is capable of turning from substantive to quicksand in no time at all.''

"The alternative is that I am mistaken in this matter. That is highly improbable.''

"Ahhh. Lefler's law number eighty-three: Whenever you've eliminated the impossible, whatever remains, however improbable, must be the truth.''

"Lefler," said Soleta, her back still to her, "I'm certain that you consider this endless recitation of your 'laws' to be charming. Perhaps some people would share that opinion. To me, however, it comes across as a mere affectation, perhaps to cover up a basic insecurity. You feel that there are some areas in which you are not knowledgeable, and so you put forward authority in many areas. Even those about which you know little or nothing. Nor are these 'laws' necessarily of your own devising. That which you just quoted is, in fact, the noted 'great dictum' formulated by writer Arthur Conan Doyle in the guise of his literary creation, Sherlock Holmes. Understand, it is not my desire to upset you with these observations. Merely a concern that we are able to work together with a minimum of friction."

The only reply she received was silence. "Lefler?" She turned and looked in the direction she had last seen Lefler.

Lefler was gone. So was the sensor array.

"Lefler?" she called again. She took a step toward the area where Lefler had just been.

And Lefler's head suddenly broke ground.

The only thing visible was her face. Her mouth was open, her eyes frantic, and she barely had time to gasp out *"Soleta!"* before she vanished beneath the ground again.

Soleta charged forward while, at the same time, holding her tricorder in front of her. She scanned the surface and skidded to a half a foot away from the edge of the newly created sinkhole. She dropped to her belly and stretched her arm out as far as she could. She was two feet shy of where Lefler had vanished.

Moving as quickly as she could, Soleta stripped off her uniform, knotting the jacket and trousers together for additional length. For weight, she grabbed up a large boulder, tied the jacket around it, and then heaved the far end into the sinkhole while clutching the other end. Her major concern was hoping that she didn't accidentally knock Lefler cold with the boulder.

The lifeline, weighted down by the boulder, descended into the sinkhole. "Come on, Robin, find it," Soleta muttered. "Come on, come on . . ."

She knew that diving in after Lefler would, more than likely, be suicide. It was illogical for both of them to die. But it was what she was going to have to do. She steeled herself, reasonably saying a likely good-bye to life, and suddenly she felt a sharp tugging at the end of the lifeline.

Immediately Soleta backed up, pulling with all her not-inconsiderable strength. The line grew taut, and she prayed that the knots would hold. The last thing she needed was for the entire thing to come apart.

She backed up step by step, never letting up on the pressure, even though the sinkhole seemed to be fighting back. And just when she thought that Lefler couldn't possibly be holding her breath anymore, Robin's head suddenly burst through the surface. She gasped, drawing in frantic lungfuls of air. Then, with herculean effort, she pulled one arm out of the mire and grabbed the lifeline. She pulled herself, hand over hand, until she was clear of the sinkhole, and then she flopped onto the ground next to Soleta, her chest heaving. It was a full minute before either of them was composed enough to say anything.

"I . . . think I found a sinkhole," Lefler finally managed to get out.

"So it would seem," replied Soleta.

"It appears the ground *is* that unstable. I'm sorry I doubted you."

"Well . . . do not do it again, and we should be fine. Fine, that is, as long as the ground doesn't dissolve under us again." She sat up, not having released her hold on the makeshift lifeline, and now she proceeded to pull it out so that she could unknot it and convert it back to its previous incarnation of her uniform. She examined her bare legs, badly scratched up by her lying flat on the surface, and then she glanced in the direction of the area where the equipment had been set up before being sucked under the surface of the planet. "So much for the sensor array."

"Actually . . ." Lefler said, and she held up the core data unit.

Soleta was surprised. "You managed to keep a grip on that even while you were sinking into the ground?" Lefler nodded, and Soleta said approvingly, "Very impressive."

"I'm nothing if not stubborn. We can get it back to the ship and analyze it there . . . right after we change into clean uniforms." As she looked over the data unit, she added, "By the way . . . I heard you starting to say something just before I sank. Something about my laws. What was it?"

Soleta hesitated a moment and then said, "Absolutely nothing of importance."

*   *   *

Commander Shelby looked around the crowded hall and couldn't help but feel how dangerously outnumbered she was.

She and McHenry had been seated in "places of honor" in the place called the People's Meeting Hall. Seated next to her was an individual who had identified himself as Yoz, and who appeared to be in some sort of leadership capacity. She could feel eyes upon her everywhere, as the Thallonians regarded McHenry and her with outright curiosity. A sea of red faces with nothing better to look at than two Starfleet officers. They chattered to each other in low tones while never once glancing away from Shelby and McHenry. Nearby her were two others who had been introduced to her as Zoran—who appeared to be some sort of aide-de-camp to Yoz—and Ryjaan, an ambassador from Danter. Ryjaan she had not met, but she knew of him; he had been present at the initial summit meetings which had resulted in the *Excalibur*'s assignment to this portion of space in the first place. Her eye caught a sword hanging from his belt, and he noticed that she was looking at it. "Purely ceremonial," Ryjaan said. "I'm expert in its use . . . but I've never wielded it in combat. With rare exception, we've evolved far beyond that."

"That's very comforting," said Shelby, not feeling particularly comforted, particularly as the stares of the people of Thallon were getting on her nerves.

"I apologize for the curiosity of my people," Yoz said, leaning over to her and sounding genuinely contrite. He extended a bowl of what appeared to be finger foods.

"For a moment I thought it was just my imagination," she said. She took a sample from the bowl and ate it delicately.

"No, I am afraid not. We Thallonians are an interesting contradiction. We have an empire that spans many, many worlds. Technically a plethora of races constitutes the empire . . . or what remains of it, in any event. But Thallon itself has always remained somewhat . . . xenophobic. Visitors from other races, even those which are part of the empire, are something of a rarity on Thallon in general, and here in Thal in particular. And certainly for outsiders to be held in a place of honor . . . it is most unusual."

"I am most aware of that, Yoz. We've come quite a long way. Thallon has gone from being a world that shunned all contact, to a world that welcomes its first visitors from the Federation. And we appreciate it greatly.''

"Do you?" Yoz was looking at McHenry with interest. "And does he?"

Shelby turned and saw that McHenry was staring off into space. She'd brought him along because he'd been working with Soleta on the history of the area. Now she prayed she hadn't made a mistake. McHenry may have seemed eccentric, but he always had a knack for rising above and beyond any occasion. She prayed he wasn't going to start backsliding now. "Lieutenant," she said sharply, and was relieved that McHenry immediately turned back to face her. "Lieutenant, I believe that Yoz was speaking to you."

"I was simply interested in your impressions of our fair city, Lieutenant McHenry," said Yoz pleasantly.

"Ah." McHenry, as he considered the question, bit into a greenish, curved, waferlike object from a bowl nearby. He smiled and looked questioningly at Yoz.

"Yukka chips. Thallonian delicacy. They're quite good."

"I'll say," agreed McHenry, crunching on several more as he thought a moment more. "Well... from my admittedly brief look around your city, and what I've seen so far... I'd say that you're all rearranging the deck chairs on the *Titanic*."

"The... the what on the what?" He looked blankly at Shelby, who shrugged, and then back to McHenry. "I'm... afraid I don't understand..."

"Oh. Sorry." McHenry leaned forward, warming to the subject. "The *Titanic* was a huge Earth sailing vessel of several centuries back, considered unsinkable. It hit an iceberg and sank."

"I see," Yoz said slowly. "And to move furniture around on a vessel that is sinking would be an exercise in futility. An indication that one is in denial that the ship is going down."

"Exactly." McHenry nodded amiably. "I mean, we're here because the Thallonian Empire has collapsed, and you guys are sitting around here like you're about to rebuild something. Like, if you can keep everything together here on Thallon, you might somehow be able to keep going with the only change in status being that you guys are in charge instead of the other guys. It's not going to happen that way."

"And do you share the lieutenant's view, Commander?"

Shelby looked Yoz straight in the eye and said, "I might not have been quite as blunt . . . but I would say that his assessment is accurate enough. You have serious problems here, Yoz, and it seems to me that you're more concerned with putting on a show for the spectators than actually trying to address them."

"This 'show' that we are putting on *is* how we are trying to address them," replied Yoz. "We are endeavoring to show the people that the Thallonian Empire—which, by the way, we will be formally renaming the Thallonian Alliance—cannot, must not, descend into chaos."

"It already has, sir," said Shelby. "The trick is to extricate it."

"Very well, then. And the way that we will extricate it is to show that there is order to be offered. And one of the fundamental means of putting forward order is through justice. Would you agree to that, Commander?"

She was about to answer when she heard the familiar whine of transporter beams. There were surprised gasps from the people watching the proceedings. They had seen matter transportation before, but most transmat on Thallon was done with sending and receiving platforms. People materializing out of thin air was not a common sight.

The beams coalesced into two forms: Captain Calhoun and D'ndai, with the transporter beams having originated from the *Excalibur*. Both of them were staring fixedly straight ahead, as if they were determined to look anywhere but at each other. Calhoun saw his second-in-command and helmsman, and nodded slightly in acknowledgment of their presence. Then he walked over to Yoz and introductions were quickly made. More chairs were immediately brought over and Calhoun sat down nearby Shelby. He was surprised to find that he was practically sinking into the cushions, and had to readjust himself so that he would not disappear entirely.

"It is good of you to be able to join us, Captain," said Yoz amiably. "I was just having an interesting discussion with your first officer. A discussion about justice."

"Really?" Calhoun looked at Shelby with raised eyebrow. "I'd be interested to hear the outcome of that discussion myself."

"I was simply saying that justice, and the means by which justice is applied, is one of the cornerstones of a civilized society. And that is what we are trying to institute here. Would you agree with that, Commander?"

"I would," said Shelby reasonably.

"And that interference with that justice would be tantamount to endorsing chaos. Isn't that right as well?"

But by this point Shelby's "antennae" were up, and she saw by Calhoun's expression that his were as well. "I would be most interested to know where this is leading, Yoz," Shelby said.

"Very well. I will be forthcoming." He leaned forward and said, "We are about to bring out Si Cwan. As far as the current government of Thallon is concerned, he is an outlaw. He has had the temerity to reenter our space. We desire to try him accordingly. Will you interfere?"

Shelby wanted to respond, but instead she waited for Calhoun to say something. But instead he simply watched her, inclining his head slightly to indicate that she should go ahead and speak. "We have a law, called the Prime Directive. It pledges noninterference. If Si Cwan is in the hands of local authorities . . . there is little we can do."

"You would not simply transport him away if the decisions being made went against him."

"That . . . would not be permissible, no," she said slowly. She looked back to Calhoun, but his expression was stony and silent. "But may I ask what crimes he has supposedly committed against you?"

"Not just against his fellow Thallonians," Ryjaan spoke up. He seemed in an extraordinarily good mood. "Against the Danteri as well. He killed a high-ranking Danteri officer. For that alone, he should face a Final Challenge."

"A what?" asked Shelby.

"Danteri law," Calhoun told her before Ryjaan could explain it. "Danteri law is very interesting when it comes to capital cases. The state can opt to execute the criminal themselves. However, the method is very humane . . . if one can call murder humane. The only one capable of gainsaying that is the family of the deceased. They can instead demand a Final Challenge. The advantage to the accused is that, if he survives or triumphs, he can go free. If he doesn't, however, well . . . it can take several agonizing days, for instance, to die of a belly wound. Any form of killing your opponent in the Final Challenge is acceptable. The 'rare exception' I mentioned earlier."

"And as we of Thallon have a new accord with the Danteri," Yoz said, "we have agreed to adopt their laws in this matter for the time being. And your law will have you stand by and take no action."

"As I said, it's not permissible. Besides . . . I suspect that Si Cwan can handle himself. And I know that our captain is a big believer in taking responsibilities for one's actions." She looked with mild defiance at Calhoun, but all he did was nod.

"Very well, then," Yoz said briskly, rubbing his hands together. "Then we are agreed . . . the accused shall be left to our judicial system."

"Where's Zak Kebron?" Calhoun said before Yoz could continue. "D'ndai informs me he's down here."

"Yes, that's correct. As a matter of fact, he's on his way up right now."

D'ndai suddenly spoke up. "Tell me," he asked with genuine curiosity, "you have expansive, liberal views on justice when it applies to one who is not, technically, part of your crew. What if it were Kebron? What if he were accused of crimes? Would you still believe that the Thallonian standard of justice should apply?"

"Absolutely," said Shelby without hesitation.

At that moment there was a roar from the observers, and Zak Kebron and Si Cwan were brought up and into view. The representatives from the *Excalibur* were relieved to see that neither of them appeared too much the worse for wear, although Kebron did seem a bit banged up. But they were walking steadily and proud, their chins held high . . . or, at least in Kebron's case, what passed for a chin.

They were not in chains, not being dragged. There were guards on either side of them, but they seemed more ceremonial than anything. In fact, they looked rather nervous. It almost came across as if Kebron and Cwan were in charge of the moment, rather than the guards or, indeed, anyone of authority.

They moved to the middle of the room and came to a halt. They noted the presence of the *Excalibur* crewmen, but gave no overt sign, no loud greeting. The moment seemed to call for underplaying emotions.

Without preamble, Yoz said, "Mr. Kebron . . . I release you into the custody of your commanding officer. You are on probation, and asked not to return to the surface of Thallon after your departure."

Brikar emotions were generally hard to read, but even Kebron seemed to register mild surprise. Then, as if mentally shrugging, he started to walk over toward the others.

And then stopped.

He turned, looked back at Si Cwan, and then back to Yoz. "What of him?"

"He is to be handled separately. He is to stand trial for crimes against his people."

"I see."

Kebron stood there for a brief time, displaying as much emotion as an Easter Island statue . . . and then slowly he walked back to Si Cwan, stood at his side, and faced the accusers.

Immediately more chatter broke out among the crowd as Shelby looked to Calhoun to see his reaction. To her astonishment, Calhoun seemed to be doing everything he could to cover a smile.

"Mr. Kebron, you are free to go," Yoz said more forcefully.

"I disagree," Kebron said calmly.

And now Si Cwan turned to him and said, "Kebron, nothing is to be accomplished by this. Whatever situation I'm involved with is of my doing, not yours. They merely consider you a pawn in this. Don't let yourself be a needlessly sacrificed pawn."

"It is my concern," replied Kebron.

"No, Lieutenant . . . it's mine," Calhoun spoke up. The captain was standing, his hands behind his back in a casual fashion, but there was nothing casual in his voice. "I appreciate and respect the ethics of all my crewmen. But I won't let one sacrifice himself needlessly. These people, and even Si Cwan, have released you. And you're too much of an asset to the ship for me to simply write you off if it can be avoided. I order you to take them up on their offer, Lieutenant."

This time, with what sounded like a sigh, Kebron moved away from Si Cwan and joined his captain. But he regarded Calhoun with a baleful glare that the captain did not particularly appreciate. On the other hand, he more than understood it.

"Si Cwan," Yoz intoned, "you are accused of crimes against the people of Thallon and an assortment of worlds in the Thallonian Empire. These include: suppressing a rebellion on Mandylor 5 . . . the execution of dissidents on Respler 4A . . ."

The list went on for quite some time, and Si Cwan simply stood there, no sign of emotion in his face. The crowd had fallen silent as well, every comment sounding like another great chime of a bell sounding a death knell.

Si Cwan only interrupted toward the end as he said, "Tell me, Yoz . . . do you have any proof that I, myself, had a hand in any of these activities?"

"Do you deny any of them?" shot back Yoz.

"I do not deny that they occurred. But there were others who made these decisions. I did not have control over everything that went on. Mine was but one voice. Oftentimes I learned of these incidents after the fact."

"So you believe that you are not to be held responsible. These were activities of the royal family. You were part of that family. Therefore you should be held responsible!"

"You would think that," said Si Cwan. "After all . . ." and he looked poisonously in the direction of Zoran, "if you would take the life of a young girl who had no involvement at all, certainly you would not hesitate to deprive me of my life." Zoran, hardly appearing stung by the comment, instead smiled broadly.

But now Ryjaan stepped forward, and he said, "You would deny hands-on involvement. We know otherwise, Cwan. We know of what you did on Xenex! And my bloodline calls for vengeance!"

For the first time, Si Cwan looked confused. His expression was mirrored in Calhoun's face, but since almost all eyes were on Si Cwan, it wasn't widely noticed. *Almost* all eyes, because D'ndai was watching Calhoun with undisguised interest.

"Xenex?" asked Si Cwan. "What happened on Xenex?"

"Do not pretend! Do not insult my intelligence!" roared Ryjaan. "You killed my father, and you will be brought to justice for it!"

"Who's your father?" Si Cwan didn't sound the least bit guilty. If anything, he sounded genuinely curious.

"Falkar, of the House of Edins," said Ryjaan fiercely. "A great man, a great warrior, a great father . . . and you, monster, you took him from me. From all of us, with your murdering ways."

And Calhoun felt the blood rush to his face.

His head whipped around and he looked straight at D'ndai. D'ndai was not returning the gaze. Instead he stared resolutely ahead, as if he found what was transpiring with Si Cwan to be absolutely riveting. But the edges of his mouth were turned up, ever so slightly, like a small smirk.

You bastard, thought Calhoun, even as he tapped his comm unit and began to speak softly into it. Shelby didn't notice, for she was watching Si Cwan's reactions to the proceedings.

"I have never heard of this 'Falkar,'" Si Cwan said. "I regret you your loss, but I did not deprive you of him."

"You deny it, then! All the more coward you! In the name of Thallonian and Danteri law, in the name of my family, I desire justice for your slaughter of my father!"

"Interesting justice system," Si Cwan said dryly. "Accusation is synonymous with guilt. Proof is not a requisite."

"It was much the same when your family was in charge," Yoz commented. "How many times did I, as High Chancellor, stand there helplessly while enemies of your family simply vanished, never to be seen again, while your justice would try them in their absence? At least we let you stand here to voice your own defense."

"You ask me to prove something I did not do, against accusations that I cannot address. How would you have me defend myself?"

"That," said Ryjaan, "is your problem."

And then an unexpected voice . . . unexpected to all but one . . . spoke up loudly. And the voice said, "Actually . . . it's my problem."

All eyes immediately turned to the speaker. To Captain Calhoun, one of the Federation visitors. He had risen from the place of honor and strode in the general direction of Si Cwan, stopping about midway between the accusers and the accused. Si Cwan stood there in bemusement as Calhoun turned to face Si Cwan's accusers. "Tell me, Ryjaan . . . did my beloved brother inform you that Si Cwan killed Falkar?"

"Yes . . . yes, he did," Ryjaan said slowly.

"Let me guess, D'ndai . . . you were trying to cover up for your younger sibling," Calhoun said, voice dripping with sarcasm. "Or perhaps you simply regarded Si Cwan as a useful tool for cementing ties with both the Danteri and Thallonians . . . the better to provide for you in your old age. Or maybe . . . and this, I think, is the most likely . . . you knew I couldn't simply sit by and allow Si Cwan to suffer for this . . . 'crime.'"

D'ndai was silent. Silent as the tomb.

Shelby slowly began to rise, sensing impending disaster, and she touched Kebron on the shoulder, indicating that he should be prepared for trouble. McHenry knew trouble was coming as well. However, he was also capable of prioritizing, and consequently emptied the contents of the Yukka chips bowl between his outer and inner shirt, since he had the sneaking suspicion he wasn't going to be getting any more in the near future.

"Captain . . ." Shelby said warningly.

But he put up a hand and said sharply, "This isn't your affair, Commander. Ryjaan . . . your father was not murdered. He died in combat, in war, like a soldier. He went down well and nobly. I know . . . because I'm the one who killed him."

There was a collective gasp of the onlookers. Ryjaan was trembling with barely repressed fury. "You?"

"Yes. You know of my background as a freedom fighter. You should likewise know that crimes against the Danteri were unilaterally forgiven by your government as part of the settlement of the worlds. You would stand there and accuse me of a crime that your own government no longer considers a crime."

"I have not rendered that decision!" Ryjaan said angrily. "I do not care what my government has or has not decided! That was my father who died on Xenex!"

"Yes, and it was your father who left me with this," replied Calhoun, touching his scar.

"This is a lie! It's all lies!" said Ryjaan. "You think to exonerate Si Cwan by assuming the blame for a crime you did not commit! You have no proof—!"

"No?" Calhoun asked quietly. He tapped his comm badge. "Calhoun to transporter room. Send it down."

Before anyone could react, the twinkling whine of the transporters sounded nearby, and something materialized on the floor next to Calhoun. It was a sword. A short sword. Shelby recognized it instantly as the sword that had been hanging on the wall in his ready room. Calhoun walked over to it and hefted it as comfortably as if it was a part of his own body.

"Recognize this?" he asked.

The curve of the sword, the carvings on the handle, were unmistakable.

And with a roar, Ryjaan leaped forward, his own sword out of its scabbard so quickly that the eye would have been unable to follow. *"Final Challenge!"* he howled.

"Accepted!" shot back Calhoun, and he caught the downward thrust of the sword skillfully on the length of his own blade.

The crowd was in an uproar, everyone shouting simultaneously.

"Come on!" shouted Shelby, and Kebron led the charge. He plowed through anyone between him and Calhoun, as easily stopped or reasoned with as a tidal wave, knocking anyone or anything in his path out of the way. Shelby and McHenry were right behind him. He grabbed Ryjaan from behind just as Ryjaan was about to lunge forward with another thrust and tossed him aside. Ryjaan went flying, landing squarely behind the place of honor, as Shelby hit her comm badge and shouted, "Shelby to transporter room! Five to beam up, now! *Now!"*

And the air crackled around them as the away team vanished. And the last thing they heard was Ryjaan screaming, "Final Challenge! Final Challenge! Honor it, if you're a man, and face me, coward!"

MACKENZIE

IX

"Captain, no! You can't!?"

Shelby and Calhoun were still in the transporter room, the rest of the away team grouped around them. Polly Watson at the transporter console had no idea what was going on, and so simply stood to one side.

"A challenge has been issued and accepted," replied Calhoun evenly. "This is a matter of justice. You said it yourself, Commander. We have to abide by local customs. The Prime Directive—"

"—is not the issue here, sir! Captain, can we continue this discussion in your ready room?"

"No." He turned to Watson. "Prepare to beam me back down."

"Yes, sir." She stepped toward the console.

"Belay that," snapped Shelby.

"Yes, sir." She stepped back from the console.

"Either you were arguing for a concept and a belief, Commander, or you were arguing for an individual," said Calhoun firmly. "It can't be that something which applies to Si Cwan or to Kebron does not apply to me."

"You're this vessel's captain," Shelby said.

"What better reason, then. I should exemplify the rule; not be the exception to it."

"If I might interject—" began Si Cwan.

"No!" both Shelby and Calhoun said.

"—or not," Si Cwan finished.

"Captain, the legality of this is questionable at best," continued Shelby. "At the very least, let's consult with Starfleet Central over the legal issues raised. You said yourself that—"

"On the first leg of our mission, you want me to drop everything and notify Starfleet so they can tell me what to do. That, Commander, sounds like an excellent way to erode confidence in this vessel's ability to get the job done."

"Permission to speak freely," Kebron said.

"No!" both Shelby and Calhoun said.

"Fine. I didn't really want it."

"Permission to return to the bridge," McHenry quickly said. "I don't think I'm serving much of a function here."

"We'll be right behind you," said Shelby.

"No, 'we' will not," Calhoun informed her. "Watson, beam me back down."

Watson took a step toward the console but eyed Shelby warily. And Shelby turned to Calhoun and said, "Captain, please . . . five minutes of your time."

He eyed her a moment. "Two. All of you out. Kebron, you look like you've been through a grinder. Get down to sickbay."

The others needed no further urging to vacate the transporter room, leaving Shelby and Calhoun alone.

"Mac, I know what this is about. It's just the two of us now, you don't have to pretend. You, of all people, can't tell me that all of a sudden you've grown an inviolable conscience when it comes to the Prime Directive."

"And you, of all people, can't tell me that all of a sudden, you don't give a damn about it."

"What I give a damn about is you, and what you're trying to prove, for no reason. This isn't about justice or the Prime Directive. This is about you needing to test yourself, push yourself. Prove to yourself that you're the man you were. But you don't have to do that! It doesn't matter who you think you were. What matters is who you are now:

Captain Mackenzie Calhoun of the *Starship Excalibur.* And a Starfleet captain simply does not needlessly throw himself into the heart of danger. Let Ryjaan rant and rave. Let him nurse his grudge. It doesn't matter. What matters is that you have a responsibility to this ship, to this crew, to . . .''

"To you?" he asked quietly.

There was none of the anger in her voice, none of the edge that he had come to expect. Just a simple, soft, "I'd . . . like to think so."

He turned away from her, oddly finding himself unable to look at her. "Before I knew you . . . I knew you," he said.

"I . . . don't understand."

"I . . . had a vision of you. It's not something I really need to go into now. I saw you, that's all, years before we actually encountered each other. I'd be lying if I said I fell in love with you at that moment. I didn't even know you. But I knew you were my future. Just as I know now that this is my future. I have to do this, Eppy. I have no choice."

"Yes, you do. And so do I. As first officer, I have a right to stop you from subjecting yourself to unnecessary risk."

"Which means this goes to the core of what is considered 'unnecessary.' " He paused a moment and then turned back to her, crossing the distance between them so that they were eye to eye. "There's a man down there demanding justice. There's only one person in this galaxy who can give it to him. I have to do this. If you claim to understand me at all . . . then you'll understand that. And understand this: I want you to stay here. To stay out of this. Do not interfere at any point. These are my direct orders to you."

Shelby, for once in her life at a loss for words, sighed, and then traced the line of his scar with her finger. "Be careful, for God's sake," she said.

"I'm not quite certain if I believe in God enough to be careful for his sake," said Calhoun reasonably. "But, if you wish . . . I'll be careful for yours."

Soleta had set up a separate research station in her quarters. She found that, while her science station on the bridge was perfectly adequate for on-the-fly research, something that required more detailed analysis likewise required relatively calm and even private surroundings. They were not entirely private at the moment, though, for Robin Lefler was with her, studying results from their scientific foray onto the planet's surface.

"You're right about these ground samples," Lefler was saying. "I'm comparing them to the results of the tests you did from ten years ago. It's similar to planting fields on Earth that have not made proper use of crop rotation. The ground has nutrients which are depleted by planting of the same crop. Thallon itself had a sort of 'energy nutrient,' for want of a better word. And the nutrients have all been drained. Except..."

Soleta leaned back from staring for what had seemed an eternity. "Except...you're coming to the same conclusion I am. That the demands placed upon it by the Thallonians themselves should not have been sufficient to deplete it."

"Exactly. I mean, this is all guesswork, to some extent. We weren't able to monitor the Thallonians on a year-to-year basis, or make constant samples of the ground. All the things that would have led to a more concrete assessment. But as near as I can tell, there's something here that just doesn't parse. And then there's that weird seismic anomaly I was picking up."

Soleta nodded and switched the data over to the readings that Lefler had picked up with her sensor web array. She watched as the blips indicating the seismic tracks arched across the screen.

"What in the world could be causing that sort of...of weird pulsation?" asked Lefler. "It's not like any sort of seismic disturbance that I've ever see—"

"Wait a minute," said Soleta. "Wait...wait a minute. Maybe we've been looking at this wrong. Computer: Attach sound attribution to seismic track. Feed available readings at continuous loop and accelerate by ninety percent."

"Nature of sound to be attributed?" the computer inquired.

"You want it to sound like something?" asked Lefler, clearly confused. "Like what? Bells, whistles, breaking glass...?"

"Heartbeat," said Soleta. "Humanoid heartbeat."

Immediately the sound echoed within the room—quick, steady, and rapid.

"You've got to be kidding," Lefler said slowly.

"Whenever you've eliminated the impossible, whatever remains, however improbable, must be the truth. Your words, as I recall."

"But this is impossible, too! You're saying that the seismic pulse we picked up—"

"—is just that, yes. A pulse."

"Aw, come on! You're not telling me the planet's *alive?!*"

"No, I'm not. Nor do I think it is. But what I think is that there is something alive beneath the surface. Something huge. That's what's causing the quakes, which are occurring with greater frequency and intensity all the time. My guess is that the energy of the planet was 'seeded' somehow, like a farmer, planting a sort of living crop. But the energy is all gone, and whatever was inside is presumably fully developed . . . and trying to get out. And when it does, whoever is still on that world is going to die."

RYJAAN

X

The mountains of Thallon were not especially similar to those of Xenex
... but they weren't terribly dissimilar, either. This was something that
Calhoun took a small measure of comfort in.

"The more things change," he muttered as he clambered up the
side of a small hill to try and get a better overview of the terrain. He
reached a plateau, pulled himself up onto it, and crept slowly toward
the edge. The purple skies matched the color of his eyes.

The region for the Final Challenge had been selected by Ryjaan.
When Calhoun had returned to the People's Meeting Hall, no one looked
more surprised than the offended party, but he had wasted no time in
selecting the area of the showdown. But as Ryjaan had been doing the
talking—including a healthy helping of boasting and chest-beating—
Calhoun had never stopped looking at D'ndai.

He passed within earshot of D'ndai as he was led past him, and in
a voice just loud enough for D'ndai to hear, he said, "I have no
brother."

D'ndai merely smiled. Clearly he was looking forward to having
no brother in the immediate future as well.

Calhoun kept the sword gripped comfortably but firmly in his right hand as he crouched on the plateau. He listened carefully all around him, remembering that Ryjaan's father had managed to get the drop on him twenty years ago. He was not anxious to allow a repeat performance . . . although, granted, when Falkar had performed that rather considerable achievement, there had been a fairly major sandstorm going on at the time. But in this case, everything was relatively calm. . . .

And the ground tore open beneath his feet.

Just like that, the plateau that he'd been situated upon was gone, crumbling into rock beneath him as the entire area shook more violently than ever before. He had absolutely nothing to grab on to. The sword flew out of his hand, swallowed by the cascade of rock, and Calhoun plummeted, rolling and tumbling down the mountainside. He lunged desperately, twisting in midair, and his desperate fingers found some purchase that slowed his fall ever so briefly. Then he lost his grip once more and hit the ground, rolling into a ball and covering his head desperately as rock and rubble rained down around him.

And from a short distance away, Ryjaan saw it all. Ryjaan, under whose feet the ground had suddenly shifted, jutting upward. He had clutched on to it, scrambling upward to avoid sliding into the newly created crevice, and had just barely escaped. But now he saw Calhoun, weaponless, with an avalanche crumbling upon him. It was as if the planet itself had risen up to smite him.

And Ryjaan, gripping his own sword grimly, waited until the trembling subsided and then advanced upon the buried Calhoun to finish the job.

"Evacuate?" Yoz said skeptically. "Because of some earthquakes?"

On the viewscreen, Soleta was speaking with forcefulness and urgency. "This is not merely earthquakes. You have spacegoing vessels that you use for exploration and travel. Use everything. Everything you've got. Get off the planet. We will bring up as many as we can as well. Fortunately enough, most of your population has already left ever since the collapse of—"

"We are not in collapse!" Yoz said angrily. "We will rebuild! We will be great again!"

And then Si Cwan stepped into view on the screen, and said, "No. You will be dead."

"Are we to listen to you then, 'Lord' Si Cwan? Traitor! Coward!"

"Save your name-calling, Yoz. It's nothing compared to the im- mediate necessity of saving our people. If you truly believe that you are acting in their best interests, you will make known to them Soleta's advice and offer. And you will do so quickly."

"You cannot tell me what to do—"

"I am not telling you what to do. I am asking you. Begging you, if that's what you want." Then a thought seemed to strike him and his tone changed into a slightly wheedling voice. "If you wish, look at it this way: This is an opportunity to make me look foolish to the people of Thallon. A nattering doomsday prophet, trying to convince them of an end-of-the-world scenario that is merely demented fiction. Those who believe and wish to leave . . . well, what use would they be to you any- way? They're faint of heart, and they clearly embrace the old ways. But those who stay with you, Yoz . . . they will be the core of the new empire that you would rebuild. They will know me to be a fraud. They will know you to be resolute and unmovable. I'm handing you the op- portunity, Yoz, once and for all, to be the leader you know yourself to be."

Slowly, Yoz smiled. "Si Cwan . . . you had a knack for being per- suasive as a prince. Even in disgrace . . . you have a turn of phrase. I shall consider it."

"Consider it quickly, Yoz. Because, whether you believe me or not, I am convinced by this woman's words. You do not have much time left."

Ryjaan felt a brief aftershock as he made his way toward the rubble, but it only staggered him slightly. Nothing was keeping the bronze- skinned Danteri from his goal.

He made it to the area where he'd seen Calhoun go down. The rocks appeared undisturbed. It was entirely possible that Calhoun was already dead, which would have upset Ryjaan no end. He wanted to be the one who ended Calhoun's life. He, and no other. But he realized that he might have to settle for whatever justice nature had chosen to mete out.

He scrambled over to the rock pile and started digging around. He thrust his hands deep into the rubble, searching, probing, trying desperately to find some hint or trace of where Mackenzie Calhoun was beneath the avalanche. Then he felt something, but it wasn't vaguely living matter. Instead it was hard-edged, rough. He grimaced a moment, for his arm was thrust in all the way up to his shoulder, and then with a grunt he pulled it out.

He held up the sword of his father. It glittered in the twilight of Thallon.

And then he was struck from the side. He went down, the sword flying from his hand, and Calhoun caught it. "Thank you," he said.

Ryjaan, his head ringing, looked around in confusion. "Where . . . ?"

"Dug myself out and hid, and waited for you. Ryjaan . . . now that it's just the two of us," said Calhoun almost conversationally, "I am asking you not to do this thing. It won't bring your father back. All it will do is cost you your life."

"Aren't we the overconfident one," sneered Ryjaan, scrambling to his feet, waving his sword.

"No. No, we're not. Just . . . confident enough." And he added silently, *I hope.*

"For honor!" shouted Ryjaan, and he charged.

And damn if he wasn't fast. Faster than Calhoun anticipated. Ryjaan's sword moved quickly, a flashing blur, and Calhoun suddenly discovered that he was backing up. Faster, farther, and suddenly there was a cut on his arm, and then a slash across his chest, and he wasn't even fully aware of how they had gotten there.

The son was faster than the father.

Or else Calhoun was slower.

Yes. Yes, that was the hell of it.

Twenty years ago, he had been something. He had been something great, something grand. He had reached the pinnacle of his life. And every activity in which he had engaged since then was a constant denial of that simple fact. He had been great once, once upon a time, at a time when—deep in his heart—he wouldn't have given himself any odds on the likelihood that he would reach age twenty. But now he felt old. Even though he was "merely" forty, he was old, not what he was. Not what he was at all. A mere shadow of the fighter he was.

Despair loomed over him . . .

. . . and there was a slash to the left side of his face. The cut was not as deep as the one which had created the scar, but it was deep enough as blood welled from it.

Ryjaan laughed derisively, sneered triumph at Calhoun, taunted him for not even giving him a decent battle.

And something within Calhoun snapped. Blew away the despair, burned it off like dew incinerated by a nova.

And Calhoun tossed the sword down into the ground, point first. It stuck there, wavering back and forth. "Come on!" shouted Calhoun. *"Come on!"* and he gestured defiantly, his fury building with every passing moment.

For a split second, Ryjaan wondered if Calhoun expected him to throw his own sword away. To leap into hand-to-hand combat, voluntarily tossing aside his advantage. Well, if that was the case, then Calhoun was going to be sorely disappointed, at least for the brief seconds of life that he had left to him. With a roar of triumph, Ryjaan lunged forward, his blade a blur.

Calhoun couldn't get out of the way fast enough. But he half-turned and the blade, instead of piercing his chest, skewered his right arm, going all the way through, the hilt up to the bone.

And Calhoun said nothing. Did not cry out, did not make the slightest sound even though Ryjaan knew the pain must have been agonizing. Ryjaan tried to yank the sword out.

It was stuck.

Calhoun brought his left fist around, caught Ryjaan on the point of his jaw, and staggered him. Then his foot lashed out, nailing Ryjaan's stomach, doubling him over. As Ryjaan reeled, Calhoun gripped the hilt and snapped it off the blade. He then reached around, gripped the sword on the other side of his arm, and pulled it the rest of the way through. He was biting down so hard on his lip to contain the scream that blood was trickling down his chin. As he dropped the broken blade to the ground, he flexed his right arm desperately to try and keep it functional, and then shouted, "Come on, Ryjaan! Still have the stomach for vengeance? Had enough?"

Ryjaan didn't say anything beyond an inarticulate scream of fury, and then he charged. Calhoun took a swing at him with his left arm, but the semi-dead right arm threw him off balance and he missed clean. Ryjaan plowed into him and the two of them went down, tumbling across the craggy surface of Thallon.

All around them were new quakes as the ground began to crack beneath them. But they didn't care, so focused were they on the battle at hand. Ryjaan intent on putting an end to his father's killer, and Calhoun . . .

Calhoun was looking beyond Ryjaan. Fury poured from him, savagery as intense as anything he'd ever felt, and it was like the return of an old and welcome friend. Suddenly new strength flowed into his right arm, seized him and drove him, and he lifted Ryjaan clear off his feet, tossing him a good ten feet. Ryjaan crashed to the ground and Calhoun charged toward him. The Danteri swung his legs around just as Calhoun got within range, knocking him off his feet, and the Starfleet officer was down as Ryjaan pounced upon him, grabbing him and trying to get his fingers around Calhoun's throat.

Calhoun twisted his head around and sank his teeth into Ryjaan's arm. Ryjaan howled, his blood trickling between Calhoun's jaws, and Calhoun tore loose of Ryjaan's grip. He slammed a fist into Ryjaan's face, heard the satisfying crack of Ryjaan's nose breaking. Ryjaan was dazed and Calhoun shoved Ryjaan back, leaped to his feet, and now he was atop Ryjaan, driving a knee into his chest, and he let out a roar as he drove blow after blow into Ryjaan's head. He was completely out of control, and part of him cried out in joy for it.

And then it seemed as if the ground all around them exploded.

Chancellor Yoz appeared on the screen of the *Excalibur,* and there was an air of controlled frenzy about him. "I am . . . a man of my word," he said with no preamble. "I have relayed your message to the people of Thallon and . . ."

Suddenly he staggered as the ground shifted under him. The picture wavered, and then snapped back as Yoz—acting for all the world as if nothing had just happened—continued, "And some of them have decided to take you up on your offer. They are gathering in the Great Square . . . Si Cwan, you recall the location?"

"Yes, I do." Immediately he headed over to Robin Lefler's station, describing the location in relation to the People's Meeting Hall so that she could feed the coordinates into the ship's computers.

Yoz continued, "Then you may direct your vessel's transporter beams to start bringing people up. Others are leaving by their own transports. You," and he began to grow angry, his pointing finger trembling. "You have frightened them, Si Cwan! I had hoped that they would be made of sterner stuff, but you . . . you have filled them with nightmare fears and they flee! They flee for no reason!"

"All transporter rooms, this is Kebron," the Brikar security chief was saying briskly. "Coordinate with Lieutenant Lefler and commence immediate beam-up of Thallonians at the coordinates she is specifying."

"Yoz, we'll bring you up, too," said Si Cwan. "For all that has passed between us, nonetheless this is your opportunity to save your life—"

"My life is not imperiled!" shouted Yoz. "I will not fall for your trickery, or for you—"

And then something sounding like an explosion roared through the palace. The last sight they had of Yoz was his still declaring his disbelief, even as the roof collapsed upon him.

The ground around them fragmented, tilted, and then oozing from between the cracks Calhoun saw—to his shock—magma bubbling up beneath them. It was as if something was cracking through to the very molten core of the planet. The ground continued to crack beneath them, like ice floes becoming sliced up by an arctic sea . . . except that, in this case, the sea was capable of incinerating them.

Calhoun and Ryjaan were several feet away from each other, and then the ground cracked between them, heaving upward. The ground beneath Calhoun was suddenly tilting at a seventy-degree angle. Calhoun, flat on his belly, scrambled for purchase and then he saw, just a few feet away, his sword. It skidded past him and he thrust out a desperate hand, snagged it, and jammed it into the ground.

It momentarily halted his tumble, but the impact tore loose his comm badge. Before he could grab it with his free hand, it tumbled down and away and vanished into a bubbling pool of lava.

The gap between Ryjaan and Calhoun widened, and Ryjaan took several steps back, ran, and leaped. He vaulted the distance and landed several feet above Calhoun. He shouted in triumph even as he pulled a dagger from the upper part of his boot. He started to clamber toward Calhoun . . .

. . . and suddenly the ground shifted beneath them once more, thrusting forward onto the lip of another chunk of land. Just that quickly, the land they were on was now twenty feet in the air. There was an outcropping from another mountain that was within range of a jump, and it would be a more tenable position than Calhoun's present one, provided he could get to it.

Ryjaan started to get to his feet, to come after Calhoun across the momentarily semi-level surface—and suddenly the ground jolted once more. The cracks radiated as far as the eye could see, as if the landscape of Thallon had transformed into a massive jigsaw puzzle. In the distance, the great city of Thal—once the center of commerce, the seat of power, of the Thallonian Empire—was crumbling, the mighty towers plunging to the ground.

The jostling sent Ryjaan off balance, and he was tossed toward the edge of the precipice . . . toward it and over. With a screech he tumbled, and the only thing that prevented him from going over completely was a frantic, one-handed grip that he managed to snag on the edge. A short drop below him, lava seethed, almost as if it were calling to him. He tried to haul himself up, cursing, growling . . .

. . . and then Calhoun was there, fury in his eyes, and he was poised over Ryjaan. It would take but a single punch to send Ryjaan tumbling down into the lava. To put an end to him. The savage within Calhoun wanted to, begged him to. And he knew that there was absolutely no reason whatsoever to save Ryjaan . . .

. . . and he grabbed Ryjaan's wrist.

"Hold on!" he shouted down to Ryjaan. "Come on! I'll pull you up!"

Ryjaan looked up at him with eyes that were filled with twenty years' worth of hatred.

And then he spat at him. "Go to hell," he said, and pulled loose from Calhoun's grip. Calhoun cried out, but it was no use as Ryjaan plunged down, down into the lava which swallowed him greedily.

Calhoun staggered to his feet, then grabbed up his sword and prepared to jump to relative safety on the outcropping nearby.

And then there was another explosion, even more deafening than the previous ones, and Calhoun was blown backward. This time he held on to his sword, for all the good it was going to do him. He was airborne, flailing around, unable to stop his motion, nothing for him to grab on to except air. Below him the lava lapped upward, and in his imaginings he thought he could hear Ryjaan screaming triumphantly at him, for it was only a matter of seconds as gravity took its inevitable grip and pulled the falling Calhoun into the magma.

Then something banged into him in midair, and he heard a voice shout, *"Emergency beam-up!"*

His mind didn't even have time to fully register that it was Shelby's voice before Thallon dematerialized around him, and the next thing he knew they were falling to the floor of the transporter room. He looked around in confusion and there was Shelby, dusting herself off and looking somewhat haggard. "Nice work, Polly." Watson tossed off a quick, acknowledging salute.

"Where the hell did you come from?" he asked.

"I was there the whole time. We monitored you via your comm badge until you were brought to wherever your surging testosterone demanded you be brought to so you could slug it out, and then I had myself beamed down to be on the scene in case matters became—in my judgment—too dire." She tapped the large metal casings on her feet. "Gravity boots. Comes in handy every now and then, particularly when the ground keeps crumbling under you." She pulled off the boots and straightened her uniform.

"You saw the entire thing?"

"Yeah." She took a breath. "It was all I could do not to jump in earlier. But I knew you had to see it through." She headed out the door, and Calhoun was right behind her. Moments later they had stepped into a turbolift.

"Bridge," said Calhoun, and then he said to Shelby, "You did that even though I gave you specific orders to stay here. Even though I told you, no matter what, that you weren't to interfere. Even though the Prime Directive would have indicated that you should stay out of it."

"Well, you see . . . someone once told me that sometimes you simply have to assess a situation and say, 'Dammit, it's me or no one. And if you can't live with no one, then you have to take action.' "

"Oh, really. Sounds like a pretty smart guy."

"He likes to think he is, yes."

Calhoun walked out onto the bridge and said briskly, "Status report!"

The fact that Calhoun was bruised, battered, and bloody didn't draw any comment from any of the bridge crew. They were too busy trying to survive. Burgoyne was at hish engineering station on the bridge, someplace that s/he didn't normally inhabit. But with the rapid changes required in the ship's acceleration, s/he wanted to be right at the nerve center of the decisions so that s/he could make whatever immediate adjustments might be required.

"We're at full reverse, Captain!" McHenry said. "I couldn't maintain orbit; the planet's breaking up and the gravity field was shifting too radically!"

"Take us to a safe distance, then," Calhoun said. "Soleta, what's happening down there?"

"The planet is breaking up, sir," Soleta replied, "due to—I believe—stress caused by something inside trying to get out."

"Get *out?*"

"Yes, sir."

The area around Thallon was crammed with vessels of all sizes and shapes, trying to put as much distance between themselves and the shattering planet as possible. The confusion was catastrophic; at one point several ships collided with each other in their haste to get away from Thallon, erupting into flames and spiraling away into the ether. Fortunately enough most of the pilots were more levelheaded than that.

"Status on the current population?"

"Most of them have managed to clear out in private vessels, sir," said Soleta. "Some chose to remain on the planet and . . ."

"Foolish. Dedicated but foolish," said Calhoun.

"We've evacuated over a thousand people onto the *Excalibur* as well," said Kebron.

"A *thousand?*" gasped Shelby. "Maximum capacity for this ship in an evacuation procedure is supposed to be six hundred."

"We've asked that they all stand sideways."

"Good thinking, Kebron," Calhoun said dryly. He turned to Shelby and said, "Looks like we'll be taking Nelkar up on their offer sooner than anticipated." Then he noticed Si Cwan standing off to the side, very quiet, his attention riveted to the screen. "Are you all right, Ambassador?"

He shifted his gaze to Calhoun and said, "Of course not."

It seemed a fair enough response.

"Sir, energy buildup!" announced Soleta.

"Take us back another five hundred thousand kilometers, Mr. Mc-

Henry. Burgoyne, have warp speed ready, just in case we need to get out of here quickly.''

"Perhaps it would be wiser to vacate the area now," Shelby suggested.

"You're very likely correct. It would be wiser. However, I think I want to see this.''

She nodded. Truth to tell, she wanted to see it as well.

On the screen, Thallon continued to shudder, its entire surface ribboned with cracks. Even from the distance at which they currently sat, they could see lava bubbling in all directions. The very planet appeared to be pulsating, throbbing under the strain of whatever was pushing its way out.

And then, all of a suddenly, something thrust up from within.

It was a claw. A single, giant, flaming claw, miles wide, smashing up through what was once a polar icecap. Then another flaming claw, several hundred miles away, and then a third claw and a fourth, but these at the opposite ends of the planet, and they seemed even larger. The screen adjusted the brightness to avoid damaging the eyesight of the bridge crew.

The process begun, it moved faster and faster, more pieces breaking away, and then the planet broke apart in a stunning display of matter and energy. Thallon erupted from the inside out . . .

. . . and there was a creature there unlike anything that Calhoun had ever seen.

It seemed vaguely avian in appearance, with feathers made of roaring flame and energy crackling around it. Its talons of flame flexed outward, and its massive wings unfurled. Its beak was long and wide, and it opened its mouth in a scream that could not be heard in the depths of space. Incredibly, stars were visible through the creature. It was as if it was a creature that was both there . . . and not there.

"I don't believe it," said a stunned Calhoun. "What the hell is it?''

"Unknown, sir," replied Soleta. "In general physicality, it seems evocative of such beasts as the ancient pteranodon, or the flamebird of Ricca 4. But its size, its physical makeup . . .''

"Oh, my God," said Burgoyne in slow astonishment. "It can't be. Don't you get it?'' s/he said with growing excitement.

"What is it, Burgy?'' asked Shelby, who was as riveted to the screen as any of them.

"It's . . . it's the *Great Bird of the Galaxy.*''

THE GREAT BIRD OF
THE GALAXY

XI

"Don't be ridiculous!" said Shelby. "That's . . . that's a myth!"

"Once upon a time, so was the idea of life on other planets," commented Zak Kebron.

The Great Bird, in the airlessness of space, continued to move its wings. It crackled with power. Extending its jaws, it gobbled up floating chunks left over from Thallon . . .

. . . and then it seemed to turn its attention to the *Starship Excalibur.*

"Uh-oh," said Shelby.

"I do *not* like the looks of this," Calhoun agreed. "Aren't baby birds hungry first thing after they're born?"

"Customarily," Soleta said.

"What if it moves to attack the other ships?"

"It doesn't seem interested in anyone else but us, Shelby," said Calhoun. "Probably because we're the biggest."

"Shall we prepare to fight it, sir?" asked Kebron, fingers already moving to the tactical station.

"Fight the Great Bird of the Galaxy?" said Calhoun. "Even we have to know our limitations."

The creature moved toward them, and Shelby said, "It seems to have a bead on us."

"I think you're right. Okay . . . move us out at warp factor one. Let's draw it away from the area and give everyone a chance to clear out."

"Incoming message from one of the vessels, sir," Kebron announced.

"Save it. Now isn't the time. Mr. McHenry, get us out of here."

The *Excalibur* went into reverse thrust, pivoted, and moved away from the shattered remains of Thallon, with the Great Bird of the Galaxy, or whatever it was, in hot pursuit.

"It's picking up speed," said Lefler.

"Jump us to warp four," Calhoun ordered, sitting calmly with his fingers steepled.

With a thrust from its mighty warp engines, the *Excalibur* leaped forward. The Great Bird, if such it was, flapped its wings and kept moving, pacing them.

"According to legend," Burgoyne was saying, "there can only be one Great Bird at a time. And when it senses its end is near, the Great Bird imparts its essence into a world, gestates over centuries, and is then reborn. I guess that's why it was 'mythological' . . . it takes centuries for the 'egg,' if you will, to hatch."

"But you told me 'May the Great Bird of the Galaxy roost on your planet' was a blessing," Calhoun pointed out.

"Obviously it was. Look at the prosperity that Thallon saw during the time of the roosting."

"But when it hatches, the planet is destroyed! What kind of blessing is that?"

"It's oral tradition, not an exact science, sir," McHenry commented.

"Thank you, Lieutenant," Burgoyne said.

"Sir, it's catching up."

"Pull out the stops, Mr. McHenry. Warp nine."

The *Excalibur* raced away, and this time the creature seemed to let out another squawk before the *Excalibur* left it far behind. It dwindled, further and further, to the farthest reaches of the ship's sensor, and then was gone.

There was a slow sigh of relief let out on the bridge. "Well," said Shelby brightly, "that wasn't too much of a chore."

"Collision course!" shouted McHenry.

The Great Bird was directly in front of them, its mouth open wide. Faster than anyone would have thought possible, McHenry course-corrected and tried to send the ship angling out of the way of the creature's maw.

No good. The *Excalibur* flew straight into the Great Bird's mouth . . .

. . . and out the other side of its head.

The ship was jolted, shaken throughout, and it was all that the bridge crew could do to keep its seats. "Damage report!" shouted Calhoun.

"Slight dip in deflector shields! Otherwise we're clear!" called Lefler.

The creature appeared on their rear monitors. It appeared to be watching them go with great curiosity. Indeed, if any of the crew were given to fanciful interpretations of events, they would have said that the creature seemed just as curious about this new life-form that it had encountered as the new life-form was about them.

And then, with a twist of its powerful wings, the Great Bird seemed to warp through the very fabric of space . . .

. . . and disappeared without a trace.

This time there was a long pause before anyone took it for granted that they were safe. And then Shelby said, "Where do you think it went?"

"Anywhere it wanted to," McHenry commented, and no one disagreed.

"Captain . . . I suggest you get yourself down to sickbay. You need to be patched up," said Shelby.

"Good advice, Commander." He rose unsteadily from his chair, and found himself leaning on Kebron. "Ah. You wouldn't mind escorting me down there, would you, Lieutenant?"

But Shelby stepped in and said, "Don't worry, Kebron. I'll handle this. After all . . . if you can't lean on your second-in-command, whom can you lean on?"

"Good point," said Calhoun wearily.

"And a word of advice: Don't keep the second scar on your face. The one is enough."

"Sound suggestion, as always."

As they headed to the turbolift, he paused and said, "Oh . . . we had an incoming message? What was that about?"

"Audio only, sir. I'll put it on."

Kebron tapped his comm board and a voice filled the bridge. A voice that was instantly recognizable as Zoran's.

And Zoran said, "Si Cwan . . . I just wanted you to know . . . I lied before. Your sister is alive. Try and find her, O Prince."

And his chilling laughter continued in Si Cwan's memory long after the message had ended.

U.S.S. EXCALIBUR

XII

It was evening on the *Excalibur* . . . evening being a relative term, of course.

Selar was in her off-duty clothes, and she looked at herself in the mirror. For the first time in a long time, she liked what she saw in there.

She was nervous, so nervous that she could feel trembling throughout her body. For a moment she considered turning away from her intended course, but she had made a decision, dammit, and she was going to see it through.

She smoothed out her clothes for the umpteenth time and headed toward Burgoyne's quarters. On the way she rehearsed for herself everything she was going to say. The ground rules she was going to set. The hopes that she had for this potential relationship. She would never have considered Burgoyne her type, but there was something about hir that was so . . . so offbeat. So different. Perhaps that was what Selar needed. Someone to whom questions such as sex and relationships and interaction were nothing but matters to be joyously explored rather than tentatively entered into.

That, Selar realized, was what she needed. Whatever this residual urge was within her, driving her forward, it was something that needed a radical spirit to respond to. Someone offbeat, someone aggressive, someone . . .

. . . someone . . .

. . . someone was with Burgoyne.

Selar slowed to a halt as she neared Burgoyne's quarters, her sharp ears detecting the laughter from around the corner.

And then they moved around the corner into view: Burgoyne 172, leaning on the shoulder of Mark McHenry. They seemed hysterically amused by something; Selar had no idea what. Just before they stumbled into Burgoyne's quarters, Burgoyne planted a fierce kiss on McHenry's mouth, to which he readily responded. Then he popped what appeared to be some sort of chips into hish mouth, which Burgoyne crunched joyously. They side-stepped into Burgoyne's quarters, and the door slid shut behind them.

Selar stood there for a long moment. This was going to be a problem. She had counted on Burgoyne to resolve her . . . difficulty with her mating drive. Perhaps a return to Vulcan was in order. Or perhaps there was another solution, closer to hand.

Selar returned to her quarters, changed into her nightclothes, and stood before the memorial lamp which burned so that she would remember Voltak.

She reached over, extinguished the light for the first time in two years—never to light it again—and fell into a fitful sleep.

In his ready room, Calhoun had just finished mounting the sword back onto the wall. He heard a chime at the door and said, "Come."

Shelby entered, and stood just inside the doorway. "I was wondering . . . I was about to head down to the Team Room and have a drink. Thought you might like to come along."

"That sounds great." He regarded the sword for a moment and said, "You know what was interesting?"

"No, Mac. What was interesting?"

"When I tried to save Ryjaan . . . I did so without even thinking about it. It was . . . instinctive."

"That's good."

"Is it?" he asked. "I've always felt my instincts were based in pure savagery."

"Your survival instincts were, sure. Because they're what you needed in order to get through your life. To do what needed to be done. But even basic instincts can change, and that's not automatically a terrible thing. Being a starship commander isn't just about survival. There's much, much more to it than that."

"And I suppose that you're prepared to tell me what that is."

"Of course. Chapter and verse."

"Well, Eppy . . . maybe—just maybe now—I'm prepared to listen."

"And I'm prepared to tell you, if you'd just stop calling me by that stupid nickname."

He laughed softly and came around the desk. As they headed for the door, she said, "One quick question: You told me that you had a 'vision' of me, long ago."

"That's right, yes."

"Just out of morbid curiosity . . . was I wearing any clothes in that vision?"

"Nope. Stark naked."

"Yeah, well," she sighed, as he draped an arm around her shoulder, "it's comforting to know that some instincts never change, I guess."

And they headed to the Team Room for a drink.

9667277